Best W.

KERi PETERSEN

Bobby Wood

LEARJET 464 JULIET

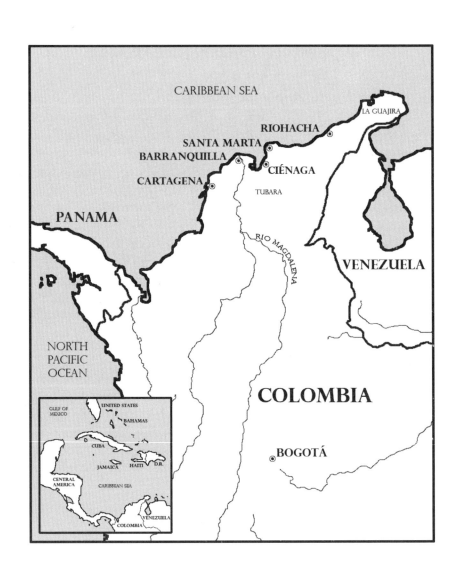

CARIBBEAN SEA

LA GUAJIRA

RIOHACHA

SANTA MARTA
BARRANQUILLA
CIÉNAGA
CARTAGENA
TUBARA

PANAMA

RIO MAGDALENA

VENEZUELA

NORTH
PACIFIC
OCEAN

COLOMBIA

BOGOTÁ

GULF OF
MEXICO
UNITED STATES
BAHAMAS
CUBA
JAMAICA
HAITI
D.R.
CENTRAL
AMERICA
CARIBBEAN SEA
VENEZUELA
COLOMBIA

LEARJET
464 JULIET

An American, A Jet &
A Culture of Corruption
that Kept them Apart

by Bobby Wood

RUNWAY
THREE SIX
PUBLISHING

PREFACE

OCTOBER 13, 2011—PLEASE, LORD, GIVE US STRENGTH AND WISDOM

The pages you are about to read were written over a five-month period from November 1981 to March of 1982.

Having lived through the ordeals and stress of my adventures in Colombia throughout 1980, I was happy to return to my regular, more sedate life in early 1981. Later, however, in fall of that same year, concerned that the details of my time in Colombia would grow dim with time, I decided to collect my thoughts and set them down in a handwritten journal.

I would sit up in bed, while my wife, Terry, slept, writing my story in longhand, and, by the end of March 1982, I had filled up twelve yellow legal pads (I still have my original handwritten copy). Whenever I would finish a good-sized chunk of writing, I'd sit down over the next few days with Ms. Midge Biaggi, an extraordinarily gifted editor who had lived and worked in Colombia for years. She would type my manuscript and clean it up a good bit, and then I would be instructed to return and write some more.

I can assure you that I lived everything and every moment in this story. All of what you will read herein is based on truth and fact. So, why call it a nonfiction novel? Well, I have had to change a number of names and a few dates to protect the innocent, and although the dialog offers a 99 percent accurate reflection of the conversations that took place, an imperfect memory can, in the end, offer only a reflection of the past and not a verbatim transcript.

As I look back at this writing from my desk today, in 2011, I can say that, yes, I have learned a lot from my trials and difficulties in Colombia in 1980. And the one thing, perhaps, I have learned the most is how much I prize my citizenship as an American. As a nation, we offer the one great beacon of hope for so many countries and good people who face lives of poverty and war.

Someone once said that to err is human but to forgive divine. I hope you will enjoy Juliet's story, and I pray that you will show mercy on those who participated in these events and who, in that time, may have lived their lives on the moral margins. For me, I know that this task could not have been achieved were it not for God and prayer. I am grateful for having survived.

—Bobby Wood, Cropwell, Alabama

A special thanks
to my wife, Terry,
and my daughter Taylor.

PROLOGUE

JUNE 15, 1977, 9:15 A.M.—SANTA MARTA, COLOMBIA, TROUBLE ON THE HORIZON

To the east, the sun had just completed its climb above the peaks of the magnificent Sierra Nevada de Santa Marta. The entire range of mountains was now cutting its way into a clear blue sky. Hardly a cloud obscured the snowfields at the highest elevations, sparkling blue-white above the lush expanse of tropical vegetation below—an emerald green glistening in the lower reaches of the morning's mountain slopes.

To the west, the Caribbean Sea lay calm, its aquamarine depths offering a complex spectrum of blues and greens, broken only by the surge of an occasional wave wrapping around one of the gigantic rock formations dotting the coastline.

And due north, rapidly approaching, a white speck in the sky.

"Santa Marta tower … Lifeguard … Learjet 464 Juliet."

"Santa Marta tower … Go ahead, 464 Juliet."

"Learjet 464 Juliet out of ten thousand feet … descending … fifteen miles north … request landing instructions."

"Learjet 464 Juliet, enter left downwind for runway three six … report abeam the tower … wind three forty at seven knots … altimeter 30.15," the words crackled over the radio in heavily accented English.

"Learjet 464 Juliet, Roger."

The sleek Learjet came on like an arrow through the clear sky, a lady in white marked only by blue and black stripes. On her tail, she proudly displayed her registration number, N464J, and the American flag.

She began her descent.

"Santa Marta tower … Learjet 464 Juliet … abeam the tower … two thousand feet, left downwind for runway three six."

"Learjet 464 Juliet … cleared to land … report on final."

Learjet 464J had already passed the sprawl of low buildings and small port facilities that was Santa Marta, as well as the airport lying a few miles south. She circled inland, to the left, to make her final approach to runway three six.

"Santa Marta tower … 464 Juliet … two-mile final for three six."

"Learjet 464 Juliet … cleared to land."

The Learjet touched down on Colombian soil at 9:23 A.M.

"Learjet 464 Juliet … taxi down three six … make first right turn … proceed straight ahead … park beside helicopter on left."

The motors stilled. The door of the Learjet opened. Three men emerged in rapid succession. First out, a swarthy American with a large black mustache named Jimmy Chagra, in his middle thirties, dressed expensively and flamboyantly in designer Western wear. Then came two younger men in medical whites: one, Miguel Parada, a slim Latino, the other, Jeff Ellis, an American of fair complexion.

This group of three waited on the tarmac for the Learjet's pilot and copilot, both of whom had remained in the cockpit for a few minutes longer, finishing their shut-down tasks.

Within a few minutes, the pilot, Tony Gekakis, a short, burly man already in his fifties, with nervous mannerisms, crawled out of the left seat. He quickly gathered himself together and stepped down to the tarmac to join the others to wait on the copilot, Steve Bolling, the final passenger to leave the plane.

Steve Bolling, a tall, well-built man with fair coloring, moved easily and unhurriedly down the steps, joining the group of four on the tarmac.

"Steve," the pilot Gekakis said, "as soon as we are through with all our paperwork, set up the stretcher with Miguel and Jeff. Make sure everything is 100 percent ready. I hear Jerry's in pretty bad shape. I understand it's third-degree burns over about 80 percent of his body. It's going to be very rough on everybody."

Bolling smiled easily and calmly as he drawled out his affirmative response to Gekakis's marching orders. Moments later, several customs and immigration officials in tropical tans approached the group, greeting them all and then indicating that they should come inside the terminal.

The swarthy Jimmy Chagra, the man with the mustache who had chartered the Learjet, quickly pulled Gekakis and the others aside. "As soon as they've checked my passport, Tony," Chagra said, with firm authority, "I've got to go up to the tower. I have to take care of something up there. I'll be right back, and then I'll go straight into town to pick up Jerry."

"OK, Jimmy," said Gekakis, "when I'm finished, I'll have to go up to the control tower, too, to file our return flight plan. Steve and the crew should be able to take right off as soon as you get back."

The copilot Bolling and the two medics, Miguel and Jeff nodded their understanding, and then the entire group of five set off with the officials for the terminal. Jimmy Chagra was the first in line. His passport was stamped quickly, and he strode off confidently, seeming to know his way around the building. He headed directly for the stairway leading to the control tower. The others presented their papers, talking briefly with the immigration official, who informed them that no visas would be required since they all would be remaining in the terminal until their departure. The pilot Gekakis also headed to the control tower to file his flight plan, leaving copilot Bolling, and the two paramedics on their own.

After almost an hour, another official appeared to the remaining group of three. He identified himself as an agent from the *Departamento Administrativo de Seguridad*, the DAS, which was the Colombian law-enforcement agency similar to the FBI and the DEA. The DAS agent informed Bolling, Miguel, and Jeff that he and his subordinates wanted to search the plane. The group went along outside, where a thorough search was made of the Learjet. The DAS officials opened everything—briefcases, small flight bags, medical cases, a box of fuel additive. When they finished, they stated that everything was in order and that nothing out of the ordinary had been found.

"*Esta limpia* (she's clean)," announced the agent in command, and he then motioned the three men away from the Learjet.

The pilot Gekakis was still in the tower filing the VFR flight plan for the return trip to the United States with their patient; they had to route first through Barranquilla to refuel because the Santa Marta airport did not provide jet fuel for anything other than official purposes. While he was away, an antiquated Red Cross ambulance, white with red crosses and the words "*Cruz Roja*" and "*Ambulancia*" painted on it, drew up near to the Learjet.

The paramedics and Steve Bolling busied themselves, making preparations to transfer the patient. Moving the stretcher into position behind the ambulance, they opened the rear doors. Although they were seasoned professionals, their faces instantly mirrored their shock of dismay and revulsion as the doors swung open to the sickening odor of burnt flesh and suppurating tissue. The ambulance was clearly not air-conditioned; the only ventilation inside was from side mounted fans that functioned only when the vehicle was in motion.

Incredibly, the man propped upright on the cot inside was conscious. His arms were swollen to almost twice their normal size, sticking out perpendicular to his body. Hair, eyebrows, and eyelashes were completely gone. His ears were ragged stubs and his skin was almost black, crisscrossed with jagged red lines where the charred skin had cracked. His tortured eyelids opened, and, when he saw the white uniforms of the paramedics, tears welled through what were now hardly more than slits.

"Oh, my God," he croaked weakly, but with joyful surprise, "you have come to take me home!"

"That's right, back to the U. S. of A.," the medic named Jeff answered, doing his best to stay upbeat.

The man then closed his eyes, his brief lucid moment gone, and he began to mutter incoherently in obvious pain.

"Home … Home … Don't let me die here," he sobbed, fitfully, without the strength to make more than a few small, mewing sounds.

Miguel and Jeff began preparing a hypodermic, having already prepped their oxygen masks, which they had been instructed to use when approaching the burn victim so as to treat him without being overcome by nausea.

Suddenly, the DAS agents reappeared. Rushing up to the ambulance, they surrounded the three men and ordered them away from the gurney and the plane. Steve Bolling protested in bewilderment. Didn't they know that this was a legitimate mission of mercy rescue flight? In all his years as a pilot, he had never heard of anything even remotely as absurd or as cruel as what was now taking place right before him. The agents were adamant. Orders had been received that the patient was not to be unloaded; he was to be returned to the hospital in Santa Marta.

Tony Gekakis returned from the flight tower; he was equally bewildered. He had not been permitted to file his return flight plan. The four men—Gekakis, the pilot in command, Steve Bolling, the copilot, Miguel Parada, the paramedic, and Jeff Ellis, the medical assistant—continued to plead in vain. Certainly, these officials could plainly see the serious condition of this burned man, lying in a sweltering, unventilated ambulance in the stifling noonday summer heat of the tropics? Certainly, they must know that it was a moral imperative to get him to the Brooke Army Medical Center back in the United States for proper treatment? Couldn't they understand that lifesaving arrangements had been made, that a team of medical professionals was on standby, awaiting his arrival?

Yet, the DAS agents remained implacable, ordering the driver to return the patient to the same hospital he had been taken from just an hour or so earlier. The ambulance left, with the four men now standing in place, helplessly watching the bounding Red Cross insignia on the white van's rear door as the object of their medical rescue mission disappeared from sight.

Moments later, the DAS agents were joined by a squad of policemen, whose leader forcefully informed the four men that they were now under arrest and were to come with them.

"Wait a minute," Steve protested, "I'd better lock the Learjet up."

"Prohibited," the agent in command snapped. He meant business.

"Miguel," Bolling called to the Latino paramedic, "tell him that there's a lot of valuable equipment inside the plane. Ask who's going to be responsible for it."

Miguel and the agent spoke excitedly for a couple of minutes. The conversation terminated with a "what can be done?" shrug from Miguel, who reported that the agent said a guard would be provided but that none of the crew was permitted to go near the jet.

The four men were loaded into an olive-drab military truck which drove them along the peaceful palm-lined road beside the sea until they came to the outskirts of Santa Marta. They caught glimpses of donkey-drawn carts, dilapidated cars, and dark-skinned women returning from market with baskets of food balanced on their heads. White teeth flashed as they exchanged greetings with acquaintances. Nearly naked children and lean mongrel dogs scrabbled in the garbage littering the streets.

The four men sat in dazed silence, eyeing the impassive guards seated beside the tailgate of the military truck, guns across their knees.

"Where are we going?" Jeff asked in a frightened voice.

"*No comprendo*," one of the guards replied.

Miguel repeated the question in Spanish. They were being taken to DAS headquarters.

Why? The guard shrugged. He didn't know.

Jeff was now breathing rapidly, licking his dry lips and darting anxious glances as if to try to find answers to all his questions. Gekakis was muttering and, true to his nervous disposition, started scratching roughly at his neck.

"This damned allergy of mine," he complained, "every time I get uptight it hits me like fire ants."

"Try to relax, Tony," Bolling said. "There's nothing we can do here in this truck. Let's see what happens at DAS headquarters; at least we know where they're taking us."

The truck was now pulling up to a dingy concrete structure, its entrance flanked by guards. Outside a red, yellow, and blue Colombian flag on its mast drooped in the windless air. The writing in large block letters above the doorway read "*Departamento Administrativo de Seguridad*"—the DAS. Once inside, the four men were hustled through the reception area and were told to be seated on a long bench at the rear. They waited. Nothing happened.

Miguel was bent toward Jeff, trying to calm his fears and instill courage and confidence into him. Jeff was a new man with the hospital paramedic service. This was his first flight outside the States on an air ambulance, and he was reacting to these ominous events with something close to shock.

Bolling took advantage of Jeff and Miguel's deep absorption to draw closer to Gekakis.

"Tony, what the hell do you think is coming down," he whispered urgently. "I'm as uptight as you are, even if I'm not scratching like hell. What's this trip really all about? And where's Chagra?"

"I don't know what's coming down any more than you do, Steve, but I'm plenty worried. Jimmy Chagra, evidently, is getting to be very bad news for us. I've made trips for Chagra before; so have you—taking him and his family back and forth, and, OK, maybe sometimes with somebody carrying big money—but all strictly legitimate. Never out of the country before. Normally, I'd not go for that, especially to Colombia. Word is around that he runs some big dope deals here in these parts. But when he called the office and told the boss that Jerry Wilson was in an automobile accident and hurt bad, I couldn't say no. Hell, Jerry and I go way back; he used to fly with me. I couldn't just let him lay down here and die."

"Tony, I have news for you," said Bolling. "I don't know who that is in the ambulance, but it sure as hell isn't Jerry Wilson."

CHAPTER ONE

I sat totally immersed in the captivating tales of Colombia—its land, its history, its people—as Dr. Plada and his lovely wife sat across from Raul and me at Mike Gordon's seafood restaurant in Miami.

Dr. Plada was a slight, well-groomed gentleman in his middle sixties, an eminent lawyer from Barranquilla, Colombia (the title "Doctor" being one that Colombians use for all professionals with doctorates and not only for medical doctors). I found Dr. Plada to be a true gentleman of the old school—courtly, mild-mannered, and an attentive listener (which very well might have been due, in part, to deafness, as I had noticed he was wearing a hearing aid).

Raul Soto was my right-hand man and interior shop foreman; he had been with my Fixed Base Operation aviation company, Air Unlimited, in South Florida, for about a year. It had been Raul, originally from Colombia, who had arranged for me to meet Dr. Plada and who was now helping *Sra.* Plada, who spoke excellent English, interpret for us.

We sat a long time over coffee and cognac, while Dr. Plada focused the discussion on the natural and cultural history of the over forty-three thousand acres of land his investment group, *La Comunidad*, owned in the Tubara region in the north of Colombia, South America. Dr. Plada went on to describe the proven oil deposits and the wealth of natural gas just seeping out of the ground in Tubara, finally closing his engaging presentation with a short pitch on how beneficial it would be for me to come to Colombia to see it for myself.

An oil deal in Colombia might be interesting. Dr. Plada had made it clear that his group did not want any major oil companies involved; they would not make enough profit. They were seeking only private investors. I had recently been working on a deal involving automotive contracts for the Colombian government, which looked as if it would indeed turn out profitably. That transaction had given me a positive attitude about pursuing further business in Colombia.

Our meeting ended with my promise to the good doctor that Raul and I would come to Colombia sometime in the near future. Raul had known the doctor and members of his family for over twenty years, and the fact that Plada was a Colombian magistrate was a good enough credential for me to gamble a little money on a quick trip to Barranquilla. I certainly realized and fully appreciated that I needed to see it with my own eyes to really know if it would be worthwhile to form a United States investment group to explore the project.

FEBRUARY 12, 1980—TUBARA, COLOMBIA, A TREK IN THE OIL FIELDS

Raul and I stepped off the Aerocondor flight to Barranquilla and were in the terminal only long enough for me, an *Americano*, to go through customs procedures. Dr. Plada and Dr. Ignas, another member of *La Comunidad*, were waiting for us. We went immediately to the Hotel Royal and started making plans for our field expedition to the Tubara area the next morning. I kept thinking about our ride from the airport. The poverty, the rickety horse-drawn carts, the dilapidated cars on the road, all made me realize how comfortable life was in the States.

Around ten o'clock, Dr. Plada and Dr. Ignas left with handshakes. As Dr. Plada was not young nor a strong man, Dr. Ignas and another *La Comunidad* partner would pick us up at six in the morning for our trip. Raul and I talked long into the night. I was getting excited now that we were getting close to seeing the gas and oil holdings, and I could hardly wait for the morning to come.

Right on time, Dr. Ignas and friend picked us up for breakfast. All I could eat was the *papas fritas* (French fries). The meat was grey, the eggs were rubbery and oily, and the rest of the food was too highly spiced. My tastes in food are not very adventurous, so this was my first lesson: Go prepared and don't plan on gourmet fare in most parts of Colombia.

In our meeting of the previous evening, Dr. Ignas, also an attorney, had not impressed me as favorably as had Dr. Plada, either in looks or personality. He was a short fat man of about fifty with a dark, pockmarked face and a pompous, self-important air. He constantly interrupted, in contrast to Dr. Plada's well-mannered attention to whoever was speaking. His actions, especially at the table, made him seem greedy. However, I decided to reserve judgment for the time being. Not everyone in the world is lovable, and certainly Dr. Plada was everything I could have hoped for in a possible future business relationship.

We rode for about an hour through the west end of Barranquilla along the north coast and finally, approximately two miles offshore, we could see three giant drilling platforms. The atmosphere seemed to charge with expectation.

We made a left turn off the highway down a miserable dirt track. After forty-five minutes of ripping the Jeep apart, we had to get out and go on foot. By this time, the sun was unbearably hot and it seemed hours before we came to a stop at an old thatched mud hut occupied by some Native American Indians. They were friendly and just as curious about us as I was about them. There was no water, no electricity, absolutely no sign of what we consider civilization. I stared in amazement, wondering how these people could survive such a primitive way of life.

After resting fifteen minutes or so, we started walking along narrow paths and under an overcast of huge trees until we were almost crawling. I could smell gas. At one spot we stopped and Dr. Ignas took out a piece of paper, lit it, and threw it down. It instantly ignited a gas pocket, flames spurting from the ground. I could hardly believe that this natural gas had been untapped and escaping into the air for untold years.

A couple hundred yards away in thick underbrush we came to the first "well." It was a rusted, cast-iron, ten-inch diameter pipe sticking about a foot out of the ground, looking as if it had been there forever. But when I looked down inside, my spirits rose again. I could see oil, pure and untouched oil, with natural gas bubbles burbling upward. There was an old can lying on the ground with some twine tied around it. We lowered it down the pipe, drew up samples and put them in bottles. I asked why the can and string were there and was told that the local Indian population used it to bring up oil for their cook fires. All these years, at least fifty, Indians had been using the oil for free, as it came from the ground, for their cooking.

After several hours of looking at other primitive but producing wells, we were tired and ready to start our trip back. By then it was two o'clock, and, even with the trees for cover, I was so exhausted by the heat I could walk only twenty or thirty yards and then have to stop to rest. The sun was taking its toll on the others, too. Soon we were separated by hundreds of yards, and it was every man for himself. My feet and legs felt as if they could go no farther. Finally, I waited for Raul to find out where the others were. He didn't know, but after about twenty minutes we saw Dr. Ignas approaching, straddled on a donkey with an old Indian leading. I didn't know that we were only about three hundred yards from the Jeep, but I gladly paid the Indian twenty pesos for a ride over to where the vehicle was parked.

The sun was getting low by that time, and I was still trying to cool off and catch my breath as the Jeep crept slowly toward the city. After a few French fries, Raul and I returned to the room, too tired to be interested in meeting that night with the rest of *La Comunidad*.

The next day brought renewed animation as we met and talked for seven hours with *La Comunidad* about starting a new oil drilling expedition. I could tell by then that my first impression of Dr. Ignas had been correct. In our discussions of the possible forms our mutual venture might take, he amply demonstrated that he was arrogant. He was a man willing to listen only to his own ideas. Introducing a new perspective or possible alternatives could not be done directly; an idea had to be slipped in through the back door and left there as if forgotten. If it looked valuable, he would later sneak up on it, gather it to his ample belly, and then present it as his own.

Obviously, Dr. Ignas had to be given all the opportunities to play one-upmanship, otherwise a person could get nowhere with him. I sincerely hoped that his attitude would not be a problem in working out what might be an interesting deal and that he wasn't such a big honcho in the group as he assumed he was. Time would tell.

FEBRUARY 13, 1980—BARRANQUILLA, COLOMBIA, AIRPLANES FOR SALE

That evening, Dr. Moreno, another old lawyer friend of Raul, came by with Dr. Ignas. We talked for some time about oil, the United States, and other matters.

Since they knew I was in the aviation business, Dr. Moreno brought up the subject of confiscated aircraft in Colombia. He told me of how he could get them released if the money was right. We talked excitedly about this new opportunity until late into the night. Raul suggested we should take a ride with Dr. Moreno into the Guajira Peninsula, to Riohacha, to look into the possibilities of the impounded airplanes.

The Guajira is the northernmost area of Colombia. Its upper western stretches are coastal desert and the upper eastern lands are fertile, with some low mountain ranges. There are hundreds of miles of deserted coastline and navigable bays. The land to the south where we were staying is more fertile and rises rapidly into the Sierra Nevada, the range of mountains with the highest peaks in the entire country.

The Guajira had long maintained its reputation for smuggling activities and in the past twenty years it had become one of the hottest places in the world for marijuana traffic and the transshipment of other drugs from other parts of Latin and South America. I was told that most of the confiscated planes were to be found there.

It sounded like a great adventure, and I readily agreed to go. We were to meet at six in the morning for breakfast and hire a taxi for the 150-mile ride to Riohacha. I didn't sleep well that night for thinking of how financially favorable this trip to Colombia could turn out to be and that if I could get airplanes like this, at a good price, it was almost too good to believe.

CHAPTER TWO

After breakfast at the Hotel Royal, we shopped for a decent-looking taxi and made a deal for two hundred dollars to take us to Riohacha. We hopped in the taxi and headed north. About twenty minutes later, just having left Barranquilla, I got my first real lesson on Colombian-American relations on Colombia's north coast.

We arrived at the bridge crossing the Magdalena River, which I would soon come to regard as my personal "gateway to hell." The bridge was manned by the *Policia Nacional* (National Police) as a toll bridge and checkpoint with six booths, three for outbound traffic to Santa Marta and the Guajira and three for inbound traffic.

It would be foolish to suppose that this checkpoint had much to do with national security and control of contraband. What it did have to do with was money, money, and more money, and I was to find out firsthand that this was where the buck stops. It was where, I had no doubt, plenty of bucks had already stopped and had found a happy home.

I was taken out of the car, having been spotted as an American. Apparently, here, in 1980, "American" always translated to mean "rich American," always an easy mark. You either paid for whatever the day's sentries thought the traffic would bear—$100, $250, $500—or you went to jail. It was all a bluff, of course, because they certainly didn't want you to go to jail. Going to jail would mean no more under-the-table money for them. Moreover, the sentries believed that all—and I mean *all*—Americans heading into this part of the country, the Guajira, were what they called *marimberos* (marijuana people), and *marimberos,* of course, were there precisely to spread money around in return for illicit favors.

Luckily for me, I was with a lawyer, Dr. Moreno, who knew the ropes, so I was released after a ten-minute check of my papers. It didn't occur to me at the time, however, that I had committed a cardinal sin. In failing to pay the guards even a token amount for allowing me to pass, I had also failed to make a single friend on the bridge. As I would find out later, the guards, although clearly not my friends and admirers, had not forgotten me. No, they had not forgotten me at all.

We continued on our way to Riohacha, taking the road to Santa Marta, which at that time was third-class or worse, full of potholes and dotted with broken-down vehicles. I was told that one thing is never done on such roads: stopping at night. This was where bandit country began, even the police were bandits. Life meant absolutely nothing here, and this included women and children. The only laws that applied along this stretch of road were survival and money.

As we approached Ciénaga, a small fishing town, we passed many wooden shacks with rusty iron-plate roofs. The overriding impression was of poverty, grinding poverty. No running water, no toilets, no electricity—nothing. At high tide, water comes inside the shacks. All their lives, the local residents had been fishing and eating fish each day, going to bed and waking up only to catch fish again the next day. Tattered children lined the road, holding up fish, hoping someone would stop and buy. Occasionally someone did.

Soon we came near to Santa Marta, called the "Gateway to the Guajira." A historic city of Colombia, its natural deep water harbor and rockbound inlets could have made it a jewel, but by 1980 the city fathers had succeeded in little more than simply transforming it into a bastardized, semi-modern Wild West town. Simón Bolívar, *El Libertador* (The Liberator), had died here; the airport was named for him. When the area was still part of Spain's New World possessions, pirate ships used its ports. Modern-day pirates in the illicit drug industries still used it, so in this respect, I reasoned, it had probably changed very little and was most likely still very wild. In more recent history, it was Santa Marta where Henri Charriere, better known as *Papillon*, was jailed after one of his notorious escapes from Devil's Island.

FEBRUARY 14, 1980—NEAR SANTA MARTA, UP INTO THE SIERRA NEVADA

About ten miles from Santa Marta, however, we turned east, bypassing the town. When I looked up and around, I saw the most majestic sights imaginable. The sun was just rising over the eastern escarpments of the Sierra Nevada de Santa Marta. The Sierra Nevada rise to well over eighteen thousand feet; sweeping up from sea level, the snowy peaks sparkled as the sunlight hit them.

These mountains are so beautiful and yet they can be so evil, I thought to myself. *The multi-billion dollar marijuana business starts right here.*

This was where the Colombian "Santa Marta Gold," considered the best marijuana in the world, was grown. Often obscured by clouds, the peaks could be seen clearly this morning. As we wound around and were given different views of the slopes, it seemed incredible and deeply tragic that what these magnificent mountains actually produced is what too many men and women often kill and are killed for: marijuana.

As I looked up, I wondered just how much marijuana had either already been shipped or would soon leave there for the United States and, even worse, how many people had died and would die there because of it, some of them, perhaps, trying to take off in their pot-laden aircraft.

About halfway to Riohacha we passed through the small town of Palomino. I was still gazing up at the mountains when Raul called my attention to something lower down. Sure enough, there was an old Twin Beech just taking off a grass strip, as if my thoughts of a few minutes earlier had conjured it up.

I could hear the engines, still running at maximum takeoff power, even though the plane was at three hundred feet in the air. It looked very heavy and was struggling to maintain altitude. Finally, I heard the engines being pulled back very slowly.

Both pilots must still have been shaking and praying, jubilant that they had gotten off the ground. I could only imagine how the adrenalin was pumping through their veins, with still over five hundred miles of open water to go and absolutely no chance of survival if an engine sputtered or quit.

It wasn't like you see it on television. There was no make-believe about it; these were men who had laid their lives on a thin knife edge of life-and-death reality, just for the sake of the marijuana trade. So far, perhaps, these *marimberos* were ahead; however, their journey had just begun, and I doubt if the thought of money even entered their minds in those few nerve-wracking minutes during takeoff, only fear and uncertainty about whether or not they were going to make it. As they disappeared into the clouds, I was certain that no small amount of relief was theirs simply because they had survived the takeoff.

February 14, 1980—Riohacha, The "Wild West" of the Tropics

The rest of the drive to Riohacha was uneventful. It was hard to erase from my mind what I had just seen. As we approached Riohacha, about ten miles out, the rutted, two-lane road suddenly opened up into an eight-lane super-highway. I thought I was seeing things, but, no, the miserable road had turned into a fifteen thousand foot runway, painted and marked like the ones in the States, right here, in the middle of nowhere.

Dr. Moreno turned to me and smiled, "What do you think of this new airport?"

I wasn't so naive as to believe it was an airport, and this most certainly was no clandestine airstrip. Here, right before me, was a military runway, and any doper using it had to be big time, well-connected or have a lot of *dinero*.

Dr. Moreno went on to explain that this was where most of the big DC-6s, DC-7s, and jets picked up their loads of marijuana. I asked Dr. Moreno how it had come to be built, and he merely shrugged, laughed, and said, "*Quién sabe?*" (Who knows?) I later learned that United States Customs and the DEA had high-altitude photographs of this installation and monitored it regularly.

Less than two and a half miles later, this monstrous airstrip had restored itself back into the same old two-lane, potholed road and a short while later, we were in the middle of Riohacha, the capital and principal city of the department of Guajira in Colombia.

Up until the pot bonanza hit the area, Riohacha had been a backward little town primarily engaged in fishing, shipping, working the salt flats, and "standard" contraband operations involving liquor, tobacco, electric appliances and the like under reasonable control, tolerated by the authorities as the inhabitants had few other sources of income.

This, too, had changed. It had become a Wild West town in the tropics. Along with Guajiro Indians in their native costume—the women in flowing robes, headbands, sandals with large pompoms, and cheeks painted black as a protection from the sun; the men in mid-calf, wide-legged wraparound pants, loose over-blouses, and straw hats—and the ever-present impoverished street people, one would also find flashy, newly-rich Colombians in sparkling pick-up trucks and four-wheel drive Jeeps sporting Rolex watches, heavy gold chains, and fat wallets. The wide gap between the extremely poor and the extremely rich—with absolutely nothing in between—was truly astounding.

Shortly thereafter, we pulled up to the airport. I started to get out of the car with the others, but Dr. Moreno said, "No, no, Bobby. You must stay."

I asked why, and he replied, "The police will think you are a DEA agent."

A few minutes later, Raul returned. He told me to remain in the car, repeating, "Bobby, it would look strange for an American to be here looking at airplanes and photographing them; only a United States drug agent would be doing that." Reluctantly, I agreed and handed Raul the Polaroid camera and a pad and pencil. I sat back to wait.

In half an hour, they were back. I was disappointed. The photos showed nothing but old "shit-boxes," the term pilots often use for abandoned planes that have been left to rust and rot for years. I concluded that I had been "had." Paying a lawyer, a taxi, as well as all the other expenses to ride to Riohacha from Barranquilla only to find nothing, well, it just seemed such a waste of time and money; but, then, on second thought, I came to realize that the experience did offer insights into Colombia's cultural and economic environment and that alone, perhaps, would be well worth the adventure.

When we stopped to eat, everyone in the place seemed to be staring holes into me, not just with curiosity, but with hostility. I had a definite sense of being threatened, but, thankfully, nothing out of the ordinary happened, so I dismissed these uneasy feelings.

When I picked up the menu, I was pleased and relieved to see that we were not beyond the last outpost of civilization—they had French fries and Coca-Cola. When we had finished, we started back on our way to Barranquilla.

Later, I was to learn that I had been right: "gringos" snooping around airports in the Guajira are definitely not welcomed and are not always so lucky.

CHAPTER THREE

Our return trip to Barranquilla from Riohacha was very hot. All the car windows were rolled down, as there was no air conditioning. We just sat there, rolling down the highway, quiet and sluggish. Suddenly, out of the clear blue, as we approached Santa Marta, Raul suggested we make a stop at the Simón Bolívar Airport in Rodadero, the luxury beach and resort district immediately to the west of Santa Marta. He had just remembered hearing about a Learjet that had been confiscated some time back, and, supposedly, it was still there. I have a special thing for Learjets, so I listened intently, more interested by the minute, trying to dredge information out of him about how the plane happened to end up there. All he could recall was that it had come to Colombia as an air ambulance and that someone had died.

Who was it? How had he died? What had happened?

Raul remembered that a lot of articles had been written about it in the newspapers a few years back, and Dr. Moreno also recalled a lot of TV and radio coverage.

"If you're going to make a decision then we had better do something but quick. ("Sonteen bot queek" was how Raul actually vocalized the words, his accented English always making me smile.)

"All right, let's do it. We're on a hunting trip for airplanes, so let's go take a look," I commanded; my sixth sense was now screaming at me.

Somewhere around four o'clock in the afternoon, we turned off the main road in Rodadero and headed across the railroad tracks into Simón Bolívar Airport. The first thing I saw was an old B-25 World War II bomber. We stopped, and sure enough, there sat the alleged first doper airplane confiscated in Colombia. It was in bad condition, as it had been there since 1969. It sat next to the airport manager's house, right beside the salty Caribbean. After a few minutes of photographing it just as a matter of general interest, we climbed back into the taxi.

Seconds later, behind some trucks, I saw the tail of the Learjet. As we got closer, it came into full view. She was beautiful, such a magnificent machine, sitting apart from the others, like a queen in exile, beside the sea, with a small white building in attendance. As we came closer, I knew I had fallen in love at first sight with Learjet N464J.

We got out of the car and walked into the terminal. It was surprisingly clean. There were only a few armed guards slouched here and there; otherwise, it was almost deserted. It was like being in any small airport anywhere in the United States—no people staring, no hostile or suspicious glances, quite a feeling of freedom. We passed through the parking area and opened a small gate leading onto the ramp.

I was even more excited as we started across the ramp, approximately one hundred yards over to the jet. I snapped a few Polaroid shots as we approached her. There she sat, a beautiful creation of man, about ten feet off the ramp, in the mud. All the tires were flattened and sunk down in the soft earth. I bent down to look underneath at the landing gear when suddenly the air exploded with excited shouts.

Raul was shouting, "No, no, don't shoot!" I banged my head on the leading edge of the wing as I jumped up in reaction. For just a moment, all I could hear was the click of machine guns being readied as the soldiers instantly surrounded us. I was scared witless to see about a dozen Colombian soldiers yelling and jamming their guns at us at point-blank range.

We immediately threw up our hands.

I didn't know what was being said. It was a bedlam of staccato Spanish, but I knew it wasn't a welcome speech. Less than a minute later, we were being escorted back to the terminal. A few of the soldiers walked over to the small white building. Little did I know at that time how much I would grow to hate the very sight of that building. We reached the terminal at the point of a gun and were hustled through the gate. It slammed after us, and, much to my astonishment, the soldiers remained on the other side. They were still yelling and shouting, but I had enough sense to keep my mouth shut

A few minutes later, the soldiers started back to the white building, which I came to refer as the "compound." We all sat down, very carefully, on a bench next to the gate. I looked at Raul and could plainly see that he was as dumbfounded as I was. I remember vividly wondering what kind of a hornet's nest we had overturned and why the furor over that plane. It must have been something very special to someone, and it was certainly a big mystery to me.

After a few minutes of conversation between Dr. Moreno and Raul, they told me what they thought had happened. The compound had been built there and the soldiers assigned to special duty to guard the jet twenty-four hours a day, seven days a week. Absolutely no one, not even a Colombian, and especially not a foreigner, was to be allowed within one hundred yards of the jet.

We had caught them napping. No one had been around in over a year and, suddenly, there we were. They had reacted hostilely because we had taken them by surprise. We later learned that they had been assigned there three years before, on June 15, 1977, and given orders to arrest anyone attempting to enter the Learjet. This was to be treated as a restricted area, especially for Americans, as several attempts had been made to hijack it.

But why? This was a burning question. I was determined to know the answer. And in learning it, I was also to learn more about corruption and crookedness on an international level, in high and low places, than I had ever dreamed could exist on such a scale.

The tumult of soldiers had now died down and, recovering some courage, I took a few more photos from a discreet distance. We departed for Barranquilla. It was just turning dark as we passed back through Ciénaga. Smoke from cook fires and dust from homecoming feet filled the air, along with the stench of rotten fish and open sewers. Poverty was still king and a fact of life here.

Back at the gateway to hell, I slumped down, turning my head aside so as not to be seen. Apparently, the guards could smell an "Americano." I was told to get out. After five minutes and another fifty dollar tip, we were allowed to leave and return to the hotel.

After my usual meal of French fries and Coca-Cola, Dr. Moreno, Raul, and I went to the room to talk. Dr. Moreno assured me again of how much clout he carried in Colombia, particularly in that region, and that there would be no problem getting the airplane out.

The summary way in which we were ousted from the Santa Marta airport made me skeptical about Dr. Moreno's alleged clout. I also felt he was overly optimistic about the "no problem" aspect of getting Learjet N464J out of Colombia.

FEBRUARY 15, 1980—HOMEWARD BOUND, DEAD SET AND DETERMINED

Dr. Moreno bade us good night. Raul and I talked about the Learjet in Santa Marta for what seemed like hours. Strangely, I should have been thinking of a multimillion dollar oil deal, but my mind was full of that beautiful airplane sitting in the mud like a captive princess. I was mystified by the all of the intrigue surrounding it, and I made up my mind to learn more about it when we got back to the states tomorrow morning.

Shortly after midnight, I had made up my mind. I was now dead set that Learjet N464J would soon be mine, and I had already started to call her simply 464 Juliet and sometimes, more familiarly, just plain Juliet. I lay awake in the dark, thinking of the special qualities a Learjet embodies, a true queen of the skies; I wondered if Bill Lear, its creator, could ever have imagined that one of his great ladies could have landed in such a predicament.

Anyone ever involved in the aviation industry shares a special feeling about Bill Lear and his Learjet. This aircraft was originally designed in Switzerland as a jet fighter. Later, it became the first production line private jet. An unmatched performance of 550 MPH and a forty-five thousand feet cruising altitude made it virtually every man's dream. The rest is aviation history: the Learjet had become the most prestigious form of executive air transportation. I was going to see to it that this Learjet was spared an ignoble and obscene decay in a Colombian trash heap or mudhole.

The next morning, as we passed through twenty thousand feet, about ten minutes after takeoff, I looked out my right-hand window. Somewhere around sixty miles to the east I could see, clearly, the giant Sierra Nevada mountains: still beautiful, always mysterious. I scanned the base of the mountains, unable to make out the town of Santa Marta. But I knew 464 Juliet was there, and I couldn't resist the tantalizing emotions and the growing excitement of the challenge before me, and, most of all, I couldn't restrain my desire to possess her. She would be mine one day, I was certain.

Most of the flight back was spent in asking Raul questions to which he had too few answers. I imagine he would have liked me to shut up, but what I was doing was trying to sort out, aloud, what was inside my head and what had taken place in the last three days, all of which would very shortly set me down in a perilous maze and change my life so dramatically.

CHAPTER FOUR

After a few days back home in Florida, I was still trying to locate the owners of 464 Juliet.

I called Insured Aircraft Title in Oklahoma and spoke with Mary Miller to request a title search. She gave me the verbal information that the recorded owner was Jet Associates of Little Rock, and that Cravens Dargan & Company in Houston were the United States insuring agents for British companies and underwriters at Lloyd's of London. I tried to telephone Jet Associates, only to find that they were out of business.

Still, I couldn't spend all of my time on this strange project. My company and family needed attention, lots of it. First of all, I liked to spend as much time as possible with my family. My wife, Terry, had been spending a great deal of time without me; although, she did, however, have her mother and our five children to keep her from being too lonely.

In 1980, my business was a good-sized operation: a Cessna dealership with parts and maintenance departments, a flight school, a charter service, an interiors shop, and a restaurant. Quite a bit of time and hard work was required to keep it running smoothly. An eighteen-hour workday was standard operating procedure for me, with help from Terry, to boot.

I sometimes wondered how I had ever let my business grow so big; but, as with other important decisions in my life, this one, too, had been made on the fly. To tell the truth, the growth of Air Unlimited was made on the basis of a host of seemingly chance circumstances and opportunities prompted by my innate stubbornness and pride and refusal to admit the word "impossible" into my vocabulary.

My family's automobile business had led me very early on to the joys of tinkering, and, ultimately, in mechanical aptitude I scored high, but I was a maverick (or, as more likely, from my family's perspective, a black sheep) who was no credit to them at all. The best thing that happened to me was that no one had ever told me what was impossible, so I would attack mechanical problems without being scared off by the naysayers.

At the same time, early in life, I was already learning to separate reality from fantasy. I often found ingenious and novel solutions to problems that more experienced people were unable to visualize because of preconceived ideas. This mechanical ability was to open doors for me later in life. As a matter of fact, it was to feed me for a good many years to come.

My idea of a great Friday or Saturday night date was to pick up my girlfriend, all dolled up, drive her down to the shop, find her a comfortable chair and a Coke, and then treat her to a fine performance of Bobby Wood rebuilding an engine. I lost a lot of beautiful girlfriends that way.

Throughout this time and for quite a few years after, I had a deep interest in racing cars, in 1959 setting the NHRA National Record for C-gas supercharged vehicles, and, for four or five years thereafter, I was actively involved in amateur racing in the Southeast.

In 1965, my grandfather decided to get some benefit out of my growing status as a racer and agreed to sponsor one of the first Funny Cars in the country. Funny Cars are serious drag racing cars that look "funny" because although they maintain the overall look and appearance of their standard showroom-model counterparts, they have been reworked to include a nitro-methane powered super-charged engine along with a significantly altered wheel-base and a much lighter composite body over the chassis. There was nothing, however, "funny" about the speeds I could achieve: well over two hundred miles per hour in less than seven seconds.

For me it was a time of fun, excitement and thrills. My automotive know-how was also attracting attention from some of the powers-that-be at Chevrolet, and during this period they sent me to California where I participated in the design of the first full-blown big-block Chevrolet prototype.

My thing was racing, however; so, shortly thereafter I turned professional, and, in 1969, I set the NHRA National Funny Car Elapsed Time record. I was participating in major meets and getting the reputation of being the "winningest Funny Car driver on the circuit." In 1969, I was chosen for Coca-Cola's Cavalcade of Stars team, on which I became one of their top runners. In 1970, I set an unofficial Speed and Elapsed Time Funny Car Record of 6.25 seconds at 236 mph.

Next year, 1971, I had a bad crash in Alton, Illinois. The car, at 220 mph, was totaled. The only thing left intact was the roll cage, with me inside. I didn't exactly walk away from it—my leg was broken and I had a concussion—but I felt, and still feel, that the good Lord was watching over me that day and, for some mysterious reason of His own, wanted me spared.

Six weeks later, I sawed off my cast and was back racing.

In 1972, I decided to give up professional racing, and I moved to Miami, Florida, where I opened Wood Engineering and, later, in 1978, Air Unlimited.

February 20, 1980—South Florida, Me and my Shadow, Raul Soto

Raul Soto, my right-hand man, was a native of Barranquilla, Colombia. Before moving to the States, Raul had been an auditor for a Colombian automobile import business. He settled in Chicago in 1965, working at O'Hare for a little over three years. The next ten years, he worked in aircraft upholstery, learning the business from top to bottom.

Raul moved to Miami in 1978. I first met him shortly after opening my Cessna dealership, where I put him in charge of my custom aircraft interior shop. His brother, Antonio, who still lived in Colombia, had worked for a department in the security section of the Colombian government. Between the two of them, they had established many connections with lawyers and officials in the Colombian immigration and customs services. Although he came from a lower middle-class family background—a constant struggle, yes, but property owners and respectable people in their community nonetheless—Raul's work gave him an excellent opportunity to make connections with influential people above his social level. Furthermore, since he was always personable and helpful, he was able to keep up these relationships on a solid basis.

At about fifty years old, Raul was eight or nine years older than I. He was short, thin, and well-scrubbed. Always clean-shaven and neatly combed, he had the Colombian habit of using cologne plentifully. He was energetic, enthusiastic, and tireless, with a good disposition and a ready smile, always willing to work. He was ambitious and loved making money, perhaps so much so that he was prone to take short cuts to get his hands on as much of it as he could.

Raul seemed to me to be an incongruous combination of "family man" and "Casanova"—engaging in casual encounters with the opposite sex, but more or less on a permanent arrangement basis. (After a certain amount of exposure to the Colombian way of life, I would discover that this was not all that unusual.)

A better second-in-command I would be hard pressed to find. Raul was my high-level "gofer" without par. He could be shown or told what to do or how to do something, and he would take to it like a flash of lightning. He was as close to a genius as there is when it came to finding immediate solutions to single-faceted problems; yet, when it came to handling long-range and complex matters that involved serious consequences if not thought out fully and dealt with carefully, he was as close to a moron as conceivable.

The most used phrases in his vocabulary of heavily-accented English were "No problem" and "I have a solution," with "Take it easy" a close runner-up. Since he was usually jovial and smiling, it made it easy for me to tell when he was upset or worried. His face would assume a bewildered look, and his eyes would glaze slightly, as if things were happening too fast for him to absorb. Our business relationship was so good that it hadn't taken us long to establish closer, more personal ties of friendship. Very simply, it was fun to be with him.

But now, however, a serious problem was emerging. Recently, I had been having some serious reservations about being taken for a walk in the garden by him in matters of financial accountability, and I knew I was going to have to check him out every step of the way. Concretely. Should things develop in Colombia concerning 464 Juliet, I would have to be able to count on Raul.

I opened my desk drawer and took out some invoices from Durant Aviation that went back almost nine months. These invoices covered a job Raul's department was doing for Durant, reupholstering 250 seats. Between interior-shop labor and materials, Air Unlimited had already spent twenty thousand dollars. Several times I had asked Raul to get at least a small partial payment, but I still had received no money. Raul had been giving me the "*mañana*" routine. He would invariably float some excuse like "When he finishes the job we will be paid in full," or "No problem," or just plain old "Tomorrow, Bobby, tomorrow."

I felt in my bones that there was indeed a problem here. I didn't want to believe Raul was stealing from me, of course, but this was not nickels and dimes, and I was beginning to suspect that such was indeed the case.

CHAPTER FIVE

One day, around the end of March, Raul walked into the office.

"Hey, *qué pasa*? (What's happening?) Are you daydreaming?"

"Right, daydreaming," I answered, sarcastically, "and I have been giving some serious thought to the Colombian deals. Time is passing, amigo. We'd better get started if we're going to do something on either one of them."

We discussed the timing and possibilities of putting everything together. First, the oil deal. I had sent the samples to the lab in Miami and had made a mental note to find out if the results would be ready soon. Second, the Learjet. I told Raul that I was having problems finding out who the owners of 464 Juliet were. I am no procrastinator and all these delays were making me chafe at the bit. I asked him to make some calls to Colombia to see if he could get us a connection with the judge in Santa Marta to find out what could be done about 464 Juliet.

It was obvious that our "no problem" attorney, Dr. Moreno, had dropped the ball and with all of his clout had come up empty-handed. Raul promised he would ask Gustavo, one of the *La Comunidad* partners in Barranquilla who had also become one of our new trusted Colombian amigos, to keep his eyes open for someone better able to handle the matter.

"Take it easy," Raul said. "We can get a connection in Colombia to get the Learjet out. It might take a little time to get the right guy is all; but, with money, no sweat."

More time passed. It was now almost the middle of April. I was still mulling over what to do about Raul, and here I was, still procrastinating.

The work day began with no indication that it would be any different from the ones in the past few weeks, but at 8:10 A.M. everything changed. Raul burst into the office with a big smile on his face and with good news in tow.

"Get packed for Colombia," he said cheerfully. "We finally have made a solid connection with the judge in Santa Marta."

Gustavo, our amigo from *La Comunidad*, had called Raul the night before, saying he had finally found a lawyer in Ciénaga who was a friend of the judge. The lawyer's name was Aldo Reyes, and we needed to contact him.

In fifteen or twenty minutes, we had made plans to leave late that afternoon. We called Gustavo, now our number one gofer in Colombia, at his home; he was to meet us that night at the airport when we arrived.

I drove home and Terry packed my clothes for a few days. She wasn't happy about my leaving so abruptly, but she drove to the grocery store to buy me a supply of crackers and candy for the trip. At least on this trip to Colombia, I would be able to vary my diet of French fries.

I got back to the office after lunch and found a message to call Mr. Arnold of Cravens Dargan & Company in Houston. Mr. Arnold told me I should contact a Mr. Dunwoody of United Aviation Assurance in New York who was familiar with the Learjet matter. I immediately got Mr. Dunwoody on the telephone.

Yes, he was fully familiar with the case. He had been handling it for the past three years, along with law firms in California, Texas, and Washington. The tone of his voice indicated a thinly-veiled desire to brush me off. Nevertheless, he told me that the law firm of Gordon & Sanford held power of attorney on the plane and had been doing most of the legal work.

Could I buy the salvage rights? I would have to make a bid that he would take up with the underwriters in England. Although he was evasive when I asked who they were, I made a verbal offer of one hundred thousand dollars. He asked how I was going to get the Learjet out, and I told him I had some connections in Santa Marta.

The entire conversation was unsatisfactory, off-key. I felt I was wasting my time and he most certainly acted as if I was wasting his. He was not openly rude, but he was definitely condescending; a big man talking to a redneck who was not in the same league at all, who knew nothing about the jet.

He was right about my not knowing what had gone on, but all I wanted was a shot at getting Learjet 464J out, so I swallowed his condescension and went along, puzzled by not only his attitude but his evasiveness as well.

At the close of the conversation, I told him I was leaving in a few hours for Colombia for a closer look. This, apparently, was a bad mistake. He suddenly became interested in what I was saying, asking a lot of questions. Once he knew that I was going to Colombia, the machinery of an affair that, apparently, had been fairly dormant up to that time began grinding into motion.

I typed up a short note with my bid and put it in the mail immediately.

It was dated April 14, 1980. As I was walking through the lobby, almost ready to leave, I received a call from Red Garglay of the FAA, who asked me to come over immediately. He had some information on 464J.

The FAA office was only about three hundred yards from my operation, so I sprinted across to save time. I headed directly for Red's office, a practice normally frowned upon, but I was in and out of the administration offices so often I'm sure a lot of the personnel thought I was an employee.

To know Red was to love him and I felt myself a lucky man indeed to be included among his friends. He was no typical government bureaucrat. Red was allergic to bullshit and useless red tape, so he was known to cut a corner or two to help someone when it was important.

"Check this," said Red, handing me a photostatic copy of a bulletin from Colombia. It had been issued by the F-2 Section of the DAS. It contained a listing, together with a brief description of and information about confiscated aircraft in Colombia. Red pointed out the item on 464J.

> *Small aircraft, executive jet type, North American registration N464J, two turbines, white with blue and black stripes, confiscated at Santa Marta Airport, finding inside six ounces of cocaine. Persons held were ANTHONY GEKAKIS, STEPHEN CLAY BOLLING, and others.*
>
> *Assignment (of plane) is pending due to the fact that the Colombian Air Force is requesting its use as the President's standby airplane. The National Police have also not been able to assign it for the time being due to the fact that it is tied in with an alleged crime of smuggling and the Superior Judge of Customs has placed it at the disposition of the Second Penal (Court) Judge of the Circuit until December 1979.*
>
> *This airplane is the famous jet ambulance.*

"Where did you get this, Red?" I asked.

"Don't worry," he said, "This is a copy for you. Just don't say where you got it."

I asked Red if either of the names, Anthony Gekakis or Stephen Clay Polling, rang a bell. No, they didn't.

"Red, I've got to rush. I was on my way to the airport to leave for Colombia when you called. I just got word that we've found a connection for getting her out of there."

"One thing, Bobby," Red warned seriously, "be careful. There's something funny about this six ounces of cocaine, but cocaine is serious. Even more important, though, is to be aware that you can get hurt bad dealing with the Colombian military."

I nodded and thanked him again as I hurried out. On the way back to

Air Unlimited I was congratulating myself on what a great friend I had in Red Garglay. Several weeks back I had mentioned that I would appreciate his keeping his eyes open for any information on 464 Juliet. I was thankful he hadn't forgotten.

Once aboard the plane, I took Red's list from my pocket and showed it to Raul.

"Let's check these facts out." We went over the short paragraph line-by-line.

Item: Description of aircraft. Correct.

Item: Jet ambulance. Correct.

So far, so good.

Item: Six ounces of cocaine in the interior. Like Red said, something funny here. I knew that six ounces of cocaine was sufficient cause for an aircraft to be confiscated, but why would somebody put up a million dollar airplane for ten or twenty thousand dollars' worth of cocaine? This would have to be investigated.

Item: the Colombian Air Force request for assignment of the plane for the service of the President. Well, they very well could have requested it, but they damned well weren't using it.

Item: The plane had been at the disposition of the judge of the Second Penal Court. We were on our way to Colombia to see the judge; probably fact.

The last item was a puzzler: Anthony Gekakis, Stephen Clay Bolling, and others. It was to be expected that there were others. But who were they? This was a question the judge might be able to answer when we saw him.

I would have to wait until then.

CHAPTER SIX

Shortly after eight that night we were back in Barranquilla. One of Raul's customs connections and the newest addition to my crew, Diego, met us and walked us straight through. No customary procedures this time. Outside the building, Raul asked me for one hundred dollars to give to Diego, which Diego accepted with a gold-toothed smile on his swarthy face. Diego would be our important point of entry and departure in the future, so he merited a good tip; I was now accustomed to the practical realities of the standard practice for obtaining these little favors.

Gustavo, Antonio (Raul's brother, who preferred to be called by his nickname, Toño, pronounced *tone-yo*), and two other new amigos in my growing Colombian "crew" were waiting. Gustavo, the playboy of *La Comunidad*, was a big, fair man in the banana business, with solid political connections, time on his hands, and the desire to hustle a buck. He was a big drinker and a big womanizer. Toño was simply a more sincere version of his brother Raul.

We rode directly to the Hotel Royal. There was quite a reception committee on our arrival. It didn't occur to me at the time, but all this VIP attention was going to cost me.

We sat in the room for over an hour talking, when Aldo Reyes finally arrived. Aldo was an attractive-looking Colombian lawyer, thirty years old, slightly taller than the average Colombian—about five ten—and slim, weighing about 150 pounds. He had crisp, curly hair and a small, well-tended mustache. He smelled strongly of Florida Water cologne, a best-seller in Colombia. His voice was pleasant.

We immediately launched into a conversation in which he told me of his intimate friendship with the judge in Santa Marta and his top-notch connections at the Santa Marta airport. It sounded a little too pat, as though he were trying to impress me with shaky credentials. Just how effective he was going to be still had to be proven, but I figured that a beginning had to be made somewhere.

I questioned him at length about 464 Juliet and tried to piece together and fill out the bits of information Red Garglay had given me. Aldo's recollection of the facts was hazy, although he did remember that the plane had come to Santa Marta to pick up an American who had been badly burned in a plane crash and who was to be taken back to the States. He recalled that some cocaine had been found inside the plane. That was all. He suggested that we ride to Santa Marta the next day to have a closer look at the plane and that he would make arrangements to speak with the judge later. I felt that we were making some progress.

When everybody was gone, Raul told me that Aldo's sister was a judge in Ciénaga and that other members of the Reyes family were in politics. Everything seemed to be on track, but I still had something of a "sit back, watch, analyze, and be damned careful" feeling about "good ole Aldo."

APRIL 15, 1980—464 JULIET UPCLOSE AND PERSONAL

I was anxious the next morning as we approached the gateway to hell. That damned bridge was beginning to get on my nerves, having rattled me all the way from Barranquilla. There was the usual bullshit with the guards—out of the car, out with the papers, and, naturally, out with the wallet. This time only twenty dollars.

I was starting to truly worry about these bridge hassles. I knew I had been lucky so far only because I had always had a lawyer or Raul with me, but I could tell by the looks and the actions of some of the soldiers that they remembered me; yes, they were simply biding their time. They didn't like gringos who didn't pay, and this was now crystal clear. They were sure I was a *marimbero*—a marijuana person—which was making my offense even greater. I was not playing by the rules and paying up, as any decent doper was supposed to understand and fully appreciate.

We crawled along the highway, five of us crowded into an old 1953 Chevrolet belonging to Aquiles, a friend of Raul's brother. We made frequent stops to refill the leaky radiator. The car was a vintage piece of crap, with oil blowing out, wires dangling from under the dash, and completely bald tires. It didn't seem to bother anyone else but me, so I resigned myself to the fact that this was normal in Colombia. Aquiles was vastly more presentable than his car. He was tall, well-built, and very clean. He had a wonderful disposition and wonderful manners. Aquiles' car, for all its troubles and breakdowns, was to become our main means of transportation for the duration of the stay.

As we passed through Ciénaga and other smaller villages along the road, my heart ached at the poverty and misery of the people, especially the children. I silently prayed for the men of character and honor in Colombia.

I knew that in such cultures, tangled up and choked off by corruption and graft, it would take extraordinarily strong men of integrity to overcome such madness and that it would take many years to move their people into the light of free enterprise. I commented on this to Aldo, whose only response was to shrug and say, "Well, you know, they don't know anything better, so they don't miss anything." I disliked his callous attitude, but again I resigned myself to accept what I saw as the reality, the Colombian way of life in 1980.

We reached Santa Marta's Simón Bolívar airport at about nine thirty. It was an absolutely beautiful morning, with the sun shining on the mountains. After an exchange of conversation and fifty dollars between Raul and Aldo and the guards, we walked out to the Learjet as if we owned it. No guns this time, no shouting.

Hey, I thought, this Aldo really does have connections. The door of 464 Juliet was unlocked and I opened it. She was still in excellent condition. Most of the radios were gone and a few instruments were missing but the radar was still there. I took a few Polaroid shots. It was a disappointment not to find any papers in the aircraft.

When I removed the nose section I was amazed to find it filled with rocks, big rocks. Almost all of the avionics were missing. The rocks had been put in the nose section to keep the plane from falling on its tail.

I took a few more photos and was surprised to find that a few of the soldiers were actually smiling at me and coming near in a friendly manner. I passed around some cigarettes. Raul told me that the men wanted me to take their pictures. I was willing. They were as excited as children to see the Polaroid shots developing right before their eyes. They had never seen this before.

I was completely at ease. We were all standing around talking about where the avionics might be when I noticed a small man in short pants approaching us with four or five soldiers. When they were halfway across the ramp, one of the soldiers shouted something I didn't understand.

Our friendly little interlude was suddenly shattered. In an instant, all the soldiers in the little white house boiled out with machine guns. The soldiers alongside us, who had just gratefully accepted the photos we had taken, suddenly backed away from us, lifting their guns and ordering us to raise our hands. I looked in bewilderment at Raul and Aldo. Why the transformation and what the hell was going on?

The small man came near, shouting in Spanish to Aldo. Aldo was beginning to reply when the soldiers surrounding us shoved their guns in our backs, motioning us to move toward the terminal. The soldiers, our buddies a few minutes before, looked as if they would blow us away if we as much as flinched. Whoever the little man was, he was sure as hell the boss around that place, with no questions asked. Raul was sweating and shaking, and so was I.

When we got back to the terminal, the sudden burst of hostile activity stopped as quickly as it had started. Everybody disappeared. The soldiers returned to the guardhouse. The little man got into his car and drove off.

Raul and the others opened up a rapid fire of questions and replies in Spanish. I watched them, especially Aldo, and asked him what the little man had been saying. Aldo was evasive. I could see that he was dodging a straight answer. All he would tell me was that the little man was an important official and that we needed permission in writing to be there. I concluded that if I asked any more questions, Aldo might decide to forget the whole thing, so I acted satisfied with his answer.

We walked upstairs in the terminal to the small restaurant. The others were eating lunch as I settled for my usual French fries, washing them down with a Coca-Cola.

As we ate, I asked Raul questions about the mysterious little man with the big clout. I hadn't been satisfied with Aldo's answer, but I believed that Raul truly didn't know who the man could have been. What I did know was that something was very, very fishy about what Aldo had told me, or, rather, what he hadn't told me.

Aldo left for a few minutes to use the phone. He was back shortly, telling us that he had set up the meeting with the judge for that very afternoon at one o'clock.

CHAPTER SEVEN

The meeting Aldo had arranged was, at least, something concrete. I calmed down.

What had just happened at the Santa Marta Airport was that I had experienced the first of a series of innumerable and bewildering mind games these Colombians would play against me. Since I had never been exposed to such games, I wasn't ready. I was still not prepared to find that everything could be absolutely perfect one minute and then, suddenly, within the blink of an eye, turn to chaos.

It wasn't the ups and downs that were so bad. It was the speed at which they occurred. It would be like standing at the altar with the bride-to-be, full of illusions, hope, and love. And after the "I do's" she sees another man, tells you to buzz off, and leaves with him. Then, two minutes later, she's back with an "I'm sorry." The human mind cannot absorb the impact of such shocks. If the highs and lows would come more slowly, most people could handle them. But the speed—the speed was the killer.

A fifteen-minute ride from the airport took us into Santa Marta. We went to a hotel on the beach with a restaurant, *La Señora*, on an open patio overlooking the bay. The view was straight off a travel poster, a tropical paradise. Well-tended palm trees and shrubbery, white sand, shapely girls in bikinis, children building sand castles and calling out to each other as they splashed in the gentle surf.

After a quick lunch, Aldo excused himself and disappeared to go somewhere, and, when finally he returned, he told us that everything was set up; the judge was waiting for us. Raul and I stood up to leave, but Aldo said, "No, not you, Raul. You stay here. The judge wants to see Mr. Wood alone."

Raul shrugged but said nothing, and sat down again. Aldo and I walked out of the hotel. He led me around the corner and into an apartment building. This seemed strange to me. I had understood that legal business in Colombia was seldom conducted in a man's home; perhaps I was misinformed.

We climbed a stairway to the third floor, and Aldo knocked on a door. A young and very pretty Colombian woman, well-dressed, opened it and greeted Aldo familiarly. We walked into a spacious living room with a balcony, the entire surroundings furnished in modern decor. The tables and lamps were chrome and glass, the sofa and chairs custom-built. A lavish and impressively rich carpet covered the floor. Two men were waiting.

One was introduced to me as Judge Valdez. He was handsome, well-groomed down to his mustache, very cordial. He seemed very young to be a judge, still in his twenties. The other gentleman, Aldo told me, was the *Procurador* (Attorney General) of Santa Marta, a heavy-set man of medium height, also with a mustache. His face was greasy, spotted with large pimples, framed in equally greasy black hair. His baggy khaki pants, scuffed black shoes, and floral shirt seemed highly inappropriate attire for an attorney general on official business.

Their un-Colombian haste to get down to business immediately was also uncharacteristic and peculiar; they launched greedily into the matter at hand—the release of the Learjet. They spoke no English and my Spanish was poor, so Aldo was our translator.

Yes, of course, they could get the Learjet released to me. No problem. Aldo relayed that this would cost eighty thousand dollars. All cash, in United States dollars, and—here, Aldo made a significant shoving gesture with his hand—all under the table.

No sign of a file in their possession. Not even a business card to establish preliminary credentials. No questions to me about the legitimacy of my claim to 464 Juliet. No explanation of why a million dollar Learjet had been abandoned for three years. No mention of possible problems that existed, just glowing reassurances that I could come to Santa Marta and pick it up, ever so easily—for eighty thousand dollars.

They hadn't prepared much of a performance for that kind of entry fee requirement—these three amateur assholes belonged with Chuck Barris on the Gong Show. My first impulse was to laugh in their faces and inform them that I hadn't just walked in off the boat. However, I had second thoughts. I would hear them out. If they believed I was stupid enough to lie down and let them screw me, then I certainly wanted to know just how stupid they were and perhaps learn something in the process.

"That sounds reasonable," I said judiciously to Aldo.

"I'd like to hear more."

Eyes gleamed, white teeth glistened. I was taking the bait. They wanted forty thousand dollars right away and, later, once the plane was released, another forty thousand. In the interim, they would be preparing the necessary legal papers. I wasn't to worry about Aldo; they would pay him out of their own pockets.

I listened straight-faced for an hour to their bullshit about how easy it was going to be. They were relaxed, expansive, and shamelessly happy in the belief that they had themselves a real dumb-ass gringo to fleece.

Let them think it a while longer, I thought. Just possibly they might be the people I would ultimately have to deal with, distasteful as this might be—the kind of people who would take any and all unscrupulous short-cuts. If I expressed my disapproval at this stage, they would surely slink back into the jungle, and I would be back at square one. On the other hand, if I played along and pretended to be accepting them in good faith, I would gain time. And what I needed right then was a lot of time. I had to find that elusive handle on how to get 464 Juliet out of Colombia.

I was already learning something about Colombian mind games. I would produce one of my own, designed to come up with a foolproof plan to avoid paying them anything before I saw their wares and to give me time to dig deeper.

I knew I couldn't make any mistakes. I needed a logical and plausible explanation for delaying the first installment of forty thousand dollars, something they could instantly understand, giving them no reason whatsoever to question my good faith. What I came up with would also have to increase my credibility. I would have to speak with authority. This would throw them off balance and keep them from finding out that I really didn't know what had happened or what was happening. Not yet.

OK, I thought to myself, *this is what I am going to do,* and, after several minutes, I began my pitch.

"First, amigos, I will need to inspect the engines for corrosion. If they have any corrosion at all, then we will have to stop right there. You surely realize that if the engines are bad, the plane is worth nothing. To buy a new pair of engines in the United States, ship them to Colombia, and install them would be just too costly. In that case, I wouldn't be interested at all in recovering the Learjet.

"You must also understand," I continued, "that a general inspection of the plane will also be necessary. I will have to bring down an expert mechanic from the States to remove some special interlocking fuel cell panels and check them with a bore scope."

I knew they didn't know what the cell panels were because I didn't myself, there is no such thing. As for the bore scope, this actually exists, but is used for a completely different purpose. "Around the fuel cell panels will be the area where any internal corrosion will be found. If the expert's examination shows no internal corrosion that will mean that the plane was in good condition, in which case, then, gentlemen, we would have a deal. I will pay you the first forty thousand dollars, you will start the procedures for releasing the plane, and I will set up my plans for removing it from Colombia."

I knew that if they fell for this strategy, I would have plenty of time to uncover all the facts I needed, still keep good credibility with them, find out if they really could deliver, and force their hands if they couldn't. And if they couldn't, in that precious time I was buying, I might be able to find out just who else in Colombia could deliver.

They discussed these points for a few minutes and got back to me suggesting that perhaps another solution would be to dismantle the plane and ship it for reassembly in the States. This required me to point out to them that the high cost of such a solution would be too prohibitive and that I just would not be interested in spending that kind of money. No, the plane would have to be flown out.

They went back into a huddle, finally smiling and agreeing that these seemed to be reasonable requests. Apparently, they were also trying to maintain credibility as prudent businessmen. I knew that the terms I had requested, which they had accepted, would require letters of authorization from the court to the chief of Aerocivil (the Department of Civil Aeronautics) in Barranquilla, allowing us to inspect the aircraft in Colombia. Also, the *jefe* (chief) of Aerocivil would have to inspect and issue the permission for the jet to fly. Even if these jokers were for real, it would still put me in control of the situation. If not, and if I had given their con game a death blow, they could still exit with grace. No matter what the case would be, I would still be able to call the shots in the immediate future.

Aldo and I walked back to the restaurant where Raul and friends were waiting.

"Well, Aldo," I said briskly, "it looks as if we're on our way. First thing tomorrow morning, let's get going on the inspection permit from Aerocivil ."

I grimly noted that Aldo was groping for an answer.

"Well," he said lamely, "I thought I'd get started on the papers with the judge, but, if you want, I'll go back to Barranquilla and stay the night."

After having been around Aldo for twenty-four hours, I could see he was disturbed and preoccupied. His mind must have been going ninety miles an hour, trying to figure a way out of this unexpected turn of events. He must've been thinking, *How am I going to maintain my credibility and still screw this* Americano *out of his money*? Without doubt, he thought of me as a "rich American," and I hadn't tried to disillusion him. He didn't want me to get away without something being left in his pocket, and he wanted to keep an eye on me.

I was satisfied with this situation. I had him off balance and had the time to keep his head a little screwed up, which gave me a little more edge and room to move around.

It was starting to get dark when we passed back through Ciénaga. Back at the hotel in Barranquilla at nine in the evening, Aldo disappeared to make a phone call. He returned to anoint himself from the bottle of Florida Water he carried in his briefcase and then disappeared with a smirk and a flourish, off again for a little diversion.

I said nothing to Raul of the mind game I had devised to keep Aldo, the judge, and the attorney general off balance. As far as I could tell, Raul had been working for my best interests in Colombia, even though he may have been scamming me back in the States. But there was always a chance that he might be involved with the others, so I was being careful.

I was nothing if not a realist.

CHAPTER EIGHT

Next morning, Raul, Aldo, and I went to the divisional office of Aerocivil at the Barranquilla airport to see the *jefe*, Luis Donado.

We waited in the anteroom for his arrival, and, when he came through the door, I could see he was not an ordinary Colombian. Donado was a huge man, well-built and clean-cut, with silver-streaked black hair. He was advised that we were waiting to see him and signaled to his secretary to bring us into his office. It was a small room, simply furnished, the walls covered with aviation pictures and the desk heaped with paperwork. He was a bull of a man, who seemed to fill the little room. When he spoke, his voice rang with authority.

I knew Donado had to see dozens of people daily with a multitude of different problems, so I was anxious to make a favorable impression and not be just another face in the crowd. I had coached Raul to tell Donado about my Cessna dealership, the flight school, and other services so that he would know I was serious and meant business. I would be happy to be of service to Mr. Donado if there was anything I could do for him stateside. We exchanged cards, I gave him my brochures, and he seemed interested and pleased to be making our acquaintance.

We told him the purpose of our visit, and he listened, offering little comment. I was certain Mr. Donado knew a hell of a lot more about 464 Juliet than he was telling me, but I didn't press him. I respected his reticence, as his position was delicate and important. I sensed that I would learn more if I waited. I had the impression that I would be dealing with an honest man in Donado.

At the end of the meeting, he was assuring us warmly that he would contact the judge to discuss the papers needed for inspection of the plane. He turned to Aldo to ask if he could have the judge's telephone number.

Aldo had been unusually quiet during the meeting. Now, he began displaying great industry, searching his pockets, rummaging through his briefcase. "How inconvenient," he apologized. He had neglected to bring his telephone book with him. Donado brushed it aside; his secretary would find it for him.

On the way back to the hotel, Aldo fidgeted. Finally, he asked to be dropped off downtown, muttering something about an errand he had to take care of for his sister. He would meet us back in the hotel. Raul, an accomplished busybody, was craning his neck out the rear window as we drove off, stopping for a red light.

"Hey, Bobby, Aldo's going into the Telecom office. He must be making some phone calls he doesn't want us to know about," he reported. With a scarcity of phone booths in Colombia, Telecom provides public telephone service.

Back at the hotel, Raul and I wondered why Aldo was behaving so mysteriously. I had a good idea, but said nothing. My "guests" were there, having a fine time. These "guests" were beginning to get expensive, real high-rollers ordering liquor and trays of food, signing my account. Their hospitality was unlimited, inviting friends they had bumped into in the lobby that I had never even seen before. Colombian drinking gets heavy, especially when it's for free, but I knew I needed their help and didn't want to look cheap, so I bit my tongue and said nothing.

Aldo returned in about an hour, looking harried and breathless. He had come back only to pick up his car and say goodbye. He had to get back to Santa Marta to see the judge. I spent the rest of the afternoon and evening watching my uninvited guests having a ball.

It was frustrating, the waiting. I did not enjoy being in a situation over which I still had almost no control. I could only wait and observe. I wondered what Aldo was doing in Santa Marta. Later that night, he phoned and told us that the judge had been in touch with Donado and that a meeting was being arranged.

April 17, 1980—Donado's meeting with Judge Valdez

The next morning I received a call from Donado. He said he was going to Santa Marta that afternoon for his meeting with Judge Valdez. We asked if we could go along. He hesitated but finally agreed.

Shortly after five he picked us up, stopping at his home to change clothing. I was surprised to see that his house was less than two hundred yards from the bridge to hell. It was in a poor neighborhood of the city, right on the corner of a main intersection. Attached to his house was a small bar and restaurant, which, he told me, he owned and his wife operated. The bar and grill was certainly not a top-notch bistro; it was, however, cleaner than average. On the wall was a print of a painting by John Pitre called *War*. It occurred to me that the salary he received, even for such an honored position as he held as the chief of Aerocivil, must not have been substantial, which spoke volumes about his level of integrity and honor. A man of his position and power in a culture of corruption could make much more than his salary. Considerably more.

Donado walked back freshly dressed and said, "Let's go."

When we pulled up to the bridge, the soldiers spotted me, giving me the usual dirty looks, but as we were in the *jefe* of Aerocivil's truck, with government stickers on the windshield, there was no shakedown. We pulled through with no questions asked, and I sighed with relief.

Donado drove like a bat out of hell, all the time maintaining a loud and enthusiastic conversation with me through Raul about his work and his five children. He wanted to send his two oldest boys to the States to become pilots.

Bingo! Suddenly, I now had something in common with Luis Donado besides five children and a passion for aviation. I needed help; so did he. He could help me; I could help him. I instructed Raul to remind Donado that I had one of the largest flight schools in Miami and that I would be very happy to help his boys get their pilot's licenses in the States.

I felt that an immediate bond had been forged, as Donado seemed sincere about advancing the careers of his boys in aviation. I assured him that this would not be difficult and that I would be glad to help his sons get work in Miami to cover part of their living expenses. He was delighted with my offer and told me that he, too, would make all efforts to help me in Colombia. This man could play a highly important role in my activities in the country. He had the final word in Northern Colombia on "fly" or "no-fly." I knew I would have to do all I could to become important to him, as he held the key to a vital element of my problem in getting 464 Juliet out of Colombia.

Donado seemed a man of good faith who would make a sincere effort to repay any obligation he might incur. Robust and smiling, he seemed genuinely pleased with this arrangement, and I felt that I could count on his cooperation.

It was around eight thirty in the evening when we reached Santa Marta. Donado was looking for a restaurant named *La Hacienda*. We finally found it, a small place with an outdoor bar and upstairs patio. When we began getting out of the car, Donado told us to wait. Bewildered, Raul and I stayed where we were, but I couldn't imagine why we weren't allowed to see the judge.

We sat there, craning our necks and fidgeting for fifteen minutes. Finally, I turned to Raul. "I can't stand this, Raul," I said, "Sneak out of the car and take a fast look. If Donado comes back, I'll tell him you have a weak bladder."

Raul flashed me a grin of conspiracy and sauntered off. He was back in a couple of minutes.

"Did you see them?" I asked.

"*Si*, I had to be careful. Donado was facing my way. He was at a table with three other men. One was military—pretty high—I didn't see him very well. I didn't see the other one very well, either. He was well dressed, young. When he turned sideways I could see he had a moustache. But, Bobby, do you know who was with them? Remember that guy in the short pants who chased us away from the Learjet? He was there, too."

I considered Raul's report. I was tempted to go take a look myself. Raul said he hadn't seen Judge Valdez, but Aldo had made sure of that by not allowing Raul to visit him earlier—so, since his general description checked out, I stayed where I was.

Donado was back in another half hour, very quiet and looking disturbed. I had no idea what might have been bothering him, but in the few short hours we had been together, I felt that I had gotten to know a little about him, and I could sense that something had not gone to his liking. But all he said was that Judge Valdez was going to prepare an official request that Donado go to Santa Marta to make a preliminary inspection of the Learjet.

As we rode down the highway, I speculated on why he was upset. Perhaps, he was angry; Donado was clearly a proud Colombian who didn't like being taken for granted. He had a position of authority and was used to people coming to him, not going to them. It also occurred to me that a problem had come up about getting the jet released that he couldn't discuss just then.

If my analysis and evaluation of Donado were correct, these were possible explanations for his reaction. Nor could I discount my deep-rooted mistrust of the judge from the second circuit Aldo had taken me to only two days before. Had Donado discovered what I suspected, that Judge Valdez was planning to take me for a walk in the garden? If this were the case and he was making no mention of it, could it be that Valdez was trying to enlist Donado's help to scam me? There were still other mysteries to be solved. I would have to be very careful.

Halfway back to Barranquilla, Donado returned to his normal good humor. He pointed out that this first step, getting the formal request from Valdez to inspect 464 Juliet, was very important. This was due to the special nature of the case. Both the President of Colombia and the Director of Aerocivil in Bogotá, Donado's superior, had asked for the plane to be assigned to the Colombian Air Force (the *Fuerza Aerea Colombiana*, or FAC) a few years back, and Donado wanted to proceed with care. He didn't want to do anything except by the book, formally and in writing. I could appreciate why, remembering that one of the scraps of information in the Colombian F-2 report Red Garglay had given me had mentioned the request of the

Colombian Air Force to use 464 Juliet as the President's standby plane.

Why had the request not been granted to Colombia's head of state? Only later would I understand more fully Donado's extreme caution and the reasons why 464 Juliet was still sitting at the Santa Marta airport.

We crossed the bridge to hell without problems, and Donado dropped us at the hotel. I groaned inwardly when I reached the room. My entourage of ne'er-do-wells—my "crew" and the ever-present retinue of freeloaders surrounding them—were hard at it again, drinking and eating. They had been kicking back all day long, sponging off the "rich *Americano*." I somehow managed to keep a cheerful smile as I greeted them. My gut told me I would need this band of amigos.

Very soon after settling in after a long day, Aldo came bounding in, smiling and confident. He announced importantly that he had set up a meeting for me the next day with Valdez. It was to be in the judge's office back in Santa Marta, at two o'clock. Since Aldo had been burning up the roads between Barranquilla, Ciénaga, and Santa Marta, maybe he was finally getting the ball rolling.

Maybe he was finally telling the truth. I would just sit back and observe.

Come what may, I would find out what was happening.

CHAPTER NINE

The next day's "commute" from Barranquilla to Santa Marta was fairly normal and included the usual bridge confrontation and payoff dance as we crossed the Magdalena River. After leaving the guard house, we headed to Santa Marta and then went directly to the same *La Señora* restaurant for lunch located a little outside the city in the Rodadero section, which is the site of some of the world's most beautiful beaches. Aldo disappeared "to set things up with the judge." (By this time, I knew that a good many of Aldo's telephone calls and quick exits were actually made for meetings of a more personal and intimate nature, the main clue usually being a "quick shower" with Florida Water.)

The core of my crew (now consisting of Raul, my faithful employee and high-level, master gofer; Aquiles, our driver from *La Comunidad*; Toño, brother of Raul; and Gustavo, the *La Comunidad* playboy and my number one, first-class gofer) and I sat in *La Señora* until almost three, eating and drinking and waiting for Aldo. I continued to be amazed at their capacity to overindulge, but one thing was certain—the price was right for them.

When Aldo returned from his extracurricular activities, whatever they may have been, he motioned for Raul and me to go with him. Going into town, he told us that we shouldn't talk money with Judge Valdez; we were just to listen to what the judge would have to say. Of course, I wondered why we weren't to negotiate with him, because it seemed to me as if we had talked some pretty substantial figures at our last meeting, but I just nodded and tried to look inscrutable. I would let Aldo play out his hand.

We parked in a small side street, cramped and narrow. After walking a few yards, we entered the stairway that opened directly into the old Caribbean-style building in front of us. Climbing to the third floor, we walked into a maze of small offices. Aldo motioned us into one of them.

We sat down beside a desk and looked around us. I had been examining the door and was now stealing sidewise glances at the papers littering a desk hoping to spot some evidence of Judge Valdez's credentials.

Suddenly, out of the corner of my eye, I saw someone so unexpected that I almost had heart failure. I couldn't believe what I had seen.

"Raul," I hissed, "did you see that man?"

Raul, bewildered, said no, he hadn't, but before he could say another word his face registered the shock of recognition. In walked the little white-haired man in the short pants who had had us thrown out of the compound at the Santa Marta airport on our initial visit to 464 Juliet and who Raul had seen at Donado's meeting the night before. This time he looked more formal, with pressed slacks, polished boots, striped long-sleeve shirt, no tie.

"I am Judge Jorge Valdez," he announced.

Shock upon shock! What the hell was Aldo trying to pull? This wasn't the same "Judge Valdez" I had met earlier with Aldo! I struggled for composure. I then found myself becoming furious with Aldo but prayed that I would not betray my rage in front of this man, who was, evidently, the *real* Judge Valdez. I had to completely regroup, blocking out my impressions of the "fake" Judge Valdez—that young, thin, and handsome Judge Valdez, with a full black mustache, that Aldo had tried to pass off on me.

This Judge Valdez, who at our "first meeting" had literally booted my entire crew out of the airport under force of arms and had denied us access to 464 Juliet, was much friendlier today, which was hardly a difficult transformation to make, considering he had almost had us shot at that "first meeting" at the airpor. No, today, this Judge Valdez simply shook hands with us and invited us to sit down. He spoke a little English, but broken, so Raul interpreted. We explained that I had bought the Learjet from the insurance company—a stretching of the truth at the time, since I did not yet have title—and that I wanted to get it released from his court. We spoke to him for a few minutes telling him who I was and establishing my credentials. He listened seriously, and finally told us that 464 Juliet was a very complex case. He reached out his hand to indicate six or eight folders making a stack over a foot high on his desk. The judge showed me documents and correspondence between the court and several law firms in the United States, also documents from Jet Avia, Inc. of Las Vegas who had leased 464 Juliet from Jet Associates. He handed me a one-page brochure of Jet Avia, Inc., showing photos of Chris Karamanos, listed as President, Jim Worden, Director of Operations, and Tony Gekakis, Chief Pilot. My anger began to subside; at least I was now starting to learn the names of some of the players in this devilish game.

I scanned hundreds of papers. There were even letters from United States Congressmen and a State of Nevada letterhead from the governor's office indicating that Chris Karamanos had been appointed to a special commission in the State of Nevada.

Then the judge showed me some photos. One in particular caught my eye. I picked it up but couldn't make out what it was, so I asked the judge about it. It looked to me at first like a photo of a very old African with no hair and indistinct features.

Then he told me: It was Bruce Allen, an American pilot who had crashed in the Guajira and who was to have been taken back to the United States in 464 Juliet. I looked again at the photo. It resembled photographic evidence of a war atrocity. The man had been burned so badly that he had no hair, his ears were almost gone, and his facial features had melted like wax. His body was charred black. It seemed unbelievable that he could have even been alive. He was sitting in a plain, upright chair, with his arms extended away and out from his body. I could almost smell his burnt flesh and feel his agony. I couldn't believe that anyone in the world could be so cruel as to place someone in his condition in that position. He should have been in a hospital, under treatment at an intensive care burn center.

My thoughts must have shown clearly on my face, because Raul kicked my foot as the judge was trying to catch my attention to speak to me. He told me that he had met with the jefe of Aerocivil and that he would write a letter requesting an official inspection. In the meantime, I should bring him all my documents of ownership of 464 Juliet.

The judge cautioned us not to go near the Learjet unless he was with us or unless we had something in writing from him. It was for our own protection, he told us; otherwise we might get shot. He smiled and remarked, "I believe you are aware that the Learjet is under military guard."

He also said he would have to study the files on the Learjet. The case had originally been assigned to and handled in the Second Penal Court, and only recently had it been transferred to the Third Penal Court, over which he, Judge Valdez, presided.

Before we left, I told Valdez I wanted to find out who "the others" were that had been detained along with Anthony Gekakis and Stephen Bolling. The judge jotted down a list of names. None of them rang a bell, so I slipped the list in my pocket to be checked out back in Miami. We told Valdez we would be back in a week or so and said good-bye.

As we walked down the steps I waited to hear what Aldo was going to say. That low-life son of a bitch, trying to screw me out of forty thousand dollars was one thing. I had suspected as much. But trying to pass off some snot-nosed kid as the judge was another. It must have been Aldo's assumption not just that I was *plain* stupid, but that I was *lily* stupid, and it was this that enraged me most. Now I understood the reason for his frantic phone calls and his sudden trip to Santa Marta two nights before. Once he knew the Director of Aerocivil, Luis Donado, was coming into the picture, he had to scuttle his original con game and produce the *real* judge.

He must have been frantic about the dangerous possibility that I would reveal his original plan to bypass Judge Valdez. Here was a man who was both sheepish and brazen. I still said nothing. I wanted to hear what his story would be. Raul sensed my rage and made unsuccessful attempts to clear the air by introducing many unrelated subjects which no one pursued. I had my emotions under control, though. If I blew it then, I knew I would regret it. Crooked as Aldo was, I needed him. I would bide my time, be patient, and let him think I was as stupid as he wanted to believe.

He began to act more confident by the minute, finally venturing to explain that the first "judge" I had met at the apartment had been the judge from the Second Penal Court and that he had decided it would be better for Judge Valdez to handle the case, which had been transferred to the Third Penal Court. He was stupid enough to have forgotten that he had introduced his friend to me as Judge Valdez. Or he might have been counting on my poor Spanish. I didn't remind him, acting as if I didn't remember the name given in the introduction.

"Yeah," I said innocently, "I guess you and the judge know best."

Seeing that I was swallowing this weak part of his story, Aldo grew bolder.

"What's more, this will cost you only seventy-five thousand dollars. I was able to negotiate it to save you five thousand," he announced triumphantly.

Raul knew and I knew what was happening. If I had to play the village idiot a little longer, so be it.

We had just stepped into the street when we heard several gunshots around the corner in rapid succession. I ducked back into the doorway, unwilling to be in the path of possible crossfire. Aldo didn't even look around; he stared at me in complete puzzlement.

"What's going on?" I asked.

"Probably a couple of *marimberos*," he shrugged indifferently at such a commonplace and ordinary disturbance.

We picked up the others, arriving at the bridge at about eight fifteen in the evening. This time the soldiers ordered me out of the car and searched me. They examined all the papers in my briefcase pockets. God only knows what would happen if I were alone, I thought.

We reached the hotel, and Aldo prepared to leave. We told him we would be back in six or eight days.

"Bobby, *un momentito*," he said briskly, "I'll be working on the papers; I'll need some money for expenses; about five hundred dollars should do it."

"Sure, Aldo," I said, taking out the money, "be sure everything is ready by the time we're back."

After he bade us good-bye, Raul looked at me in disgust. "Why did you give him the money?" he demanded. "You should have told him to wait until he's done something."

"Look, Raul," I answered, "so far, that five hundred is the best investment I've made. At least, Aldo's connected us with the right judge. We'll talk about it later."

Next morning, once on board the plane in Barranquilla, I sat back and stared out the window looking toward Santa Marta, thinking about 464 Juliet, Aldo, the fake judge, and the real judge.

"Raul, I tell you the way I see it. I know Aldo's a snake, but I don't mind dealing with snakes as long as I get in the last bite. Right now, he's all I've got. What we've got to do is find a way to get close to the judge. I don't think Aldo's all that close to him. Sure, he acts with us as if the judge is in his pocket, but look at how Valdez kicked his ass, and ours, out of the airport the other day.

"I don't even think Aldo's the judge's gofer, and I wouldn't be a bit surprised if the judge knows, or at least suspects, that Aldo was attempting to pull off a scam on us without cutting him into the action. I think this real Valdez caught Aldo with his pants down. I'm pretty sure Valdez wasn't there at the airport just by coincidence, but he's playing his hand very close to his chest. At this stage, I may not know exactly what the connection is between them, but I feel in my bones that the best way I can protect myself is to go along with Aldo and work at the best way to get in solidly with Valdez."

Raul was nodding thoughtfully. It was a little complicated for him, but he was following my reasoning. As for getting close to the judge, Raul understood that Aldo could certainly help.

"Take it easy," Raul reassured me, "We've got plenty of solutions. I promise you."

CHAPTER TEN

I was up bright and early and at work around seven thirty. Glad to be home.

Red Garglay's document and Judge Valdez's list of names were in my hand. I had gone over the information and the list at least twenty times, trying to piece something together with little success; but, at least, I had the six names of those who had flown to Santa Marta in 464 Juliet—Steve Bolling and Anthony Gekakis, whose names I already knew, plus Jeffrey Ellis, Miguel Parada, Jamiel Alexander "Jimmy" Chagra, and Jerry Lee Wilson. They were just names to me, nothing rang a bell.

Time to see Red Garglay, again, I thought. As Red had access to a few "classified" computers, maybe he could check out the names I had been given and get me some background on who they were. I walked over to see Red at about nine fifteen in the morning.

"Red, I got this list of names from the judge in Colombia. These are the people who brought 464 Juliet into the country. I thought maybe you could check them out for me. I'm curious to find out what role they played and to see if I can find any connection as to why there's so damned much secrecy and mystery about the whole matter."

"How were they involved in it?"

"All I know is that they were arrested in Santa Marta."

"One of these—Chagra—rings a faint bell. I'll call one of my sources at customs." He picked up the phone, asked for his friend and gave the tail number of the Learjet and the six names, with the request that he would like any available information as quickly as possible.

"Sit a while and catch me up on what's going on," he invited. "They'll be back to me in about a half an hour."

I told him about my latest trip and then we got onto other subjects, mostly automotive, as I had been tuning up Red's car for him for the past three or four years. We discussed the alcohol-water injection system I had helped him install in his Mercury, and its resulting mileage improvement.

At about nine forty-five, the phone rang. His friend was on the line. Red's brief "Yeah's" were quickly turning into "How about that's" and "Wow's." He was busily scribbling as he listened.

When he hung up, he looked at me and said, "Bobby, you got a real hornet's nest here."

"Come on, Red, don't keep me in suspense."

"Well, first of all, this Jimmy Chagra has been involved in the marijuana and cocaine business for some time. They have a file on him a mile high, stretching back for years. Hell, he's in jail now. The funny thing is, he's still under one hell of an investigation—and that is classified. Jerry Lee Wilson? Also a record on various drug smuggling operations. No information on the others, only that they were detained along with 464 Juliet in Santa Marta.

"My advice to you, Bobby, is to be very careful." He went on, "These boys are real heavies in the drug business and, jail or not, something is funny about it."

I asked what made him say this and he told me.

"When my connection tells me it's classified, this means that they have something important. Otherwise, they would have given me a full rundown. So, when I don't get what I want, I know something big—really big—is going down. But, say, there's probably something you can find on this in the old newspaper files."

"OK, I can look into that," I said, "but, actually, I'm not too concerned right now. I just thought it could throw some light on what had happened, and it very well may have had something to do with all the paperwork I'm involved in trying to get 464 Juliet out of Colombia. It's the paperwork that I've got to concentrate on right now. One thing I'm going to need as soon as I get the release is a ferry permit. Do I get that from you?"

"No, you'll have to get it from the International FAA Office at Miami International," Red informed me, "but Bill Everett over there is a good friend of mine, so just let me know when you need it and I'll ask him to get it moving for you."

I thanked Red for all his help and left with a promise to keep in touch.

If this book were complete fiction, Bobby Wood would immediately become like James Bond and do a brilliant job of researching and learning, effortlessly, everything about Jimmy Chagra and Jerry Wilson, finding out why such heavies were involved in a mission of mercy, but that isn't what happened.

Being a single-minded person, my all-consuming interest in 464 Juliet was to get her released, and for me, a task like this requires a kind of tunnel vision. I was dealing with the present and pressing realities of first establishing ownership of the plane, then getting Judge Valdez the papers he needed so he would authorize the Colombian Aerocivil to inspect the plane, and then, finally, orchestrating the complicated logistics of making 464 Juliet airworthy again. On top of that, I was running a full-time, demanding business.

From a position of 20/20 hindsight, I believe that had I known then all the ramifications of the involvement of Jimmy Chagra, Jerry Lee Wilson, the United States federal government agencies, and Colombian central and regional government agencies in this matter, I very well may have written off my efforts up to that point and dropped them. It may be that my burning determination to get 464 Juliet released subconsciously blocked out any side issues that could have affected the outcome.

So, since this is a factual account, the truth of the matter is that I knew nothing at the time of all those involvements. This was strictly a case of truth being stranger than fiction. Despite the fact that during February and March of 1980 the national media were covering the latest news on Jimmy Chagra, my nose had been to the grindstone in a universe light-years away from him and all the news he had created. What I learned came piecemeal, and after the fact.

Red's information had aroused my curiosity, however, and I decided to ask my good friend Jim Burkett, a top-notch private investigator and polygraph expert, what he might know about Jimmy Chagra. I had used his services several times before and knew he could deliver.

Burkett had been in law enforcement in the Hollywood, Florida, Police Department and the Palm Beach County Sheriff's office. He had gone into business for himself in 1973. Before entering police work, he had been a United States Navy diver, and he must have been a good one. I knew that after his retirement, he had been in charge of special effects for the underwater demolition scenes for the James Bond movie *Thunderball*. In fact, he had appeared in many of the scenes.

"Jim," I said, "I need a rundown on a couple of names."

"What are they?" he asked.

"I know they're on the customs database, but what they have is mainly classified. I know they're involved in drugs, but I don't know much more, except that they were on the Learjet I'm trying to get released from Colombia. You already know it's the jet ambulance that was sent down to pick up someone who got burned down there—they're Jimmy Chagra and Jerry Lee Wilson."

"Chagra? Jimmy Chagra? Hey, fellow, you've got to be kidding. Wait a minute; it's got to be somebody else. Somebody with the same name. Do you have an AKA?"

"Sure. Jamiel Alexander Chagra."

"Yeah, it's one and the same. You mean to tell me you've never heard of him?" Jim asked incredulously.

"Never did. Come on, Jim, tell me about him," I said.

Burkett explained that Chagra had figured in newspapers all over the country earlier that year. He knew Chagra had been picked up after having jumped a big bail the day he was to have been sentenced on a cocaine conviction somewhere in Texas and that he had been re-arrested and finally sentenced. He also knew Chagra was allegedly involved in the murder of a federal judge in 1979.

"I don't remember all the details," Burkett told me, "but it will be a simple matter to run down some information from the newspaper morgues, if you want me to do that."

I assured him I did, and he promised he would get back to me soon, adding, as he was preparing to hang up, in a joking tone of voice, "Next time you have a real hard job of investigation like this, get a high-school kid to do it."

"Just a minute," I said, "I do have something else." I outlined to him the problems I was having getting the information I needed to establish the current title to 464 Juliet. I needed to know where to start; I had gotten nowhere with Dunwoody at United Aviation and had a feeling I was being jerked around.

"I'll get back to you in a day or so and we'll talk about it then," he promised.

Good as his word, Jim came to the office two days later and handed me a folder with copies of several newspaper articles.

"I found myself an assistant," he said. "My wife, Kitty. I was busy and she dug up some of the information you wanted from the files. Here's the story on Jimmy Chagra," and we then looked over the articles that Kitty Burkett had prepared for me. She had arranged them chronologically and, then, for good measure, prepared a synopsis of the most important events the stories covered. The clippings covered a period from January 1979 through spring of 1980 and dealt with Jimmy Chagra's arrest, arraignment, trial, and conviction on drug trafficking charges; his bail jumping prior to sentencing; and, finally, his re-arrest and sentencing.

There were also reports on the assassination of Judge John Wood (no relation) that took place the very day Judge Wood was to preside over Jimmy Chagra's trial. Many of the articles mentioned Chagra's activities in Colombia and his connection with 464 Juliet as a substantial part of the evidence leading to his indictment.

The first article, dated January 28, 1979, was written by Lou Cannon for the *Washington Post*. It dealt mainly with Jimmy Chagra's brother Lee who had been murdered before Christmas of 1978. It provided some interesting information on the background of the Chagra family in general, and specific information on Jimmy Chagra that touched on my personal interest in the matter.

The article, "Texas Gambler-Lawyer's Death Leave Few Clues," described Lee Chagra as the Southwest's most flamboyant lawyer, widely considered the best at the business of representing accused narcotics smugglers.

> *In 1978, he won acquittal in Ardmore, Oklahoma, of a group known as the El Paso 10, then charged with the most massive marijuana smuggling operation in Oklahoma history. Since 1973, federal officials had made Chagra the subject of a long and persistent investigation to link him to drug smuggling in three countries.*
>
> *Upon his death, federal officials seized his files, which the surviving family members believed the authorities were using to zero in on brother Jimmy, in whom they showed interest since the summer of 1977, when he persuaded Jet Avia, a Nevada air charter service, to fly to Colombia to rescue a burned pilot whose plane supposedly had crashed while engaged in drug trafficking. Chagra and the rescue crew were detained by Colombian authorities but ultimately were released without being charged.*

The federal officials, apparently, were a little more than "interested" in Jimmy Chagra. There was a UPI dispatch from Midland, Texas, dated February 27, 1979, headlined, "Chagra's Brother Arrested in Vegas."

> *Jamiel Alexander "Jimmy" Chagra, brother of slain El Paso defense attorney Lee Chagra, was arrested Monday on a secret five-count narcotics indictment handed down earlier in the day.*
>
> *United States Attorney Jamie C. Boyd said the indictment covered Chagra's activities in Texas, Florida, and the Republic of Colombia from June 1, 1977, to June 1, 1978. The charge specifically charges Chagra with conspiracy to import marijuana and cocaine and distribute the drugs …*
>
> *… Lee Chagra's death, an assassination attempt on an assistant United States attorney and alleged racketeering, prostitution, gambling, and narcotics currently are the subject of federal grand jury investigations in El Paso and San Antonio in Texas and by grand juries in Las Vegas, Seattle, Wash. and Florida …*
>
> *… Boyd said the federal grand jury indictment of Jimmy Chagra was part of the wide-ranging investigation by all the panels.*
>
> *"This indictment is an outgrowth of an intensive grand jury probe expected to continue for as long as a year or more," Boyd said. "We have*

called forty witnesses already, and we anticipate calling as many as two hundred before it is over."

With respect to the grand jury probe, another UPI dispatch, also dated February 27, 1979, carried an interesting sidelight concerning 464 Juliet:

> *One person mentioned as a possible witness is University of Nevada Regent Chris Karamanos, operator of Jet Avia in 1977 when one of the company planes was seized in Colombia, South America, and the crew detained. Colombian authorities said narcotics may have been involved in what owners of Jet Avia said was an air ambulance airlift for a burn victim.*
>
> *The plane had been chartered by a man named Chagra in El Paso, Texas, who boarded the plane en route to Colombia and was one of the first to be released when authorities seized the aircraft ...*

A few facts were emerging in the light of this new information I had. First and foremost, it became very clear to me that somebody, or, rather, a lot of somebodies were out to get the Chagras. In fact, somebody had already "gotten" Lee Chagra. Second, the "federal officials" mentioned seemed to be basing much of their case against Jimmy Chagra merely on his presence aboard an air ambulance flight dispatched to Colombia to rescue a United States citizen burned in a recent flight out of Colombia alleged to have crashed during a drug operation. Chagra and the rescue crew were detained by Colombian authorities but were ultimately released without being charged. If these investigations of the Chagra's had been going on since back in 1973, somebody, it seemed, was getting desperate, reaching out very far, perhaps even stretching the limits of the law in order to enforce it.

Jimmy Chagra was indicted by a Midland federal grand jury to face trial in Austin on May 29, 1979. That date, May 29, was also the day that marked a new chapter in the series of articles I had. On that very day, Judge John H. Wood, Jr. was assassinated early in the morning of the day he was to begin presiding over Jimmy Chagra's trial. From the *New York Times*, "Federal District Judge Assigned to Drug Trial is Shot Dead in Texas," an article by John M. Crewdson:

> *San Antonio, May 29, 1979—A federal district judge who was scheduled to preside over a major narcotics conspiracy case was shot and killed this morning as he stepped from his apartment on the city's north side.*
>
> *Judge John Herbert Wood, Jr., apparently the first federal judge ever*

to be murdered, was 63 years old. Neighbors said he had walked a short distance from his doorway to his late model, pale green car when he was felled by a single shot.

The police and FBI agents emphasized that they had no information thus far linking the judge's murder to any of the narcotics cases in which he had been involved. But Fred Kraus, Judge Wood's administrative assistant, said that in his view there was "bound to be a connection."

Judge Wood had been under guard by the United States Marshal's Service, but the bodyguards were removed in December at his request. The protection was ordered after an assassination attempt Nov. 21 on James W. Kerr, an Assistant United States Attorney here who had prosecuted a number of narcotics cases before Judge Wood's court. Mr. Kerr was not harmed and no arrests have been made in that case.

Judge Wood had been scheduled to preside at what promises to be the most important such case brought here in recent memory, that of Jamiel Alexander Chagra, 36, an El Paso native and professional gambler who is charged with importing more than 20,000 pounds of marijuana into this country over the last few years.

The Chagra case, which has attracted considerable attention for months throughout the Southwest, was to have begun today in Austin, Tex., but was delayed after Mr. Chagra was re-indicted on more stringent charges earlier this month.

… There have been reports that federal and state narcotics officers have identified Lee Chagra, who was 44, as the "kingpin" behind an El Paso-based network alleged to have smuggled massive quantities of cocaine and marijuana into this country from Colombia.

Lee Chagra was indicted by the federal government in Nashville in 1973 on narcotics charges, but the case was dropped after two years, in the fall of 1977; however, Judge Wood was quoted as having told Lee Chagra in his courtroom that "everyone in this area knows that you've been the subject of a grand jury investigation ever since the Tennessee indictment."

The next phase of the Chagra case covered by the articles dealt with early August 1979 and reported his trial. An article in the *New York Times* by Molly Ivins, describes high points of the proceedings:

Austin, August 9, 1979—The prosecution ended its case today in the drug smuggling trial of Jamiel (Jimmy) Chagra, a case that is part of a web of Texas intrigue with strands that lead to more than one murder and to numerous insights into the widening drug trade in the Southwest.

Prosecutors describe Mr. Chagra, a thirty-six-year-old professional gambler, as the "kingpin" of a narcotics empire. The Chagra family sees him as the victim of a law enforcement vendetta against his slain older brother, who had a reputation as the best drug defense lawyer in the West.

Jimmy Chagra is charged with organizing and managing "a continuing criminal enterprise;" specifically with conspiring to import some 80,000 pounds of marijuana and nearly 20 pounds of cocaine, worth millions. He faces life in prison without parole if convicted.

He was a carpet salesman before he became a gambler in Las Vegas— gambling, his attorneys say, is not a habit but an occupation.

Mr. Chagra is being represented by his younger brother, Joseph, and Oscar Goodman, who has represented a number of Las Vegas casino figures accused of having ties with organized crime.

Mr. Chagra's case is of particular interest because it was originally scheduled to be tried before Federal District Judge John H. Wood Jr., who was shot to death May 29 outside his San Antonio home. Investigators are focusing on "drug interests" in that case.

Despite rumors here of involvement by organized crime, testimony by prosecution witnesses suggests that Mr. Chagra's alleged drug dealings were not always highly organized ...

... The Chagra case also recalls an assassination attempt last November against Assistant United States Attorney James Kerr, who had been pursuing Lee Chagra. Mr. Kerr later sought the indictment against Jimmy Chagra but is under round-the-clock protection and is not trying the case.

Lee Chagra was murdered during a robbery at his office in El Paso last December 23. There were three Chagra brothers from a Lebanese family in El Paso. Lee, the oldest, was an honors graduate of the University of Texas, where he was president of the student body and later editor of the Law Review. He began his legal career in El Paso, defending poor people, often Mexican-Americans, but his practice became increasingly oriented toward defending those accused of narcotics violations.

He was indicted in Nashville on a marijuana smuggling charge, but the charge was dropped because it was not brought to trial quickly enough. His most famous victory as an attorney was freeing the "El Paso 10," a group charged in Ardmore, Oklahoma, with smuggling 17,000 pounds of marijuana.

Lee Chagra had tangled repeatedly with both Mr. Kerr, a vigorous prosecutor, and Judge Wood, a staunch Republican with a reputation for being tough on narcotics offenders. Three men have been arrested and charged with the killing of Lee Chagra, with the apparent motive of theft of a large sum of money Mr. Chagra had in his office.

The jury deliberated only two hours before convicting Jimmy Chagra of "continuing criminal enterprise" in drug trafficking. He was to have been sentenced on September 6, 1979, but failed to appear, thereby forfeiting the four hundred thousand dollars in bail, and was rearrested in Las Vegas in early 1980. His delayed sentence was handed down on March 29, 1980, giving him prison terms of fifteen and thirty years and a fine of $125,000.

The chronological account appearing below will help put some of the events in the careers of Jimmy and Lee Chagra into proper perspective. The major part of the information was condensed from newspaper articles; a few facts were found in magazine articles.

EARLY 1970s—Lee Chagra's career as successful defense lawyer of narcotics related cases begins.

JUNE 20, 1973—Lee Chagra and forty others arrested on an indictment by a federal grand jury in Nashville, Tennessee, on marijuana trafficking charges.

LATE 1973—Lee Chagra finds that his home and office phone records and IRS records have been subpoenaed as far back as 1970.

MARCH 1975—Chief Judge of the Middle District of Nashville dismisses federal grand jury charges against Lee Chagra, after two years. The judge's memorandum states that the "indictment was obviously and fatally defective" adding that it was "so worded as to be utterly meaningless and, therefore, the indictment charged nothing at all."

SUMMER 1975—Jimmy Chagra allegedly scores in fifty-four-thousand-pound marijuana operation in Massachusetts. Feds were unable to prove it.

DEC. 30, 1976—Jerry Lee Wilson and others charged with smuggling seventeen thousand pounds of marijuana when group was caught red-handed in Ardmore, Oklahoma.

APRIL 11, 1977—Federal Prosecutor James Kerr goes to Nashville, Tennessee, to review 1973 indictment against Lee Chagra.

MAY 1977—Kerr interviews Jack Stricklen, one of the members of the Nashville group who by this time was serving a prison sentence on another charge. Kerr offers Stricklen a choice: talk about the Chagra's or be charged with a "kingpin" indictment.

JUNE 15, 1977—464 Juliet confiscated in Colombia. Six ounces of cocaine found on board. On board, among others, Jimmy Chagra and, reportedly, Jerry Wilson.

AUGUST 1977—Trial of Ardmore group. Lee Chagra defends Wilson and others and was able to get charges dismissed, as the Justice Department had used false testimony in their eagerness to convict the defendants.

OCTOBER 20, 1977—Judge Wood dropped his "bombshell" regarding investigations of Lee Chagra's involvement in smuggling.

MARCH 1978—Jimmy Chagra allegedly successful in unloading fifty tons of Colombian marijuana in Florida.

NOVEMBER 21, 1978—Assassination attempt on federal prosecutor James Kerr. Next morning FBI agents confiscate Lee Chagra's gun collection.

DECEMBER 23, 1978—Lee Chagra murdered in his high-security office.

FEBRUARY 27, 1979—Jimmy Chagra arrested in Las Vegas. United States Attorney Jamie C. Boyd announced that the indictment covered Chagra's activities in Texas, Florida, and Colombia from June 1, 1977 to June 1, 1978.

FEBRUARY 28, 1979—Jimmy Chagra arraigned on six counts of drug trafficking, conspiracy to import marijuana and cocaine and distribute the drugs. Trial set for May 29, 1979, in Midland, Texas, where none of the crimes was committed, and to be heard by "Maximum John" Wood.

MARCH 1979—Chagra tries to have Wood removed from case because of Wood's close friendship and "nonprofessional relationship" with James Kerr.

MAY 20, 1979—A "superseding indictment" is brought against (approximately) Jimmy Chagra of "continuing criminal enterprise"—the "kingpin" charge involving ten years to life imprisonment and no parole.

MAY 29, 1979—Judge John H. Wood, Jr. assassinated as he left his home the opening day of what was to have been Jimmy Chagra's trial.

AUGUST 1, 1979—Jimmy Chagra's delayed trial begins under a new judge.

AUGUST 15, 1979—Chagra convicted of six charges of original indictment and the kingpin charge. Sentence scheduled to be passed September 5, 1979.

SEPTEMBER 5, 1979—Chagra fails to appear for sentencing. Forfeits four hundred thousand dollar bond.

FEBRUARY 22, 1980—Chagra recaptured in Las Vegas. Put on three million dollar bail.

MARCH 29, 1980—Chagra sentenced to fifteen years and twenty-five thousand dollars on first charges, and thirty years and one hundred thousand dollars on kingpin indictment.

CHAPTER ELEVEN

Since my meeting with Judge Valdez, my first line of priority was to get to the number one man in Lloyd's of London to get some action going on my offer for the salvage rights to 464 Juliet. If I could deal directly with the decision maker, I could speed up the process. I was getting nowhere with Mr. Dunwoody at United Aviation Assurance, Lloyd's United States representative.

I called Steve Sloan, my United States lawyer, and Jim Burkett, my investigator, to see if they had any leads. No news at all, good or bad. Disappointed, I tried calling Mr. Dunwoody two or three times during the day, but couldn't reach him. I was becoming seriously concerned that I was being jerked around and needed to come up with something positive.

A few more days passed in getting nowhere. Raul walked in one day and said that he had spoken with Aldo about the jet and with Gustavo, my number one gofer, about the oil deal with *La Comunidad*. The news perked me up. Gustavo had mentioned that he had a good connection, Alfredo Escobar, the son of the Minister of Justice, who might help me in Colombia. I should have thought of Escobar myself; I knew him well, as we had worked together previously on a government automobile contract. He would be an excellent connection.

Raul also remarked on how protective and jealous Aldo had acted concerning our making any separate contact with Judge Valdez, to the point of quoting the judge as saying that all contact should be through Aldo and Aldo alone. I had strong doubts that such a prohibitive and exclusionary order had come from the judge. A more logical explanation would be that Aldo was afraid we would expose his original plan to cut Valdez out.

"What a self-important blowhard that Aldo is," I said. "He's afraid we might make a deal directly with the judge and that he won't get anything." We laughed and laughed at Aldo, as we both were sure that when it got down to the last stretch Valdez would probably be the one to cut Aldo out of the picture anyway.

I kept trying to reach Dunwoody, leaving messages for him to return my calls, which he didn't do. So I decided to try another tack. Once again I contacted my lawyer, Steve Sloan, and my investigator, Jim Burkett, and asked them to meet at my office that evening.

They got there about eight o'clock, and we sat down to shoot the bull for a while. I briefed them on the latest developments in Colombia. Timing was getting to be crucial. I had already set things in motion with Judge Valdez, who stated that we needed documentation of ownership to take to Colombia. The lack of action from United Aviation Assurance was bothering me—I had misgivings and suspicions that my efforts to buy the salvage rights had stirred a sleeping giant. My single conversation with Dunwoody was the only concrete indication of this, but his original condescension and then sudden curiosity were very unusual.

My proposal was simple.

"Look, you guys, I'm up against a brick wall. I'm getting nowhere with 464 Juliet. I'm putting up—if I get her out—a ten thousand dollar reward to the first of you to hook me up to Lloyd's number one man handling the 464 Juliet claim. Just get me a name and a number. If you two want to work together to split the money, that's fine with me. But, understand, if I get the information first, the deal is off."

Sloan and Burkett were elated, full of great ideas. They knew that I wasn't just exercising my jaws; they knew when I said I would do something, it went. If they produced, they would get paid. Both Sloan and Burkett were highly capable, and I felt sure they would have something for me in short order.

The next morning, I went to my bank to see Jack Wood (no relation), but a good friend. He was the vice president handling my firm's account since its beginning. Jack already knew my plans, so I updated him on the new developments in Colombia. This visit was to request a loan of one hundred thousand dollars. My credit with the bank was excellent; company deposits were almost a million dollars by my second year of dealing with them. As there was no time to prepare updated financial statements needed for a loan of that size, I would put up two of my airplanes as security.

"When you need it, come on in and we'll take care of it all the same day," Jack had told me.

It's a good feeling to have a banking connection with that kind of confidence. I had worked hard, though, to put myself in that comfortable position, so I felt I deserved a little of the credit, too.

The afternoon of that same day Jim called.

"Are you sitting down?" he asked. When I told him no, he added, "Find a chair—I have your number one guy in England."

I rushed to my office to take the call there. Jim gave me the name of the

Lloyd's underwriter, C. E. Heath & Company in London, and the name of their aviation claims manager, Mr. Peter Nash, along with the telephone number.

"Terrific," I said, stunned at having the information in less than twenty hours. I didn't so much as try to find out how he had unearthed it in my hurry to place an international call, even forgetting that the five-hour time difference meant that it was nighttime in London.

Next morning, May 6, I was on the phone with Nash. His voice was very British; he was polite and cordial. I first verified that I was talking to the right person, the man who had been handling the matter of Learjet N464J. He assured me that this was indeed the case and that he represented all the underwriters involved in the case and had been working on it since 1977. Wonderful, I thought.

I told him that I had talked with Mr. Dunwoody at United Aviation Assurance, Lloyd's American representative, and had made, and had then posted, an offer to Dunwoody of one hundred thousand dollars for the Learjet, adding that I had spoken with him only once and that Dunwoody had never returned my follow up calls. I explained that I had just learned that C. E. Heath was the principal acting for the underwriters and was calling to find out if any action had yet been taken on my offer of April 14, sent to Dunwoody over three weeks earlier. I also told him that I had been to Colombia, had spoken with the appropriate judge with proper jurisdiction and was confident I could get the Learjet released.

It was surely only Nash's British courtesy and innate gifts of prudence and kindness that prompted him to hear me out and not hang up on me immediately. What he told me was, to say the least, highly unexpected. It was also the turning point of the whole affair for Lloyd's of London, and for me.

"Mr. Wood," he said, "I am sure you are an honorable man acting in good faith, but I believe you are mistaken. Learjet N464 Juliet is currently being flown by the Air Force in Bogotá, Colombia."

I stifled a gasp of surprise and made a rapid decision to try to match his calm, British manners.

"Mr. Nash," I began cautiously, thinking back on Dunwoody's strange behavior, "is your information hearsay, or are you basing it on something substantial and factual?"

His reply was decisive and confident.

"Our lawyers and representatives in the United States have assured me that this is the case—I have no reason to believe that it is not completely reliable information."

"Mr. Nash," I continued, "in the face of what you have just told me, I know you might think that this is a practical joke or that I am insane, but please hear me out, and then check it. I left Colombia just ten days ago and while I was there I personally inspected 464 Juliet at the Santa Marta airport."

I filled in the facts I thought would be of interest: That the radios were gone; that the nose was full of rocks; that all the tires were flat and sunk six inches into the mud; and, finally, another small but important detail, that the airplane was full of mud dauber nests that had been there for years. I explained to Nash that an act of God would have been necessary for that Learjet to be flying in less than the ten days since I had last seen it—much less for it to be in Bogotá flying in the Colombian Air Force.

Peter Nash's British reserve was shattered. Shock reflected in his voice, and I knew I would have to give him time to digest this information and investigate. I merely added that I was a well-known and reputable businessman in South Florida and that he could call my bank or the local FAA for references. I assured him that I had no reason to lie.

I knew he was stunned. The idea that his company and the other underwriters had paid out a million dollars on a possible false claim must have made his blood run cold. Plus, the hundreds of thousands in attorneys' fees and expenses—only to learn that somebody just might be pulling a monumental scam on his firm.

Nash was maintaining his professional manner with difficulty.

"Please, Mr. Wood, let me look into this. I will call you the soonest possible."

I thanked him, urging him to be sure to call me back and not to give me the Dunwoody treatment. He promised that he would indeed call.

I leaned back in my chair and took a deep breath. What I had to do was to analyze the implications of this bombshell of a conversation and to examine every possible reason for Nash's conviction that 464 Juliet was being flown by the Colombian Air Force. From whom could he have gotten this information? Why had it been given to him? I even began to wonder if we were talking about the same airplane. *No,* I told myself, *this is not fantasy. There's bullshit all around, but the Learjet sitting on the tarmac is definitely not bullshit. She's for real—it's the same 464 Juliet that I saw with my very own eyes.* The paint was old, and the numbers hadn't been repainted. Even more convincing, I had examined the serial number plate on the door, and it showed years of dirt and dust. No, it was Peter Nash at C. E. Heath, not Bobby Wood, who had been getting jerked around, I concluded.

A thought lurking in the back of my mind was coming to the front faster and faster: Could a person, or persons, unknown possibly be screwing Lloyd's of London. Giving them false information about the Learjet and collecting lots of money. I couldn't imagine how these unknown persons could think that the truth would not get back to Lloyd's, but obviously they had thought they were covered. I was confident that Mr. Nash would be on the line with me as soon as he checked me out and learned that my facts were the true ones.

MONDAY, MAY 12, 1980—CUTTING A DEAL FOR 464 JULIET

I had spent a lot of time on the telephone the previous four days tracking down more information on 464 Juliet. The title search had arrived from Insured Aircraft Title, still showing the registered owner as Jet Associates of Little Rock, Arkansas. I already knew the firm no longer existed. The lien on the plane for over six hundred thousand dollars was assigned to Cravens Dargan & Company as United States agents for the London group.

Trouble here, I thought, studying it. *I know the plane doesn't belong to Jet Associates, even though it's still in their name. What I need is a clear statement concerning the title as a starting point.*

I knew Lloyd's had a policy not to allow any property they insured, even if they had paid the claim on it, to be registered or recorded in their name. This policy was designed to protect them from any liability that might arise during the interim or off-the-record ownership of such property. I had a gut feeling that this would present a problem in Colombia. I had been learning the hard way that Colombians are nothing if not nit-pickers, and that they would catch this and ask why, as the owner, I didn't have a title search mentioning me as the owner of register.

I was pondering this point when my secretary buzzed me and said there was a long distance call on line two. I picked it up. The static on the line indicated it was an overseas call.

It was Peter Nash calling from London. Even more polite and cordial than before, he informed me that after our conversation of the previous week, he had sent an investigator to Colombia who confirmed everything I had reported. He didn't know why or how, or give me any explanation, as to why his firm had been led to believe that 464 Juliet was being flown by the Colombian Air Force. He was angry at having been given this erroneous information and did not want to go into details, but he assured me that his principals were eager to do the correct thing.

I read between the lines. What he seemed to be conveying was that he had discovered that someone—he wouldn't say who—had obviously been lying to them.

We discussed my proposal to purchase the plane, and after twenty minutes we had agreed to terms and a price of $150,000. Ten thousand dollars of this figure was to be a non-refundable deposit. The balance would be due in six months, on November 13, 1980. I would have six weeks from the time I signed a contract to remove the aircraft from Colombia.

One major stipulation of the contract was that I would bring the jet out of Colombia legally. By legally, he meant through the courts, with all the legal documents to avoid future problems. The $140,000 balance would be interest-free. Also, if at the end of the six-week period—by July 10, 1980—I had not secured release of 464 Juliet, my ten thousand dollar payment would be forfeited, and Lloyd's would have the right to rescind this conditional sale contract.

I had been the one who had first mentioned the six-week period as I felt the release could be obtained in that length of time. This estimate was my first and, thank the good Lord, last major mistake in dealing with reality.

I agreed to all the conditions set forth by Peter Nash, high with jubilation. Nash gave me the telephone number of Paul Engstrom in California, a legal consultant of Lloyd's through their representatives Cravens Dargan & Company. Nash knew Engstrom well and would see to it that Engstrom received the power of attorney, giving him final authority from that time forward regarding 464 Juliet.

I told Nash I would go straight to the bank and wire him the ten thousand dollars so that he would have it the next morning. As soon as he received it, he would send me a telex confirming all the points of our agreement. He would also send me a telex addressed to Judge Valdez in Santa Marta in the exact wording I gave him:

> *JUEZ 3RD PENAL DEL CIRCUITO SANTA MARTA, COLOMBIA*
> *RE: LEAR JET N464J S/N 24-164, 2 TURBINAS*
> *PLEASE ACCEPT THIS TELEX AS AUTHORITY FOR MR. ROBERT*
> *E. WOOD, JR. TO EFFECT THE REMOVAL AND TRANSPORTATION*
> *OF THE ABOVE AIRCRAFT FROM SANTA MARTA, COLOMBIA, TO*
> *MIAMI, FLORIDA, ON BEHALF OF HIMSELF AND UNDERWRITERS*
> *FOR THEIR RESPECTIVE INTERESTS.*
> *PETER J. NASH*
> *C. E. HEATH & CO., LONDON, ENGLAND*
> *FOR AND ON BEHALF OF LLOYD'S UNDERWRITERS AND*
> *COMPANIES*

I explained to Nash that this was exactly how the judge had instructed the telex to be written, and that it was to be included with other papers I would have to take with me. Nash agreed that as soon as he had received my deposit he would send what I needed. In the meantime, he would immediately contact Paul Engstrom and have him get started on the contract.

I was so excited after we rang off that I had a hard time concentrating on my next step, but I felt that I was beginning to gain control over the future and destiny of 464 Juliet in Colombia. I had finally made an official beginning to the most complex, frustrating, mind-bending task of my life as a businessman. I still thought that the big push was to be one of beating the Colombians at their own game, but that was only one stretch of a longer and much harder path I would have to walk, crawling sometimes, even backtracking and attacking again from an altogether new starting point.

The ten thousand dollars was transferred that afternoon, and I spent the rest of the day with Raul, working out what we would do on our return to Colombia.

The next morning, I called Paul Engstrom in Los Angeles and introduced myself. Engstrom said he had already spoken with Peter Nash and knew the background. He spent some time questioning me about how I had become involved in this case that had lain dormant for three years. At the time, I believe, he was a little skeptical about me, but he was pleasant and interested.

We spoke for an hour or more about details of our contract and how I would fulfill it. Engstrom told me some of the history of the matter, mostly the efforts expended to get the Learjet released. He also mentioned that the law firm of Gordon & Sanford in California had been handling a good part of the case. Gordon had held the power of attorney on the Learjet but now it had been given to Engstrom. I was also told that the underwriters had already paid out over a million dollars and were now further than ever from getting the plane out of Colombia. I told Engstrom I would call him after Peter Nash had confirmed receipt of the money and that we would go into more detail at that time. I was greatly impressed at the way Engstrom handled himself, very positive, very professional. It was a reassuring feeling to talk with someone who knew what he was doing.

I had absolutely no idea at that moment of the nature of the sleeping giant I was awakening.

CHAPTER TWELVE

Now that the big push in Colombia was imminent, having secured the conditional sales contract for Juliet, I had to put an end to my procrastination about dealing with my right-hand man, Raul.

Fact: I needed Raul and I enjoyed being with him. I didn't speak or understand much Spanish. Raul had, I believed, served me very well up to that time in interpreting for me, but I had always been extremely careful in interpreted conversations to be reasonably sure that he was telling it like it was—both coming and going.

Up to now, he had performed and delivered in the initial skirmishes. In the future, however, the battles would become more crucial—I would have to concentrate skillfully on observing the facial expressions, body English, and other nonverbal communications of those I would have to deal with. I simply wouldn't be able to monitor Raul at the same time. So now I had to deal, once and for all, with his performance on my turf; specifically, I had to address the pilfering that was going on under my nose at Air Unlimited.

I recognized that, in order to succeed, I would have to use his weaknesses to my own advantage. I had to ensure his continued cooperation when we started the next, more serious phase, of full-dress battle on his turf in Colombia. And being a good businessman, I figured I ought to get some kind of return on what amounted to around twenty thousand dollars I had unwittingly "invested" in my friend and employee Raul.

So, on Wednesday morning, May 14, I gathered all the invoices from Durant Aviation into a folder and drove over to their installation near the Miami International Airport. I asked for the manager, Mr. Waters, and, when we sat down in his office, I explained why I was there.

I showed him my invoices for close to twenty thousand dollars. He told me he was familiar with the account and that he knew Raul and his brother. Calling his accountant, he asked for the file of Raul Soto.

When it was brought to us, Mr. Waters showed me a stack of photocopied checks and invoices that Durant had paid to Raul. There were copies of checks—from $150 to $2,000—all made payable to "Raul Soto." I couldn't believe that it had grown to such proportions.

I had been paying him, his brother, and a helper their salaries for over nine months and had never collected a dime. What was worse, they had been coming to Durant to work at night and collecting additional salaries, plus what they had collected for all the materials I had paid for. In my rage, all I could think was that that son of a bitch had been screwing me, but good—for almost a year.

I tried to keep my composure in front of Mr. Waters, apologizing for taking up his time, then leaving. I was fuming inside. Back at the office, I decided I needed a little time to cool off to decide how to tackle Raul and how to turn this twenty thousand dollar debit into an asset.

I went home early and spent a peaceful hour or so playing with my children, pushing everything else from my mind. My three-year-old daughter was really a doll, and the presence of such lovable innocence made the dog-eat-dog world seem to go away.

Next morning, however, I was thrust back into that same old canine culture when I buzzed Raul to come into my office. I had the Durant folder in hand as he came in and said good morning.

"Let's take a ride down to Durant," I said neutrally, "and collect some money."

Raul was nervous. We talked very little on the ride over to Durant. I was curious to see how far he would carry the charade, and I figured I would learn more about his mentality this way than by any other means I could think of.

Raul didn't want to go in by the main lobby; he took me to the shop entrance and asked for someone whose name I wasn't familiar with. He was sweating; I could see small beads on his forehead. He stuttered a little and his eyes were slightly glazed. When he was told that his friend was not there, I said, "Never mind, we'll go to see the manager."

He looked at me and said, "Let's go to the car. I have a problem. I have to talk to you."

Raul had finally reached his breaking point, but that no-account SOB had gone almost all the way down the line with his con. When we sat down, I told Raul that I already knew what he had been doing. He admitted everything. After it had all poured out of him, we sat a few minutes without a word.

"I'll pay you back," he blurted out. "I promise you, I'll pay it back. But please, don't tell my family." He had tears in his eyes.

I assured him I would say nothing to his family. He said he would move his belongings out of Air Unlimited and thanked me over and over for my promise not to tell his family. I knew then that I had a better measure at least of this Colombian's mentality and that there was a serious gap somewhere in his power to think ahead and to avoid complications that might arise in the future from past and present actions.

I looked seriously at Raul for a few seconds, and then asked why he had done it. He gave me several excuses, but deep inside, he really didn't know. What was worse, I thought, a hundred years from that time, if he were still alive, he still wouldn't know.

Many of the Colombians with whom I had dealings were like Raul. They really couldn't give any logical reason for such actions, except that they saw an immediate opportunity to steal and just couldn't resist. No thought about the reckoning *mañana*; no thought to the consequences of their criminal behavior; *mañana* is just another day. And perhaps worst of all, they had no respect for the intelligence of their fellow men.

After a few more minutes, I told Raul I would be willing to forget the whole thing, but that I would expect him to repay me, some day, and to give me his loyalty in the matter of 464 Juliet, in which there was so much at stake. I described to him what I expected of him and assured him that I not only expected it, I demanded it.

Almost like a child, Raul was happy again—even though embarrassed—and very relieved, too, almost as if he were reassuring himself that *mañana* really had taken care of itself.

I had been waiting for this same Wednesday for another and better reason than simply confronting and resolving my issues with Raul. Today was the day that the telex for the judge would arrived from Nash, and when it did, my spirits soared. I read it over and over, finally calling the now contrite Raul into my office to share the news. Now, I had it in my hands—in writing. Now, no one could interfere with my dealings in Colombia. I had what the judge wanted, along with the other papers, everything I needed to get rolling.

Suddenly it occurred to me that I had overlooked something on the telex printout. I snatched it, up and my fears were confirmed. It said, at the bottom:

COPIES SENT TO UNDERWRITERS IN NEW YORK
ATTENTION: MR. DUNWOODY, UNITED AVIATION INS.
ATTENTION: MR. PAUL ENGSTROM, ESQ.

"Raul, now Dunwoody knows about this; I have a bad feeling about him. Just the way he acted on the phone with me spells trouble. He has connections with Gordon & Sanford in California, and I know they're not going to take this lying down. It's like a slap in the face to them, but more serious. All their wheeling and dealing down the drain, all because of some redneck in Miami."

I was upset, and warned Raul that we had to move fast. "Let's leave for

Barranquilla tomorrow. You call Aldo and Gustavo tonight and have them meet us."

I immediately rushed over to the bank and arranged for the loan of one hundred thousand dollars. It was just as Jack had said: it took only an hour.

While we waited for the papers to be drawn up, I showed Jack my papers and the telex. Jack liked the whole deal and boosted my spirits enormously by showing his complete confidence in my ability to pull it off successfully. I left with one hundred thousand dollars in cash.

Back at the office I gave a rapid-fire series of instructions for matters that had to be attended to in my absence. Most of the employees knew by then something of what was going on and were excited at the possibility of having a Learjet on our 135 Certificate. I also called to get preliminary figures on insurance for the airplane.

My wife was excited about 464 Juliet, too, but not happy about my leaving again. She didn't mind a day or two, or even more if I came back as scheduled, but she always worried when I was delayed. It was hard to make her understand that things don't always go the way one expects in Colombia, and there was no use trying to explain this.

CHAPTER THIRTEEN

MAY 15, 1980—BARRANQUILLA, ENCOUNTER AT THE GATEWAY TO HELL

As we stepped off the plane in Barranquilla, Raul's friend Diego from customs greeted us just like old buddies and escorted us right through. My Colombian "crew," Gustavo, Aldo, Toño, and company, were all there waiting with smiles. At the Hotel Royal, I was greeted enthusiastically at the front desk; the manager came over to welcome me back.

We talked late into the night. Aldo was satisfied with my telex of authorization and the other documents I had for Judge Valdez. Everything seemed great. Even the renewed and voracious eating and drinking didn't annoy me. Everyone was relaxed.

The next morning after breakfast we got ready to set out for Santa Marta, taking two cars because Aldo would be staying over at his home in Ciénaga. I rode with Aquiles and Aldo in the 1953 Chevrolet. Raul, Toño, and a friend followed in the second car.

As we approached the bridge, I turned to make sure Raul and the others were still behind us. My heart almost stopped—they weren't there: We were almost at the bridge. Raul was still not in sight. I was beginning to panic. From what had happened at the Santa Marta Airport I knew I could count on Aldo for no help at all. He knew the bridge routine, but was too fearful of his own ass to stand up, as my lawyer, and insist upon my rights.

I sat in the seat and looked straight ahead, trying for a casual look, as if everything was normal. I was scared shitless and didn't dare move for fear of being spotted by the soldiers. Aquiles reached out to hand the toll money to the guard and I could see the soldier called Gonzalez, who had always hassled me, walking around to the front of the car. The "I've got you by the balls now, gringo" look on his face told me that Gonzalez was finally at the plate for his innings at bat.

He yelled at a few of the soldiers as he motioned for Aquiles to pull over to the right. The soldiers came running, immediately opening doors, ordering us out. I barely had my head clear of the roof when Gonzalez and another soldier grabbed me and roughly led me across the highway to a small white guard house. I knew, just from the fact that they hadn't asked for my papers, that I was marked for special treatment.

I glanced at Aquiles and Aldo, standing there, just staring. They were keeping their mouths shut, making no move to come to my rescue. The guards shoved me into a small room, about six by eight feet. Directly ahead was a small cot pushed up against the wall; to the left was another cot, turned sidewise.

Gonzalez began shouting at me. I didn't understand a word he was saying and kept repeating, "*No comprendo, no comprendo*," which seemed to madden him more by the second. I realized he was in a hurry, because he motioned urgently for me to face the wall and empty my pockets on the cot. I started removing the money and other items from my clothing when the other soldier slapped me on the back of the neck and hissed, "*Rapido!*" This I understood. They were in complete control. I was helpless.

I instantly took everything from my shirt and pants pockets and laid it on the cot. I saw the small guard smile greedily at Gonzalez when I laid down my wallet, thick with over two thousand dollars inside.

Gonzalez again grabbed me and turned me to the left. He motioned for me to take off all my clothes and face the wall again. After I was completely stripped, he bent me over the cot with my hands against the wall and stood to block my view of the other soldiers. I could smell his rancid sweat.

As I stood there braced for a knife to be stuck on my ribs it dawned on me: those bastards were either going to rob me or plant drugs on me, not kill me. My mind was beginning to operate with some logic. They wouldn't have made me strip if they were going to kill me; that would be too obvious. The next thought that occurred to me was that if they planted drugs on me, they would get nothing. What they wanted was my money … and to teach me that they called "the shots."

I tried to turn my head slightly to see what the other soldier was doing. Gonzalez grabbed my hair and slammed my head to the wall. I stood there, motionless, very cautious but not quite so frozen with fear. I knew it was my turn in the barrel, so I just gritted my teeth and kept my mouth shut.

Less than a minute later, another soldier walked in and took hold of my shoulder. I turned around, very slowly, expecting another blow on the head. To my surprise and relief, Gonzalez and the other soldier had disappeared.

The new arrival motioned for me to dress, and I put on my clothes in record time. When I picked up the wallet, I could tell that some of the money was still inside. If I could make it outside, I knew I would be safe. The soldier signaled for me to leave and escorted me rapidly out the door.

No soldiers were outside except for five or six on duty around the toll gate, as if nothing had happened. Aldo and Aquiles were halfway across the highway. They came rushing over to me with loud and anxious inquiries about whether I was all right, and expressions of relief when I said I was.

Gee, thanks a lot fellows, I thought bitterly.

In less than five minutes, Raul and Toño pulled up to the bridge and parked behind Aquiles' car. Raul stepped out and Aquiles yelled, "*Raul, venga, pronto.*"

Raul came running anxiously toward us. When I told him what had just taken place he was in a frenzy of fury at Aldo and Aquiles and concern for me.

"What kind of a two-bit lawyer are you, Aldo?" he stormed, and then in the same breath, "Bobby, are you all right? Did they steal money from you?"

Aldo, with shrugs and doleful expressions, was defending himself self-righteously.

"Raul, they held their guns on us. They told us to stay where we were and keep our mouths shut—I could do nothing."

Raul delivered his opinion of Aldo's explanation by spitting vigorously on the dusty highway, and again he turned to me to ask if they had taken any money.

"This is very serious," he kept repeating, "very serious."

"Just forget it," Aldo spoke up, "if you make problems, they won't ever forget it."

Aldo was running true to form, showing his real colors. I could see he was made from the same mold as the bastards who had just stripped and robbed me. If I were to survive in Colombia, I could count on only three people— me, myself, and I.

I walked away from Raul and Aldo, and stood for a few long moments by the guardrail, thinking.

"Raul," I finally commanded, "get over here. I want to talk with you. In private."

Raul was still repeating, "This is very serious," as he joined me. He was genuinely upset and wanted to do something. I now knew what I wanted to do, but I was checking to see if Raul thought it would be feasible. I quickly outlined my plan.

"Listen, Raul, I want to do something about this. If I let these mothers get away with it, it's going to happen over and over again. I have to call their bluff. The only way I know to make them lay off is to create a big scene— right now—and rub their noses in it. I want these assholes to be good and sure that here's one gringo who's not going to take it."

We would be coming across the bridge often with parts, fuel, and mechanics, and I had no intention to go through this frightening, time-wasting, and expensive bullshit forever. Raul was in complete accord. He knew exactly how far such a situation could get out of hand.

"*Si, si*, Bobby," he nodded vigorously, "we'll give it to them."

We started toward the booths where the soldiers were standing. Raul asked me to point out the soldiers who had robbed me. As I was looking for them, one of the soldiers came over and asked what was going on. Everyone was suddenly acting innocent, but we weren't convinced. I couldn't see Gonzalez and the other soldier; they were long gone. At that point, Raul had one of his quick brainstorms. He asked who was in charge. The soldiers were beginning to get the picture and were uneasy: we were serious and were sure as hell going to have some scalps.

Raul informed them that I was a very important government man from the United States with many political friends in Barranquilla, including Magistrate Plada of *La Comunidad*. More nervous and helpful by the minute, the soldiers gave us the commandant's name: Major Hernandez. As Raul was speaking, most of the soldiers slowly began to edge away. They were becoming increasingly aware that there was going to be trouble over this matter, and all were busily professing phony innocence with outstretched hands, raised shoulders, and bewildered faces.

We went immediately to the National Police headquarters in downtown Barranquilla, and, after a short period of time, we were advised that Major Hernandez was at his home. Raul did some name-dropping, so they phoned Hernandez, who requested that we meet him there.

Around ten thirty, we pulled up before the major's house. It was in a poor neighborhood with dirt streets and donkey-drawn carts parked along the road. Major Hernandez invited us inside, offering us a cool drink and letting us know he was completely "*a la orden*"—at our service. After we explained what had happened, Major Hernandez assured us that he would start an investigation and get my money back.

I told Major Hernandez that exactly eight hundred dollars had been taken. We agreed that the reason they hadn't taken it all was that, if they had taken it all, I would have had a far superior case against them. By leaving part of the money untouched, they very cleverly were attempting to destroy my credibility and boost theirs, since, after all, who would rob a man of only part of his money?

Again, the major promised he would get to the bottom of the matter, and we all left for the bridge again. Major Hernandez took Raul in his car and told us to follow him. I knew that Raul would do some serious talking to the major, including more name dropping, and that we would most likely have some protection in the future.

We got back to the bridge again shortly after midday. The major was impressive and military as he sternly questioned the soldiers, and I could see at once that he had their attention. While he talked, I tried to spot Gonzalez and friend but they weren't there. At least by that time, all the soldiers knew me, and I made damned sure they got a close look so that they would recognize me in the days to come.

After the major finished talking with his men, he returned and told us that the guards who had taken my money were not there but that he would have the money returned and see that they were punished. Raul asked the major if we could have a letter from him on official stationery that we could present to the guards on the bridge if we ever had any further problems.

"Of course," said the major, "come by my office tomorrow and pick it up. In the meantime, use this card," and he took one out and wrote brief instructions on the back authorizing us to pass unmolested.

We thanked the major and started out again for Santa Marta. I rode with Raul and Aquiles; this time I was taking no more chances with Aldo. Raul told me of the talk he had with the major when they had ridden together. Like everybody else, Major Hernandez was looking for a piece of the action. Being higher in rank and with more to offer than his men in the rank and file, he could indulge in the luxury of "requesting" what he wanted—a .357 Magnum. If I would bring him the gun the next time we came to Colombia, Hernandez could assure us that we would never again be subjected to unfortunate incidents at the bridge. Raul had told the major that this would be "no problem" and suggested that it would be advisable for the major to meet us at the airport when we arrived to make sure the Magnum didn't fall into somebody else's hands.

"Did I do right?" Raul asked.

"Sure," I replied, "Hernandez seems willing to give us further protection— we just got a free sample. It's not unreasonable. You take care of it, and I don't want to hear another word about how you handle it. Just get it done."

Raul had a real talent for handling these situations that arose so quickly, and he knew how to "shop around" for a price that was right.

I learned a lot about the Colombian culture of graft from this incident. It gave me some new insights into the age-old game of quid pro quo— "something like this" for "something like that." I also learned that it paid to go to the top, always being sure to have something the other person wanted or needed. If not, forget it. Nor did it pay to be cheap. These two elements would be my keys to opening doors in Colombia.

Without them, failure was inevitable. And failure was not an option.

CHAPTER FOURTEEN

We resumed our interrupted journey to Santa Marta, stopping first at Aldo's father's house in Ciénaga to telephone Judge Valdez and explain the delay in arriving for our appointment.

This was the first time I had seen Ciénaga except in passing. The streets were narrow and unpaved, except for those circling the town square. Life here was poor. Grimy and naked children stood sucking their thumbs in rotten wooden doorways. Even children of five or six were playing completely naked in the streets. Others wore tattered clothing. Here and there, right alongside the miserable shacks were well-built houses with scrubbed, well-dressed, children on the porches. Women passed by barefoot in the dust, balancing huge containers of water on their heads. It was a primitive way of life, and I remember wishing that my wife and children could see it.

In front of the Reyes house, several children were playing a loud and enthusiastic game of soccer in the dirt. Their ball was made of compressed paper, semi-round and bound together with knotted twine. I was impressed at their ingenuity at constructing a soccer ball of paper and twine that would stay together in the dirt and rocks.

As we walked up to the front door, Aldo's father, a man around sixty-five years of age, arose from an old rocking chair on the porch. He was courteous as he shook hands with us. I was amazed at how clean the women kept the house, despite the dogs and cats freely roaming in and out the open door. There were swarms of flies that everyone ignored. Aldo's mother and the rest of his family were friendly and hospitable. The whole family was in politics, in a small and purely local way, and all seemed to be intelligent and outgoing.

Compared to their neighbors, they were rich people, although by our standards they would be people of moderate means. Next door lived others so poor that they had no money for clothing or diapers for their babies—not even the money to buy soap or to heat the washing water to keep the clothing clean. The contrast was like going from Beverley Hills into the Watts ghetto of Los Angeles, but here the distance was less than ten feet apart. I did not know it at the time, but the Reyes house would become the storage depot for my Learjet parts.

Aldo announced that the judge was waiting, and, as we were already three hours late, we left at once. I sat in the back seat with Raul, looking over my documents, full of confidence once more.

May 15, 1980—Santa Marta, Hidden forces at work

At three thirty in the afternoon, we finally got to our appointment with Judge Valdez. He was cordial and invited us to sit down, but there was a certain reserve in his attitude. He immediately handed us some papers to examine. They were brochures and circulars. I recognized the name of the company, Jet Avia, Inc. The brochure showed photos of three men. One was of Chris Karamanos with a caption of professional information that also stated he was president of the company. The second was Jim Worden and the third, Tony Gekakis, whose named had been listed as one of the crew of 464 Juliet when she arrived in Santa Marta on June 15, 1977.

I reminded the judge that he had shown me these before.

"Yes," he said, "but these are new ones—they were just given to me."

I was confused. Had Raul misunderstood and interpreted incorrectly what the judge had said? I asked Raul for a replay. No, there had been no misunderstanding.

Valdez then asked if we knew a lawyer from Cartagena named Ortiz and another from the States named Masterson.

"Never heard of them," I answered, still puzzled.

Valdez went on to tell us that the previous afternoon they, Ortiz and Masterson, had come to his office to discuss the release of the Learjet. That was when he had received the new Jet Avia brochures. Valdez had informed them that Mr. Wood, owner of the airplane, had already been to see him. Then Ortiz had brought out documents showing that he was representing Gordon & Sanford of California and that he and Masterson were there also on behalf of Jet Avia. Masterson insisted that Jet Avia owned the Learjet and that he had never heard of a "Mr. Wood." Furthermore, Masterson had "reminded" Valdez that his own Colombian court records would prove that Chris Karamanos, President of Jet Avia, was the rightful owner of Learjet 464J and, thus, that Mr. Wood had no claim whatsoever to the airplane.

This was going to be difficult. It was a fact that Colombian records for the past three years had shown Chris Karamanos as the owner. Karamanos had, in fact, gone personally to Santa Marta shortly after confiscation of the Learjet and everyone concerned had accepted him as the true owner, just from association and not knowing that he had only leased it from Jet Associates.

My immediate task would have to be one of showing the judge that these people were not shooting straight with him.

The visit from Ortiz and Masterson was no coincidence. They were there to wreck my plans. All the confusion about "ownership" and "use" of the plane was no longer accidental or an honest mistake. Someone, upon learning of my trips to Colombia, must have sent these men to the judge to try to make a fast switch or take last-ditch action, using either falsified or expired documentation. My suspicion that I had awakened a sleeping giant was now confirmed.

I showed the judge my documents and assured him that all of the claims to the aircraft had been paid off a long time back and were no longer valid. Raul explained, step by step, to Judge Valdez, how I had become the new owner, as supported by the telex I had received addressed to Judge Valdez. It read exactly as he had requested.

"Yes," said the judge, "but all this created confusion, problems. I can't release the jet to you, or to anyone else, until I have complete, absolute proof of ownership, documents updated and notarized by a Colombian Consulate in the United States."

We talked at length. I wanted to make clear to Valdez the full chain of events leading to my present ownership of 464 Juliet. I started by showing him the title search stating that in 1977, the airplane had actually been owned by Jet Associates of Little Rock, Arkansas, thereby proving that Chris Karamanos could not be the real owner. The title search established that Lloyd's of London, the insurer, had paid off all claims and that the plane had then reverted to them. I also explained that Gordon & Sanford's power of attorney had been revoked; Paul Engstrom was now the legal representative for Lloyd's of London—as borne out by his name showing on the telex.

It was a slow and laborious process, but I wanted Judge Valdez to understand fully the succession of events—how Jet Avia had leased the plane from Jet Associates, how all claims had been paid off over a year and a half before. I thought I had made it amply clear that Karamanos had only been leasing the plane and had no right to claim ownership, much less have documentation to support his claim.

By then, it was well into the evening. The judge was still somewhat confused, but not so dubious as he had at first been. At the very least, he was again willing to proceed with the matter should certain conditions be met. He wrote down in detail what he wanted. One item, in particular, was a poser: he wanted a written statement from Chris Karamanos indicating that Jet Avia was selling me the plane.

I was beginning to think that Judge Valdez might not be very smart.

Once more, Raul went through our rationale—Karamanos, president of Jet Avia, had never owned the plane, therefore he could not sell it. Jet Associates, originally the owner, was no longer in business. The only one who could sell the plane was Lloyd's of London, which they had done, selling it to me.

Slowly, slowly, ever so slowly, the judge was getting the picture. However, he maintained that I would have to prove, beyond any shadow of legal doubt, that I was the rightful owner. He wanted an affidavit from Lloyd's stating every detail, from the first day onward, of how everything had transpired.

This excessive caution on the part of Judge Valdez told me unmistakably that hidden forces were working to prevent me from removing 464 Juliet. Just what these forces were, how many were operating, and why they were opposing me, I didn't know. But I did know I was playing in the major leagues—there were just too many big-time lawyers, moneyed people, and powerful official bodies in the act. I wondered if Jimmy Chagra's involvement had anything to do with it and sensed that it did. There were buried mysteries—perhaps cover-ups—and I felt that a lot of people would look very bad if these were unearthed and brought to light.

As we went through some of the old documents, the judge pointed out one indicating that the President of Colombia had requested the plane for his personal use, which I already knew from Red Garglay's document. Valdez told me that the President had ordered it to be inspected and made airworthy by the Air Force, but that it had been condemned as being unairworthy. The inspection had been made in late 1978, at which time it most certainly would have been unable to fly "as is." I later learned that although the Colombian Air Force had mechanics qualified for some jet classes, the Learjet was an exotic and rare bird to them, and they were completely unqualified to give any opinion at all. So to save face, they simply condemned it. Their document of unairworthiness would create quite a problem for me.

All these complications, I could now see, had Valdez scared of making the wrong move and leaving his back wide open. He wanted to be covered, every way.

We left the judge on good terms and I told him that I would return in a week or ten days with all the proofs he wanted. I assured him that I would clear up all the confusion about who the real owner was.

On the way back to Barranquilla, we dropped Aldo in Ciénaga. This suited me; I wanted to talk with Raul. I expressed my fears that it was going to be a monumental task to convince the judge of my real ownership and to provide him with the airtight documentation he was determined to have. I was also disturbed by the appearance of the two legal types, Ortiz and Masterson, trying to beat me in getting release of the plane. I simply couldn't believe that anyone, even Aldo, would think that the kind of documentation they had would be effective in the long run, especially a lawyer, who must surely have been aware that legal documentation had to be in existence somewhere.

Raul told me that such tactics were fairly normal procedure in Colombia, that Americans are considered gullible. I saw it a little differently. It occurred to me that the tactic had not been intended primarily to succeed, only to delay, to discourage, to put another obstacle in the way so that perhaps I would give it up and go back home empty handed.

I realized that what I would have to do was to wear two faces there in Colombia to make any progress. One face would be a dumb, rich gringo willing to play—and pay—by their rules and to remain outwardly oblivious to their malicious con games. The second face I would keep hidden. This side would take each situation as it arose, analyze it and use every means available to make their rules work to my benefit, without their knowing. I would have to create an illusion that they were winning while it was actually I who would succeed.

Raul was delighted; it was the kind of situation he liked. He was enthusiastic about helping me create the illusion. While we talked, my mind was still mulling over the riddle of the two attorneys who had visited the judge the day before.

"Raul," I said, "I think I know what happened, and it was no accident. Where it started was with Dunwoody, that New Yorker from United Aviation Assurance. When I talked with him, I had a feeling I was stirring up trouble. I was right. I think those two lawyers were sent down here because of that phone conversation with Dunwoody.

"All it took was for Dunwoody to see his copy of Peter Nash's telex to know that they were giving me a contract to remove the jet. I'm sure he got in touch with Gordon & Sanford right away. I believe one of them, or both of them, were lying to Lloyd's about the Learjet—telling Lloyd's it had been flying in the Colombian Air Force. Now Lloyd's knows better. It's got to be Dunwoody or Gordon, or both, who are trying to keep me from getting 464 Juliet. They must be plenty worried. If I get her out, can you imagine how bad they will look? Over a million bucks and the plane is still salvageable. They're trying to save their asses is what they're doing."

At that point I made a decision: If I didn't get 464 Juliet out, no one else would either. I could have been wrong, but I didn't believe so. I would turn their game back on them and muddy up the waters so much as to actual ownership that it would take years to clear—by that time the jet would be worthless.

I stressed to Raul that I couldn't prove exactly who had told Lloyd's that 464 Juliet was flying for the Air Force, since official documents did exist showing that this had been the intention. I could, however, stake my life on the fact that only two people had received copies of the telex Peter Nash had sent me—Paul Engstrom and Dunwoody. Since Engstrom had been chosen to handle the matter directly with Lloyd's from that time on, it left only Dunwoody, or, by inference, Gordon & Sanford. Although I could be wrong, this is where my logic inevitably lead me.

I cautioned Raul that we couldn't mention to anyone, and certainly not to Aldo, what our plans would be. We would sit back, listen, collect information and analyze it. We would not have much help from the States; our only known asset up to this point was that we could give the bank assurance that we had ownership of the Learjet, even if just provisional for forty-two days.

We were going to have to develop a few more assets and one of these, as I saw it, was to get firmly and comfortably into bed with Judge Valdez. Without him, we might as well have quit right then and there.

When we reached the bridge we were ordered to pull over. It was a different detail than the morning shift, but I figured they might have heard what happened that morning, as they weren't so nasty this evening. I handed them Major Hernandez's card. As the group around me read it, I could see six or eight other soldiers talking in low voices to each other. One made a move toward us, but another stopped him, adding an explanation in Spanish.

As we drove off, Raul explained that the soldier reading the note had warned the other to lay off—I was a friend of Major Hernandez. As soon as we had our letter from the Major's office at National Police, Raul was sure we would be saying adios to our problems at the bridge. Any troublemaker would be putting his job at risk in the face of written support by Major Hernandez. It felt good to have another amigo, yet another small but very important asset.

MAY 16, 1980—BARRANQUILLA, DR. PLADA INTRODUCES DR. JULIO SALGADO

The next morning we went to Major Hernandez's office first thing. He instructed his secretary to prepare our letter and when it was finished, he signed it with a flourish and fixed his seal to it. It looked official and impressive.

Hernandez drew Raul aside for a few minutes of private conversation. Raul afterward reported that the major was reminding him not to let me forget the Magnum—he also thought it would be nice to have a special holster and extra clips. He had reassured Raul that we would have no more trouble at the bridge. He had given his soldiers firm orders not to molest the *Americano* or to delay him in any way. I was relieved to be finished with the nightmares about passing through the gateway to hell.

Raul had another good idea. He told Aquiles to drive us over to Dr.

Plada's office. Dr. Plada, our chief contact at *La Comunidad*, worked at the palace of Government, and we needed him to ask if we could get another letter from the Governor stating that we were in Colombia on important oil negotiations. Nothing was to be said about the Learjet, of course. Another letter might give us a little more freedom of movement should other kinds of problems arise.

There was nothing very palatial about the palace of government. Hundreds of people were coming and going and just milling around, most of them poor, judging by their clothing. The inside was dirty and cluttered. The creaky elevators were operated by old women in black: widows of pensioners, as I was informed by Raul.

We got off on the fourth floor and went down the hall to Dr. Plada's office. It was shabby and dingy with papers stacked everywhere. The Colombians are champion paper shufflers, and Dr. Plada was no exception.

He was happy to see us, inviting us into his inner office. This room was small, only about nine by twelve feet with the usual quota of piled papers and folders. I couldn't help but wonder how he ever found anything. We talked about the oil project and the steps I was taking to find an American investment group. It was arranged that we meet that night at Dr. Ignas's home.

Raul finally broached the subject of our interest in the Learjet in Santa Marta. Dr. Plada recalled the incident, and he remarked that he would be glad to help us in any way he could. I was particularly interested to learn that he knew Judge Valdez and that he would call the judge to give me a good recommendation. This would enhance my credentials with Valdez as Dr. Plada had actually seen my operation in Florida and would mention it. Also, as Plada was a magistrate holding a high government position in Barranquilla, I knew this would make a good impression on Judge Valdez.

When Raul finally led into telling Dr. Plada what had been going on at the bridge, the doctor was shocked and outraged at the behavior of the National Police. Raul told him about Major Hernandez, showing him the letter we had just picked up.

Dr. Plada suggested that perhaps he could get us something even better.

With no further explanation he picked up the phone and placed a call to the Governor of Atlántico, the Colombian Department of which Barranquilla is the capital. Raul gave me the gist of the conversation. Dr. Plada had asked the governor for a letter mentioning our names, addressed "To Whom It May Concern," stating that we should be given any help we might need and be treated with courtesy and consideration.

When Dr. Plada hung up, he sincerely apologized for both himself and for the Governor for how I had been treated. He would try to make sure it never happened again, and he would help in any way he could. Dr. Plada was, without any doubt, one of the truly rare non-corrupt public officials that I met in Colombia. His concern was not pretense; he simply had not been aware of the treatment many Americans had been receiving in Colombia.

During our conversation, Dr. Plada informed us proudly that he had been named as a candidate for the Supreme Court in Bogotá. I was happy to hear it. Dr. Plada was a man of real stature, who deserved the honor of sitting on the bench of the Supreme Court.

At the end of our visit, Dr. Plada told Raul that if we ran up against any legal problems in Santa Marta, he had a good lawyer friend, Dr. Julio Salgado Vasquez, who might be able to help us. Dr. Salgado had been a Justice of the Supreme Court and was now practicing law in Bogotá with offices in Barranquilla. Unquestionably, Dr. Salgado was one of the most respected men in Colombia and, certainly, one of its keenest legal minds; the government frequently called upon his expertise to decipher and clarify the fine points of Colombian law.

We arranged to pick up our letter from the governor's office around four thirty that afternoon, and left with warm goodbyes and soaring spirits. We were lucky, Raul felt, to have such powerful support. Dr. Plada and his connections were almost a guarantee of an end to our problems with the local police, as the doctor naturally didn't want us to get discouraged and drop the oil project so important to his future business.

We drove over to the Barranquilla airport to see Luis Donado whom we spotted by the Aerocondor gate. As we stood there talking, two young men walked up, whom Donado introduced as his sons, Fernando and Donado Jr. They were fine-looking young men. Donado Jr. spoke no English, but Fernando had been studying the language and spoke it well. Donado invited us to the restaurant upstairs for a drink, and we could see that his sons were the apples of his eye.

Donado's sons were both interested in hearing about my flight school in Miami and excited at the prospect of attending. Donado Jr. already had four hundred hours of flying time. Fernando had been attending the Colombian Air Force Ground Training School.

The bond between Donado and me was growing stronger daily, and I felt that our relationship would be long-lasting. We told him we would have to leave, as we had an appointment at the Governor's office, and I invited him and the boys to be our guests for dinner. We would meet them at the hotel at six thirty that evening.

At the Governor's office the letter was ready, impressive with its stamps and seals. Together with Hernandez's letter, it would give us some protection, and I considered it another asset to my credit.

At the hotel we found a message at the front desk from Dr. Plada that the meeting that night with Dr. Ignas had to be canceled and that he would call us the next day.

Donado and his sons arrived for our dinner date and we resumed our conversation about my business in Florida. After dinner we talked longer. Fernando offered to stay the night and take us to the airport for our return trip to the States. I was glad to get to sleep. During the past six hours, at least eight persons had been in our room, drinking and eating, most of them half drunk. The liquor bill was over $250, which even Raul felt was getting out of hand.

MAY 17, 1980—BARRANQUILLA, THE OUTLOOK IS BRIGHTER

The next morning was unusually clear and fresh for Barranquilla, without the usual smoke and haze in the air. From the window of Room 402 of the hotel, the Sierra Nevada de Santa Marta could be witnessed in all its splendor. The majesty of these mountains never lost the power to shake me, and I always involuntarily contrasted their beauty with the ugly events that took place in their shadow. Even the town of Santa Marta, over fifty miles away, was visible. It seemed to float on the air, a dream city, full of secrets. One of its secrets—464 Juliet—I wondered if I would ever be able to unlock.

Like a paleontologist, I had discovered and unearthed a few bones of information on something mysterious that had been buried for a long, long time. At that time, I had no idea of the size and nature of the mystery that would gradually flesh itself out into a chain of events that included men who played the smuggling game for keeps, the horrible and prolonged death of an American, and insights into the cynical and cold-blooded way this part of the world really operated.

Raul nudged me out of my reverie with a "*Qué pasa?*," and I told him I was thinking about Learjet 464 Juliet. Truly, I was thinking of her sitting across the water like an angel with its wings clipped, far from home, wondering if she would ever fly again.

"Take it easy, you're going to do it," Raul insisted. "Very soon. You'll see. I promise you."

His confidence plus the happenings of the day before lifted me out of my doubts and, with a "Let's go," we headed downstairs. Donado Jr. met us in the front lobby, and his brother Fernando then drove us all to the airport in his father's truck. Times were improving, I thought, being chauffeured through Barranquilla in the vehicle of the head of Aerocivil.

The airport was crowded and after standing in line for half an hour we were informed at the desk that the flight was full. In spite of our confirmed reservations, we would have to wait until the next day for a flight to Miami.

I was getting ready to launch into a hot argument, but Raul took me aside.

"Give me fifty dollars," he said, and without further explanation he took the money and left. In five minutes he returned, his face creased with smiles, with two tickets to Miami.

"How did you do it?" I gasped.

"No problem"—Raul's stock answer in such situations—"The station manager was glad to oblige. That's how it's done."

"You're one smart, Colombian, Raul," I complimented him, and we laughed happily.

CHAPTER FIFTEEN

MAY 18, 1980—MIAMI, OWNERSHIP RIGHTS TO 464 JULIET

We were in Miami before noon. I couldn't wait to sink my teeth into a good old-fashioned U.S.A. hamburger. Being a meat and potatoes man and a junk food junkie, I stopped for us to have some solid food and even ordered French fries.

Back at the office, my first priority was to call Paul Engstrom.

"Paul, I got back today from Colombia. I ran into a serious problem about 464 Juliet."

"What's wrong?" he asked, with concern in his voice.

"I went over to Santa Marta with my lawyer for another meeting with the judge who has custody of Juliet to get started on the legal processing of the documents required for releasing her. The first thing he told me was that he had just had a visit from a pair of lawyers—one Colombian, the other American—representing Gordon & Sanford. They were there in Santa Marta working on the release of the airplane. They were claiming that Jet Avia was the owner and that I had no claim to it. Do you know anything about it?"

"No, nothing at all. Gordon doesn't have power of attorney any longer. I find it very strange."

I told him what I believed had happened in the States concerning the telex Nash had sent. Engstrom gave no indication as to whether he agreed or disagreed, but he listened seriously and didn't attempt to laugh it off or tell me I was imagining things.

We discussed the points of the contract he was drawing up between Lloyd's and me, and he told me he would send a copy when it was typed in final form. After I had looked it over, I was to call him back for further comments. He assured me that he would try to prepare it to avoid any further problems, at least concerning the legal aspects of ownership of the Learjet.

The next day and a half dragged while I waited to receive the copy of the contract. It arrived at noon and I took it to Fort Lauderdale for Steve Sloan to review.

"Sit down and let me read it," he said, and with his usual all-seeing eye, he spotted a few weak points. The weakest was, in fact, something that did not appear in the contract. Nowhere did it say specifically that I was the owner.

"Look, Sloan, this could mean real trouble. I know that judge. Somewhere in here it's got to say that Robert E. Wood, Jr. is the legal owner. It's got to be spelled out, very clearly. If not, I've got problems, because I know for sure that it will be challenged in Colombia."

We decided we'd better go visit Paul Engstrom and immediately called Los Angeles to arrange an appointment for May 29. Time was of the essence.

When I got back to the office, my lovely, patient wife, Terry, had been waiting for an hour and a half longer than the time I had promised to be back. As a peace offering, my first words were, "Let's go to that good Chinese restaurant you like," and she gave me a forgiving kiss as she handed me my messages.

One was from Gordon & Sanford in California. I couldn't believe my eyes. Why in the world would they be calling me? And what a hell of a lot of nerve. I knew it had to be about 464 Juliet and my dialing finger was very itchy, but I decided not to return their call. *Keep them guessing*, I told myself. The tables were turning, and they could do the worrying for a change. I would keep them off balance. Then, the very next moment I was wavering— maybe Gordon could help me. Finally, I took myself in hand and gave myself a lecture in the difference between reality and bullshit and that gut feeling that had seldom failed me. That did the trick. It only took once for me to learn a lesson, and, after what had just happened in Santa Marta, I wasn't going to give anyone even a remote chance to screw me twice. This was one of the wisest decisions I ever made.

MAY 29, 1980—LOS ANGELES, MEETING WITH PAUL ENGSTROM, ATTORNEY

Sloan and I left for Los Angeles on May 28 in the afternoon in order to make our appointment with Paul Engstrom the next day. A taxi took us to his office the following morning, May 29. As I sat facing him in his beautifully appointed office, I thought how fitting the elegant background was for the tall, well-tailored, distinguished attorney. The fine furniture gleamed and the thick carpeting muffled our footsteps.

We sat a long time talking. I gave him a step-by-step account of what had happened to date in Colombia, being careful to make the distinction between what I knew as fact and what I suspected might be fact—or fiction. I told him everything except how I was going to get the plane out. This matter I would keep to myself. In truth, I still hadn't fully pieced out every step of the strategy I would use. However, I assured him, and truthfully, that I was in complete agreement with Lloyd's—it had to be legal or not at all.

The point of the contract concerning ownership came under serious discussion. Exhibit 7, Page 3, Paragraph 3 stated: "Air Unlimited shall have no ownership rights in the aircraft ... until ... ," and thereafter gave the conditions to be fulfilled. I knew this negative wording would be spotted by Judge Valdez, and I tried desperately to convey to Paul that this would make it impossible for me to convince the judge that I was the real owner. Colombian law, legal opinions, and juridical concepts are based on Napoleonic Law and not on English Common Law as are ours in the States. Very broadly speaking, English Common Law assumes a person is right until proven wrong while Napoleonic Law assumes a person is wrong until he can prove he is right. In criminal law, the difference is even more striking: In our system, a man is innocent until proven guilty. In theirs, a man is guilty until proven innocent.

After much discussion, Engstrom felt that I had a point, but he had to take care of the best interests of Lloyd's. We finally agreed that the original contract, as written, be placed on file with the FAA in Oklahoma, but that the contract the judge would receive in Santa Marta would contain one small change. Exhibit 7, Page 3, Paragraph 3 would now read: "Air Unlimited shall have only those ownership rights in the aircraft which are set forth in this document."

This point turned out to be very critical, as even the new version was eventually questioned and challenged in the Judge Valdez's office. Engstrom and I shared the unspoken knowledge that money was going to have to change hands at one time or another. I started to approach the subject indirectly, but Paul interrupted, me, politely but very professionally.

"Bobby, I don't even want to think about, much less discuss, paying off anyone or doing this in any way that is not 100 percent legal. Just remember, the Learjet has to come out of Colombia through their legal system. All papers and documents must be authentic, official, and blessed by the Colombian courts. Please keep in mind that these stipulations are called for in your contract. Make sure that when and if you do get the plane released it is completely legal; otherwise, you have violated the contract."

Engstrom's strictly legalistic attitude was very reassuring and confirmed my impression that I was dealing with someone completely aboveboard who would not jeopardize his position or his client's with any hanky-panky about the release of the jet. This exchange of words told me more about his character than anything else could have done. I felt I had someone I could trust.

Another reassurance that Engstrom was a highly ethical man to be trusted was his desire not to know anything about my future tactics. This proved to me that if anything did go wrong, it would not be Engstrom who passed on information that might hinder my progress or land me in trouble.

"Let me give you a detailed run-down on everything I know and maybe it will give you a better picture of what you're up against," Engstrom said. He then went on to tell me what had happened at his end. He was called in on the case the first day N464J was confiscated, and had tried every possible legal means to get her out. In late 1979, Dunwoody came into the picture, as manager of United Aviation Assurance. He had told Dunwoody of his efforts in trying to resolve the insane incident and gave him the information he had received from the State Department.

Engstrom brought out the files of thousands of pages—telexes, affidavits, depositions, letters from Senators and Congressmen—three years of paper work. I could appreciate how very complex the matter truly was. Engstrom continued by allowing that John Gordon of Gordon & Sanford had contacted either Dunwoody or himself—he couldn't remember exactly how the first contact had been made—but he remembered that it was in late December 1979 or early January 1980, after Dunwoody had reopened investigations in Bogotá and in the United States. Dunwoody had told him that Gordon & Sanford were representing an organization in San Francisco with connections in Colombia that were supposedly the specialists in recovering confiscated aircraft from that country.

He interrupted his narrative to remark, "Bobby, you must understand that in the last three years I have been contacted by at least fifteen or twenty soldiers-of-fortune who said they could get the jet out. When you first came into the picture, frankly, I thought you were another one. But since you were willing to put up your own money to prove it, I changed my mind."

"Anyway," he went on, "at that point I had already told Dunwoody I was giving up and wished him the best of luck. Next, on March 3, I received a phone call from Gordon saying he could get the jet out, and I referred him back to Dunwoody. On March 14, Dunwoody telexed me to say he was considering retaining Gordon and giving him power of attorney on 464 Juliet. It was May 6 when Dunwoody advised me that Gordon had been given the power of attorney on May 5. He also told me that 464 Juliet was currently in use and being flown by the Colombian Air Force and that a scheduled release date of May 28 had been set."

That coincidence rang a bell.

"Wait, Paul," I interrupted, "May 6 was the day I talked with Peter Nash in London and informed him that 464 Juliet was sitting stripped in Santa Marta and had not been flown since it arrived there three years before. I had spoken with Dunwoody over three weeks earlier, on April 14, telling him the present condition of the plane. And yet, sometime between April 14 and May 6, Lloyd's had been told that the jet was flying for the Air Force down there. Also, Peter Nash had no knowledge of what I had told Dunwoody verbally, nor did he have knowledge of my written offer for the salvage rights. No wonder my first call to Nash caught him off guard."

But why hadn't Dunwoody investigated my story? I quickly assembled facts, deductions, and dates in my mind.

Fact: Dunwoody's unmistakably rude and condescending tone in our single telephone conversation on April 14.

Deduction: He had been weighing the credibility of one unknown individual, a man with a "deep South" accent named "Bobby Wood," against a known and well-established, big-time San Francisco lawyer and found Bobby Wood lacking.

Fact: Dunwoody's report to Lloyd's sometime in late April or early May, and to Engstrom on May 6, that the plane was being flown in Colombia.

Deduction: The news that the plane was in operating condition automatically meant it was worth more than just salvage value. Obviously this was more palatable to him and to his principals, Lloyd's of London. It would certainly be what he wanted to believe.

Fact: Gordon had already spent considerable effort and money on the project. He was promising the release of an airworthy plane on May 28.

Deduction: Mr. Dunwoody had burned his bridges behind him when he represented to Lloyd's that the plane was flying. He had misinformed them, intentionally or unintentionally. He had put his money on Gordon, who he thought was the winner. He had painted himself into a corner with Gordon. Bobby Wood could be swept under the carpet and not be able to shake off the dust before Gordon had delivered. By that time, Bobby Wood would no longer be a problem, or even an embarrassment. I was finding out that my own countrymen were also playing mind games with a lot of people, including me.

Engstrom may have been aware of my deductions, but was noncommittal and remarked only that it was quite a mess, and he hoped I could pull off a miracle and untangle it. I was fairly sure that he and Lloyd's had found out what had been going on when he told me that he would send Gordon a telex reminding Gordon that he was off the case. He returned in a few minutes.

"This should make it clear to everyone concerned that Gordon is officially out of the case," and handed me a copy, which read:

> LOS ANGELES CA 05/29/80
>
> PMS•JOHN GORDON ESQ. DELIVER DON'T PHONE.
>
> GORDON & SANFORD SAN FRANCISCO CA
>
> THIS WILL CONFIRM OUR TELECONS OF 5-20-80 WHEREIN I ADVISED YOU THAT THE INSURERS OF N464J HAD TENTATIVELY AGREED TO SELL THAT AIRCRAFT TO AIR UNLIMITED/ROBERT E. WOOD, JR., AND THAT ALL ACTIVITIES BY YOU RE THE AIRCRAFT'S RELEASE SHOULD CEASE IMMEDIATELY. YOU AGREED TO DO SO.
>
> NOW BE ADVISED THAT A CONDITIONAL SALE OF N4643

HAS BEEN CONCLUDED TO WOOD AND ANY AUTHORITY OR
AGREEMENT YOU MAY HAVE HAD IS RESCINDED. THANK YOU FOR
YOUR EFFORTS ON INSURERS' BEHALF.
    SINCERELY,
    PAUL W. ENGSTROM
    ENGSTROM, LIPSCOMB AND LACK

"This looks good," I said, "Now all we need is to have this affidavit translated and notarized at the Colombian Consulate."

"It's just across the street," Paul told me, "and I've already advised her that we're bringing the papers over—by the way, the Consul is a lady."

I was greatly impressed with Consul Clara Munoz de Yust, and she was indeed a lady, from her impeccable posture to her well-manicured fingertips. She was a true *señora*, about fifty years of age, immaculately dressed, with every hair in place. She reminded me of an eighteenth century aristocrat. After telling her what we needed, she told us to return around three that afternoon; the affidavit would be translated and notarized, with full consular authentication.

Paul Engstrom had a lunch appointment, and with the three-hour jet lag, Sloan and I weren't hungry, so we walked around sightseeing and talking. At two thirty we picked up Paul and returned to the consulate. *Señora* Yust came out to greet us and handed us the most thoroughly official-looking papers I ever saw. They were absolutely blazing with stamps, seals, and signatures and seemed designed to impress anyone who would receive them. We returned to Paul's office to pick up the rest of my documents.

While I was gathering up my papers, Engstrom walked over to me with a sheet of paper in his hand, which he held out to me. "You know, Bobby, after you left at noon, I was thinking about the problem you ran into at the Colombian judge's office, the matter of the lawyers who said they represented Gordon & Sanford. I remembered this telex from Gordon that I got a couple of weeks ago. Maybe it will shed some light on what happened."

The telex was dated May 15, 1980, and read:

> *PMS PAUL ENGSTROM LIPSCOMB AND LACK*
> *ATN: PAUL ENGSTROM LOS ANGELES, CA*
>   *PURSUANT TO RETAIN AGREEMENT AND POWER OF*
> *ATTORNEY DATED MAY 5, 1980, THIS OFFICE ACTIVATED CONTACTS*
> *WITH AMERICAN EMBASSY BOGOTA, AMERICAN CONSULATE*
> *BARRANQUILLA, MADE PERSONAL INSPECTION OF LEAR JET AT*
> *SANTA MARTA, REVIEWED FILE WITH JUDGE JORGE VALDEZ,*
> *3RD CIRCUIT CRIMINAL JUDGE SANTA MARTA, ASSOCIATED*

*COLOMBIAN COUNSEL AND UNDERTOOK NUMEROUS OTHER
ACTIONS TO OBTAIN RELEASE ON MAY 28.*

*JUDGE ADVISED THAT INTERVENTION AND UNAUTHORIZED
INSPECTION BY WOODS' AGENTS MADE IMPOSSIBLE IMMEDIATE
RELEASE. ADVISE YOU CONSULT FAA RECORDS TO DETERMINE IF
AUTHORITY TO THIS OFFICE FROM TOM DUNWOODY IS SUBJECT
TO CANCELLATION BY YOUR OFFICE AFTER CONSIDERABLE
EXPENSE ADVANCED AND RELEASE CLOSE AT HAND.*

*IF NO INTERVENTION NO "SALE" IS POSSIBLE BY COLOMBIAN
GOVERNMENT AND NO "CONDITIONAL SALE" BY INSURERS IS
POSSIBLE SINCE INSURERS NOR COLOMBIAN GOVERNMENT
PRESENTLY HAVE TITLE TO SELL.*

JOHN G. GORDON

Engstrom made no further comment, nor did I utter the "I told you so."
I was on the point of blurting out, but later, in the elevator, I did say so to my
lawyer, Steve Sloan, who nodded and commented that he was beginning to
understand what I was talking about.

"Thank you, Paul," I said, promising to keep him updated weekly.

His parting words of encouragement were simple, "Get 464 Juliet
out." His warmth made me feel he was solidly on my side and that he had
confidence I could do it.

Sloan and I went back to the hotel to pick up our luggage. He wasn't
happy about leaving that same night for Oklahoma, but there were no flights
that would put us there early in the morning.

"Sloan," I urged, I've already spoken with Mary Miller at Insured Aircraft
Title. She said it would take four or five hours to complete our paperwork
and file it, so we've just got to get there tonight. Otherwise, we'll have to stay
over tomorrow night and we'll lose another day."

We arrived in Oklahoma City around eleven and checked in at the
Ramada Inn. Sloan was grumbling about what a slave driver I was, that the
restaurants were closed, no bars open, and so on and on and on. I promised
to wine and dine him when we got back to Miami.

MAY 30, 1980—OKLAHOMA CITY, MEETING WITH INSURED AIRCRAFT TITLE

Next morning, at nine, we went to Insured Aircraft Title located across
the street from the FAA filing center. This is the principal, in fact, the *only*
FAA documentation office in the United States. Every American aircraft
in the world is registered here. Every contract, bill of sale, lien, and other
important aviation document. All under one single roof.

Many times in the past I had spoken with Mary Miller whenever I had needed title searches or information about aircraft documents, so I felt as though I was meeting an old friend. She took us into her office. I commented on the vice president sign on her desk, asking if she was that important executive.

Smiling, she replied, "Only when things can't get done properly."

Mary was a petite young lady around thirty years old, married, with two sons. She was attractive, well dressed, and a real whiz at her job. We spent about half an hour to give her the picture and discussed the points of my conditional sale contract with Lloyd's at length.

"I know and you know that, in all truth, I am the owner of 464 Juliet," I said, "but nowhere does it say that Robert E. Wood, Jr. is the owner. I need some kind of documentation, legal and notarized, that will make it extremely easy for the judge in Santa Marta to understand that this is the case. There is some opposition here in the States trying to undermine my dealings with the government in Colombia. The credentials and documentation I take to Colombia this time must be absolutely airtight."

I went on to explain that my dilemma was even more complicated by the judge's lack of knowledge of the English language, and that I was afraid I couldn't get across to him the reason for the forty-two-day time period stipulation.

"I'm not sure, either," Mary said, "but let's go over to the FAA and see Mrs. Swimmer. She's a good friend and will help if there's any way. We'll get her to give us a notarized statement, complete with all the ribbons, that your papers and documents are on file with the FAA. It will be on government paper, and will be 100 percent official."

Mary thought it would be a good idea for me to take out a title insurance policy guaranteeing that I was the official and legal owner. They would write it for six hundred thousand dollars.

"That would positively prove you are the titled owner," she assured me, "and it would guarantee that you would collect the money if anything happened. I'm sure the judge would consider this additional proof. The only thing is, Bobby, it will be expensive."

"How much?"

"Right at $1,050 plus taxes," she informed me.

I assured her that it was very reasonable considering what was at stake. I also privately figured that should Gordon & Sanford go to Santa Marta with any more superseded documents to try to convince the judge that they were the owners or put doubts in his mind, that this policy would be insurance of another kind—foiling their efforts and ensuring that if I didn't get the jet out, no one else would, either.

Mary went on, "I can give you an updated title search showing Air Unlimited/Robert E. Wood, Jr. as the recorded owner."

Beautiful, I thought, *this is the frosting on the cake. Now, no one can disprove that I am the real owner.*

All the legal documents I had would have been ample and readily understood in the States, but Colombia was another matter. Proof after proof after proof was required there.

Mary was one sweet and helpful girl. She patiently spent the next five or six hours typing, running over to the FAA, notarizing, and getting my package ready. At four o'clock she finally announced, "Bobby, if this doesn't get you what you want, nothing will."

Sloan and I were elated; a perfect three days, and a complete lock on 464 Juliet. With heartfelt thanks, we bade Mary goodbye and left for the airport. The flight wouldn't leave until six thirty, so I had plenty of time to call my wife.

My son Jay answered the phone and his "Hurry, Mom, it's Dad" told me something was up. Terry got on the line. "I've been trying to get hold of you since morning," she said. "Raul needs to talk with you right away—something about the judge in Santa Marta. He's at home, waiting for your call."

I hung up, telling her I would call back.

In two minutes, I had Raul, who had been sitting by the phone, to pick it up at the first ring. He lost no time. "Aldo called this morning. The judge called Aldo and told him that the same two lawyers, Ortiz from Cartagena and the other from the States, had been at his office again yesterday. They are still telling him they are the owners of 464 Juliet. They brought him documents and a letter from Gordon & Sanford saying that they have the power of attorney. The judge is very confused. He wants to know what the hell is going on. Aldo says we better do something but quick."

"Raul, I have good news. I have absolutely all the proof the judge needs to show that I am the real owner. Absolutely, positively, no more confusion for the judge. I just left the FAA and will be home tonight."

I instructed Raul to go immediately to the house and get four or five hundred dollars from Terry. Then he was to go directly to Miami International Airport. If he hurried, he could catch the 7:00 P.M. flight to Barranquilla. If he missed that, he was to take the next flight to Bogotá or to Panama; but, either way, he was to bust ass to get to Barranquilla this night. He was to get his wife to phone Aldo to meet him at the Hotel Royal tonight. I put in a strongly worded warning that he was not to screw up.

Then, I went on; he was to be at the doorstep of the judge's office the next morning at eight o'clock and wait. He was to inform the judge that I had been in California with the representative of Lloyd's of London and also in

Oklahoma City to conduct our business with the United States Government's FAA office. That I would be in Barranquilla that same night and that we would all meet the following day.

Raul was to be very persuasive and insistent. He had to get it across to the judge that when I got there the judge would see with his own eyes that I had all the documents notarized by the Colombian Consulate and that I had proof positive of ownership. He was also to tell the judge that I also had proof that Gordon & Sanford's power of attorney had been rescinded.

"Don't talk," I urged, "just throw something in a suitcase and get over to my house to get the money. One other thing: Call Alfredo Escobar in Bogotá tomorrow and ask him to go to Barranquilla to be there tomorrow night. That will be the right time to introduce him to the judge. Valdez knows Alfredo's father is the Minister of Justice and this will reassure him about doing business with us. I'll call Terry to tell her you're coming over."

"Wait, don't forget to get Alfredo his present," Raul said, reminding me that he had asked for us to bring him two derringers when we next returned to Colombia. "That will make him more than happy to come to Barranquilla."

I told him I would and hung up. Sloan was trying to figure out what all the frenzied conversation had been about, but I had to put him off until I called Terry back to tell her what the plan was.

After phoning Terry, telling her to expect Raul, to give him money, and to keep him moving, I turned to Sloan. "I've got to do something about those sons of bitches in San Francisco. They're still trying to screw me up with the judge. Damn it, they know I'm the owner of 464 Juliet now. They're still trying to cover their asses by trying to shoot me down."

I blew off steam for a couple of minutes. On the flight back to Florida, I did some thinking out loud with Sloan about developments in Colombia.

"Look, Sloan, you know and I know that for three years the best legal brains in England, the States and Colombia have been trying only the good Lord knows how many different angles to get 464 Juliet out. I'm not doing anything that hasn't already been tried. So what I need to do is to come up with a different angle, one that hasn't been thought of up to now. Someone has been overlooking something, and that includes me. I've got to find out what it is.

"I know several things for sure," I continued.

"Number one: almost anything a person wants to do in Colombia can be done with money. Lloyd's has money, so let's strike that.

"Number two: I am reasonably certain that every possible legal detail has been thoroughly investigated. However, if by remote chance something has been overlooked, we should keep that one open.

"Number three: the airplane belonged under the jurisdiction of the

Department of Magdalena where Santa Marta is located, and not in Bogotá."

"So it's probably here, in number three," I concluded, "that most of the problem originates. The only one who can shed light on why it's been here for three years is the judge. There might be some political ramifications and complications out of Bogotá, because the Learjet had been given to the President and the Air Force. But I believe the key is Judge Valdez. I think I'll have Gordon & Sanford under control once I see the judge. Then I'll have time to concentrate along these lines."

I went on, thinking out loud.

"One thing I don't understand is why our government hasn't helped. The flight was a bona fide international air ambulance trip. The United States and Colombian governments should have helped, even if just to appear humanitarian in the eyes of the world. I have a gut feeling that some important information is lacking and that the matter goes deeper than we, or, any others, may suspect." By now, I had some specific and concrete information about Jimmy Chagra, and the thought that his involvement must have something to do with this mystery kept nibbling at the back of my mind, but I kept that to myself and didn't tell Sloan.

I made a mental note. *When I get back to Colombia, I am going to look over Judge Valdez's papers again to try to clarify this puzzling point and perhaps shed some light on what 464 Juliet's flight had to do with why Bruce Allen had been forgotten or ignored. Why was an American pilot left to die alone in a strange land, even if he had flown there to run drugs or to perform some other criminal errand for Jimmy Chagra?*

CHAPTER SIXTEEN

Terry took me to the airport early in the evening on May 31. It was a rough flight to Barranquilla, with thunderstorms over Cuba. I read and re-read all my documents with growing confidence. I was sure I would get a quick release of 464 Juliet.

Raul, Aldo, Toño, and Gustavo were all waiting for me at the airport, escorting me importantly through the long line of people waiting to clear customs and immigration. I was glad to let Raul and friends take care of passport stamping and the other red tape.

"Where's Alfredo?" I asked as we got into the car. Raul replied that Alfredo hadn't been able to come that night but would be there next evening. Alfredo would be glad to help us.

"You did talk to the judge?" I demanded next. Raul nodded vigorously. He had done it first thing. Valdez would be waiting for us in the morning.

Aldo had been out of the act too long for his liking.

"Bobby, all those other people are making Judge Valdez very nervous." Aldo sounded very nervous himself, fearful of any possibility that his deal and his fee might be endangered. "I hope you have something good," he said anxiously.

I assured him that my papers would calm the judge's nerves.

Next morning, June 1, at seven, we left for Santa Marta. No problems at the bridge, just a routine check and dirty looks. We drove slowly. Aquiles' 1953 Chevy had not grown any younger since my last trip. The valves were clicking loudly and the cords were showing on the tires. The road was worse than ever, I could have sworn new potholes had developed in my short absence.

We stopped at Rodadero to leave the rest of the group while Aldo, Raul, and I went to the judge's office. He showed up about ten, in a good mood, but he did indeed seem nervous, wary and more reserved than at our last meeting.

He lost no time in expressing concern as to why, if I were the owner, other people were coming to him to get release of the Learjet, claiming they were the owners.

I took out my new papers and we went through them slowly, one by one. I put special emphasis on the principal ones, particularly those, that had been officially translated into Spanish and authenticated by the Colombian Consulate in Los Angeles.

Judge Valdez read them carefully, asking questions during his examination of the contents. The Spanish version of the affidavit that Paul Engstrom had written was of particular interest to the judge. It explained, from Exhibit 1 through Exhibit 11, all the steps that had been taken to make me eventually the owner. I pointed out to the judge that these had been notarized by the County Court of Los Angeles as well as authenticated by the Colombian Consulate. I also showed him how all the other documents had been stamped by the United States Government FAA office in Oklahoma. All had their pretty ribbons, gold seals, and lots of stamps. These decorations are important in Colombia, nothing is considered official without them.

The title search was next scrutinized by the judge. "Look," I said, "Right here it says *Recorded Owner—Air Unlimited/Robert E. Wood, Jr.* Also, sir, look at this," and I showed him the official statement from the FAA indicating that all my documents were on file there. I strongly emphasized that this document was on official United States Government paper, duly sworn and notarized by United States Government officials.

The judge was showing more and more satisfaction with what I had brought him. He was particularly pleased with the Insurance Title policy proving I was the correct title holder of 464J. Six hundred thousand dollars' worth of proof is a lot of proof.

Another half-hour and the judge seemed fairly well convinced that I was the good guy and that Gordon, Ortiz, and friends were the bad guys. However, Judge Valdez was nothing if not thorough.

"Well," he hedged, "all this looks good. Yes. But I can't accept it as completely legal yet. You see, I don't have the Los Angeles Consul's signature on file here in Santa Marta. We want to be 100 percent sure ... You must take all these papers to the Ministry of Foreign Relations in Bogotá. They will pass on their legality and advise me if they can be recognized in Colombia. And, at the same time, they will confirm the authenticity of the signature of the Colombian Consul in Los Angeles and the legal translation you have here."

It was loud and clear that the judge was going to make 100 percent sure and was passing the buck higher up. *Damn*, I thought, *another Colombian* mañana—*more bullshit, more stamps, more seals.* I was beginning to wonder if Colombian toilet paper had to have seals.

Here, I concluded, is where my friend Alfredo Escobar in Bogotá could help us.

"Raul," I suggested, "mention that I am planning to retain the services of Alfredo Escobar, the son of the Minister of Justice, and that perhaps it would be a good idea if the two of them could discuss it to see what the best course of action would be."

Apparently the right name had been dropped. The judge's eyes widened with interest. He immediately replied that he would be most honored to meet Alfredo Escobar. Raul went on to say that Escobar had mentioned that we could count on his father's support should any problems arise in Bogotá. This pleased Valdez enormously, which was understandable—one of his main concerns was to protect his seat on the bench.

It looked as if I had been right in the third point I had outlined to Steve Sloan a couple of nights earlier on the plane from Oklahoma to Miami: Judge Valdez *was* the key. The political ramifications and complications out of Bogotá, and the judge's desire to resolve them, were what would put him solidly on my side. Once I gave him what he would need to cover his back, his full cooperation would be forthcoming.

I told the judge that we would go to Bogotá that night and ask Escobar to visit the Ministry of Foreign Relations to take care of the matter of the re-authentication. We would be back in two days. I urged that he say nothing to the Gordon & Sanford contact, Ortiz, about the matter. I promised that we would have every *t* crossed and every *i* dotted concerning my legal ownership of the Learjet.

I wanted badly to stop at the airport to see 464 Juliet, but the judge advised me that we absolutely could not do this until we had a legal order. The order would be issued once all the papers were legalized. He added that he had not written the official letter requesting Luis Donado to inspect the plane since he had to show complete impartiality in the face of the visit of Ortiz and the American lawyer who were claiming they represented the legal owners.

His closing remark was very illuminating.

"Once you return from Bogotá with all your papers legalized, we can proceed. And if a problem arises, it will be the responsibility of the Ministry in Bogotá—not mine."

We stopped at the restaurant to pick up the rest of the crew and left for Barranquilla. While passing through Rodadero we saw a road block ahead. The soldiers were searching cars for contraband.

"I don't like this … ," I muttered to Raul.

"No problem. You have your letters with you."

We were motioned off the road and one of the soldiers, spotting me, started blowing his whistle. I began getting out, but Raul was ahead of me, explaining who I was, that I was not a *marimbero*, and then he slipped the man a twenty.

The soldier told us we could go. We needed no second invitation. Raul explained to me that even with the letters, it was still a good idea to pay a "leetle."

We reached Escobar that same afternoon by phone. He said he would meet us at the Bogotá El Dorado Airport at customs. I wanted no problems with the two gold-plated derringers I had brought with me as his gift.

I decided we would keep the room in Barranquilla rather than pack everything up to take to Bogotá. Aldo and Toño said they would be willing to stay and take care of our things for us. Imagine that. Those boys were all heart.

Alfredo Escobar met me and Raul at the ramp of the Bogotá airport as we stepped off the plane. He flashed his credentials at several immigration officials. One of them removed his hat, bowed and shook Escobar's hand warmly. Escobar looked important, well-groomed with an expensive hand-tailored suit; he might have been a Senator or a Minister himself.

When Raul whispered that the derringers were in his suitcase, Escobar merely nodded, smiled, picked up the suitcase, took it over to the counter, and removed the derringers openly, with not a glance to see if there were watching eyes. He slipped them in his pocket. At the customs counter, he again brought out his credentials and out we went. Two exit guards were preparing to check my bag, which Escobar forestalled by mentioning his name. The guards politely excused themselves. Clout was a very comfortable thing to have in Colombia, I thought enviously.

Escobar had reserved us a room at the *Tequendama* Hotel, and after checking in we sat down to give him a complete rundown. He was interested. When he heard my offer of a five thousand dollar retainer plus expenses to be our "consultant" with the ministry until we got 464J released, he became very interested. I felt that a fee would get his full attention and be a good, preventive measure against, what I was now calling, the "*Mañana* Syndrome."

Also, if Escobar delivered he would definitely have earned his money.

"Alfredo, one thing is very important, and I want to give it to you up front," I said. "You've got to convince Judge Valdez that your father will back him up if any problems develop in Bogotá."

Alfredo saw this as no problem and promised to go with us to Santa Marta as soon as he had gotten the papers re-notarized and re-authenticated in Bogotá.

"I've already called the Ministry," he added, "and they said they would give it their immediate attention."

We had a long session in which I told him about Gordon, Ortiz, and possible other interested parties who were trying to hinder us or who might try to see that we didn't get the deal done.

"Look, Bobby," he said seriously, "you won't have any further problems with at least this part of your work in Colombia. My father is an important man and my family commands a lot of respect. I can help you, believe me."

I was in high spirits when he left, and Raul assured me that this amigo was another valuable asset.

Next morning, June 2, we went directly to the Ministry of Foreign Relations with Escobar. I didn't even have to go inside. When he returned, I quickly realized that he had been giving it to me straight the night before—he had *palanca*—leverage. All the documents were ready. It had taken only two hours and had cost only thirty dollars.

Raul and I checked out the documents and it was clear, absolutely, without any shadow of a doubt, we had incontestable Colombian government approval of the legality of my documents. Normally and under the best of circumstances, two weeks would be a highly optimistic estimated waiting period, even if no questions arose during the process. Alfredo Escobar had done it in two hours. It was done solely on the name and reputation of this man and his family.

Had I gone there alone, I was convinced, someone surely would have remembered that 464J had been a serious national problem, and then higher-ups in the government would have had to be found to give an "opinion." Even more incredible, only the affidavit was in Spanish, the rest of the papers were all in English. I could never have gotten them notarized and authenticated without Escobar, because each page would first have had to go back to the Colombian Consulate in California to be officially translated and notarized.

I had been sick with worry for three days, but now my stomach was back to normal. When Alfredo, Raul, and I arrived back in Barranquilla and went up to the room we found the usual crew, my five steady and true amigos plus four new ones I had never seen before. Judging from the number of liquor bottles and empty food trays, I had been the absentee-host of yet another party. I was embarrassed and annoyed at having Alfredo see all those slobs treating the room like a pig's trough. However, Alfredo took it in stride and acted as if he weren't fully aware that all of them were taking full advantage of a free ride.

The next day was cloudy with a slight drizzle when we started to Santa Marta. It seemed to soften the ugly approach to the bridge. We were ordered to pull over for a paper check. Nothing indicated a hassle, today, but just a slight air of insolence hung in the air. Alfredo caught it at once.

Without a word, just a small hand signal to me, he stepped out of the car, impeccable, beautifully tailored. As the guards came near, Alfredo pulled out his identification and with complete authority said, "I am Alfredo Escobar.

My father is Minister of Justice of the Republic."

These resounding words impressed them, to judge from their expressions and the way they snapped to military attention. Alfredo even saluted them, like a general reviewing the troops. He motioned me to join him, and he put his arm across my shoulder.

"I hear there has been some misunderstanding here in the past," he began sternly. "I want everyone here to know that *señor* Wood is a personal friend of mine and of my father's. I would consider it a personal insult if *señor* Wood is not given proper treatment here. He is not a *marimbero*. He is a United States aviation consultant. We are working together on important projects."

His tone softened and grew friendlier. "On the other hand, I would consider it a personal favor if he is given proper treatment."

The transformation was instantaneous and almost comic. Suddenly wide gold-toothed smiles appeared on previously insolent faces. One of the guards with a well-developed instinct for polishing apples even shook Escobar's hand vigorously and assured him that he was completely at our orders, at any time. Quite a barrage of bullshit was laid down within a couple of short minutes. As we pulled away, Raul and I nudged each other and exchanged glances, both of us trying to stifle our guffaws.

Another small and amusing aspect of the trip was that Alfredo said nothing about Aquiles' piece-of-shit Chevy, which was in even worse condition than before.

Alfredo was the perfect gentleman, completely at ease, even in that derelict heap.

We were in Santa Marta by nine thirty and drove straight to Judge Valdez's office. His secretary, Beatriz, told Aldo that he was to telephone the judge at home as soon as we arrived. Aldo phoned and told us the judge would like us to join him there. This was a big step forward. In Colombia, a man's home is definitely his castle. To be invited to the judge's home represented an enormous vote of confidence. Of course, I wasn't foolish enough to think that anything short of Alfredo's visit had opened the door, literally and figuratively—the judge couldn't very well have excluded me and Raul from the invitation. But whatever prompted it, a precedent was established and in the future we were to meet more often at his home than at his office.

Judge Valdez lived in Rodadero. About three blocks from his home, we ran into a road block. The occupants of a military Jeep ordered us over and out. When I stepped out, two of the soldiers grabbed me roughly and began a search. Alfredo was having none of this. He shouted at them. One of the soldiers turned to grab Alfredo, when he suddenly recognized the name he had heard. It was plain to see that they realized they had screwed up, but good.

Immediate apologies were made. They were stammering out explanations that an American prisoner had escaped and they thought … more apologies. The two soldiers were even trying to brush off Aldo and to straighten my clothing that had been disarranged in their search. How could they help us? They were *eager* to know.

A minute later we were before the judge's house. Aldo self-importantly instructed us to wait until he had advised the judge of our arrival, a suggestion I could see Alfredo took not too kindly, but he didn't challenge it.

The Valdez property was beautifully tended, absolutely spotless, with a manicured lawn and freshly painted breezeway. This was to be my first visit to an upper-class Colombian home.

Aldo returned, inviting us to enter. Inside, he introduced Escobar and Judge Valdez. The judge was clearly pleased to have Alfredo as a guest in his home. He invited us into a small den at the far end of the house, taking us through a hallway that glistened with cleanliness.

We were asked to sit down, offered refreshments. I had my usual Coca-Cola, the others had whiskey. It was a special mark of courtesy that the judge had made, who served the drinks with his own hands, an unspoken indication that our meeting would be informal and casual. Valdez and Alfredo carried the bulk of the conversation.

After these necessary well-mannered preliminaries, the judge was ready to approach the real purpose of the visit. He inquired, very solicitously, about the Minister's health. Alfredo took the cue. After thanking the judge and assuring him that his father was in excellent health, he got down to the case at hand, also politely and indirectly.

"As a matter of fact, Dr. Valdez, I was discussing this matter with my father just the other day, telling him about the consulting I am doing for *señor* Wood," he said smoothly. "When I told him that we would be visiting you here in Santa Marta, he mentioned that he was as anxious as all of us are to get this matter successfully concluded and that he would help us in any way possible to do so."

This was music to the judge's ears, just what he wanted to hear: His smiles became more frequent and broader, and he paid particular attention to everything Alfredo had to say.

When Alfredo handed Judge Valdez my documents, he said, "I personally saw the Minister of Foreign Relations, who hand carried these to be notarized. They are completely legal and I am certain you can now go ahead with the full assurance that you are acting in the best interests of all concerned."

Valdez was lovingly examining the seals and stamps, nodding approval and interjecting an occasional "very good" or "excellent" as he went through them.

"These are in perfect order," he announced finally. "Now I can issue the official order for inspection of the Learjet. I will inform the *jefe* of Aerocivil in Barranquilla and get the matter moving."

The rest of the conversation was between Alfredo, the judge, and Raul speaking for me. Valdez was ignoring Aldo in his interest in a new-found amigo. At the same time, Raul's stock with the judge had apparently gone up. The judge spoke to him in a friendly manner and gave him what I felt was another vote of confidence.

"Here, Raul," he said, "I'm giving you my home number on my card. Sometimes I am difficult to find—or you may need to call me from the States." And to Alfredo, he said, "You should have it, too, just in case you need to call me urgently."

Aldo was seething. He had tried hard to keep his special status as the sole contact with the judge. Now the judge was sidestepping his plans, and Aldo couldn't do a thing about it but try to smile through clenched teeth.

When we finished our business, Alfredo asked the judge if he could spare us a few more minutes to go to the airport for a look at the Learjet. "Of course," replied Valdez, "I'll take you myself, in my Jeep."

Raul grinned at me as we went outside. He stepped into his place with a flourish that said plainly, "Imagine this, the judge is driving us to the airport. We're coming up in the world."

Fifteen minutes later we pulled up to the airport. As we walked across the ramp, a few soldiers approached us. The judge motioned imperiously that everything was fine.

We sure enough, indeed, had come up in the world.

CHAPTER SEVENTEEN

JUNE 3, 1980—SIMÓN BOLÍVAR AIRPORT, A VISIT TO 464 JULIET

I was hoping that our promotion upward in the world would now become a permanent arrangement with the military personnel of the Santa Marta Airport. This, in fact, didn't turn out to be the case. The presence of Judge Valdez and an important-looking man such as Alfredo Escobar had made them roll over and behave like trained circus cats, but once the "tamers" were gone, they would be after us fang and claw for whatever tidbits they could get.

"*Qué belleza* (what a beauty)," Alfredo exclaimed as we approached 464 Juliet. He was clearly excited; it was the first time he had been close to a Learjet and even her sad condition could not detract from her classic lines. While Alfredo and Judge Valdez walked around her, I quietly asked Raul to mention that the plane was still unlocked after three years and that the major part of the equipment had been removed. I felt that this would accomplish two objectives.

First, it would put me in a better bargaining position, as the value of the plane had obviously been lowered by the pilferage. And, second, it would put the judge on the defensive, because he would be losing face with Alfredo, who could see that the seizure stickers had been broken. At the same time, I would give Valdez a chance to regain lost face by re-establishing his authority in no uncertain terms in Alfredo's presence.

I was right. Raul had scarcely finished pointing this out when Judge Valdez was motioning the soldiers to come near. Indicating the seals, he began angrily inquiring about who had flouted his authority and who had dared to break them. Naturally no one knew. The seals had been broken for years.

After delivering a strong, general tongue-lashing, he then gave them specific orders to arrest anyone who came near the jet. If caught breaking in, the thief was to be shot first and questioned later.

I asked if the judge had the keys. He didn't, but he would check with the DAS office at the airport. He assured me that it would be secured and resealed. I had my doubts about how long the new seals would remain unbroken, but at least Valdez was making some kind of effort to keep down further pilferage.

"Alfredo," I said, "ask the judge if I can show him what's in the nose." I figured that a request from Escobar would carry more weight with the judge than from me.

"What for?" Alfredo wanted to know.

"Just ask him—you'll see," I urged.

The judge was a little reluctant to allow this inspection, but, as I had thought, he didn't want to turn down Alfredo's request; so he nodded yes.

I lost no time in taking a screwdriver out of my pocket (which I just happened to have handy) and quickly removed the top nose panels to expose the avionics compartment.

Both the judge and Alfredo were amazed.

"What is this?" Judge Valdez demanded. "What are all these rocks doing here?" He motioned to the group of soldiers to approach, and in a minute we had a crowd of around twenty onlookers.

I explained to everyone, through Alfredo, that this was where the avionics boxes had been, and started heaving out some of the rocks—actually a lot of them were small boulders over eighteen inches in diameter. After the removal of around two hundred pounds of rock they could see that the avionics racks were empty.

"The equipment that should be in here is worth about two hundred thousand dollars; it's all been stolen," I announced.

This information prompted the judge to deliver a new tirade at the soldiers. I had overstated the value of the missing avionics; I could replace them for about forty-five thousand dollars, but brand-new they would probably have cost close to the higher figure. But I wanted Judge Valdez to take the thefts very seriously.

"Why would someone put rocks inside after stealing the radios?" the judge wondered.

I demonstrated the reason by walking around to the nose and lifting the whole front of the jet about a foot off the ground.

Everyone looked at me as if I were Superman, in complete disbelief. I gently set it back down and explained that the rocks had been used to weight the nose so that it wouldn't lift up and fall on its tail. Learjets, I explained, are very critical in the weight-and-balance area, which was why we would have to replace the rocks we had removed for the demonstration.

The point I had wanted to make was well taken. I felt sure that the judge would do his best to secure the plane in order to keep all-important face, and I was happy to note that he was not angry with me for revealing the extent of the thefts: He promised earnestly that he would order the soldiers to watch closely in the future, and took them over to the compound to issue further instructions.

Raul and Aldo were speculating about who could have taken the radios and avionics boxes when I got back to them, and I gave them my thoughts on the matter.

"Let's not kid ourselves," I said, "we all know damned well no one could have taken them without the soldiers at least knowing about it. I guarantee they either took them or looked the other way, for a price, so that someone else could take them."

They were both sure that this was how it had happened. I instructed Raul to spread the word around to military personnel, Avianca mechanics, and any others concerned that I would give a five thousand dollar reward for the return of the equipment—not just part, but every damned piece. At least the offer of a reward would get them thinking.

We departed about three thirty in the afternoon, arranging to see Judge Valdez the following day to sign a letter of authorization for him to proceed, and that I would assume responsibility for all court costs that would be incurred in his investigation. Alfredo spoke privately with the judge for a few minutes before we took off.

When we were on our way, I turned to Alfredo and asked him what he thought about the judge.

"I don't know," he answered thoughtfully, "but I can see he's a little nervous over the whole thing. When I was talking with him a few minutes ago, he asked again if I was sure my father would help in case any problems arose. Valdez is worried about repercussions in Bogotá, not in Santa Marta. You know, of course, that the case was originally in the Second Penal Court of Santa Marta and then was transferred to him in the Third. You have to remember that it was a very notorious affair—not your 'usual' confiscation. Valdez is aware of a lot of factors that he hasn't mentioned, I'm sure. He dropped a few remarks to me about some deals made in 1977 between Bogotá and the United States government and between the Magdalena Department (state) government and the United States. He didn't mention any names, though, and he didn't give me any concrete information. What I think he wanted to let me know was that he was being cautious because so many different levels of Colombian government had been involved."

Alfredo went on describing the departmental, national, and international aspects of the confiscation as he saw them and in the light of what information the judge had dropped. He mentioned again that Valdez knew that arrangements of some kind had been made between higher officials in Magdalena and Bogotá and that the jet was to be confiscated when it arrived in Colombia. All the persons involved were to be arrested. The deal had fallen through. He didn't know why, but certain key people in Bogotá had put pressure on others in Santa Marta. Because the case had so much publicity, it was getting to be a hot potato. And because a great deal of confusion was building up about who was going to get paid, either under the table or aboveboard, the fate of the jet was consigned to limbo.

He continued. At the time 464 that Juliet had been confiscated, it was to become the property of the Department of Magdalena where Santa Marta is located. However, this law was changed some time later, and since then, all confiscated aircraft were considered the property of the central government in Bogotá.

Here Alfredo digressed a few moments.

"We Colombians are very regionalistic people," he said. "We don't often stick together as Colombians, but we close ranks very fast as Bogotános, or as other people from their respective departments, like Antioguia, Magdalena, or Atlántico. So what happened, I gather, is that someone in Bogotá tried to push around the courts in Santa Marta, and Santa Marta was having none of it. With all the in-fighting, and with no one knowing who was going to pay whom, the Learjet has been consigned to limbo."

All of this made a great deal of sense to me. Suddenly, Alfredo switched to a related, but different subject.

"Bobby, be honest with me, how much are you having to pay the judge?"

I was caught off guard, and his question put me in something of a dilemma. I had been warned not to tell anyone that I was paying the judge anything, much less the figure. I was also concerned about the possibility that Alfredo might use such information to have the judge removed from the bench, but couldn't really see this as a serious possibility. On the other hand, Alfredo would naturally want to know something about this fact of a matter in which he himself was involved, and as he was to receive his own fee for the help he was giving in obtaining release of the plane, I decided to tell him what he wanted to know. He might have good advice to offer on how I could best handle this part of the deal.

I took a breath, cast off caution and told him Judge Valdez was to get seventy-five thousand dollars, which included Aldo's cut.

He digested the information for a few seconds and finally offered his comments.

"Bobby, don't pay him anything until I give you the word. Seventy-five thousand is a lot of money, and I don't want you to get screwed. Believe me, if there's anywhere in the world this could happen, it's in Santa Marta."

"Actually, Alfredo, it's not Valdez I'm worried about. It's that so-called lawyer of mine—Aldo. He's supposedly the one handling all the financial arrangements. He won't let me open my mouth with Valdez about this part of the deal. That's what makes me nervous. If Aldo's planning to screw the judge—and I don't put it past him—the judge would more than likely think it's me."

"I see what you mean … so, that's all the more reason to wait until I tell you it's the right time," Alfredo warned.

I mentioned that during our visit to the house, Raul had slipped two thousand dollars to the judge that he had requested, but added that Valdez had not been Rauling me for money and that I thought it would not be any problem to wait until I had Alfredo's go-ahead.

"I don't think Valdez will take me for any walks in the garden," I added. "He knows by now that we are the owners of title and that if he doesn't honor his deal with us, his chances of getting money from somebody else will be slim. But I feel more secure having you here to oversee and monitor exactly what's happening in my dealings with the judge. That way we can take it step by step and reduce the risks."

Alfredo assured me that he would make certain that no one in Colombia would screw around with the legal aspects of the matter.

CHAPTER EIGHTEEN

Next morning, it looked like a fine day and it turned out to be just that. We had taken Escobar to the Barranquilla airport for his return trip to Bogotá, and we were watching his plane depart when Luis Donado, our friend from Aerocivil, walked in.

"Bobby, you're just the person I'm looking for," Donado said. "I've been trying to call you. It would be a good idea for us to go to Santa Marta today and take a preliminary look at the Learjet. I have a couple of Avianca mechanics available, and it's a good opportunity to get your project moving."

I was nodding eagerly.

"Look, all we're going to do is go through some motions," Donado said. "This will give me a solid basis for recommending that you bring in a Learjet mechanic from the States to do the official inspection. We honestly don't have anyone down here who can give us a qualified opinion."

"Great, this way I can get a first-hand idea of the actual condition of 464 Juliet. That's important," I agreed.

I was delighted to see Donado taking the initiative, not merely helping when asked.

"Bobby, you'll have to pay the mechanics. I don't have a budget for anything like this. What's more, it would look better if I appeared completely impartial, just carrying out instructions. I'll see that they charge you what's fair."

I told him I understood completely and that I was in complete agreement, thanking him sincerely for arranging everything.

Donado gave us instructions to go down to the Avianca maintenance building and ask for Manuel. Manuel knew about Donado's plan. We were to make the financial arrangements and be back at Donado's office to leave around eleven.

Manuel was waiting for us with another mechanic. We agreed on payment of three hundred dollars for both of them, which I felt was a fair price. We had some time to kill, so we told the mechanics to meet us in the restaurant and that we would buy them lunch.

Donado arrived a little after eleven, apologizing for being late. He wolfed down a sandwich, we finished our Coca-Colas, and then we left, first making a stop at Donado's home to pick up his boys, Donado Jr. and Fernando.

We reached the Santa Marta Airport in the early afternoon, unloaded ourselves, and started for the gate. For a moment I thought I had been whisked back into the past—a short, white-haired man suddenly appeared trotting toward us out of nowhere. A second look assured me that it wasn't that same angry little man in short pants who I now knew to be Judge Valdez. He was, however, giving us a loud argument about going over to 464 Juliet.

Donado finally shut him up by showing this little man his credentials. Baratta was his name. He had worked there for Aerocivil for about six years and was the assistant airport manager. He was highly embarrassed when he realized that he had been giving his superior a lot of lip, and his belligerence swiftly turned to smiles and words of welcome.

I was amazed as we approached the Learjet, not a single soldier came near. They had seen the exchange between Donado and Baratta, and some of them knew Donado by sight, so they were being very careful.

The inspection lasted only twenty minutes, the mechanics dutifully informing Donado that they were unable to make a proper inspection since they had no manuals for the jet and were unfamiliar with the factory inspection program.

Donado picked up the ball, turning to me and informing me in his most professional and official manner that I would have to bring a Learjet mechanic to Colombia to perform the preliminary inspection. He even apologized, saying he was sorry, but in order to determine if the jet could be made airworthy, he would require expert opinions on the matter.

"That's too bad," I went along, "but I can bring a mechanic down next week."

Both Donado and I were enjoying the game, as we both knew that the inspection was farce since there were no Learjet-qualified A & E mechanics to make such an inspection. However, our act would serve as a solid basis for Aerocivil, under Donado's command, to make their official recommendation that an outside Learjet mechanic be requested. That way I knew I would get straight information, and, since I am a mechanic, too, I would be allowed to participate in the inspection and see things first-hand.

We left the mechanics and the two Donado boys at the airport and went straight to Judge Valdez's office. Valdez was surprised to see Donado. We talked a few minutes, and during our conversation Valdez mentioned that he was executing the formal inspection order. He would have it in the mail the next day and would appreciate an immediate response. I told Valdez that I would be back in less than a week if necessary, for the inspection. Valdez was pleased that I would be allowed to bring in American mechanics to do the inspection.

While Donado and the judge were discussing the contents of the inspection order, Raul and I moved over to the window. While we stood there, I spoke to him in a low voice.

"Raul, I need to have another look at the files on 464 Juliet to get some more information. Ask Valdez if we can see them for a few minutes. Tell him my lawyers in California want me to confirm some dates or something he'll believe."

"No problem," said Raul, sauntering back toward the desk.

He politely and respectfully conveyed my request to Valdez, who, after a moment's hesitation, handed over the files. He was involved in his conversation with Donado and apparently saw nothing unusual about our needing the information.

As I thumbed through the reams of paper, I could see that all the names I had seen previously were still the same, there were no new ones. Finally, I spotted something interesting: the word *cocaina* (cocaine). It appeared several times in the text, along with the names of those originally arrested, plus the commander of the Magdalena Police Department, director of the Judicial Police, several names of those who seemed to be police officers, and the commander of the police post at Rodadero. It looked like a report on the inspection of 464 Juliet. I knew something was wrong here; the plane had already been inspected on its arrival June 15, 1977.

I whispered to Raul to read it, while I continued leafing through other papers. Raul read it and handed it back. He knew what I wanted and that he shouldn't speak yet. I was anxious to hear what he would have to report, but kept my face blank and jotted down a few dates.

When Valdez and Donado finished their discussion we rose to leave. I thanked Valdez and handed him back his files. "Did you get what you, needed?" he asked.

I told him that I had found a couple, but that I would get the rest the following week.

We stopped off at the airport to pick up the others, had some Cokes and got into the truck. As we slowed down near Ciénaga and stopped to get gas, Aldo was just passing in the opposite direction on his way toward Santa Marta. With great screeching of brakes, he stopped, turned around and came racing back to us.

"Where have you been?" he asked, clearly worried to see that we had been in Santa Marta.

I told him that we had been to inspect the Learjet with Donado, and had gone to sign a few documents for the judge. Aldo looked as if he had just bitten into a lemon, his face full of dismay and anger. But as Donado was there with us, he had to restrain himself and limit himself to asking why we hadn't stopped by for him.

Raul and I both knew that Donado was not a man to ask for pick-up service for Aldo, but all I said was that Donado had been in a big hurry to get the Avianca mechanics back to town.

Aldo was very unhappy about having been left out in the area where he felt he had special status, in dealing with the judge, but in Donado's presence he had to grin and bear it. All he could say was, "Yes, I understand."

We told Aldo about the inspection and the documents we had signed and informed him that we would leave for Miami in the morning and return in five or six days.

Donado walked over to pay for the gas, giving Aldo the opportunity to take out some papers and receipts and to hit me for money. He wanted eight hundred dollars. However, I handed him three hundred, telling him that it was all I had on me. Aldo graciously accepted it.

I had been finding out that payments and pay-offs involved mind games falling into special categories of their own. Aldo, for example, was greedy and always had dollar signs in his eyes. I was now making it a practice never to give him as much as he asked for. I was sure I was doing the correct thing because he never argued or indicated that he was dissatisfied.

I had heard an old Spanish saying that goes something like this: "Music not yet paid for is played sweeter." Well, the musicians that were playing for me must have belonged to a different union. They expected something even for tuning up, and I was willing to pay for their music a few bars at a time. The trick was to judge how much. Once a scale or an amount had been established, a precedent had been created, and future payments had to adhere to the same general level. Otherwise, the recipient was insulted by the low value placed on his worth, and the quality of his music went down. Also, it didn't pay to be cheap; a man had to be remunerated according to his stature and worth, scaled to how badly his services were needed. They hadn't just walked off the boat, either—they knew they were indispensable and had a sure instinct for what the traffic would bear.

All the protocol connected with ordinary tips and routine bribery, not to mention extraordinary mind games involving money that were suddenly initiated had led me to set up the "Wood Five-Pocket Accounting System." The right front pants pocket disbursed Colombian bills in small denominations; the right rear, large denominations. The left front was for small American bills, and the rear, large bills. The left shirt pocket contained at all times twenty dollars' worth of Colombian money, which was replenished as needed, and often, from the right front pants fund. My five-pocket system worked well. It eliminated a lot of haggling that would have taken place had all the money been displayed during the bargaining process.

During the drive back after the "preliminary" inspection of 464 Juliet, Donado confided in me that he was facing a problem regarding his younger son, Fernando.

"This is something that has been on my mind for a long time," he said seriously, "and I need your advice and help." He went on to tell me that about twelve years previously, Fernando had suffered a seizure, possibly epileptic, and that three years before, he had been refused entry into the Air Force on the basis of his medical record indicating the single seizure. There had been none since that time.

"Fernando doesn't want you to know about it, but I feel I have to tell you, because more than anything else in the world, Fernando wants to be a pilot."

"Donado, is it definite that he is epileptic?" I asked.

"No, it's not; that's where I need your help—to get a definite yes or no."

The tone of Donado's voice revealed his concern and misery for his son, and I sincerely wanted to help him any way I could, regardless of 464 Juliet or any other consideration.

Above all, I felt he deserved more than a snow job, so I told him straight out that I knew that if Fernando had really suffered an epileptic seizure, even a single one, and even if he had been only six months old, he would never be able to obtain his pilot's license. However, if the diagnosis had not been definitely confirmed, he could be tested with the newest medical equipment to settle this point once and for all.

That was what Donado wanted, a chance for Fernando either to realize his lifelong dream or, if this did not turn out to be the case, to pick up the pieces and set his course in another direction. I asked Donado to get together any records he had and that I would arrange an appointment with a specialist in Miami for a complete examination.

Donado had tears in his eyes as he thanked me and told me that he would be forever indebted to me for my help. I was embarrassed by his naked emotion and gratitude, and tried to lighten his mood by saying that what I would be doing was minor and that the *major* thing was for us to hope and pray that Fernando would be airworthy.

By mutual and unspoken consent, we turned to another subject, specifically Donado's years in the Colombian Air Force. He had been a pilot, with over six hundred hours in the B-25 Mitchell, the same type of plane Doolittle had used for bombing Japan. Donado was interested and impressed to learn that I had a Douglas A-26 bomber. I reached into my briefcase to give him an 8-by-10 inch color photo. His expression showed that he was reliving old memories.

"Yes," he said, "it's a beautiful plane, very beautiful. I had about fifty hours in the Douglas, too."

Bringing out my wallet and removing my pilot's license, I pointed out that I was also type-rated in the Douglas A-26. He was viewing me at once as one military pilot to another, but I had to inform him regretfully that I hadn't flown in the military, and used the Douglas for pleasure. However, we talked about military aircraft the rest of the way back and were cementing our already established bonds more and more firmly.

Arriving at the hotel, we spoke for a few minutes about my plans for the next trip back to Colombia in four or five days. I mentioned that I would be coming in a Cessna 402 with tools and parts for the Learjet. He foresaw no problems, but cautioned me to advise him of my flight to see that I had no problems.

I was consumed with curiosity to find out what Raul had to tell me about the document he had gone over in the judge's office. The moment the door had closed, I asked him about it.

"Bobby, there is something very, very funny about the confiscation of the Learjet," Raul began. "Like you gringos say, something smells of the rat." His butchering of the saying made me smile.

"What do you make of it? How do you interpret it?" I asked, wanting to learn if Raul had been getting the same vibrations I got.

Well, first of all, in Raul's opinion, the document didn't make sense. The Learjet landed in Santa Marta at 9:30 A.M. on June 15, 1977. The plane was inspected by the DAS and the local police. The crew were all arrested less than three or four hours later. Nothing was found inside the jet besides the usual medical equipment and flight related articles.

Then, several days before July 4, 1977, it was re-inspected by the commander of the Magdalena Police Department, the director of the Judicial Police, several officers, and the commander of the police post at Rodadero. And when this large and impressive search party opened the door of the Learjet that day, right inside, what did they find? A box without a lid containing three cans of Prist, a jet fuel additive, and a plastic bag with approximately fifty grams of cocaine. I had seen a photograph as one of the exhibits in the judge's files, and had noticed at the time that the evidence had been extremely well arranged in a composition that made a real star of the little bag of cocaine. The only thing missing was an arrow pointing to it so that all could notice it.

"Something is wrong here," Raul said flatly.

I didn't have to be hit over the head, either. Besides having been inspected on arrival by two different police agencies, the Learjet was unlocked during that time. And why were so many different police agencies sent to the latest inspection—this sounded like a classic overkill. Also, even the stupidest of smugglers would never leave fifty grams of cocaine in open view, just screaming to be seen. On top of which, no one on board the jet could have put the cocaine there in that time period—they were all in jail. Even if they were free, why would they go back and plant evidence to incriminate themselves?

"You're right," Raul said excitedly, "and you can bet it was planted there by the Colombian officials so that they could confiscate the jet. I saw that photograph, too, and it was too neat and pretty. Sure, I know the Santa Marta people. I know the police put it there. Nobody else had any reason to put it there."

We digested another tough piece of information. The crew had been sent to Bogotá. This didn't make any sense. Any charge brought against them would be under the jurisdiction of the Department of Magdalena, where the alleged crime had occurred. Still another strange fact had been revealed in the document. The crew had been originally held on the charge that they hadn't filed a proper flight plan and therefore were technically violating Colombian airspace, and, yet, the airport officials finally admitted that they did, in fact, file a proper flight plan.

I was convinced of another obvious fact, too. Jimmy Chagra may very well have been involved in drug smuggling, but not at all likely a mere fifty grams, brought *into* Colombia, worth twenty-five hundred dollars at most, in a Learjet valued at well over a million that had been chartered in his name, and, finally, for a mercy mission that was a bona fide fact. No way was I buying this.

Raul and I went down to the dining room to join the Donado boys for dinner. Donado Jr., Ferdinand, and Raul were consuming the rice, plantains, and fried meat with gusto; I still stuck with my original menu of French fries and Coca-Cola. Gustavo, our *La Comunidad* partner, had arrived, as I had asked him to stop by before we left. We talked about my progress in the United States concerning funds for the oil drilling exploration. I told him that Pan Am Labs in Miami had finished the oil analysis and that the samples had turned out to share, within 1 percent, the same content characteristics of the crude found in Venezuela. This was encouraging news to him. I also informed him that my lawyers were drawing up drafts of several contracts so we could start arranging for financing. I presented all this progress as a little further along than it actually was, however, as my priorities were a little different from his at the moment. Although I remained basically interested in the oil deal, I had shelved it with the idea of getting back to it once 464 Juliet was released. But, eventually, the stumbling blocks *La Comunidad* put before me would make the deal completely unrealistic. They were only willing to do the deal at percentage figures way out of line with normal investment practices. I would pass on the opportunty, bowing out of an undoable deal.

When we finished in the dining room, we all went upstairs, and I helped everyone finish up "the last supper" of snacks and candy bars that I still had left in my suitcase.

Before dropping off to sleep, I reminded Raul that I wanted to get up early to stop at the American Consulate on the way to the airport to see if they could recommend a good translator to work on some of the documents that were starting to accumulate, as I felt this would save a great deal of time and trouble and spare me the torture of some of Raul's "off-the-cuff" versions that often left a lot to be desired.

CHAPTER NINETEEN

The offices of the Consulate of the United States of America were located on the road to the airport, so it was not going to be out of our way to stop there on the way to catch our flight back to Miami. Since this would be one place Raul wouldn't be needed to "defend" me in Spanish, he went off with our amigos to do a few last minute errands, with a reminder from me to be back in half an hour or so.

I was a little surprised to see that it was pretty much of a poor-boy operation. I wasn't expecting resplendent Marine Guards at attention or the United States coat of arms, but there was not even the smallest flag on display and I could only conclude that if the United States was trying for an image in this corner of the world, it must be very low-profile. It was the same inside, a plain and utilitarian arrangement of four or five small offices with a small waiting room plainly furnished.

I took my place in line before one of the glass windows and could see a few of the members of the staff on the other side, busy with papers and talking with visitors. Within a few minutes it was my turn.

"Nice to be able to speak English," I said to a middle aged man who asked if he could help me. I introduced myself and explained that I was there to see if the Consulate could recommend a translating service for some work I needed done.

As I talked with him, another official walked into the side office and seemed to be trying inconspicuously to point me out to someone else that I couldn't see.

It seemed strange, but I put it out of my mind. However, a few seconds later, a man came out of the same side office and walked over to the counter where I was standing.

"Are you Robert Wood?" he asked, and, when I told him I was, he asked if he could speak with me inside.

I picked up my briefcase. He motioned for me to go to the first door on my left which opened into a small room with a bank of gray file cabinets and an old battered desk.

"I'm Harry Gilbert," he said, handing me a card that identified him as the Consul of the United States for Barranquilla.

"So you're the mysterious Mr. Wood," he began, "I've been wondering when you would show up."

The "mysterious Mr. Wood" was mystified. What in the hell did he mean by that remark?

"What is your business here in Colombia?" he wanted to know.

I took a closer look at Mr. Harry Gilbert. He was a pale man in his early forties, with a stern and rather humorless face, and a general appearance that could easily lose him in a crowd.

However, I was fast becoming as curious about him as he seemed to be about me and I was unwilling to let him quiz me about what I was doing until I could get some indication of why he wanted to know. If Mr. Gilbert wanted to play some kind of game, I would give him selective information and then listen to what he had to say.

"I'm in the aviation and petroleum business."

"What type of aviation business?"

"I'm the Cessna dealer in Miami, but at present I'm here negotiating an oil contract with Magistrate Plada."

"What oil contracts?"

"Specifically, for forty-three thousand acres in the Tubara region," I answered, thinking to myself that this meeting was developing into a real inquisition.

"If your oil contract is for property in the Tubara region, what have you been doing in Riohacha and Santa Marta?" he shot back at me.

"Well, sir," I said seriously, "my trip to Riohacha was actually undertaken as a favor for some friends in the FAA and in U.S. Customs. You know how it is; they collect information here and there and shoot it into the computer. Sometimes it fills out some blanks for them. They asked me to make note of all United States aircraft registration numbers I saw in the smaller airports nearby, and Riohacha was one they mentioned in particular."

I opened my briefcase and pulled out my file that had a listing of confiscated aircraft, putting on an act of exaggerated caution as if I were handling classified material; and pulling out the list marked "Riohacha," I handed it to him.

"Why are you keeping track of United States Airplanes?"

"Mr. Gilbert," I was very earnest and honest, "I'm not at liberty to discuss this with anyone. It's a confidential matter. My instructions are to turn in the list when I get back to Miami."

"What about the Learjet in Santa Marta?" he asked. "Are you interested in that?"

"Oh, yes. I stopped by to see it. My friends in FAA mentioned it was there. It looks as if it's been there a long time." Now that I had been able to move the ground a little from under his feet, I wanted to keep him talking to find out more. I mentioned that the confiscation of planes seemed to be a real problem in the area and that the Consulate must have to do a lot of processing of the legal aspects, that it must be very confusing.

This proved to be the right bait. I had been casting for a minnow of information and what I hooked into was a whale.

"Do you know an attorney named Gordon in San Francisco?" he asked.

I struggled to keep my face from reflecting my utter amazement at this unexpected turn of the conversation. He had unwittingly given me the answer to a question that had been burning in my mind. *This is where the "something" is wrong, right here in the United States Consulate in Santa Marta.*

Without a pause, I replied, "No, sir, I don't believe I do."

"He's an attorney who has a representative in Cartagena. He's a specialist in recovering confiscated aircraft here in Colombia."

I let no more than polite interest show on my face. I had learned enough and didn't want to push my luck.

"Really," I remarked, "there are plenty of confiscated planes here, that's for sure. Anyway, I'd better get going, I have a plane to catch. By the way, can you tell me who does translating here? That's what I came in to find out."

"Boston School of English is good," he said, and jotted down the address and telephone number. I thanked him.

As I was preparing to leave, he said, "Make sure you come by and see us next time you're here. If you need any help, just give us a call." He was playing it safe, just in case I was an undercover agent.

"Thanks a lot. Bye."

Raul was waiting outside.

"I was getting worried—what took so long?" he wanted to know.

"Problems, Raul, problems," I said. "Someone here is keeping tabs on what we're doing." I outlined to him the strange interchange I had had in the Consul's office, and then both of us sat silent for a few moments. Raul had put on his thinking cap, to judge from the intense expression on his normally smiling face.

"Bobby," he finally spoke, "you know none of us would be telling anybody what we're doing. No outsider knows."

I agreed that none of our group could have passed along information, but added, "You're wrong about no outsiders knowing."

I thought to myself, *Harry Gilbert knows too much. Gordon wouldn't have us monitored here, much less have us followed to Riohacha. He may have friends around, but that seems far-fetched. Someone might have called him or— Wait. Gilbert mentioned that Gordon had a representative in Cartagena—that's it. Ortiz is Gordon's associate in Colombia; he's the one who went to see Judge Valdez, and Gilbert must be friends with Gordon and Ortiz. Still, I can't see Gilbert having me followed just as a favor for them. Sure, he'd let them know if he stumbled onto something about us … but … Ah, the hell with it. I'm wasting time trying to figure something out that's immaterial right now. But I have an idea—let's do something to make Gilbert, or whoever, work for his money."*

I outlined my plan to Raul. When we reached the airport we would go see his buddy, Diego, at customs. We would give Diego one hundred dollars every time we arrived in Barranquilla to "forget" to put us on the immigration list.

Raul would get Diego's telephone number so that we could advise him of our arrival. When we got there, he would simply stamp our visas and escort us outside.

Raul was sure that Diego would welcome such an arrangement. When we got to the airport we went directly to see Diego, whom Raul briefed regarding our plan. Diego was wearing a flashy, gold-toothed grin as he nodded that he understood and accepted our offer. We told him to be sure to keep his ears open in case anyone was inquiring about us, and Diego said he would.

It suddenly occurred to me that Aquiles and Toño could do some gofering for us while we were in the States that might save us some time and money. I instructed them to go to the Santa Marta airport and speak with Mario there at Avianca to find out if he could uncover some leads on the missing radios. I would pay them for their time, and, come what may, perhaps we would get lucky.

"Be sure they spread the word around," I told Raul as I handed him four hundred dollars for their expenses.

We departed Barranquilla on runway four, making a slight left turn northward. I was sitting in my usual place next to the last seat on the right and peered out the window toward Santa Marta where Juliet still sat imprisoned alongside the sea. I sent a wordless prayer to the Sierra Nevada to guard her well, and a message to her not to lose faith—nothing was going to stop me from freeing her.

Raul seemed to sense my mood. He gave me a comradely punch on the arm and a warm, "Don't worry, Bobby, you'll do it."

"You're damned right we will," I said, "the only question still is when. It seems like forever."

I would just have to play it smarter than the rest, I resolved. It was like a puzzle. I had to hold onto each piece and see it clear while I searched for the next. I had to find the rest of the pieces, fit them together and concentrate on every step. Let Gilbert, Gordon, and whoever else there might be spend their time worrying about us. We wouldn't waste ours worrying about them. We would let the chips fall as they may and spend all our time and energy on getting Juliet her freedom.

When the taxi pulled up in front of my house my youngest daughter, Jaime, was on the front porch with Terry. They came running to hug and kiss me. Greta, our German shepherd, stood on the sidelines wagging her tail. It was wonderful to come back to something so authentic and uncomplicated as this simple welcome home.

CHAPTER TWENTY

What I wanted more than anything else I could think of was to spend a quiet and contented evening with my family. However, when Terry, Jaime, and I went inside, Terry mentioned that Jim Burkett had dropped off another packet of newspaper clippings for me and mentioned that it contained the accounts of the confiscation of 464 Juliet and crew. The itch to know more returned in full force, and I had to go through them, even before sitting down to a good meat-and-potato man-dinner.

The next day, June 6, I re-read the articles in greater detail, and, as I had suspected from the clippings I had already read as well as from the information Raul and I had been able to glean from our hurried examination of a few of the documents in Judge Valdez's office, it was a strange saga indeed. For every question that was answered, two new ones sprang up in its place, like the mythical hydra-headed monster of Hercules. How could a routine, although dramatic, mercy mission have mushroomed into such a sinister and tragic event? I was beginning to understand more of the complications that had been making my task such a difficult one.

Most of the clippings were from Las Vegas newspapers and therefore the news was presented from the point of view of local interest, although a few of the follow-up accounts brought in national and international ramifications. Several of these are given below. The first, from the *Las Vegas Sun* of June 21, 1977, carried bold headlines:

> Colombia Holds Las Vegas Men
> *By Penny Levin and Tricia White, SUN Staff Writers*
> *Six men including four Las Vegans are being detained in Bogotá, Colombia, after flying a mercy mission to transport a burn victim who allegedly received the injuries in an airplane accident and later died.*
>
> *The men, identified as Jet Avia, Ltd. pilots Tony Gekakis and Steve Bolling, both of Las Vegas; Mercy Ambulance paramedics Miguel Parada and Jeffrey Ernst also of Las Vegas; James Chagra, an El Paso,*

Tex., businessman and real estate investor, and Jerry Lee Wilson, address unknown, departed from the United States in an effort to take a man tentatively identified as Bruce Allen to the burn center at Brooke Medical Center in San Antonio, Tex.

Colombian newspaper accounts allege the men were detained after an abortive attempt to remove the patient from the country.

Mike Leavitt, a Jet Avia, Ltd. attorney who is in Bogota, said "no charges have been filed against the men, there is no drug investigation and they are being detained for a violation of technical air space."

Late Monday, Leavitt announced Allen was dead (June 20).

In a statement issued Monday, Las Vegas-based Jet Avia, Ltd. confirmed one of the airplanes and four Las Vegas men were being detained by Colombian officials because it (the aircraft) "entered the country without filing technical air document."

The SUN has learned, however, that two international flight plans filed by the jet pilot through Miami International Airport were "in order, accurate, and complete documentation existed authorizing the plane's entry into Colombia," said Robert Norris, operations officer at the Miami flight service station.

Reports out of Colombia indicate the four men were successful in removing Allen from the hospital and loaded him aboard a waiting Learjet leased by Jet Avia, Ltd. when police surrounded the aircraft and arrested all aboard.

The SUN has learned it was Chagra who hired Jet Avia, Ltd. to pick up the burn victim in Colombia. A spokesman for both Mercy Ambulance and Jet Avia, Ltd. in Las Vegas reported the victim was supposed to have ,third-degree burns over 70 percent of his body. Arrangements had been made last week by Jet Avia, Ltd. for the burn victim to be admitted to Brooke General Hospital in San Antonio Texas.

The Jet Avia, Ltd. spokesman said a passport was picked up in Texas for Chagra, who joined the flight at its next stop Atlanta. The plane's final stop Tuesday was in Ft. Lauderdale.

Two international flight plans were filed Wednesday from Ft. Lauderdale with the Miami flight service station. The first scheduled a stop in Port-au-Prince, Haiti; and the second flight plan scheduled the plane's final destination as Santa Marta.

A military aide contacted by the SUN at the United States Embassy in Bogota said no officials at the embassy could comment on the status of the missing Las Vegans or other passengers.

A follow-up story appeared the following day, June 22, 1977, by the same two *SUN* staff writers recapping the facts given in their June 21 account, and adding that Colombian federal agencies were now investigating the detainment. From the article I learned:

> *To date, efforts to free four Las Vegas men being detained by Colombian secret police in Bogota are snarled in international red tape … The six Americans were detained after arriving aboard a Learjet leased by the Las Vegas firm of Jet Avia, Ltd. on a mercy mission to evacuate an American burn victim who later died.*
>
> *… UPI Tuesday reported the burn victim was the "pilot of a plane that wrecked in the Guajira Peninsula, a remote area of Colombia known as the center of marijuana and cocaine trafficking."*
>
> *The Jet Avia, Ltd. spokesman claims the men are being detained because of "illegal alien entry," based on improper paperwork.*
>
> *He said the permission to fly into the country without proper passports and visas was obtained from a Marine sergeant at the United States Embassy in Bogota.*
>
> *The spokesman said Jet Avia, Ltd. was operating under rules provided in the International Flight Information Manual, published by the United States Department of Transportation in April 1976.*
>
> *The Learjet, which is reportedly being held as evidence in Santa Marta at the Simón Bolívar airport, is valued at more than one million dollars.*

As mentioned, most of the articles were from Las Vegas newspapers and as four of the men detained along with confiscation of the Learjet were Las Vegans, it was understandable that the local media would give them the most coverage. Two Las Vegans were released July 7, along with Jimmy Chagra and Jerry Lee Wilson, the only members of the group heretofore under investigation for drug trafficking.

How had they been able to walk? I searched through the accounts trying to find a clue. There was nothing.

The newspaper accounts covering these first releases also contained other interesting facts.

Las Vegas Pilot, Paramedic Return After Ordeal in Colombia
  By Tricia White, SUN Staff Writer
  Looking worn but healthy, pilot Tony Gekakis and paramedic Jeffrey Ellis arrived Thursday at Hughes Executive Airport and were greeted by a swarm of relatives, friends, and news media.
  Happiness at the homecoming of the two Las Vegans, detained in Colombia, South America, for the past three weeks, was dampened by the

knowledge that two additional Las Vegans remain in the custody of Santa Marta, Colombia, police officials.

Gekakis and Ellis were released Wednesday but pilot Stephen Bolling and paramedic Miguel Parada continue to be detained for "further investigation," according to the returned men.

They arrived after taking a commercial airline flight from Barranquilla, Colombia, to Miami, Fla., and connecting with a second commercial flight in Dallas, Tex. Aircraft leased by the Las Vegas firm of Jet Avia, Ltd. transported the men to their final destination at the Hughes Air Terminal in Las Vegas.

Jet Avia, Ltd. spokesman and corporation partner Chris Karamanos and Mercy Ambulance General Manager Bob Forbuss were the first to speak with the man as they transported them from the aircraft to the terminal in a gold Mercedes Benz.

"No charges were ever filed against any of us. All they (police officials) kept saying was that we were under investigation," said Ellis.

Both Ellis and Gekakis also agreed that the reason their two colleagues are still in custody may be Colombian officials wish to take permanent custody of the Learjet 24 aboard which they arrived in Santa Marta.

A total of five Americans arrived aboard the aircraft June 14 to transport a severely burned United States citizen, identified by Jet Avia, Ltd. as its former pilot, Jerry Lee Wilson, to a United States Hospital.

Texas businessman James Chagra, who had chartered the jet from Jet Avia, Ltd. of Las Vegas, accompanied the four Las Vegans.

Upon arrival in Santa Marta, the men attempted to pick up the burn patient, who was actually Bruce Allen of Sunland, N.M., but were taken into custody by police authorities. .

Gekakis said Thursday the men first encountered Wilson at the DAS (secret police) office where they were taken for questioning.

Allen later died of his injuries.

"It's a shame they had to let a man die just to have an airplane," said Ellis after being reunited with his wife, Renee, at the airport.

Both men maintained that any illegal drugs aboard the aircraft "had been planted to keep the airplane."

…during a Wednesday telephone conversation with Parada, one of the two remaining prisoners, he explained that police claimed they found cocaine aboard the jet, which implicated both Parada and Bolling in continued investigation …

… Both Wilson and Chagra, also released … Wednesday, accompanied the two Las Vegas men on the flight to Miami, where they parted company, Gekakis said.

Questioned on the attitude of Colombian authorities toward the detained Americans, Gekakis said, "Somebody took it upon themselves to be both judge and jury where we were concerned."

… Ellis said the only drugs aboard the plane were medical supplies taken to treat the burn patient and "none were any stronger than aspirin."

Gekakis said police officials had searched the Learjet three times before declaring that they had found drugs aboard.

This was not the first time the fact had come to light that the Learjet had been searched previously, before the small quantity of cocaine had conveniently been "discovered" in plain view inside the door, and that a lot of unrelated people had felt it was planted so that the aircraft could be confiscated.

After six long, hard weeks, two of the crew who were least likely to have been implicated in drug traffic were still being held in Colombia. Here is an account from the *Las Vegas Sun*:

Las Vegas Men Awaiting Colombian Jail Release

Two Las Vegas residents, detained in Santa Marta, Colombia, since June 15, are tentatively scheduled for release Saturday, the SUN has learned.

During a telephone conversation with the paramedic Miguel Parada Thursday, he said attorneys hired to represent the two men introduced legal motions Tuesday calling for an end to their detainment.

"The F-2 police department admitted that they threw my scissors in the box. Everything looks good for me and for Steve, too, but I don't know if they will let me back into the United States right away," said Parada.

The Las Vegas paramedic earlier had reported that secret police refused to release Parada and pilot Stephen Bolling, claiming that illegal drugs had been found among their personal effects.

Parada said police authorities had conducted several searches before declaring that drugs had been located in a fuel box, along with the paramedic's medical scissors.

Pilot Tony Gekakis and paramedic Jeffrey Ellis, two Las Vegans detained along with Parada and Bolling, were released July 6 and returned home two days later.

The two released men confirmed that three police searches had been conducted of the Learjet 24 "air ambulance" aboard which they arrived, before authorities declared the presence of illegal drugs aboard.

The two Jet Avia Ltd. pilots and two Mercy Ambulance paramedics arrived in Santa Marta June 15 as the crew of the jet, chartered by reputed gambler James Chagra of El Paso, Tex. for a "mercy mission."

Chagra chartered the jet from the Las Vegas firm of JetAvia. Ltd. to allegedly transport an American burn patient identified as former Jet Avia Ltd. pilot Jerry Lee Wilson. The actual burn patient, identified as Bruce Allen of Sunland, N.M., later died after the evacuation attempt was halted by Colombian police authorities.

Wilson, present in Santa Marta when the jet arrived, Chagra and the four crew members were taken into custody and detained in a Santa Marta Prison.

Wilson and Chagra both were released with the two freed Las Vegans.

The returned Las Vegans alleged that police authorities who continued to detain their colleagues were seeking some method of acquiring permanent custody of the medically-equipped jet, valued at more than $1 million.

Former Jet Avia Ltd. pilot prisoner Wilson was charged last December in Ardmore, Oklahoma, with "possession of marijuana with intent to distribute" after state narcotics police confiscated 276 bales of Colombian marijuana, valued at $12 million street value, at an industrial air park outside Ardmore.

Thursday the Ardmore trial of Wilson and nine co-defendants entered its fourth day. Attorney Lee Chagra of El Paso, Tex., brother of James Chagra, is defense attorney for Wilson.

A community-wide petition drive in support of the two men who continue to be detained has sparked hundreds of letters and telegrams to both South American and United States officials concerning their plight.

Parada said Thursday that both he and Bolling were "very depressed" and "the only thing keeping us going right now is knowing that Saturday may be the day and there are those people in Las Vegas who haven't forgotten."

This article brought out an interesting sidelight. Jerry Lee Wilson hadn't been aboard 464 Juliet, as original reported. Where had he suddenly come from? Another interesting fact that emerged was that Wilson apparently had returned to the States just in time for a trial in Ardmore where he was to be defended by no other than Lee Chagra.

A task force of federal and state agents had seized a DC-4 with seventeen thousand pounds of top-grade marijuana in Ardmore, Oklahoma, on December 30, 1976. By New Year's Day, it was a big story and the defendants were being called the El Paso Ten. Jimmy Chagra's name was never officially mentioned, but it was assumed that he had masterminded the scheme. Trial on this case was pending when the 464 Juliet incident took place. Lee Chagra's defense had been a brilliant victory. The defendants had been caught with seventeen thousand pounds of marijuana. Ten smugglers, two airplanes, and four U-Haul trucks had been seized in a trap. And, yet, Lee Chagra had been able to break down the government's testimony, mainly because the prosecution had been so eager, almost rabid, for convictions that it destroyed its own case.

Unfortunately, there was only one clipping from the Colombian press. This had appeared in *El Tiempo* of Bogotá and was dated August 5, 1977, which was the date when the last of 464J's crew were released. It was a recap of key facts in the case, and, inasmuch as the information was closer to first-hand than all the others, it was the most interesting.

> Jet Ambulance Occupants Freed
>
> *The well-aired episode of the air ambulance of Jet Avia of Nevada came to a close yesterday morning before the Colombian Courts when the superior judge of customs in Santa Marta declared that the aircraft did not enter the country with contraband, and set the members of its crew at unconditional liberty.*
>
> *The crew had also previously recovered their liberty without any conditions from another judge who was aware of the allegation made concerning them regarding a few grams of cocaine found in the jet-hospital.*
>
> *Criminal lawyer Pablo Salah Villamizar, who was retained by the president of Jet Avia, Chris Karamanos, to represent those charged, went down to Santa Marta and conducted both cases which closed yesterday when it was adjudged that no evidence whatsoever existed regarding drug trafficking. Thereupon, the Criminal Court of Customs established that the aircraft was engaged in a humanitarian mission, had done nothing contrary to the rulings and regulations of Aerocivil and could not be considered as having brought contraband into the country, for which reasons (the aircraft) could be returned to its owners in the United States.*
>
> The Episode
>
> *The facts material to these investigations are in public domain, since the incidents had wide coverage in communications media.*
>
> *Bruce Allen, North American citizen, was picked up in the Guajira, a victim of grave burns sustained, apparently, when a plane engaged in drug traffic caught fire.*
>
> *Allen was taken to the Santa Marta Hospital where he was given the scanty treatment available in that medical center.*
>
> *On June 14, United States Citizen Chris Karamanos, President of Jet Avia; which provides, among other charter services, use as an air ambulance, telephoned the physicians of Santa Marta Hospital, stating that one of his aircraft had been chartered to airlift a burn patient being*

treated in that hospital, and requesting a report on whether the patient was indeed in the hospital and, if so, his physical condition.

The hospital authorities, as they later stated in the legal proceedings, replied that indeed they did have a foreigner, name unknown, as a patient in the hospital who had sustained severe burns and that the hospital did not have facilities to

provide him with treatment that would give any chance of survival. They added that there had been no warrant for the arrest of the patient and that he was not a prisoner.

Therefore, the following day, June 15, a jet ambulance belonging to Jet Avia contacted the control tower of the Santa Marta Airport requesting permission to land, which was given. After landing, the pilot went personally to the tower and handed in his flight plan.

While this was taking place, Bruce Allen was transported to the airport in a Red Cross ambulance, which was done through written order for dismissal signed by the physicians. However, the police intervened and halted the airlift operation. The North American patient was returned to the hospital, where he died a week later.

Procedures

The Jet Avia airplane was inspected three times without anything of a suspicious nature having been found; however, on a fourth search, it was said that several grams of cocaine were found. As a result of this, the crew, the two paramedics who had come to pick up the burn victim and a private citizen were detained and placed at the disposition of ordinary justice.

The private citizen, the pilot and one paramedic were first released, but a warrant was issued for arrest of copilot Stephen Bolling and paramedic Jose Miguel Parada, for drug trafficking.

Later, upon petition of attorney Pablo Salah Villamizar, Bolling and Parada were released unconditionally on that particular charge, but were immediately detained anew by order of the Superior Judge of Customs, Fabio Marquez Quevedo, who stated that he would investigate the alleged contraband in the aircraft.

Bolling and Parada were thereupon called for questioning, which was heard in the presence of Dr. Salah-Villamizar. He, at termination of the questioning, requested immediate release of the persons charged, on the grounds that no crime of smuggling existed, nor were any of the rules and regulations of Aerocivil violated.

The judge concurred, stating that he would no longer hold the crew, and issued his opinion whereby the individuals were unconditionally released.

Thus ended the incidents involving arrival in Colombia of a jet

ambulance that had come to airlift back to a United States hospital a
seriously injured burn victim, who later died. These events were widely
reported in the national and international media. Certifications were
received from such sources as the Governor of Nevada and several United
States congressmen addressed to the Attorney General of Colombia and the
judges to the effect that the aircraft and its crew had been on a mercy
mission which, in the end, they were prevented from accomplishing.

No one, apparently, not even the Colombian officials, had taken very
seriously the mysterious presence of a few grams of cocaine which had shown
up, in plain view, upon the later search of the plane, almost three weeks after
the first search had been made. Why, then, had three of the plane's occupants
and Jerry Lee Wilson, who had appeared suddenly out of nowhere, been
released, and why had the copilot and one of the paramedics been held? It
seemed almost as though they had been considered as hostages, or at least
human collateral to ensure that some unknown measure or measures might
first be taken.

It was very strange.

There was another article included with this third group that was dated
October 6, 1978, and had to do with 464 Juliet, even though it appeared
fourteen months after the episode had been concluded. It was a report on
what seemed to be a United States Justice Department release and was picked
up and distributed by the Washington office of the Associated Press. What
was very interesting was the new interpretation of old facts.

> Jet Avia-Linked Drug Probe Reopened
>
> *WASHINGTON (AP)—The United States Justice Department has*
> *reopened an investigation into a drug smuggling incident involving an*
> *aircraft owned by Jet Avia, a Nevada-based air charter service.*
>
> *Sean Holly, in charge of Justice Department investigations involving*
> *Colombia, said Wednesday he is asking for an update on the case because*
> *of intense pressure by several Congressmen. He declined to identify the*
> *Congressmen, but said they weren't from Nevada.*
>
> *The principal partner of the company is Chris Karamanos of Las*
> *Vegas, a member of the University of Nevada Board of Regents.*
>
> *The incident occurred on June 15, 1977, when a plane furnished by*
> *Jet Avia flew into Santa Marta, Colombia, on what was purported to be a*
> *mission to rescue an American burn victim.*
>
> *The Nevada State Journal quoted Nevada state government and*
> *Drug Enforcement Administration sources as saying Karamanos' company*
> *is the target of federal and state investigations for alleged drug smuggling*

activities which occurred on Jet Avia planes.

Files dating back to 1973 in the Jet Avia office show that the original partnership included Karamanos, Dr. Harold Fiekes, Dr. Elias Ghanem and Allen Glick, a wealthy Las Vegas casino operator. In 1975, the Nevada Secretary, of State's office revoked the company's corporate status because it failed to list its officers.

In the Colombia incident, Karamanos said he was contacted by James Chagra, a Texas businessman, to pick up an emergency burn victim.

Aboard the Learjet were pilots Anthony Gekakis, Stephen Bolling and Chagra. Also aboard were two paramedics from Mercy Inc. of Las Vegas. Initial press reports in Nevada said the mission's aim was to rescue former Jet Avia pilot Jerry Wilson, but Holly said Wilson was also aboard the Jet Avia mercy flight with the other five men. "There is some question about who ordered what," Holly said. "It sounds a little odd that someone can call up and get a $2 million aircraft to zip right off to Colombia."

The Jet Avia plane entered Colombia without filing a flight plan or obtaining proper visas for the crewmen and passengers. Holly said it appears the crew tried to get Allen out of a Santa Marta hospital but failed. Allen died a day later.

The Jet Avia men were arrested and were initially charged with drug smuggling. Holly said reports showed that cocaine was found on the Learjet. Colombia police reported. 75 grams of cocaine were found, but all evidence remains in Colombia, he said.

Eventually all the ,men were released and a Las Vegas paper quoted Karamanos as saying he had paid $250,000 in "legal fees" to get Miguel Parada, a paramedic, and Bolling out of jail.

"It is my understanding that when the men were released they were not exonerated. They were released provisionally," Holly said.

Karamanos said last week he regarded the Colombia incident as "old. news." He said the aircraft did not belong to his company, but was leased from another firm.

He said Jet Avia is no longer flying as an air taxi service although the partnership remains and the company planes have been leased out.

One thing this article revealed to me for sure was that Mr. Sean Holly, the Justice Department investigator, just didn't know how to separate bullshit from facts, or else he was lying for reasons of his own. The first seven paragraphs of this article may very well be true. From that point on, we are given a lot of fairy tales.

First, Wilson was not aboard the Jet Avia mercy flight with the other five men. Granted, there had been a lot of confusion about his presence aboard the plane in initial reports, but it had definitely been established that he had not gone to Colombia aboard 464 Juliet. Just how he had gotten there was still an unanswered question, but surely the Justice Department knew full well that he had not been the pilot or a passenger.

Second, in spite of Holly's statement about there being a question about who had ordered what and "it sounds a little odd that someone can call up and get a two million dollar aircraft to zip right off to Colombia," there was actually never any question who had chartered the flight. It was Jimmy Chagra—no question at all. Also, the owners and the crew had originally been told that they were going to rescue Jerry Wilson, with whom they had formerly flown. Rescuing an injured buddy seems pretty adequate motivation for them to have been willing to fly to Colombia for this purpose.

Third, 464 Juliet had suddenly undergone a big inflation in value; now, instead of a million dollar baby, she suddenly had become a two million dollar baby in Holly's Five and Ten Cent store.

Fourth, 464 Juliet scarcely zipped "right off." Arrangements had been made to bring the patient back to an intensive care burn center in Texas, telephone calls had been made regarding his release, and burn specialists had been consulted on medication and treatment for the return flight. Four incorrect statements in one sentence had to be a professional journalists' record.

Fifth, "The Jet Avia plane entered Colombia without filing a flight plan or obtaining proper visas for the crewmen and passengers." Official Colombian records show that the Jet Avia flight plan was filed and was perfectly in order. Visa's are not required for Colombia; passports are required. The two paramedics did not have passports; however, Jet Avia officials spoke with the officer in charge at the American Embassy in Bogotá and were assured that as long as the two paramedics remained at the airport, there would be no problem about their lack of passports.

Sixth, Holly said "it appears the crew tried to get Allen out of a Santa Marta hospital but failed. Allen died a day later." Holly is wrong twice over. The crew did indeed get Allen out of a Santa Marta hospital (where they *failed* was in not leaving Santa Marta with him), and Allen did not die a day later, but, rather, six days later.

Seventh, Mr. Holly has also upped the figure on the amount of cocaine "found" on the plane to seventy-five grams instead of fifty. Naturally, he doesn't mention the conclusion, even of the Colombian courts, that it had been planted and found in plain sight in the middle of the aisle on the fourth search. He was correct in saying that "all the evidence remains in Colombia."

Eighth, "It is my understanding that when the men were released they were not exonerated. They were released provisionally," Holly said. This is also pure, unadulterated bull. The fact is that all six were released unconditionally. Then two of them were detained again by another court and eventually released unconditionally for a second time.

These statements by the head Justice Department investigator made me very suspicious, especially in view of the fact that, on our timetable of events, James Kerr was hard at work, trying to get together enough information to slap a heavy indictment on the Chagras brothers. And on November 21, 1978, about six weeks after this article appeared, an attempt was made on Kerr's life.

CHAPTER TWENTY-ONE

The next morning, June 7, 1980, I drove up to Fort Lauderdale to see Bill Jones, the owner of Jet Care. I had spoken to Bill several times before about needing a crack mechanic to go to Colombia to put 464 Juliet into at least minimum condition so that we could get her back to the States to do a complete "demate," a complete overhaul of all the components of the airplane, xrayed and inspected: windshield, wings, engines, avionics, all of it.

Bill buzzed Jeannie, his secretary.

"Would you page Dave Pearson for me," he said, and a few minutes later, Dave walked in.

Dave Pearson was a slight, lithe man about 5' 8" and weighing maybe 125 pounds, in his middle thirties. Inside this small frame was a giant of a mechanic. Actually, his slender build and catlike agility allowed him to get into impossibly cramped places. He had an infectious laugh and boundless enthusiasm for any job he undertook.

Bill introduced us and added that I needed some work done. "Shoot" was the first word out of Dave's mouth. I could see immediately that he was exactly what I was looking for. Bill, Dave, and I sat for almost two hours discussing every possible part and tool we would have to take to Colombia. Dave stood up when we finished, saying he wanted to get started on the list and to see what items the parts department had in stock. I wrote Bill a check for three thousand dollars as a deposit and told him we would probably be leaving on June 10.

I joined Dave in the parts department to find out if his passport was valid.

"Sure," he replied, "I can leave whenever you want."

"Great. As soon as you're finished here, come on down to my place and we'll start chasing whatever else we need. We're going to use my 402 Cessna to carry the stuff down."

I had a beautiful 1975 402B Cessna Business Liner, tail number 82921, with low-time engines and in excellent mechanical condition; we could use her for the trip. Later that afternoon, I phoned Mike Ashley, an old friend about my age, thirty-nine years old or so. An excellent pilot, I asked him if he would fly to Barranquilla with us and then take 82921 back, as I intended to remain in Colombia for some time. Mike, like Dave, was an eager beaver with a highly positive attitude, something I knew in my bones we couldn't do without to get this job done.

"Sure," he agreed, "when do we leave?"

"Why don't you come down this Sunday afternoon and help us load. We'll leave early, around seven Monday morning."

I discussed details with Mike, and we settled on a price, arranging to meet on Sunday at two o'clock in the afternoon. Terry walked in as I was hanging up.

"What's this about Sunday?" she asked suspiciously. Her tone told me that she was not going to be very pleased with the news. "Look, honey, I've got to be back in Colombia this Monday."

"But you just got back," she wailed.

"I know. But please don't fight me on this. Timing is very important now and I need your support, not an argument. I'm going to be real busy these next few days getting together the things we need, so be a doll and help me. It'll all be over soon."

When Raul came in I gave him strict instructions to stay right beside me and be available for the next few days.

"No problem. What do you want me to do first?"

"Right now you can take my truck and run the aircraft jacks down to the overhaul shop. Stay there while they reseal them and bring them back. I'll be here. I'm going to be working on the 402."

Friday and Saturday were a blur of activity as we gathered parts, supplies, even water hoses and ten pounds of condensed iced tea. Dave was right there all the time, busy with his share of the preparations.

Mike arrived a little after two on Sunday afternoon. The four of us spent some time in my office, mostly to tell Dave and Mike about 464 Juliet. Mike remembered hearing lots of the conflicting stories about the plane and was interested to hear about it first-hand. We finally cut it short to get into the loading operation.

Mike took a long look at the load, another at the 402, and then still another, longer look at me.

"You're not going to take all this shit, are you?" he asked incredulously.

"Mike, I have to. You know it's impossible to get parts like this in Colombia."

"Well, yeah, but let's not get killed trying to get them down there, either," adding philosophically, "let's get a scale and see just what kind of an overload we're talking about."

Piece by piece, we catalogued the weights and when we had finished and added up the total—998 pounds, almost half a ton over gross for the plane.

Mike gave me a long, hard look.

"Are you serious, Bobby?" he wanted to know. "If one of the engines even farts, we're going down. And don't forget, we have the mountain in Haiti to climb over. Then five hundred miles of open water."

I wasn't very happy about the "what if's" either, but I reminded him that I would be there with him.

"But, seriously," I said, "this 402 is the best one around. I personally tuned the engines and adjusted the fuel injection. We won't have any problems."

"What about the Feds?" he wanted to know.

"Don't worry. We'll leave early, before they open. Even if we get caught overweight, it's my license, not yours. Besides, Raul has been on a diet and we're all going to take a shit before we take off."

This broke the ice. Mike laughed, and said, "What the hell, if we crash, I'd rather it be with a long-haired hippie like you. Maybe I'll kiss you before we crash."

I felt my hair. It really was getting long. I forgot when I had last had a haircut.

We got busy again, removing all the seats except two for Raul and Dave. By the time we had finished packing in our supplies it was so crammed that the only way to get to the cockpit was by crawling over the boxes and jacks. Even in the two seats behind the pilot's and the copilot's the only leg room available was by extending them over the jacks.

After fueling the 402 we all stepped back and took a long, critical look. Mike spoke first, in his usual direct manner.

"Ah, shit, it'll never fly. Look—the struts are almost collapsed—the tires are almost flat."

"Hell, Mike, I'll fix that. Hey, Raul," I yelled, "bring me the air hose."

I must have put almost one hundred pounds in the tires. There was no sense using the gauge as I had already set them at seventy pounds and, to tell the truth, I really didn't want to know. I stepped back and looked at Mike.

"OK, how's that, Mike?"

He was still not happy, "What about the struts? They're bottomed out, that's for damned sure."

"Don't worry," I told him, "I'll taxi real slow and as soon as we get over eighty knots or so, we'll have enough lift on the wings—if they don't fall off—to take the pressure off the struts."

"And what about landing?" he demanded, "When we get to Haiti we'll still be overgrossed by four hundred pounds."

"Ah, c'mon, Mike," I wheedled, "I'll grease her on."

Dave and Raul were standing there, just listening. Raul was getting a little nervous, but wasn't sure if this interchange was serious or just horsing around, so he tried to laugh with not much success.

The truth was 82921 was so seriously overloaded that it was preposterous, and, as sometimes happens, our subconscious reaction to the pressure of nerves came to our rescue. All of us burst out laughing uncontrollably, until we had tears in our eyes.

When we were finally able to calm down, I looked at Mike. "Mike, all joking aside. We've got over eight thousand feet of runway here. It'll be cool in the morning and the engines are purring like kittens. Sure, it's a risk, but it's a calculated risk.

We all went back to the office, had a few Cokes, and tried to top each other's jokes about Cessna 402B 82921. We knew she was so bloated that she was going to waddle like a bow-legged duck as she taxied and tried to take off, but what the hell. It was all just another adventure.

I kissed Terry goodbye at six in the morning and drove off to pick up Raul. We were at the airport by six fifteen and found Dave waiting for us. Mike showed up around six forty. "I told my wife to keep the radio on from seven o'clock on to listen for any plane crash report," he joked.

It was a clear morning, still cool, the sun already over the horizon. As we climbed into the Cessna we had to stop and wait for Raul to disentangle himself. His foot had caught between a jack and a tool box tied together by chains and the more he struggled the more he became ensnared. His face became red from exertion; he was puffing and sweating, cursing in Spanish one minute and calling upon different saints for help the next. We all collapsed in laughter. I kept poking him in his round and solid ass, telling him to move it. Finally he was in the clear and we were able to enter. I went in last, securing the door.

Both engines started like a Cadillac. After a few minutes of warm-up and going through the checklist, I gently eased the throttles forward. She didn't want to move. I looked at Mike and smiled as I pushed them forward to about 50 percent power. I drew a breath of relief as she started, slowly, to roll. Mike looked at me with a quizzical expression and shook his head. Both of us were casting worried glances at the tip tanks as I taxied ahead. Again we both smiled, ever so cool, and Mike shook his head again.

We finally lumbered painfully down to the end of runway nine left and started doing the engine run-up. Dave was smiling and cutting up as I looked over at Raul. Raul wanted to laugh, but, at the same time, I could see he was saying his "Hail Mary's" and making secret little Signs of the Cross.

"Hey, Raul," I said to distract him, "the right engine is running real rough. How about changing sides with Dave? That way, if it quits, we won't be too heavy on the right side."

Beads of sweat were standing out on Raul's forehead and he was trying to join Dave and Mike in their outbursts of laughter.

The tower wasn't yet open as it wasn't quite seven o'clock. I eased the power up and taxied into position. "Props forward, mixture rich, boost pumps on high," I called out.

Fuel pressure—OK.

Oil pressure and temperature—in the green.

NQW 82921 was coming to life as she eased past eighty knots. I held her down until she read one hundred knots and then eased back gently on the yoke. She surprised me by flying right off.

"Gear up, flaps up," I called. Thirty feet off the runway, I nosed her back down and watched the airspeed climb, fairly easily, through 125 knots. I eased the power back to thirty inches and pulled the props back to twenty-five hundred RPM. "What a sweetheart." I thought as I scanned the instrument panel. Everything in the green.

Passing through four hundred feet, I punched on the autopilot and set the rate of climb at five hundred feet per minute. Then I reached over and cut off the boost pumps. Then, slowly and very deliberately, I sat back and folded my arms, beaming like a proud father at his well-behaved child.

"Mighty sweet," Mike said. "She's a real ever-lovin' sweetheart."

The sun was well over the horizon as I leveled her off at eighty-five hundred feet and punched the altitude hold button. I centered the Miami VOR on my No. 1 NAV for Bimini, about 105 degrees and punched NAV TRAK on the autopilot. After two minutes, I pulled the power back to twenty-eight inches and twenty-three hundred RPM.

Mike, Dave, and even Raul were amazed at the Cessna's performance. "Like a Swiss watch," Mike commented. Once in the air 82921 acted as if she didn't know she was almost a thousand pounds overgross.

Four hours and fifteen minutes later, we were on a one-mile final for runway nine at Port-au-Prince, Haiti.

"Gear down, flaps fifteen degrees," I called out, "on short final, full flaps, props forward."

I was making what is called a "power-on" landing, which means I had a controlled rate of descent rather than a "flare" type touchdown.

"Easy on the struts," Mike warned me. I nodded.

I let her fly herself down and she came in with an ever so slight squeak of tires.

"Beautiful," Mike approved. "I didn't even feel her touch."

After a short refueling and clearance of our papers, we taxied out of the fuel pit. The tower gave instructions to use nine left for takeoff. It was getting hot, around ninety-four degrees and humid.

"I don't like nine left," Mike muttered, looking worried. "We need two seven."

I knew what he meant. We would be taking off right into the mountains. With the intense heat, I knew 82921 would be very sluggish and would require a lot of runway.

"Me, too," I agreed. "If we have any problem, I'd rather crash in the water. Still, we have a twelve-knot headwind and that's better than having it on the tail. So what the hell, let's try nine."

After the run-up checklist was complete, I eased the throttle forward. When it was up to thirty-six inches, I could tell she was going to be heavy. Cessna 82921 seemed to take forever getting to eighty knots, but she passed it slowly and laboriously got up to ninety-five knots. She still didn't feel like she wanted to fly, and she ate up more runway.

"Rotate," Mike called.

"No, she's not ready," I said, concentrating on squeezing a few more knots of groundspeed. Finally, we reached 105 knots. I eased back on the yoke, ever so gently. "Shit, Mike, she's like lead," and just as the words were spoken, she got off with great protest, and I called for gear up.

Mike had his hand on the flap selector and called, "Flaps up," but I overrode him with an immediate, "No! She doesn't want to climb." I knew we were still in "ground effect" and needed some more altitude. I eased her up to fifty feet and nosed her back down to a level altitude.

"OK, flaps up," I instructed.

Slowly, very slowly, the airspeed climbed to 115, 120, and, finally, 125 knots. The houses and telephone poles seemed very close as I pulled her up to a three-hundred-feet-per-minute rate of climb. Power was still set at maximum takeoff. Gently, I gave her a fifteen-degree turn to the left and eased the power back to thirty inches and twenty-five hundred RPM.

Both of us were sweating profusely, and it wasn't just from the heat. I looked sidewise at him and he looked sidewise at me. We exchanged our tight little smiles that said volumes. His was saying, "You crazy bastard," and mine was replying, "Yeah, I know, but we made it." Mike just shook his head and looked back at Raul, who was still fervently crossing himself. Dave was just grinning, he was unflappable.

"What about getting over the mountain?" I asked as I turned her to a 270-degree heading.

"I don't know, Bobby ... The mountains are a lot lower if we keep heading west. But, hell, look at the clouds. Those damned thunderstorms are right where we have to turn south and we can't see the tops of the mountains."

I looked out to the left and saw a small hole in the clouds and beyond the mountain tops.

"Look, Mike, let's keep on a two seven zero heading for about fifteen miles and then back to ninety-degrees east, heading back over the airport. By that time we should be to seven or eight thousand, and then we turn south. What do you think?"

"Our choices are not unlimited. Let's go."

The Cessna was beginning to behave and to feel a little more responsive in an outside air temperature around seventy degrees. In about fifteen minutes, we were back over the airport at six thousand feet. I made a right turn to heading one eight zero and stared at the clouds and mountains ahead.

"What do you think, Mike?" I needed all the support I could get.

"Shit, I don't know. It's going to be close. The clouds are covering the tops pretty fast."

I eased the power up to thirty-two inches and pulled her up to five hundred feet per minute. As we climbed, there was a hole of only about three hundred yards through which we could see the peaks. The mountains rushed toward us. At seventy-five hundred feet, the clouds closed in, now leaving only about one hundred yards of clear visibility of the peaks. Mike and I were tense as I eased the power up to max take off and pulled her up to one thousand feet per minute. The mountain peaks were slipping by at only about three hundred feet below us as we passed over them, our sighs of relief cutting off abruptly when we caught a down draft that dropped us almost five hundred feet before we stabilized. Thank God we had made it to the other side of those jagged peaks.

We now knew the worst was over. I eased the power back and punched on the autopilot. The skies were clear and beautiful as we left the area of the island, and the five hundred miles of open water stretched ahead of us without a blemish.

I glanced back at Raul and would have given a hundred dollars for a photograph of his face. He was wringing wet, shaking and swallowing convulsively, and at the same time, trying to smile. His face was puckered up like a little kid on his first roller-coaster ride. We all burst out laughing.

"*Qué pasa*, mother fucker?" I asked him in great good humor, and he answered with a lengthy and colorful expletive of his own in Spanish.

For the rest of the two-and-a-half hour flight, 82921 behaved like a true thoroughbred. However, approaching Barranquilla, about twenty-five miles out, it was obvious that we were in for some rough weather. The skies were jet black in front of us, even though the control tower was reporting scattered clouds and eight-mile visibility. As far east and west as we could see, there was not a single opening. We were committed to fly through it.

"Look at all that shit," I complained to Mike. "I think we'd better start down and hope we can get under her. That storm's over forty thousand feet high; it'll break us apart."

"Yeah," Mike agreed, "but even so, we're going to take a beating. There's a lot of rain in those clouds."

I eased the power back and started a five hundred feet per minute descent. The clouds were boiling black ahead. I nosed her down to fifteen hundred feet per minute and slowed to 130 knots.

Seconds later, we were in it. I set the autopilot for five hundred feet per minute as Mike was checking the approach plates. We were down to two thousand feet, being bounced unmercifully. The rain crashed against the windshield so hard it felt solid.

"Check the chart for obstacles, Mike, I'm going down to a thousand feet." Bracing myself against the violent pitching, I punched off the autopilot and asked Mike for a heading.

Mike was studying his charts intently, and called out, "Go to the VOR." I spun the H.S.I. and centered the needle to show a 190-degree heading.

"I'm down to nine hundred feet. We can't go any lower. The DME shows eleven miles and we should be over downtown Barranquilla now."

The movement of the rain was incredible; it felt as if we were in an automatic dishwasher churning and tossing jets of water on the plane. Suddenly, without any warning, we broke out. There were puffy white clouds, blue skies, a complete transformation from a minute before. Barranquilla was directly below and for the first time in my life, I was happy to see it.

"Cessna 82921 cleared to land on runway four," came over the radio.

"Gear down, flaps fifteen degrees," I sang out as I made a left turn onto final. Another greased landing, and several minutes later we pulled up to customs. I half-expected Raul to kneel down and kiss his native soil as we emerged from the plane, but now that he was safe and sound, he decided to act the role of the intrepid international traveler and behaved as if the flight had been nothing out of the ordinary.

CHAPTER TWENTY-TWO

A moment after I stepped out of the plane, I forgot all about Raul—I knew something wasn't according to plan.

"Where's Donado?" I asked. I couldn't see him anywhere.

Raul told me that he would look in immigration, and I called after him to check on Aldo and Aquiles, as well.

Several immigration officers were walking toward us, and, when they got near, two of them took our passports and the others began looking inside the plane. Raul returned, reporting that no one had seen Donado. As we were talking, one of the immigration officers motioned for us to go inside. Mike gave him our general declaration and a copy of our flight plan. Raul's friend, Diego had appeared and cleared our passports and visas, handing them back to us. No apparent problems, but I was uneasy.

"Raul," I said, "something is wrong. No one has asked about the cargo."

I had spoken too soon. A short and officious customs officer was asking about the load manifest. Raul looked at me, and I acted as if I didn't understand.

I told Raul to explain that the parts and tools were here only for making an inspection and would be returned to the States. If the man had any questions, he was to be informed that Donado, *Jefe* of Aerocivil, was expecting them.

His only acknowledgment was a grumpy and non-committal *"Si,"* followed by an instruction that we should move the airplane over next to the Tavina hangar. *What is going on here*, I wondered.

"Where the hell is everybody?" I yelled at Raul.

"I don't know. I called them and told them to be here," he answered.

I had no choice but to crawl into 82921 and taxi over next to the west end of the terminal, about two hundred feet from Tavina. I shut off the engines and waited for Raul and the customs officials who were walking over slowly, behind Dave and Mike.

I could see we were running into a problem, to judge from Raul's face and violent gestures. When they got near, I asked him what the matter was.

"Bobby, he's saying the duty for these parts for import is three thousand dollars."

The scene was building up into a typical gringo shakedown. That was why the official had made me move the plane, so that no one from the customs office could witness what was going on.

"Tell him that these are used parts and worth only about a thousand dollars. Besides, they were not brought here to import, just for an inspection. They'll be taken back out," I instructed Raul.

Several minutes of increasingly violent verbal exchange took place between Raul and this man I decided to call Grumpy. At one point, Raul trotted over to tell me that the price had been reduced to two thousand dollars; otherwise, the parts would be confiscated. Grumpy looked adamant and angry, his face fittingly flushed. I called Mike over.

"Mike, you know the Tavina people. See if somebody over there can help us."

Aquiles and Toño finally appeared without Aldo. Raul yelled for them to get over there, fast. Both of them were soon into the fray hot and heavy, yelling as loud as everyone else.

I just stood back and watched the meaningless verbal aggression, trying to figure out some solution to this unforeseen problem. I knew it would be getting out of hand shortly. Then I had an idea. What was good enough for Caesar was good enough for Bobby Wood. I would try the old "divide and conquer" tactic.

I walked over and took Grumpy and Raul aside, telling Raul that I would give Grumpy four hundred dollars and not a dime more. This was still too much, I felt, but it would save us a lot of bullshit. I knew that I could let them confiscate everything and get it back the next day when Donado was there. However, it was more than likely that some important items would be stolen and I most certainly didn't want that to happen.

Raul conveyed my offer. It clearly was far below Grumpy's expectations and an insult to a man of his "position" because he began to strut off toward his men, ordering them to confiscate everything.

"Raul, get over there fast and spread the word that I have offered four hundred dollars and won't go a cent higher. You know what to do; lay it on 'em good and thick."

Raul didn't need any further instructions. He was on familiar ground and knew his own way around in this graft game.

As he was giving his pitch the other customs men quieted down, and I could see a couple of them nodding thoughtfully. They were considering the advantages of a small feast over no feast at all. Grumpy was having no part of it. It was becoming a matter of pride with him, something rare in those parts. He kept shaking his head, yelling "No!" and strutting back and forth. He acted as if he would like to walk away from them completely, but couldn't quite bring himself to do it.

Raul and Toño were old hands at keeping the fires going, and they added fuel as needed. Small conferences would be held between two or three of the men, and then they would move off and regroup. In the midst of all this, Mike returned and said that no one at Tavina wanted to interfere as they had to work around the airport and didn't want to lose any amigos.

"Just wait till those bastards want something in Miami," I commented. After a few minutes, I realized that I wasn't being very smart and apologized to Mike. He understood.

We stood together by the wingtip of 82921 and watched the show.

"What the hell is going on?" Mike asked curiously.

I explained to him what had taken place.

"All they want is money. It's boiling down to a matter of how much. I've made them an offer and I'm hoping it's one they can't refuse." Mike laughed. I continued, "I think it's time for the next move. Let's see—Hey, Raul."

Everyone waited as I came near. I came all the way into the group, stopped, glared, threw up my hands, and yelled as loud as they had a few minutes before.

"Tell them all to fuck off. I'm mad now. Tell them to go ahead and confiscate this shit so we can go the hotel. We'll get it tomorrow and not have to pay a dime."

Without another word, I turned, walked off, and returned to my place, folding my arms and standing like an Indian chief who had spoken.

My outburst brought some new action. Now the others were beginning to argue with Grumpy. He put up strong resistance for several minutes, but we could see that he was weakening. Mike was shaking with laughter, but trying to keep a straight face.

I had to get behind the plane to keep them from seeing me laughing so hard I couldn't control myself. They looked like a flock of barnyard roosters fighting with each other to cover a hen.

In a couple of minutes they had all calmed down and walked over. Raul gave me the money sign; I took out four hundred dollars and handed it to Grumpy. After all, he was the boss.

"OK," Grumpy ordered, "get it unloaded and out of here."

I asked Dave to get Toño and Aquiles to bring the car around, and motioned Raul over to the side of the plane.

"Get the boss man to come over. Tell him I want to talk with him," and Raul trotted off, returning with Grumpy. I turned my back to the others and held out my hand in which I had folded a one hundred dollar bill. As we shook hands, he glanced down and his sour countenance brightened visibly. I thanked him for being a reasonable man, and this, plus the "little extra" for him partially broke the ice. I could see that his pride was still smarting, so I explained, through Raul that I was not a rich *marimbero*, just a poor man like he was, and that the money I had was all I could give them. This was the right thing to say—it put us on the same footing, which saved him face—and, along with the extra money, it had shown respect for his rank. I was learning.

We all shook hands and parted amigos. Just then Aquiles and Toño pulled up in their cars. It took an hour and three hundred feet of rope to tie the jacks on top of the vehicles. Parts and boxes were bulging out of trunks and windows, bumpers were close to dragging on the ground. In the end, we had to hire a taxi to transport the rest of our group.

Mike made arrangements to leave the plane parked inside the Tavina hangar and we all departed for Aquiles' house to store the parts overnight. We had no illusions about trying to transport them to Aldo's house in Ciénaga at night in those heaps.

Later that night, Donado's boys came over. Dave was an immediate hit with them, as he was with Aquiles and Toño. Toño was especially happy to have the distinction of being taller than Dave, and glad to see that all gringos weren't giants.

Everyone was fascinated by Dave's talent for imitating bird calls, which they were willing to listen to as long as Dave would perform. Language was no barrier for Dave; he seemed to understand what everyone said to him by some kind of osmosis.

I asked Donado and Fernando if they would like to stay the night and help us the next day to take our equipment over to Ciénaga. Since anything that had to do with planes was meat and drink for them, they were happy to accept.

Aldo made his appearance around eleven. I was furious with him for not having met us at the airport and glared at him coldly while Raul told him what had happened.

"But I left my car for you," protested Aldo. "I had to go back to Santa Marta to see the judge."

Aldo couldn't even tell a decent lie, much less the truth, I thought to myself disgustedly. Raul and I had called Judge Valdez earlier that evening and Valdez hadn't seen Aldo in three days. On top of that I could smell liquor on his breath and see lipstick on his shirt. If he had, in fact, seen a judge, it was for sure a lady judge.

While Aldo was still trying to establish that he was blameless, the phone rang. It was Donado. Raul gave Donado an account of what had taken place with the customs officials and Donado apologized for not having been present to help us. It had been absolutely necessary for him to be in Cartagena on a government matter, and was calling to say that he was still tied up and could not return to Barranquilla until the next night.

Donado told Raul to call Judge Valdez first thing in the morning to remind him that Donado had still not received the formal request for inspection of the plane. It was urgent. Raul suggested that we could go to see Valdez the next day when we took the parts to Aldo's house in Ciénaga.

I was disappointed to be losing another day, but was becoming accustomed, to the old Colombia ailment—the *Mañana* Syndrome.

A few minutes later the phone rang again. Aldo leaped to answer it as if he were expecting it, and he was not wrong. It was for him. He turned his back to us and spoke in a low voice so that none of us could hear the conversation. When he hung up, he opened his briefcase, took out his bottle of Florida water and a clean shirt and disappeared in the bathroom.

He emerged looking good as new and made his exit, ready for action. He announced he would see us at his house the next day.

We sat around making a few lewd comments on Aldo's active love life and kidding Raul about how Aldo made him look like a bush league Romeo. I was well aware by this time, after my visits to Colombia, that it was a standard practice for many Latin men to keep a sharp eye out for as many extra-marital relationships as they could handle and remarked that Colombians were endowed with two extraordinary pieces of equipment—cast iron stomachs and steel pricks. Fernando translated this to the others, who burst out laughing, since the words for "iron" and "steel" in Spanish—"*hierro*" and "*acero*"—rhymed and thus turned the remark into a clever couplet that made me sound like a real wit.

After our bawdy interlude at Aldo's expense, we got back to serious matters—the radios. Raul had already checked with Aquiles and Toño to see if they had any news for us, but they still had no information. He had also spoken with Mario at the Santa Marta airport, who had reported that he had a few leads but nothing definite as yet.

JUNE 10, 1980—BARRANQUILLA, MY 402 CESSNA AND A JOB WELL DONE

In the morning, at breakfast, while I ate my French fries, I couldn't take my eyes off Dave who was wolfing down everything in sight, dousing it with *aji piquin* (a hot sauce) and heaping on seconds. Dave was a man for all seasons and all countries, I could see that clearly.

We all went over to the Tavina office about nine thirty. Mike had already fueled 82921. He now filed his flight plan and was rarin' to go. I had tried to talk Mike into going to Santa Marta with us to take a look at 464 Juliet, but he had refused.

"Look, hippie," he had told me, "you're going to have enough problems here getting it out. I'm not going to spend the next month or two in jail in that hellhole. I've done my job, now you do yours."

He was half-joking, but in all earnest he had spent a lot of time in Colombia in the past five years and knew that Murphy's Law was especially applicable in Colombia. Anything that could possibly go wrong there certainly did.

Cessna 82921 cranked to life as Mike waved goodbye. We stood there for several minutes watching as Mike pulled her off the runway. She was light now, climbing almost like a jet, and looked as if she was reaching for the stars. Mike turned northward, heading home.

CHAPTER TWENTY-THREE

With Mike gone, we left the airport quickly as it was going to be a busy day.

"Did Aquiles get the truck?" I asked Raul. We had arranged the night before to rent a vehicle to have mercy on the two overloaded cars that had taken our cargo to Aquiles' house.

"Yes," Raul replied dubiously, "but I don't think it's in great shape." Since Raul was always one to foresee "no problems" and wear an enthusiastic smile, I was immediately aware that this was, for him, a highly qualified statement.

Thirty minutes later we pulled up in front of Aquiles' house.

There it sat, in all its splendor—a 1947 Chevrolet half-ton flatbed with three-inch-diameter cut tree trunks for side stakes. Half of the left front fender was completely eroded by rust. It had no windshield. An old man, the owner, was energetically polishing the hood with an old red rag, standing back to observe the results of his efforts.

"What's this piece of crap?" I whispered to Raul. "It won't carry all this load. Besides, even empty, I don't think it will make it."

Raul conferred with the old man, asking if the truck would take fifteen hundred pounds of parts. A lively conversation with many gestures ensued. The old man, his face shining with pride in his "beauty," was listing to Raul its special features, such as heavy-duty rear springs and dual rear wheels. I was aware that it had dual rear wheels; the only thing that worried me was that the right rear had only one tire on it.

The old, man concluded his sales pitch by slapping the good fender firmly, announcing, "The cab isn't so good, but she's a real *burro* (workhorse)." Dave was standing on the sidelines, laughing—it was as if he understood every word, and after a few minutes, I could see that it was funny, too. None of us wanted to hurt the old fellow's feelings, since it was obvious that his truck meant more to him than his wife.

We loaded her up and set out like a caravan of gypsies, Aquiles in the lead position with his 1953 Chevy and the 1947 flatbed following. Less than six blocks from the bridge we heard a loud boom, and Aquiles' Chevy quickly slowed and settled to the side. It was his right front tire. Aquiles sheepishly told me that his spare was also flat. We examined the one that had blown; it was worn past the first three cords and the part that had blown was a "boot" he had put in the week before.

After an hour or so, we had improvised another boot that was enough to get us to a place where they sold tires. This establishment in no way could be called a store. It was a dirt-floor shed with a sheet metal roof. No fancy tire tools or air machines, everything was done with a sledge hammer and tire spike. I was dubious about finding anything at all here that would be suitable for Aquiles' Chevy, but everyone dug around and in a short time, we had four brand new 6.7' by 15' tires. It would have been difficult to find them in the States. Aquiles was beaming as he examined his four new tires and the spare, as if he now knew he could get another twenty-seven years out of the car.

Reloaded and ready to get back on the road, we departed for the bridge. As we approached, the soldiers were laughing and pointing to the pair of antiques—certainly none of them could have mistaken us for *marimbero*s in this poor-boy caravan.

We were ordered to pull over for a document check as they had spotted Dave as a newcomer. Raul handed them our passports, and Dave and I stood apart from them, waiting, when I noticed Raul and the soldiers arguing.

Raul called me. I walked over and Raul handed me my passport with a worried expression and the news that "we got problems."

He showed me the stamp, pointing out that it was for twenty-four hours. That jerk at immigration had given us only 24 hours on our visa status. Raul explained that we were going to be in Colombia illegally after 3:00 p.m. that same afternoon. If we tried to come back through the bridge after that hour, we would be put in jail. That was what Raul had been arguing about with the soldier—they hadn't wanted us even to leave the bridge and were preparing to arrest us right then, even though we had Major Hernandez's letter.

Raul was finally able to convince them that we weren't in the country illegally until after three. I was thinking that if they had been smart, they would have just let us pass and then would nab us when we came back that night. I thanked heaven for their stupidity.

"Let's go to Immigration right now and get this straightened out," I said and then instructed Aquiles and the Donado boys to stay and watch the truck. I didn't want to find it stripped when we got back.

Twenty minutes later we were at the downtown Immigration office and Raul spent another twenty minutes explaining our situation to the immigration officer on duty. He was very sorry, but very firm. Nothing doing.

We walked outside for a conference.

"What do we do now?" I asked Carlo's.

"I don't know," he said. "We have to be out of the country before midnight or we'll be arrested. He wouldn't even let me talk to the officer in charge."

I was getting angry. My common sense told me that this was going to be a show of that other common Colombian syndrome, the *Dinero* Syndrome, but I couldn't understand why the official had been so bashful to call it to my attention. Maybe he was used to more private negotiations.

"Look, Raul, let's come up with one of your solutions. We'll stay out here—you go back and give the guy fifty bucks to let us talk with *Numero Uno*. I'm sure he'll do it. Then you give *Numero Uno* whatever he wants within reason. Just get us a visa for a week or so. You know what to do."

Dave and I sat outside waiting, and I gave him a rundown on how this system worked, and on how the Colombians needed to be greased to keep the official machinery moving. Raul was soon back, and his smile told me that he had been successful. He motioned for us to go inside, whispering that he needed three hundred dollars, and that things were taken care of.

We walked inside and were introduced to a nice-looking Colombian official, *Numero Uno*. A few minutes of polite conversation, an "I apologize for the 'inconvenience,'" a couple of signatures, and the exchange of three hundred dollars, which *Numero Uno* gracefully accepted, we were handed our passports, stamped with new visas for two weeks. Very generous, I thought to myself, we got here on bargain day; we got an extra week. I also thought how nice it would be if some day one of these Colombians would pucker up and give me a kiss while they were screwing me.

After my lecture to Dave half an hour before on the endless variations of the shakedown, he was getting another hands-on demonstration of how it worked. He just shook his head and laughed as we came out of the building and said philosophically, "Well, Bobby, at least you know what to expect by now."

We got back to the bridge and pulled up behind to assume position in our "convoy," only to be met by another group of soldiers also wanting to see our passports. As we showed them the new visas, the original soldiers who had shortly before been giving us a hard time joined the others and wanted to see, too. They were displeased; it was obvious, as they slammed the passports together and shoved them back at us.

"Where are your papers for these parts you are hauling?" they wanted to know.

At this, one of the Donado boys spoke up and said the parts were for their father, Luis Donado, *Jefe* of Aerocivil. They pointed to their house, only a block away. Raul brought out the letter from Major Hernandez.

"Raul, I'm tired of this shit. Tell them I demand to see Major Hernandez, now. Ask him to come over here."

Raul reminded them of Major Hernandez's orders and that he had punished the men who had robbed me before, and assured them that this time, the major would take an even firmer stand with anyone who disobeyed him. While Raul was addressing them, one of the men whispered something to several others, and they nodded reluctantly and drifted away.

Raul told me that several of the soldiers were new on the job and hadn't known about the earlier trouble. This was probably the case, but I knew that soldiers were changed often (possibly to let everyone share the wealth) and that they would all be on the alert for even the slightest irregularity in our papers. Major Hernandez or no Major Hernandez, they'd be over us in swarms.

Raul had to agree with me, saying, "Yeah, Bobby, you're not very popular here."

About twenty-five miles beyond the bridge, the old Chevy truck started bucking badly and ground to a halt. We all got out and stood respectfully around the remains, but the old man showed no sign of worry. He reached behind the rear seat and pulled out a greasy carburetor. I offered to help him, but he proudly shook his head and waved off my offer. Raul made a sign for me to move away, so I joined the others. A few minutes later the old man mounted to the single seat in the truck, turned the key and we were all astonished to hear her crank right up. He turned to us with a smile that said, *See, just like new*, and he patted the dashboard as if the Chevy were a thoroughbred horse that had just come in first at the Kentucky Derby and as if he were the only trainer in the world that knew how to handle her.

Dave's reaction to the poverty and ugliness as we passed through Ciénaga was the same as mine had been the first time. His normally smiling face turned serious and thoughtful.

"That's a hell of a way for people to have to live," he remarked. "Look at those kids; it's terrible."

We pulled up to Aldo's house about three thirty in the afternoon. Aldo was sitting in his father's rocking chair dozing and when he opened his eyes they looked like two holes burned in a blanket. Raul and I made a few indelicate remarks about Aldo's delicate state of health, which Aldo accepted with his usual foolish grin.

The family came out to greet us warmly, Aldo's mother scurrying back into the house to bring out a pitcher of ice water. The Reyeses were a family of substance; they had a refrigerator, the only one on the block. It sat proudly in the dining room and was equipped with a lock to discourage the theft of its contents. We were shown a back bedroom and a section of the dining room where we could store our parts and equipment.

I asked Aldo to call Judge Valdez to see if we could go over and pick up the letter for Luis Donado. The judge was not in his office, but we reached him at home. Aldo spoke for several minutes and when he finished he said he would go over and be back in about an hour.

"Just a minute, Aldo," I said firmly, "Raul and I are going with you."

Reluctantly Aldo grunted, "OK." It was clear that he still wanted us to have as little direct contact with the judge as possible.

The judge came out to greet us and to usher us personally into his home with a "Raul, Bobby, how are you?" He seemed glad to see us. He asked about our trip. We told him the details and mentioned the parts we had brought down, adding that we had a mechanic with us.

Judge Valdez wanted to know where the mechanic was. We told him Dave was waiting for us at Aldo's house with the Donado boys rather than to bring the whole group to the judge's home. Slowly and delicately we led into the subject of getting the release of 464 Juliet, provided, naturally, that the inspection turned out OK.

"Two weeks should do it, I think—three maximum," Valdez said. "I should have all the paperwork finished by then." There was hesitation in his voice. He didn't sound completely confident and, worse, he avoided looking directly at me.

I was studying Valdez intently. My limitations with the language had forced me to analyze and interpret pauses, speech patterns, body English, eye contact—the unspoken languages—and I was getting bad vibrations.

I wanted to ask about how he was going to prepare the papers. I seriously doubted that this would be easy. The indecision in his voice made me wonder. Was this matter truly within his competence? I still was not sure. And did he have the legal expertise to do it? Since the plane had been there for three years and had been involved in so much red tape already, I knew it couldn't be released by a mere signature and a magic wand.

I hid my misgivings. "Very good," I approved. "I have almost everything here with me to make it airworthy, so from that point of view, I don't think we'll have any problems."

Also, slowly and delicately, I brought up the subject of the two lawyers who had visited Valdez claiming they were representing the "real" owner. Were they, in fact, in the game?

"No, yours is the correct documentation, in my opinion. They would have to produce something truly extraordinary to disprove what you have presented," the judge stated.

This visit, our second invitation to his home, nevertheless had special significance inasmuch as Alfredo was not with us this time. Although his tone was still professional, our relationship was becoming less formal.

We asked Judge Valdez if he would be going to the airport the next day for inspection of the jet. Valdez didn't know if he would be present or not, but he reached into his desk and brought out a legal-sized sheet of paper.

"You will be needing this," he said. "It's the formal request from the Third Penal Court requesting an inspection of 464 Juliet."

Raul gave me the gist of the document. A wave of elation swept over me. Finally, after all the bullshit and ass-kissing, I had in hand the first legal authorization that represented the first step toward rescuing 464 Juliet. It read as follows:

LEGAL ORDER FOR INSPECTION

In Santa Marta, on the twelfth (12) Of June nineteen, eighty (1980), such date and time being indicated in the decision dated June 7 of the same year, the seat of the Third Court of the Penal Circuit was removed to the offices of the Simón Bolívar Airport of the same city for the purpose of performing the Official Inspection previously decreed. Present were. the honorable judge, together with his secretary and Mr. Luis Donado, Chief of the Central Technical and Security Unit of Aerocivil, North Zone of Barranquilla, the latter appointed as the expert, from whom the honorable judge received sworn statement in conformance with the dispositions of Articles 157 and 270 of the C. de P.P. and 191 of the C.P. (legal codes governing such activities), that he would fulfill faithfully and to the best of his ability the dUties required of him. Duly empowered, the office of the Court was moved to the site where aircraft JET N464J subject of this order, was located. The designated expert, after arrival at the site, was given the following list of questions:

1. He was to indicate the class, make, type, etc., of the aircraft.

2. Present condition of the different parts of the aircraft.

3. What elements or appurtenances were presently missing in the aircraft.

4. If the aircraft was airworthy, and its approximate commercial value in accordance with the present condition of the plane.

At this stage of the task, the Aerocivil expert states that at this time he is unable to give an exact opinion on the condition as this would take too much time, but that the following week said opinion will be in the judge's hands.

The order having been carried out. this document was signed and witnessed by all those concerned, who first read and then signed it.

The Judge(Signed) JORGE VALDEZ

I was biting my tongue to keep from asking about working on 464 Juliet after the inspection had been completed, but decided not to push my luck. An inspection didn't seem like much, but it was a lot more than anyone else had been able to get done in the past three years. So I cautioned myself to take it easy, not to push, and to take one step at a time, politely asking, "May I," at each occasion.

Jubilation was in the air as we drove back to Ciénaga. We discussed Valdez's cautious attitude, but we were happy that he had at least moved us forward as far as he had. At Aldo's house we picked up the rest of our party and departed for Barranquilla.

Dave seemed pleased about the go-ahead to start work the following day and was tickled by my poorly concealed excitement. He beamed at me like a father whose son has just found his first bicycle under the Christmas tree. He knew how long I had been waiting for this, and could understand my excitement.

After dinner we talked more about the big day coming. The Donado boys were not about to be excluded from this one—both were clamoring to help. My assets were growing to include Junior League amigos, and I was happy to accept their offer.

Dave had introduced Fernando, Donado, Aquiles, and Toño to poker while they had been waiting for us in Ciénaga, so they were all eager to try their luck. Of course, I joined the table. For a switch, we were now able to teach this little group of Colombians something about American "mind games" that evening—the bluff. Dave and I thoroughly enjoyed parting them from a few of their *pesos*.

I was holding a full house—three jacks and a pair of threes—when the phone rang. Raul answered; it was Donado. He was informed that we had our precious inspection order, and it was arranged that we meet at his house next morning at 7:30 A.M. He spoke with the boys a few minutes. Then we all turned in for the night.

CHAPTER TWENTY-FOUR

There was a fever of intensity in the air as we pulled up to Donado's house. It was a fine morning and I was riding a mental high. All my previous frustrations had been swept away as if they had never existed.

Donado came out to greet us with a cheerful "Good morning," and acknowledged the introduction to Dave with a smile and a hearty handshake.

"Where's the mechanic?" he asked, looking around inquiringly.

"You just met him," Raul said, "Dave is our mechanic." Donado's face was a study. It was an embarrassing situation for him; Dave's very youthful appearance and his slim, boyish build took several years off him, and Donado had obviously expected someone similar to himself, a counterpart, exuding authority at every pore.

However, he extricated himself gracefully by saying with complete sincerity, "I hope you're as good as Bobby says you are."

Dave, with his usual good humor, just laughed. He was secure in his expertise as a top Learjet A & P (airplane and power plant) mechanic, and totally without the vanity of a man less well-prepared to do the job; so, it never occurred to him to interpret Donado's misunderstanding as an insult.

We were waved on at the bridge and treated to another of Donado's bounding races across the foot of the peninsula, arriving at Aldo's place a little after nine.

Donado's eyes widened as he viewed all the parts and tools we had brought down.

"*Dios mio*, you brought all this down in the 402?" he asked incredulously.

When we assured him that we had, he just shook his head and made a rapid comment which Raul told me was, "You've sure got balls."

We had packed everything in the truck but the jacks and tires, as these wouldn't be needed for the inspection. With all these parts, as well as Fernando, Donado Jr., Toño, and Aquiles in the back, and Donado, Aldo, Raul, Donado, and me in the front, the truck was carrying a substantial load, which did absolutely nothing to reduce our breakneck speed as we continued our journey to the Simón Bolívar Airport.

On our arrival, Donado asked us to wait while he went upstairs to talk with the airport manager, returning in a few minutes with a "*Vamanos* (Let's go)." We got back in the truck and drove around to the north gate which Donado Jr. opened for us. As soon as we were inside the ramp area, the fussy old man we had met before—Baratta—emerged, shouting and waving his hands, motioning Donado to stop.

He hadn't recognized Donado, and, as we came to a halt, his expression immediately changed, revealing an "I screwed it up" look.

"I'm sorry," he began, "but that gate was supposed to have been locked."

He was torn between eating crow and displaying his authority. Donado, not even acknowledging Baratta, imperiously drove on over to 464 Juliet.

"Boy, she's pretty," Dave remarked as we pulled up to the left of the jet. As Donado went over to talk to a soldier a little distance away, I felt this was a good time to instruct Dave in a matter involving cooperation, face, and public relations regarding this all-important inspection.

I indicated that he and I would go into a huddle so that our signals would be straight.

"Dave, you've probably figured out that Donado was a little off-balance when he saw your young and smiling face and that you're about the size of his kids." Dave nodded and smiled.

I went on, "Now, I want you to act like you're God Almighty. When you get started on the inspection, don't say 'I don't know' or 'I'm not sure' or anything like that. Speak with complete authority. Give orders like you were a shop foreman and leave nothing to be questioned. When Donado gets back, spit out orders of priority, and Raul and I will jump to attention."

"Don't worry, I'll make you jump."

"One more thing, Dave, make Donado feel and look important. He doesn't have any experience with this type of inspection, but he has to keep face in front of all these people here. Invite him to assist you. I know he'll say no and tell you to go ahead on your own. But it's important to consult him, and it's important for him to have the chance to decline."

"Shoot, I'll handle it. Don't worry."

When Donado returned, Dave walked over to him and with a respectful and serious air, got down to the formalities.

"Mr. Donado, would you like to supervise my inspection or tell me how you would like it to be done?"

Donado was surprised and pleased to be shown the respect his position demanded. He also looked relieved to be given such a fine opportunity to avoid a possibly embarrassing situation. "No, no," he said gravely, "proceed on your own. Just give me a written report."

Dave and I didn't dare exchange looks, but we were both pleased at this outcome since it would give us a free hand to do as much as we wished and an opportunity to make a scrupulous evaluation of the condition of 464 Juliet.

The scene was set as Dave motioned for Raul and the rest of the crew to come over. He took command like a Napoleon.

"Bobby, get an inspection pad and pen. Raul, Fernando, get the batteries and set them up behind the left wing. Toño, Donado—set the tool boxes by the cabin door."

We all leaped to obey.

"Let's do a walk-around inspection while the boys are setting up," Dave suggested and I nodded, pad and pen in hand. As soon as we were out of earshot of the others, I whispered, "Make it look bad." He nodded agreement.

Dave examined and rapped out instructions. I jotted as fast as I could write. "Corrosion here … corrosion here … ," he pointed out. I made notes. "This panel to be pulled … that panel to be pulled …," I continued writing. "All the vortex generators missing; damn, someone made sure this thing would never fly." Dave was not faking his concern about these missing components—since they controlled the airflow over the ailerons they were absolutely essential to the aerodynamics of the Learjet.

This went on for about thirty minutes. When Dave got to the tip tanks, his stern, professional act broke down. When he had the fuel caps open he burst out laughing, "It's been a few months since they emptied the garbage," and he reached inside the fuel tank, pulling out beer cans, coke bottles, newspaper sheets, and even yellow tags from another plane. Everyone crowded around to see what he had dug out. Donado's lips twitched. I could see he wanted to join the laughter, but he was a professional and an important official of Aerocivil and had to show concern at the serious nature of the matter. And this was a very, very serious matter: There is an inflexible taboo in any country in the world against tampering with the fuel system of any airplane.

Dave was quick to observe Donado's reaction, and he instructed Raul to give them a preliminary cleaning saying that he himself would do the final cleaning and seal the tanks.

Next Dave ordered an inspection of the cabin. I opened the door, which Valdez was supposed to have had locked the previous time we were there, but hadn't. Dave looked at me in bewilderment as we stared at the stripped radio panel.

"Well, at least the radar is still there," he said and then continued with his verbal list. "No oxygen, no emergency air; also, no pilot's oxygen masks. Note that all passenger oxygen masks are also gone." He next walked toward the back of the plane and pulled out the bottom portion of the rear seats. "It looks like they missed these," he commented.

Donado stuck his head in the door, with an inquiring look and a "What's that." Dave pointed to several avionics boxes.

"Give me a couple of minutes," Dave said, and he quickly went to work. In less than five minutes he handed me an AVQ 75 DME, two 1014 transponders, and an emergency battery for the standby artificial horizon.

"Bobby, you're lucky they didn't know these were here," and I heartily agreed as they were worth at least four thousand dollars.

Dave pushed the seat back into place and pulled the top of the rear seats forward, to climb into the baggage compartment. "You're not so lucky here," he said. "They got the HF radio. Write it down." I scribbled obediently.

We moved outside and examined the miscellaneous parts for a few minutes. Donado mentioned that he had a radio technician in Barranquilla who could check the radios. I didn't want this, as I planned to have them repaired in the States, but I nodded my head and said that would be nice.

"Next, we'll pull the nose panels," said Dave. I knew he would be stunned when he saw the rocks inside. I had mentioned this to him before, but now he would see it for the first time. I was right; he just stood there shaking his head, as if to say, "What will they think of next?" He ordered them to be taken out to check the radio racks for damage and to remove the rocks around the oxygen and emergency air tanks.

"Hold the nose down," Dave ordered, and Raul and Fernando jumped to grab it while we removed the last of the rocks. "We don't want her falling on her tail."

After a careful inspection of the racks and tanks, Dave was satisfied that no visible damage had been done.

Donado stood by, very intent on the inspection, and concerned about the wanton damage and pilferage. "I'll do some investigating on my own," he promised, "this is a serious matter."

The sun was overhead by that time and scorching the tops of our heads. Aquiles was our "Coca-Cola boy." He had established a bottle brigade to quench our thirst but it was time to take a breather in the shade of the east end of the compound. We were only about fifty feet from the beach and the breeze blowing from the water refreshed us. On a clear day the skyline of Barranquilla could be seen across the bay.

Alongside me, Donado gestured toward the group of soldiers who had been keeping out of our hair all that morning, hanging out in their compound. Donado mentioned that he had questioned them about the missing radios when we had first arrived that morning. Apparently they wanted to make themselves as scarce and inconspicuous as possible and not have to answer embarrassing questions.

After a short break, I whispered to Dave to give some new orders and put us back to work. He ordered a renewal of activities and we moved back over to 464 Juliet. Raul spotted the arrival of Judge Valdez and his secretary, Beatriz, who were duly removing "the seal of the Third Penal Court to the offices of the Simón Bolívar Airport" thus making the inspection "official."

"Here comes the big cheese," I whispered to Dave, "get back into your act."

Dave grinned and said, "Shoot, if you want I'll give him a couple of wrenches and work his ass off," and then, louder and with an all-business look on his face, "Bobby, pull the hellhole cover. I'll, get the batteries ready and you can hand them to me when I'm inside."

"I don't want to seem dumb, Dave, but where is the hellhole?"

I wanted to know. Dave told me to wait and see, and in a few seconds had taken a screwdriver and removed a panel located on the bottom of the fuselage, between the engines.

The panel opening was only about twenty-four inches by twenty-six inches. Dave squatted down and slowly stood up inside the hellhole. All that could be seen of him were his legs from the hips down.

"Hand me a half-inch wrench, and I'll get these old batteries out of here," Dave shouted. I lay down on my back and handed him up the wrench. He looked down at me and said, "Now you know why it's called the hellhole—it's pure hell just getting inside, not to mention working once you are in there. Stick around, I'm going to need you to help me with the batteries."

In five minutes, he shouted, "OK, here comes one. Don't drop it."

Dave pushed his body back against the opening, sucked in his non-existent gut, squeezed the battery down between his stomach and the other side of the opening, and I lowered it down once it was clear.

"You'd better lay off that fattening Colombian food, Dave," I warned him. "If you gain a couple of pounds, you wouldn't be able to do that."

Dave called for the new batteries and I handed them up to him. I could hear grunts and muffled curses and see Dave's legs bracing and replanting as he struggled inside the fuselage. In about fifteen minutes, he crawled out, wringing wet.

"OK. Electrical is done. Get me the hydraulic fluid and we'll service the reservoir."

I walked over to the truck, and Valdez approached, greeting me with a friendly but professional, "*Como esta*, Bobby?"

"*Muy bien, gracias*," I replied, equally formally. We were both aware that we had to appear to be at arm's length and couldn't look to be overly friendly in the presence of the soldiers.

"I can see that you are all busy; please go on with your work. I will stay over here with Donado," Valdez observed.

He, too, wanted to know where the mechanic was, and I pointed to Dave, still wiping the sweat from his eyes. The judge looked first at Dave and then back at me, just as incredulous as Donado had been. "He looks like a *nino* (boy)," was Valdez's comment.

I had Raul explain that Dave's diminutive size was an invaluable asset in addition to his high technical qualifications, and that the judge could see for himself as soon as Dave would get back into the hellhole. Valdez watched as Dave again disappeared into the fuselage. Turning to join Luis Donado, I saw Valdez walk off, chuckling to himself and shaking his head in amazement.

After Dave finished in the hole, we climbed into the cockpit and Dave flipped on the master switch. We were glad to see there were no major electrical problems. All the lights for fuel pressure, oil pressure, generator, stall warning, and the others lit up perfectly. Then Dave turned on the auxiliary hydraulic pump. It started building the hydraulic pressure. Next, we lowered the flaps, slowly and cautiously. They creaked and groaned in protest, they were dry and badly needed lubrication. When they were fully lowered, we extended the spoilers or speed brakes.

Our next step was to inspect these parts of the plane. After getting out of the plane, we headed under the fuselage. Dave snapped down the gear doors, which loosened several mud dauber nests that cascaded over us. We had to come out from under the plane to shake the dirt from our hair and clothing, while the rest of the crew were having a laugh at our expense. Dave quickly turned the tables on them, however, when he ordered them to take long screwdrivers and clean out all the nests while he removed the engine covers. Their grins disappeared. Nobody wanted this dirty job.

After removing the lower engine covers, we spent the next hour pulling the oil screens and fuel filters. They were surprisingly clean and we found that another piece of luck had fallen to us: the fuel controls still had jet fuel in them, which had preserved the interior diaphragms and seals. Had they been dry we would probably have been in for some serious problems.

After a thorough examination of the engines, we installed new filters and screens and refilled the engines with new oil. We also installed new igniters on both engines. Dave spent the next half-hour inspecting wheel wells, flaps, controls, spoilers, and ailerons; and I resumed my secretarial duties, taking his dictation.

We were putting on a good act and could see that Dave's stock was going up with Donado and Valdez. It was a fact that Dave never wasted a single second, and Valdez remarked, "That mechanic isn't going to overlook anything."

When we were finishing the inspection, I drew Dave aside into a private pow-wow. "Tell me honestly, no bullshit. Will she fly? Do you think she's worth taking back?"

"You're lucky. She's in excellent condition, especially considering she's been here for three years next to salt water. The corrosion is only on the surface; it'll clean up easy. The engines look good on the outside. With three days of ball-busting work, we'll fly her away."

I had been sure of all this myself, but I had wanted to hear it from Dave, as he was much more qualified than I to pass a final opinion.

"Great," I said, "but don't let Donado and Valdez know. Tell them that it seems to be in fairly poor condition but that you feel, at this point, that it can be repaired. Point out that some of the areas affected by the corrosion are in semi-critical condition and that something has to be done—and soon—to preserve it; otherwise, it will be nothing more than scrap metal."

I also warned him not to commit himself to an opinion on the engines; they would have to be run before their internal condition could be determined. And that there was a small amount of corrosion in the fuel cells that would have to be treated immediately.

"What I want, in short, Dave, is that you convince them we're not talking about a million-dollar airplane anymore and that, very soon, they won't have anything. This will put a little pressure on the judge to get the lead out of his ass and do something pretty quick about the release."

Dave was already two steps ahead of me. His face lit up and he said, "Don't worry. I have just the thing to get them off the pot. Let's go in the cockpit a minute."

We climbed in and sat in the pilot and copilot's seats.

"Now, what we're going to do is this, Bobby. I'm going outside and will stand next to the left engine. When I yell and ask you to hit the start switch, hit the switch; wait two seconds, then hit the air ignition. Wait another two seconds and turn them both off at the same time. Don't screw up, and do it in that exact sequence."

"Dave, you SOB," I said, "are you going to give them the old 'stuck vane' routine? Damn, why hadn't I thought of that!"

It was a brilliant idea. When they heard those igniters cracking they would shit in their pants.

"You've got to be the one to tell Donado," I told Dave. "I don't think I can play it straight. If you do it, it'll get their attention."

Dave climbed out and walked around to the left engine.

"Wind her up," he yelled. I turned on the battery master and hit the start switch. *One thousand one, one thousand two,* I counted. Air ignition on. Immediately the air igniters cracked like a whip. One thousand one. One thousand two … .

"Stop," Dave called. I turned everything off and jumped out.

"What happened?" I asked.

Donado, Valdez, and everyone else came hurrying over. The stage was set.

"I don't know," Dave said, "let me check something." He climbed on the wing and stuck his head in the engine air inlet. Several seconds later, he looked at me and said, "Let's try her once more."

Everyone was standing close by. Dave ordered, "Crank," and I went through the same procedure. Then Dave ordered me to stop. I left the air ignition on and turned off the start switch, to make sure they heard the ignition cracking. Then I turned off the air ignition and jumped out.

"What's wrong, Dave?" I wanted everyone to pay close attention.

"Did you hear that cracking noise?" Dave demanded, but before I could say I had, Valdez wanted to know what was wrong, and what the noise had been. Donado was also very curious. Dave was ready for them.

"The engines haven't been run for such a long time that the vanes in the compression section are starting to lock up due to the corrosion. That popping noise is made when they break loose. If one of the vanes comes loose while it's running, it'll blow the engine into a million pieces." He looked around at his audience to impress on them the seriousness of the matter. "These engines have to be serviced very soon. If not, they won't be worth the price of scrap metal," Dave made this pronouncement with great solemnity and finality, the curtain falling on a command performance.

Donado then stepped forward and took charge. This was an area where *he* was in control.

"Dave," he asked, all professional, "what can you do to correct this problem?"

Dave explained that there was a special solution for compressor corrosion. The engines were first washed down with the solution and then soaked it in. With the engines running on idle, they were sprayed again with the solution. This would cure the problem. "But we can't wait much longer," Dave warned.

Our little mind game was something of a calculated risk, but one well-worth taking. First of all, our demonstration of a non-existent critical condition was much more dramatic than just listing ten or twelve smaller but very real problem areas that did require immediate attention, but which would have been hard to explain due to their more technical nature.

Second, Donado and Valdez were now convinced of Dave's expertise, and Donado, as the court-appointed "expert," notwithstanding his lack of experience with Learjets, was being placed in the limelight and would have to produce an answer everyone had been waiting for to the question of whether 464 Juliet could be made airworthy.

"Yes, it's obvious," he agreed. "The engines must be serviced very soon." As Donado spoke, I could see a "seventy-five thousand dollars down the drain" look cross Valdez's face, which gave way to a flood of relief as Dave said, reassuringly, "I'm sure they will be OK as long as we act fast," and then he turned to me asking, "The oil pressure came up OK, didn't it?"

"Thirty pounds before I shut the engine off," I replied. Dave nodded, satisfied.

After several minutes of related conversation, Donado was ready to decide on the question of 464 Juliet's chances, and he turned to Dave to have it straight.

"Mr. Donado, I can repair it to airworthy condition, with help, in five or six days. There is no question in my mind that it can be made 100 percent airworthy, provided it is done soon."

Judge Valdez's expression revealed that he was now off the hook with regard to earning his fee. However, he was now under pressure to expedite the release of 464 Juliet I hoped.

Donado was speaking to Dave, telling him to have the crew pack up the equipment and secure the plane. "Bring me a written report to my office in the morning," he said, "and we'll do whatever is necessary to expedite this matter."

I also had a request. "Luis, I am going to have to take the NICAD batteries out to take back to the States. They have to be deep cycled by a special charger and I'm sure there isn't one in Barranquilla. Would this be all right?"

Donado wasn't familiar with NICAD batteries, but he turned to Valdez to ask if Valdez would object to this. Valdez seemed dubious about letting any part of 464 Juliet out of Colombia. He immediately wanted to know what was wrong with the ones we had used in the inspection. I told them that they had been borrowed, and that new ones would cost around five thousand dollars apiece, which I would not have to spend if I could recondition the old ones. This answer seemed to satisfy him, as he finally gave his approval, albeit grudgingly.

While Donado and the judge spoke together we cleaned up and prepared to go. Dave had the key. The door was electrically operated, and, now, with the batteries installed, we were able to lock it up for the first time in three years. Valdez left us, asking that we telephone him the following day.

We walked over to the loaded truck, all of us, excepting Aldo, looking as if we had spent the day in a pigpen. Aldo was a real expert at getting out of the dirty jobs, but I had no complaints about my other amigos—they had done a great job. We got aboard the truck and headed back toward Barranquilla, stopping to drop Aldo and our equipment in Ciénaga. Dave and Donado spent most of the trip talking about 464 Juliet, with Dave at one of Raul ears and Donado at the other. Raul's look of concentration and his swiveling head, going back and forth, made him look as if he were watching a tennis match while delivering a bilingual commentary for two experts.

By this time, Donado seemed most impressed by Dave and had given him an official seal of approval. He also acted pleased that 464 Juliet had been found potentially airworthy, satisfied that he had been the fount of authority during the inspection.

After a much-needed shower and a hearty meal of French fries for me and seven courses for Dave, we sat down to prepare the inspection report to give to Donado the next day. Dave wanted to know if we were going to start the repairs right away.

I was wondering myself, and I turned to see what Raul thought about it.

"Well," he said slowly, "we're supposed to call Valdez in the morning." My heart sank; I could see that Raul was doubtful, too. "We'll see Donado first thing in the morning."

The fact that neither Donado nor Valdez had mentioned anything about commencing the work was an ominous sign, and I could see that we were going to have yet another reoccurrence of the *Mañana* Syndrome.

Toño and Aquiles had already joined us and a knock at the door announced the arrival of Fernando and Donado Jr. Dave, who by this time had finished the report, got up to greet them, advising all that he had the deck of cards ready and asking if he should call room service for food and drink since we now had a full house.

JUNE 12, 1980—BARRANQUILLA, ANOTHER OBSTACLE AND OUR RETURN TO MIAMI

The next morning, we were at Donado's office shortly after eight. I could see him on the telephone through the glass window. He was laying down the law to whoever was on the other end and looked as if he was in a bad humor. However, when he saw us, he smiled and motioned for us to enter. After exchanging greetings, we sat down and Dave handed Donado the report.

I took the bull by the horns immediately, "Do you think we can start work tomorrow?"

Donado laughed, a little shamefacedly. "No, it doesn't work that way here," he said. "First, I have to write a formal report to Judge Valdez. After he receives it, it's up to him to decide when you can begin."

My heart sank. I had suspected there might be another delay, but I hadn't been quite ready to face the fact that this would be the case.

"How long will it take, Donado?"

"Take it easy, Bobby. I'll try to take care of it this week. It might be a good idea to go back to Miami and keep in touch with me and the judge from there. In the meantime, I'll try to get things moving."

I was bitterly disappointed, but tried to force a smile. We had, after all, made a giant step forward the day before, and I didn't want to spoil that. So I mustered up a cheerful tone and replied that I understood, and, that, yes, we would plan to leave after we had talked with Valdez. I thanked Donado again for all his help and support, promising to call him within a few days.

When we stepped out of Donado's office into the open-air second-floor corridor Raul pointed out an old Lockheed T-33 jet fighter that we could see on the field below.

"That's our modern Air Force," he remarked.

"Don't knock it," I reminded him. See those small holes in the nose? Those 50 caliber machine gun bullets are just as deadly now as they were in the 1940's."

"That may be true," Raul replied, "but these old jets sit around broken down more than they fly. In the last five years they have only shot down a couple of marijuana planes."

"Maybe so," I said, "but I still wouldn't want to be the one they're chasing."

We returned to the hotel, and in the room, along with our usual crew were three new faces. Everyone had just finished an "on the house" breakfast special. I had not been in a good mood to begin with and I wanted to throw them out bodily, but Raul came to their rescue and asked them to leave as we had to make some important phone calls.

We placed the call to Santa Marta, and the operator called us back about half an hour later. Raul went through the regulation few minutes of polite inquiries about health, etc., with the judge before I nudged him impatiently to get on with the real reason for the call.

My spirits continued to droop as I listened to Raul's "*Si, señors*" and "*Comprendos,*" which indicated clearly that the *Mañana* Syndrome had reappeared in full force. I turned around and walked over to the window, staring at the mountains, chafing with frustration.

After Raul finished this unsatisfactory conversation, he told me that the judge had been pleased with the inspection but had to wait until he got the official letter from Donado before we could touch the jet. Dave sensed that something was wrong, and asked what was going on.

I gloomily told him that we would have to go back to Miami and return later since Valdez had informed us we could do nothing until he received Aerocivil's recommendation in writing.

"Everyone here in Colombia is scared to death about doing something wrong with 464 Juliet. There's nothing we can do but wait, but I not going to do the waiting here and listen to the *mañana*s for another day. I'm getting out of here."

Everyone put forth an effort to cheer me up which I appreciated, but I still felt frustrated and resentful and growled non-stop while we packed to leave. To add to my general bad mood, when we arrived at the airport we were informed that the flight to Miami had been canceled. Our only option was to go to Bogotá and catch a later flight to Miami that evening, which we did.

I wasn't going to spend another night there, not for anything in the world.

CHAPTER TWENTY-FIVE

Terry, my sons Jay and Jeff, my oldest daughter Terri, and my "baby" Jaime sat around father at the breakfast table. I felt like an honored guest. Terry had fixed me my favorite breakfast—eggs just right, crisp bacon, my old Alabama standby, grits, and a large, cold glass of fresh-squeezed orange juice. Everyone was sitting listening with rapt attention as I gave them a G-rated version of dad's adventures in Colombia. They were laughing about the struggle with the mud dauber nests in 464 Juliet, and how Dave had managed to change the batteries in the hellhole, complete with huffs and puffs and 'shoot's.' Terry, who was aware of the darker side of the frustrations and problems, leaned close, shot me a wicked look, and whispered, "You sound just like Captain Kangaroo."

I couldn't top that, so I got up and armed with lots of hugs and kisses, started for the office.

The next couple of days were spent in revising my parts list, ordering additional items, and in updating all my connections on progress in Colombia regarding 464 Juliet. I spoke with Paul Engstrom in California, who was highly satisfied with my compliance with the conditions of obtaining legal documentation. Peter Nash in London was also pleased to know that I was fulfilling the conditions of the contract. Jim Burkett and Red Garglay both were given lengthy accounts of the results of the latest trip.

I also visited Jack Wood at the bank. He was a little concerned at the endless delays, but since he was a retired Air Force colonel, he could relate to the "hurry up to wait" situation, which he knew was standard operating procedure for Colombia. In fact, Jack had been exposed first-hand to the *Mañana* Syndrome as his bank had a Navajo that had been confiscated in Colombia, and they were having their share of problems, just as I was.

JUNE 17, 1980—MIAMI, ED JACKSON, An unfortunate soldier of fortune

By June 17, I was finished with what I had to do in Miami and was getting itchy to get going. July 10, the day marking the end of the six-week period I had for getting 464 Juliet released, was drawing nearer, and my timetable was getting badly screwed up. I called Raul into the office so that we could place a call to Donado to find out whether the necessary exchange of reports and letters had yet passed through the machinery of Colombian red tape. While I was outlining to him the questions I had for Donado, my intercom buzzer sounded and I picked up the phone.

"Mr. Wood, there's a Mr. Ed Jackson here to see you," the receptionist announced. I told her to send him in, asking Raul to excuse me, that we would get back later to the call to Colombia.

A few seconds later, in walked Ed Jackson wearing an expensive ten-gallon cowboy hat on his head, heavy gold around his neck, and a wide smile on his face. Ed was a real Wild West character, complete with a laconic cowboy way of talking, goodhearted and happy-go-lucky. Rumors floated around from time to time about his involvement in drug smuggling, and it was a fact that he had been busted once in a DC-6. There were also rumors that he was an informant. Whatever side of the street he was working, I felt, was his own business. In any dealings I had had with him, he was always "legitimate"—i.e., he had rented 152s and 172s, occasionally, for instruction and local flights only, and I had never run into any problems with him.

At that time, I owned and operated a comfortably successful Cessna dealership and FB0. It shouldn't come as a surprise to anyone to learn that everyone in the aviation business in South Florida would—some sooner, some later—learn the score, even if the majority of them never once played the game. My business was my livelihood and on my end it was kept clean. This was not always easy. I walked a tightrope to keep it that way, and the constant and unremitting concentration to maintain balance over a narrow strip of neutral ground was what eventually prompted me to divest myself of it and get into a related, but less demanding, line of the aviation business.

It would be foolish to suggest that all of the wide variety of people I dealt with on a daily basis were pillars of society. I had a few simple rules for conducting my business and keeping it legitimate: Anyone who had the price of an airplane or equipment was welcomed as a customer and I maintained confidentiality. If a buyer said he was Mickey Mouse and wanted the bill-of-sale sent to Disney World, I didn't question it. If I was paid in cash from a paper bag full of money, I didn't ask for bank references. However, once the transaction was completed I would make the deposit at my bank, and that was the end of the deal. I also strictly enforced the rule that charters of multi-engine and high-performance aircraft were flown only by our own pilots, who were hand-picked, highly reputable professionals. With regard to smaller craft, anyone who rented these was well aware that anything questionable found in them after their return to our ramp would be turned over to the authorities, together with names. Nobody was going to mess around with my equipment. Sure, I could spot who was into drugs. Orders for long range equipment, portable ground-to-air-radios and such equipment were unmistakable clues.

Besides that, a good many of my cloak and dagger customers didn't use the cloak very much; they were very open about their activities and recounted their hairbreadth escapes with great enthusiasm and attempted to top each other's stories with great relish.

So, as I say, a lot of soldiers of fortune passed through my doors and I guess ole Ed Jackson fit into that category.

"What's happenin', Bobby?" Ed drawled.

"Keeping busy. What about you? Haven't seen you for a long time."

"I was over at Hanger One and just thought I'd drop by." We talked about who was doing what and where for several minutes when the phone rang. I excused myself and answered. It was Red Garglay.

"Hey, Red," I said, glad to hear his voice, "I just got back from Colombia and am almost ready to go back again."

Red was calling to give me the good news that his friend at International had my ferry permit lined up.

"That's 464 Juliet, isn't it'?" he asked.

"Right," I confirmed, "464 Juliet. Red, I'll call you back in a few minutes, OK?"

It was OK with, Red, and we hung up.

"Did I hear right? 464 Juliet?" Ed Jackson repeated. "What do you have to do with that plane?"

"I've been working on getting it out of Colombia for almost two months," I told him.

"Are you crazy?" Ed wanted to know. "Are you serious?"

"Sure," I said, puzzled. "Why? What do you know about it anyway?"

Ed laughed. "Enough that I sure wasn't going to get myself killed trying to get her out."

"What the hell do you mean? I got a lot riding on this, level with me."

"Well, Bobby, first of all, there are some real bad dudes involved. Besides, the United States government has been watching her with real close interest ever since that federal judge was killed. I tried to get it out last year and … ."

"Hey, Ed, back up there a minute. Start from the beginning. I need to know this. It's important."

"OK, sit back, and I'll tell you," and this was Ed's story.

"I was in Santa Marta, oh, I guess it was March of 1979, trying to get a friend, Dan Birch, out of jail. That's when I found out about the Learjet. Some people—some connections—told me what had happened and everything about why it was still sittin' there. So I went by and took a look at the plane. I got the N number off it and came back to the States. I contacted my banker. He was affiliated with the First National Bank of Little Rock. I told him I thought I could get it out. My banker told me that if I could make a deal, he could make a deal.

"Who could I make a deal with? Well, let's just say some friends down there who could arrange to give me a three-minute head start. Well, I was back here in the States for only two weeks to make the arrangements."

"What kind of arrangements?" I asked.

"With the bank for $250,000 to get the airplane returned. The original deal was for fifty thousand up front, but there were all kinds of things they wanted me to sign. Stipulations and all that shit that I couldn't go for. Hell, they had a million things I couldn't go for. You know, if this happened or that happened, I owed them fifty grand. So I just worked it out through my banker and he saw to it I was protected for the $250,000."

"Did you get to work on it?" I asked.

"Hell, no! Nobody would let me get near her. What did I carry down? Just a battery and a few tools, that's all. See, there was only one of the batteries missing."

I mentioned to Ed that I had found both batteries when we had inspected the plane, and he laughed and said, "Well, Bobby, one of them batteries you got is courtesy of ole Ed Jackson."

He resumed his story.

"Well, anyhow, I carried the battery down and gave it to my Colombian friends who were going to install it and get me the three minutes. Of course, like I said, I had never been able to inspect the plane. They'd never let anybody mess around it—Who?—the police, that's who. You had that problem, too? I'll be damned.

"My friends had it fixed that I was to wait until this certain shift was on, you know, at the airport. There was a girl who spoke pretty good English who did our talking between us. Her name was Mabel. Not like the telephone company, but in Spanish they pronounce it like that: "Ma Bell." Her father was a doctor there, in Santa Marta. She had a brother; he was one of my connections. They made arrangements for me to go to the airport when the special shift was on duty. It was early in the morning. Anyway, when I inspected that airplane, I decided right then and there that I wasn't going to fly it, not under any circumstances. Jesus, all the instruments were out of it and the nose was full of rocks. And corrosion, all over the control surfaces … all over. It was hard to tell where else it might be. It didn't have nothing. I mean, you couldn't convince me that I should get in there and just fly it off without getting to run it. What they wanted to do was say, 'OK, start engines,' and then 'Go.'"

I interrupted to ask what he had been going to do for jet fuel.

"Jet fuel? There was plenty of jet fuel, not out of the ground, but in fifty-five-gallon drums. Shit, they wanted $1,280 per drum. And they had a whole truck full. I guess it was for some dopers; I don't know. Anyway, we had the batteries in, and they wanted to get it started and running. But I had another problem. See, at that time I had a plan where I was going to take this guy out of the jail down there. I was going to do both things at once: get him out of jail, then make a run for it to the airport, pick up the Learjet, and get back home.

"At the time, see, the DAS had a helicopter, a Bell 47J at the north end of the airport. We didn't have keys or nothing, but we had a plan to get them and swipe the helicopter and then bring him back in it to the airport and make a run for it to come home. No shit. That was the plan. And when I got back, I'd be $250,000 richer and old Dan would be back at home, free."

"What soured it?" I asked.

"I'll tell you what soured it, that Learjet's what soured it. I always thought I'd fly in just about anything if it'd start, but—huh-huh—I couldn't see no way to fly that baby, no way. I got to thinking that I'd be getting up to the end of the runway and have to abort, and, then, I'd be back with my buddy in the Santa Marta jail. Even so, I might have tried it if I could've come in there, you know, started it and run it up to see if the engines developed full power and how much power they would pull. But no way was I going to land the helicopter at the end of that runway, jump in the jet—they were going to have the engines already running—and then just blast off into whatever with a three-minute head-start and be gone. No way."

We were both laughing when he finished the story of his aborted hijacking and rescue attempt.

"And what about your buddy in the Santa Marta jail?" I asked.

"Oh, we finally got him out. A different way."

"How?"

"Pay-off and snatch, a combined operation. He was allowed out now and then, under guard, to go into town. Of course, you had to pay for this. These passes usually lasted for six hours. One day, the right guard was his escort, see, and we paid him off and he let Dan go. That way we had a six-hour start."

"How did you get him out of the country?"

"We had an airplane waiting," replied Ed. "He didn't go commercial ... we had a Queen Air waiting. Anyway, we got him home and that was it. But, hell, about that Lear, I didn't feel bad about not getting it out. My friends down there said that only God knows how many people had tried to snatch her over the years, but no one ever succeeded. There were a lot of other airplanes there too, even an old B-25."

"The one on the right as you go into the airport?"

"Yeah, that's it. It didn't look like it would fly, though."

I told him it had been there since the late 1960s and was the first doper captured in Colombia. Both of us laughed at each other. Ed probably was thinking I was as crazy as he was. The funny thing was, I suspected he might just be right.

CHAPTER TWENTY-SIX

June 19, 1980—South Florida, Raul paints the town red

The first thing on my list that morning was to call Red Garglay. He had been helping me coordinate my ferry permit and had told me it should be ready that day. Before I could dial his number, however, Raul trotted into the office, with a "good news" look on his face. We had not been able to get through to Donado the day before, and I was sure that Raul had finally been able to make the call.

"Donado told me he would have his report finished for the judge by this Friday," he announced happily. This information lifted my spirits. We were getting some action.

"When does he want us to come down?" I demanded. Raul didn't know, but he had a sizable shopping list that Donado wanted us to bring down for him when we came.

I looked over the list. It was mostly parts for his truck, but he had included one item that gave me some misgivings: three gallons of red Imron paint for his truck.

"This paint's going to be a problem," I told Raul. "It's against the law to carry paint in a passenger plane, especially the Imron thinner. It's flammable. They won't carry it on a passenger plane. Dammit, Raul, you should have thought of that."

Raul assured me that he had a solution. He would pack it in a toy box and send it as luggage. No problem.

I wasn't happy with his solution, remarking, "It's your ass, not mine. Just don't get caught." Raul nodded.

"Let's call Valdez now; it's early and he's probably at home." I reached for the phone and dialed the operator. While we waited, I explained to Raul, "Tell him you'll be down Friday and that you'll bring Donado's report to him by hand. Don't sound pushy. But we've got to get the lead out of his ass. Don't forget my deadline with Lloyd's runs out July 10." While the number continued to ring, I gave Raul yet another valid reason to give Valdez for our trip. We had, in fact, landed some bona fide leads on the radios stolen from 464 Juliet, and we had some people in Santa Marta to see about them. I also reminded Raul that the most important thing was that he should try to pin Valdez down on how soon we could start working on 464 Juliet.

After several tries, the operator finally had our Santa Marta number ready.

"*Como esta, Sr. Juez* (Judge)?" Raul inquired respectfully. The judge apparently was very well, I gathered, from the happy expressions of satisfaction from Raul, and the judge was equally pleased to find Raul in good health.

They finally got down to business, and I sat there impatiently, waiting to hear what Raul had found out. "Valdez didn't mind at all that we called him at home," he began, after hanging up. "Everything is OK. He said it wasn't necessary for me to bring Donado's report, that he would get it in the mail in two days. It will take about a week to write an order from the court for us to start work. One funny thing—he said that when I came to Santa Marta about the radios I should stop by and see him—alone, without Aldo."

"Why do you think that is?" I asked.

"He didn't say. Just that he wanted to talk to me. I think it's a good sign," was Raul's opinion.

I was very curious as to why Valdez wanted to see Raul alone, but whatever the reason, this was a new development and might be important.

We spent most of the day gathering up Donado's parts, which amounted to around $375, most of it in paint. When we got back, Raul lugged it to the interior shop and carefully packed it into a large carton.

"See, Bobby," he stood back to admire his work, "nobody'll ever know what's inside. It looks like an ordinary package."

"I hope for your sake they don't drop it."

"Bobby, it's going as luggage. They won't drop it."

I leveled a look at him that said I was washing my hands of the matter, and again warned him that it was his neck on the line, not mine. Actually, I had to admit, Raul's carton did look a lot like every other carton that many Latins typically pack up for return trips home, seldom having enough suitcases to carry the great bargains and purchases they have made while in the States.

JUNE 20, 1980—SOUTH FLORIDA, AN UNSETTLED WEEKEND, DISAGREEABLE NEWS

It was two thirty when I got back to the office from my trip to take Raul to the airport. Terry walked in with a "Back already?"

"Raul must be in the air by now," I remarked.

"You know, Bobby, this is getting to be pretty expensive. Are you getting anywhere with it?"

She was not complaining, just asking. I felt she deserved a serious answer but couldn't bring myself to tell her exactly how much the frustration and delay was taxing my brain and my emotions.

"Yes, I'm getting somewhere with it," I said slowly. "I think I have a handle on it. I'm sure I can pull it together. I have faith. Please have it, too."

She smiled, nodded, and patted me on the cheek.

Our serious moment was interrupted by a phone call from Aerocondor Airlines. The minute I heard who it was I groaned to myself and thought, *Oh, no.*

"Is this the management of Air Unlimited?"

"Yes, it is."

"This is Mr. Rodriguez. We have a box down in the baggage area that has been damaged. It has an Air Unlimited label on it, and the name of Raul Soto on it. I wonder if you could come down here as soon as possible."

"Well," I lied, "I don't know what it's all about, but I'll be glad to come down there. We do have an employee named Raul Soto ... ," and I took down the instructions for finding Mr. Rodriguez.

Thirty minutes later, I was in Mr. Rodriguez's office.

"Come with me, Mr. Wood," he said. I went with him to the baggage area and my worst fears were confirmed. There was the carton sitting on a luggage dolly, in a large inch-deep puddle of firetruck-red paint. A trail of the paint led to the outside area.

"Would you please open it, Mr. Wood?"

I made a motion to begin tearing open the wrappings, and suddenly realized that I was not supposed to know anything about the package, so I stopped and turned to Rodriguez.

"Just a minute. Are you sure it's legal for me to open this? It isn't my property."

Even though I had told Raul that it wasn't going to be my ass that got in trouble, Raul's ass was comfortably resting in an Aerocondor seat thirty-five thousand feet in the air, on its way to Colombia. I was damned sure going to cover mine on the ground right there in Florida.

"This isn't yours?"

"No, sir," I said seriously. "Raul Soto works for me, that's all. It's my company's label, but that doesn't mean the box is mine."

"Well, let's open it anyway," he said. When we had the top off, we could see that two lids had burst off their one-gallon cans when the carton had been dropped. Inside was a gory mess. Fortunately the cans of thinner had remained intact and their labels were completely drenched in paint.

"This is a serious offense, Mr. Wood," I was told. "It's extremely dangerous to take flammable material aboard an aircraft." Since this was the dialogue I had written and delivered to Raul the day before, I could only nod and agree.

"You're 100 percent right, Mr. Rodriguez," I replied, "You'll have to see Raul Soto about it. I came down here to try to be helpful …" and went on to try to establish myself as an interested but innocent bystander.

We had several minutes of discussion which included threats of prosecuting Raul. As a favor, I agreed to clean up the Aerocondor equipment, to remove the package, and to take it back to Air Unlimited to await Raul's return. Needless to say, I ruined a good pair of pants, a shirt, and a pair of shoes, not to mention the back of my El Camino. It was nine at night by the time I got back to my place and cleaned up the parts that had not been ruined. As I worked at this messy job, I was designing the broadside Raul would receive from me as soon as I saw him again.

I spent the rest of the weekend waiting to hear from Raul. I knew it was difficult to place outgoing calls from Barranquilla, especially so through a hotel operator. Sometimes it took sixteen hours or more.

Finally, around ten o'clock Sunday night, the phone rang. Jay answered it, telling me that it was long distance, with Raul on the other end.

"Bobby," Raul said anxiously, without any preliminaries, "we got some problems. Aldo has been in a car accident. He's in the hospital at Ciénaga."

"How did it happen? Is he badly hurt?" I wanted to know.

"Take it easy, Bobby," Raul said. "He's going to be OK; he's just cut and bruised—real bad. But we got more problems than Aldo. You remember that lawyer from Cartagena? Ortiz? He's involved somehow. I don't know how, exactly. I'm going to Ciénaga tonight and see Aldo tomorrow. But Bobby, we got a bigger problem than these."

"What do you mean bigger? Hell, it can't get much worse."

"You know Diego? At customs?"

"Yes, I knew Diego at customs. What about Diego?"

"When I got here the other day, I saw Diego. He told me that an American government agent had been around asking about you and me."

"What? What kind of agent?" I asked.

"Diego didn't know. The man showed him a badge. He asked how often we were there and what our business was. Lots of nosy questions."

I told Raul that I would fly down in the morning. He was to check the first arrival of Aerocondor and Avianca and that I would be on the first. I would be the last one off the plane and he and Diego were to be there to meet me and make the usual arrangements, except that we would go around the left side of the building. Raul wasn't to screw up. He was to try to see Aldo that same night, not the next day, to find out what had happened so that I would know immediately upon my arrival.

My head was spinning as we said goodbye, and I needed to sit down and digest all the unpalatable morsels Raul had just served me. I outlined to Terry what had happened, and asked her to get me a suitcase ready for morning.

JUNE 23, 1980—BARRANQUILLA, ALDO OUT-OF-POCKET

The Aerocondor had landed in Barranquilla ten minutes before and unloading was delayed. The ground crew was having trouble with the portable steps. It was sweltering with the worst heat and humidity of the day, around two in the afternoon. Slowly the passengers started to deplane, cursing heartily in Spanish and wiping the sweat from their faces. There was no such thing as ground air conditioning or ventilation, and I was, as planned, the last one off the plane.

Raul and Diego were waiting and motioned me to walk toward them. After about fifty feet, they turned and walked to the side entrance to immigration. After a quick one hundred dollars for Diego and a couple of stamps, we moved outside where the usual crew, minus Aldo, was waiting.

I had to have a Coca-Cola so we stopped to pick up some cold bottles to take in the car. I was still trying to dry off the sweat that had been drenching me.

"OK, Raul," I finally said, "let's take one thing at a time. What about the papers from Donado? Did you get them?"

Donado had signed them Friday afternoon. Raul had a copy at the hotel for me. The original had had to go through official mailing. Raul had called Valdez and told him that we would see him that night or the next day, whatever I wanted.

"When can we start work? Did you ask him?"

Raul reported that Valdez had wanted to talk about that subject when we saw him.

"What did he want to talk privately to you about?"

Raul nudged me and brought a stubby finger to his lips.

Oh-ho, I thought to myself, *what is this all about? A private conference?*

I changed the subject to ask about Aldo. Aldo was all right but would have to stay in the hospital for another three or four days. I asked what the story was about Ortiz, the agent trying to horn in on the 464 Juliet deal for the California firm of Gordon & Sanford.

"You're not going to be very happy about this, Bobby," Raul began, "but they're trying to start more trouble."

"Just start at the beginning, Raul," I said patiently.

"Well, last night Aldo told me that he got a call from Ortiz about lunchtime on Saturday. Ortiz wanted Aldo to meet him that night at the Hotel Royal."

"Did Aldo say why he agreed to meet Ortiz?" I wanted to know.

Raul's brow creased. "Well … he said it was to protect your interests."

I snorted. I knew how Aldo protected my interests—like a fox in a chicken coop. I asked Raul to continue.

"Well, when Aldo arrived at the hotel, there was a message for him to meet Ortiz in the bar. Ortiz was with an American. Aldo said he didn't remember the American's name, but thought the man was from Nevada. They talked about the Learjet most of the evening, and asked him a lot of questions about Bobby Wood. What his business was, what kind of a person he was, what connections he had in Colombia," Raul said.

I was very curious to know what Aldo's answers had been as I was sure he had been very skillfully pumped. Raul said that the two men eventually got around to talking about Aldo, which was, of course, Aldo's favorite topic of conversation. They were interested in knowing what role he had been playing in getting the Learjet released. I had a pretty good idea that Aldo had painted himself as the prime mover.

Aldo also told Raul that Ortiz and the man from Nevada had offered him twenty-five thousand dollars to go to work for them and convince the judge that Ortiz represented the true owners. Ortiz claimed he could come up with documentation that would make my claim look bad and then, if Aldo could get them the jet, there would be an additional bonus.

"And what did Aldo say?" I inquired.

Raul just shrugged. "Aldo said he turned down the offer … but *quién sabe?*"

I was incredulous. I couldn't believe those men had been so stupid. Aldo, yes, but how could they imagine they could succeed? The only conclusion I could reach was that I had covered my advances sufficiently well that they hadn't been aware that Aldo was—I'm sure to his great regret—beyond the point of no return.

Still, I was seething as we dropped my bags at the hotel and left immediately for Ciénaga. I didn't even give a thought to the soldiers as we swept across the gateway to hell, as I was back to questioning Raul.

I wanted to know about the accident. Raul continued the story.

The three of them—Ortiz, Aldo, and the man from Nevada had talked and drunk until after four Sunday morning. All Aldo remembered was the car turning over and over, and, finally, someone pulling him out. It had happened about ten miles from Ciénaga. Raul had seen the car. Aldo had been lucky; the car was totaled with the roof crushed in. The only thing that had saved Aldo, Raul thought, was that he had been drunk. He had only needed fourteen stitches, but he was badly bruised. His eye was black and his nose purple and swollen. I figured that if Aldo hadn't taken over eight hours of solid boozing to make up his mind whether or not to sell me down the river, he wouldn't have been in his predicament, and said as much to Raul.

"The only reason he didn't switch sides was because Alfredo is involved, and he knows we are in tight with Donado. Besides, he knows that we have all the right documentation now. The only reason he said no was because he had to. It was too late for him to do business with anyone else."

While Gustavo and Raul engaged in an energetic and emphatic discussion about Aldo, I sat back, withdrawn into myself and willing myself to gather together my inner resources so that I could continue. I have always been a devout believer in God, and I prayed to him for strength. I had been so busy, I had almost forgotten that He was there but as I prayed, rattling over that road to Ciénaga, I truly felt His presence and was comforted.

From that night forward, when the pressures threatened to overwhelm me, I would pray and I received the strength to go on and the wisdom to act. In my heart, I knew that without divine help I could not finish the task I had set for myself. I was re-armed to deal with my present realities. As for the agent asking about us, I would forget it ever happened. I had done nothing illegal and if that person thought I had, he was just chasing his tail. As for Ortiz, he and his group were obviously desperate if they were seeking out Aldo for help. They were no longer a threat, just an annoyance.

As for Aldo? As an ally, he was a weak vessel and left much to be desired. But it was a reality that I still needed him for many reasons. Our airplane parts were stored in his house, which was a convenient and safe depot. He had some connections here that could either help us or harm us, and we obviously would prefer help. Furthermore, in spite of his initial attempt to bypass Valdez and pull a hit-and-run scam, he had connected us with the right person. And I still knew almost nothing about the financial arrangements that he and the judge had set up. Nor had Valdez given me the slightest clue concerning this important point. Aldo had to be included to the bitter end. He could make waves when, right then, even a ripple could sink us. I would still have to play the village idiot and would do it as long as necessary.

"Raul," I came to life, "when we get to the hospital, let's act very concerned. Play it up big, and don't give him any clues that we are onto him."

Raul thought it would be the best course of action. He and Gustavo then launched into speculation about the effect of the accident on Aldo's love life, Raul translating the choicer items for me, both of them laughing like hyenas.

We got to Ciénaga around six in the afternoon and pulled up to the hospital. It was only a small white cinder block building about thirty feet wide and sixty feet long. There were no separate rooms for the patients, it was like a military barracks with sheets hung between the beds to give a small amount of privacy.

A nurse pointed out Aldo's "room."

Aldo hadn't seen us come in and was enjoying an animated and smiling conversation with a pretty young nurse. At the sight of us he underwent an instant transformation. His head fell weakly back onto the pillow and his face became etched with pain. He extended a limp arm and moaned softly, just barely managing to get out, "Bobby … Raul … how kind of you to come."

True, he did look bad and I was sure that every bone and piece of flesh on his body ached. But he acted as if he were ready for last rites, and he put on a magnificent performance for all of us, which we acknowledged with worried looks, advice to take it easy, and general concern for the patient.

We chatted gently with poor Aldo for half an hour and as we prepared to leave, he looked at me dolefully. "Bobby, I have no, insurance or money to pay my hospital bills. Can you let me have a thousand dollars?"

I knew I couldn't aggravate his critical condition by refusing; so, I murmured, "Sure, Aldo. I only have six hundred dollars, though. I think that ought to cover it."

"Thank you, Bobby," he moaned, with lips trembling, while reaching out with his bandaged arm in great effort to accept the money. We assured him that we would be back the next day and tiptoed out.

Raul was his old, brisk self as we got back to the car. "Do you want to go see Valdez?"

"Did you bring the copy of Donado's paper?"

Raul had forgotten it in the hurry to get to Ciénaga, so we decided to head back for Barranquilla and call the judge from the hotel.

In the car, I suddenly remembered Raul's package and the red paint. "Raul, you SOB, you really got me in trouble in Miami. Aerocondor called me after you left, and I have news for you. They did drop the package, and I had to go to the airport to clean up the mess."

"I know," Raul said.

"How the hell did you know?"

He burst out laughing, and, between gasps, explained that he had been sitting on the right side window seat and saw the carton containing the paint drop from the top of the loaded baggage dolly and hit the corner … and then bounce back onto the bags.

"All of a sudden the red paint was pouring over the suitcases and dripping like blood. I slid down in my seat and picked up a magazine to pretend I had seen nothing. I was afraid they would come looking for me. Every time someone came down the aisle, I would slide down farther. I thought the plane would never leave."

He started laughing again, as he described the scene at the Barranquilla airport when the passengers found their paint-streaked bags.

"They were cursing and raising hell," he said happily, "even the unloaders had red hands."

I couldn't help laughing myself, and we both roared at the comical aspect of the sad consequences of Raul's eternal optimism.

When we got back to the hotel, we placed a call to Judge Valdez who invited us to meet him shortly after noon the following day. Raul mentioned that we had been to visit Aldo in the hospital. The judge had known about the accident but had not gone to see Aldo, which I felt was an unmistakable indication that Valdez was not very interested in Aldo's welfare.

In the meantime, Raul had taken out our copy of the Aerocivil document, which he had had translated for me. It was short and to the point.

REPUBLICA DE COLOMBIA
DEPARTAMENTO ADMINISTRATIVO DE AERONAUTICA CIVIL
Barranquilla, June 20, 1980 BQTL-423
Third Penal Court of the Circuit Santa Marta
With reference to your official memorandum No. 448 of May 26, 1980, I list below the results of the inspection made on the aircraft LEAR JET at the Simón Bolívar Airport in the City of Santa Marta.

On June 12, 1980, in the presence of members of your court and the Administrator of the Simón Bolívar Airport of Santa Marta, a technical inspection was made of the aircraft identified with Registration N464J, LEAR JET, Model 24, Series 164, with the following results.

The undersigned followed the questionnaire prepared by your Court, and reports as follows:

1. Aircraft LEAR JET, Model 24, Series 164, built in 1966, by LEAR JET INDUSTRY OF THE UNITED STATES, white with blue stripes, apparently abandoned on the premises of the aforementioned airport.

2. In accordance with information obtained, the aircraft in question had been parked more than a year at the Simón Bolívar Airport. For this reason, and in accordance with orders from the Air Force, as per specification AlOCE, the plane proper, its power plant and other elements composing said aircraft, had to be inspected.

3. In view of the above, in order to continue operation of the aircraft, it is necessary to change certain parts such as the brake assembly for the main landing system, its wheels and the set of wheels for the nose landing system. All the hydraulic system lines must be changed as well as the motor lubrication system and other items which the manufacturer specifies must be changed after six months of use of said aircraft.

4. For this reason, until the technical work and change of the parts mentioned above have been done on the aircraft, it cannot be passed as airworthy at this time as its local test flight must be made which will determine whether or not it is airworthy once the work has been completed.

Therefore, bearing in mind the present condition of the aircraft, its approximate value is estimated at more or less U.S. four hundred thousand dollars.

NOTE: The undersigned recommends that the interested parties obtain the services of a technical expert in this type of aircraft since there are no authorized shops (in Colombia) for doing work on this type of plane.

Very truly yours,
(signature)
Luis Donado
Chief, Technical Control Unit

Everything looked OK, but I was not happy about the value of four hundred thousand that Donado had assigned to 464 Juliet. However, it suited me better than the million dollars it would be worth once it was repaired and operating.

There was another lesser stipulation that was unnecessary: replacement of the hydraulic system lines. These were mostly braided stainless with a standard life of around ten years, but I felt sure we could get around that. Donado had also made a mistake on the age of 464 Juliet. It was manufactured in 1968 and not 1966 as written. This made it worth less than it actually was.

All in all, I was pleased.

CHAPTER TWENTY-SEVEN

Another urgent matter for me to deal with was Raul's "private conference" with Judge Valdez, but, as he had cautioned me not to ask him about it in front of the others, I had to wait. I found my chance when Fernando Donado showed up around ten-thirty to find out if I needed anything. I asked him and Aquiles, to go out and scout me something to eat. I had heard that somewhere nearby there was an "American style" place that made fair hamburgers. I was hungry for something more than potatoes, so I gave them money to get a burger for themselves and to bring some back for me and Raul.

As soon as the door had closed, I turned to Raul. "OK, Raul, talk. Why did the judge want to see you alone?"

"He's fishing," said Raul, giving me a knowing look.

"What for?" I asked, puzzled.

Raul began on an oblique tack. "Remember how many times we talked about getting in with the judge?"

I nodded.

"Well, Bobby, it looks like he wants to get in with you. He came right out with it. He asked me if I thought you would be interested in getting into the 'business' with him."

My jaw dropped. I stared open-mouthed at Raul. "You mean the judge is into marijuana? Raul, stop jerking me around."

"I promise you, Bobby," he said earnestly, "he has his own plantation—a big one—a brand new airstrip, new equipment, everything. All he needs is a good connection in the States. You know how scared he always acts? He's looking for somebody he knows he can trust. He likes you. He feels safe with you. That's what I think."

"But Raul, he's a judge," I said. "Every move I've seen him make has been to cover his back, to protect his position as a judge. Look how it was until Alfredo got into the picture—Valdez wouldn't move until he knew he was covered up there in Bogotá."

"Bobby, you don't understand," Raul insisted. This was one of the rare times he lost patience with me. He sat me down and instructed me on some new Colombian realities, realities I hadn't known existed ... .

"Listen, Bobby, how much do you think a judge—even a big judge—makes?"

I hadn't any idea.

"Not as much as I do," Raul informed me. He went on to explain that no Colombian in his right mind would seek an official position unless he had a substantial outside income. Or unless he wanted that position so that he could generate an outside income. If that person came from a wealthy family, fine. If not, there were other ways to supplement an insufficient income.

That was the basis for the ingrained institution of bribes. The bigger the job, the bigger the bribe. This went from bottom to top, beginning with those pitiful excuses for policemen at the bridge, thugs who literally couldn't feed their children on their tiny salaries and therefore were motivated to further dehumanize themselves by degrading those who had to cross their turf.

Other officials with even greater ambitions branched out into even more lucrative enterprises. Of course, the most profitable of all was "the business." This was especially true on the north coast of Colombia. Until recent years and the marijuana bonanza, very few opportunities existed for them. Now that the boom was on, everyone was getting a piece of the action.

When Raul finished, he sat back, folded his arms and glared at me. "This is how it is in Colombia."

I nodded thoughtfully and sat there, thinking over what Raul had just told me about life in Colombia. I knew I had to figure out the best way to deal with this the most recent head game to be waged—specifically, Judge Valdez's invitation to tango with him. One thing I knew for sure, I couldn't indignantly reject his proposal and push his hand off my knee like an insulted virgin. He would drop me and everything connected with me—464 Juliet—like a shot. Needless to say, I was not going to fall into his arms, either. If I had been interested in an illicit affair, I could have accepted offers from far better prospects than Judge Valdez. I could see that this was a mind game I would have to play with great care.

I got back to Raul. "Are you positive the judge is involved directly, or is he fronting for somebody else?"

"I'm positive the judge is all in. We talked for a long time. He's just nervous about asking you is all. And whatever happens, he doesn't want Aldo to know anything about this. Another reason why he's nervous about asking you is that he said he doesn't want to do anything to screw up the jet deal."

Well, I thought, since it was the judge who was mentioning the priority of the Learjet, I could use this as a reasonable stall on replying to his offer. I would work on convincing him that, yes, possibly, I could be interested, once

I had 464 Juliet safely out of the country.

Raul went on, "He felt that since you're a gringo and in the aviation business, maybe you've done some deals. That you're just being careful with him, too."

This I could use. If Valdez thought I might be "available" I could counter move. I could let him think he was courting me, persuading me, wearing down my resistance. But I would have to come up with a very good and logical reason for being reluctant. A tempting possible advantage of playing the game this way occurred to me. Valdez's desire to bypass Aldo suggested misgivings about Aldo's honesty. If this was the case, then the judge might reveal just what kind of a deal they had regarding release of the plane.

Aldo's insistence on exclusivity in handling the money end worried me. With all the secrecy, I had never had any way of leaning on Aldo to keep him honest with Valdez.

I had no illusions about possible pitfalls in this new mind game. It could be dangerous, very dangerous, if Valdez found out what I was doing. I had to play my role perfectly.

"Raul," I said, "this is too good to be true. It's the best way of all to get in with the judge—by letting him try to get in with us. But we can't let him take the upper hand. What I want you to do is to go back to him and tell him that you talked with me about doing business with him but that I was a little skeptical and that I sell a lot of airplanes to people in the "business" and that from what I have-seen lately, the problem is in the quality of the merchandise—almost everything coming to the States now is just green shit. That everyone is promised Colombian Gold, but when it gets here it's just junk. Tell him that if he can come up with a top-of-the-line, pure Gold, then I would be interested. I'd send him all the customers he can accommodate. If not, no problem. We'll still be friends. You might also mention that I've been approached by a lot of Colombians to go into the business but that I always turned them down because of the quality problem. Stress to him that I can produce if he can produce, then drop the subject and let's see what his next move is."

I was sure that his next move would be to want to talk with me personally and my move would be to do nothing—make him wait. Make him try to "sell" me on what he could produce.

I spoke to Raul with a lot more assurance than I felt. We were moving into an area that was heavily mined with dangerous booby-traps, not the least of which was that mysterious surveillance by someone from the United States government I seemed to be under. It would be one hell of a note to be busted for a fake interest in the "business." I would have to cover myself from all points of the compass.

I reminded Raul to stress first and foremost that I was heavily committed financially to the costly procedures of getting release of 464 Juliet, and that the quicker we could accomplish that task, the quicker we could get on to other matters.

We had finished our conversation by the time our amigos returned. The burger spot had been closed but they hadn't wanted to come back empty-handed so they handed me a bag of French fries, which I pecked at with little appetite.

Tuesday, June 24, was a hot day, even at sun-up; so, we decided to make an early start to Ciénaga and Santa Marta. At the gas station, Aquiles filled the radiator and his gallon jug for spare water, which he kept under the hood alongside the radiator. At the bridge, there was only an ID check, and we continued on our way.

When we pulled up in front of the hospital, both double doors of the entrance end of the patients' "barracks" were thrown open. We had a full view of the large room, all the way back to the rear wall.

"Look," Fernando yelled, "there's Aldo."

Aldo had seen us, too. He scurried out of sight and must have sprinted back to his bed because he was settling the sheet over himself as we came in.

"What are you doing out of bed, Aldo?" I scolded, with a concerned look on my face. Aldo gave me a piteous glance and moaned that he had been to the bathroom, that there was such bad service, that no one had been attending to his needs … We all nodded in commiseration.

Aldo wanted to know if we had seen his car, and I told him that we had first come to see him. That was more important. We would look at the car later.

"Aldo," I asked, "What am I going to do for a lawyer? I know you're not able to do anything yet, but I need someone to help me … ."

Aldo interrupted anxiously, and the look of pain at the thought of being dealt out at this stage of the game was very real.

"Don't worry about that, Bobby. I've talked to my brother, Gomez, in Bogotá about that. It was the very first thing I thought about after I regained consciousness …"

I bet it was, I thought.

" … and he's coming down to help us and to take care of the papers. He's an excellent lawyer. Don't worry. He'll stay as long as he's needed. No, no, no, everything will be just as it was." Aldo was becoming frantic in his effort to convince me that I would be in good hands.

It was time to give him a little reassurance. "OK, Aldo. But you make sure he takes care of everything. You're the only one who has the inside connection with the judge and we really need you."

The color came back to Aldo's face and he calmed down.

We talked for a short time about Donado's papers and told him that we were going to see the judge. He again became uneasy, but as there was nothing he could do about it, the only thing he could do was to apologize for not being able to go with us. We comforted him by saying that we would stop again on our way back to keep him informed of the results of our talk with the judge.

Our appointment with Valdez wasn't until 12:30 so we had some time to kill. I told Raul I would like to run over and take a quick look at 464 Juliet, just to be sure she was all right.

"No problem," Raul replied, and to Aquiles, "*Vamanos.*"

The airport was almost deserted when we arrived. There were almost never any private aviation activities in Santa Marta, due to the large number of clandestine strips across the area.

The big event of the day at Simón Bolívar airport was the arrival of the Avianca flights, and we had appeared at a quiet hour.

We parked, passed through the abandoned lobby and tried to open the gate. It was locked, so we took the quick expedient of jumping over the low wall. Our feet had scarcely touched the ground before Baratta, the fussy and bureaucratic assistant administrator, flew out and ordered us to stop. He motioned to the dozing guards taking a mid-morning siesta in the shade of the compound. They half-opened their eyes and got slowly to their feet with no show of enthusiasm whatsoever. Baratta was getting no support from the guards but he nevertheless launched into a loud and vehement tirade, stating that the gate was locked, we had no permission to enter the area, and that we must leave.

Raul was giving Baratta back as much lip as we were getting, mentioning the names of the judge and Luis Donado, pointing to 464 Juliet and to me, and making other loud noises. Neither of the two was listening to the other, both were yelling at each other at the same time. We finally left. Raul turned to fire a final salvo, warning Baratta that he would soon be put in his place.

When we arrived at Valdez's house, his Jeep was not in the driveway. Raul knocked on the door, informing *señora* Valdez that we were there and would wait outside for her husband. Valdez returned shortly, greeting us with a smile and a hearty handshake.

When we had been ushered inside his den we were served cake and coffee. During this time the usual foreplay concerning the state of each other's health went on, plus an account of the morning visit with Aldo and our most recent encounter with Baratta.

Finally, we were ready to talk about 464 Juliet.

Raul showed Valdez our copy of Donado's report. The judge read through it and said that he should be receiving the original in the next day's mail. He nodded as he examined the contents, murmuring "*muy bien*" at intervals.

"When can we start the repairs?" I wanted to know.

"I should have the papers ready in about a week. I'll let you and Raul know."

Hoping to exert a little pressure, I remarked that I hoped it would be soon since I was paying my jet mechanics a full time salary while we were waiting. I debated whether I should also mention my deadline which was rapidly approaching but was fearful of rocking the boat yet. I needed to be more solidly "in" with Valdez before hitting on him too hard.

Even by this time, Valdez was showing signs of hesitancy and uneasiness regarding the initiation of work on 464 Juliet, which somewhat upset me. Why in the hell was he dragging his feet? I also had the feeling that Valdez was waiting for me to bring up the subject of his "business," and, as my plan was to let Raul do the initial talking, I wanted to avoid getting into that matter. So, we talked aimlessly for a few minutes until the judge found a safer topic of conversation.

"Are you having any luck with the radios?" he asked.

"No," Raul answered, "but I have a few leads."

The judge told Raul that he would help if needed and that he would see that the thieves were jailed if caught.

"I have an idea it's the airport personnel," I said. "Mario at Avianca knows more than he's telling," and I dropped the subject. "I'm going back to Miami tomorrow, but Raul will stay here for a day or so, following up the leads on the radios. I'll be back next week."

The judge nodded, and we rose to leave. When we were walking to the car, Valdez motioned to Raul to drop back to talk with him in the far end of the driveway. They spoke in low tones with their heads together for several minutes. When Raul returned to the car the judge stood by the door, waving and smiling.

Raul said nothing about his conversation as we drove off, so I was sure it had been about the "business." I was curious to hear what had been said and if Raul had followed my instructions. However, this would have to wait until we had some time alone together.

We stopped in Ciénaga to inspect Aldo's car. Raul had not exaggerated. It was totaled. Then back to the hospital to tell Aldo how lucky he was and to report on our visit with the judge.

In the couple of hours we had been gone, Aldo had made remarkable steps toward recovery. He had obtained good mileage from his role as an invalid, but he now realized it was time to drop it.

"What did Valdez say?" were his first words.

"He sent his best wishes and hopes that you will soon be better," I told him. His eyes brightened. "But, Aldo, you know this is getting expensive for me. I need you, and I hope you will be out of here soon. I'm not a rich man, and it seems to me that everyone is dragging their feet. When we started this, you told me it would take a few weeks, but it's over two months now. You have to start pushing Valdez."

"Yes, yes … I know … but my accident has slowed me down temporarily. My brother, though, will speed it up. He is a very important lawyer in Bogotá."

I could tell by Aldo's reaction, and by the questions he asked and didn't ask, that he hadn't the slightest idea of the legal aspects and processing for release of 464 Juliet. What Aldo was concerned with was the money.

"You didn't talk about money with the judge, did you?" he whispered.

"Of course not, Aldo. You said never to discuss that with him." He was relieved and went on to explain that this was the way the judge had wanted it. When the jet was released, Aldo was to receive the money and would give Valdez his share.

"You know judges can't take money under the table," he said, adding, "It's illegal."

It was all I could do to refrain from bursting out laughing at this news, and I had to turn away and say something to Raul to control myself. When I was able to talk again, I bent down and spoke in a low voice to Aldo.

"Just to make sure there is no confusion, how much do you get out of the deal?"

Aldo explained that Valdez was to get fifty thousand dollars and that his own share was to be twenty-five thousand, hastening to add that his own cut had to cover his considerable expenses of a fee for his brother Gomez, telephone calls, gas, legal papers, and his own time.

"Sure, I understand, Aldo. I just want to make sure that the seventy-five thousand dollars covers everything."

Aldo assured me it did.

We left Aldo a happy and fairly healthy man as we departed for Barranquilla.

When we got into Aquiles' "limousine," Raul was chuckling, remarking that Aldo would make a great Colombian judge. We all burst out laughing at the idea of Aldo in public office. He would be able to screw things up on an even more monumental scale than they already were.

Aquiles and Raul chatted with each other in the front. I leaned back in my corner of the right rear seat, lulled by the clicking harmony of the loose valves in the engine. I withdrew into myself and stared out the open window at the ocean. My life in the United States seemed light years away. I was in an alien world, very real and very much around me. The endless problems and vicious games were taking their toll and clouding my mind and soul. Again I prayed silently for the forbearance and wisdom to keep the two worlds separate, hold on to reality, keep my inner identity intact while playing my different outward roles for the judges, the Aldos, the corrupt officials, and crooked lawyers, all waiting to pounce the moment I became vulnerable. I had to part the clinging strands of the complex spider web to reach 464 Juliet trapped in the center. I had to avoid being trapped myself. God would give me direction and strength.

It seemed like only a few minutes before we pulled up to the gateway to hell. After a routine check, Aquiles eased the car forward, only to halt when one of the soldiers blew his whistle and pulled us over to the side of the bridge. He gestured to the others to join him, and he advanced toward us. His uncertain gait and flushed face indicated that he had been drinking and was in an ugly mood.

"*Pasaporte*," he snarled at me.

Before I could reply, Raul was out of the car, telling the sergeant who I was and holding up Major Hernandez's letter.

"I know who he is," the sergeant grated out. "He's the gringo who has made problems for us here. We have a name for him. *Sr. Un Buendia* (Mr. One-Fine-Day). Because one fine day he will make a mistake and we will get him. All the other gringos pay here. He's the only one who doesn't."

Raul had the guts to give back as good as we were receiving, which discouraged the other soldiers from getting involved in the argument, but the sergeant continued bellowing and cursing us, raging like a maddened bull. Finally Raul was able to draw him aside, and I saw him slip a bill in the sergeant's shirt pocket.

I kept my mouth shut until he returned to the car and, when we drove off, I launched into him for having given the man the money.

"Wait, Bobby," he protested, "that guy is crazy. He told me that Hernandez won't be around all the time to protect you, and he's right. He said that one day, one night … they'll get you. They will, too. I know how they are. Don't report this to Hernandez; it will only make them meaner. Let's pay them a little, five or ten dollars. Just enough to keep them in a good mood. Then we won't have any more problems."

I was fuming, but knew Raul was right, so I agreed that we would do it his way. None of us liked it, but it was not too much to pay for our peace of mind. Besides, I was not deluding myself. I would equally be a partner to corruption when I would be paying off Valdez, through Aldo.

Back at the hotel, Raul and I took a walk outside, and I asked him what the judge had said when he had pulled Raul over to the side earlier. Raul gave me a wide smile, grabbed my hand and shook it. "We are een like fleent," he announced, pronouncing "In like Flint" in a most stereotypical Latino accent.

"The judge was a little disappointed that we didn't bring up the business while we were there," said Raul. "He's anxious to know what you want to do. But I fixed everything. I told him you could send him many clients—he liked that. And when I told him that you weren't interested unless he could give you pure Gold—he was telling me 'Yes, yes ... I have the best quality ... I deliver only Gold ... not green.' Oh, yes, he wants you to be certain of that."

Raul had apparently done a good job. The judge was now defending his merchandise and eager to persuade me. I fervently hoped that he would be motivated to speed along the release of 464 Juliet in my absence, as a demonstration of good faith.

Raul was excited, saying, "Bobby, I'm sure this will help get the Learjet out faster. You know how to work things. Maybe when you get the judge a few connections, we'll all be rich."

I was strongly tempted to warn Raul not to get too carried away because there would be no pot of Colombian Gold at the end of the rainbow, but decided against it. Raul needed all his wits about him, and I was afraid he couldn't think ahead far enough to play the role of a "double agent." It would be better for the judge to see those dollar signs in Raul's eyes shining bright and clear.

I would wait to tell Raul after we got 464 Juliet safely back home.

CHAPTER TWENTY-EIGHT

In the morning while Raul was helping me pack to return to the States, I gave him further instructions. After he took me to the airport, he was to go back to Santa Marta to talk with the judge. Just talk, with no particular stated reason, feel him out, study him, watch his eyes, and listen closely to how he answered questions. Raul was to learn everything he could about the judge so that I could understand him better. He was also to go to see Mario at the airport to see if he could pick up some information on the radios. When he had done everything, he was to return to Miami in a couple of days. Judge Valdez was to be informed that I was making plans to be back in a week or so.

We arrived at the airport by nine, spoke a few minutes with Luis Donado, and after a few last-minute instructions to Raul, I left for Miami.

I was in the office before eight, waiting impatiently for Raul's arrival. Everyone at Air Unlimited was full of questions about the release of 464 Juliet, especially Terry. When Raul finally entered, he wore a small proud smile, indicating that he had no bad news.

"*Mucho trabajo* (a lot of work)," he said importantly. "I spent most of my time in Santa Marta."

"What about the judge?"

"He's still a little nervous, but he said we could probably come down after July 4."

I was disappointed. "Damn, Raul, why so long?"

"He's trying to get his papers done right. That's what he told me," said Raul.

"Fine, I want him to have them done right, too, but what's he stalling around for? My contract expires on July 10."

"I know, Bobby ... ," and, then, Raul brought up the subject that really interested him—the "business."

"Valdez wants to get started. He asked lots of questions about you, the kind you asked me about him. He really likes you. He's anxious to talk with you."

I nodded and changed the subject to the radios. Did he have anything new on this?

Raul said he had been to the Santa Marta airport and talked with Mario. Mario promised he would have some leads by the time we got back. Raul had also met someone named Tomás, who ran the control tower, who thought he knew where some of the radio equipment could be found. Also another Colombian, named Manuel, who worked for Baratta, could also possibly help.

"You can talk to them when we go back. Both of them are in the 'business,' too."

"Are you serious?" I wanted to know.

Raul nodded. "Everyone in Santa Marta is in it. Well, most everybody," he stated positively. "Tomás can be important, because he's *jefe* of the control tower. He says who lands and who doesn't. He tells me his family has a plantation—they load lots of planes right there at the airport. The military helps them load, refuel—everything. When we go back, we should go and talk to him. Even if you don't do business, make him happy."

He didn't have many details first-hand about Manuel, but, still, Raul insisted, this Manuel could help us, too, so I should talk with him.

Damn. I could hardly believe the "business" was that open. No wonder one couldn't get a decent meal in Colombia—everybody with a patch of land was planting it in marijuana.

I was on the phone most of the day of June 28 trying to reach several pilots who might be available to fly 464 Juliet out of Colombia. I had talked with a dozen the month before with no results. The minute I mentioned 464 Juliet in Santa Marta, they were all suddenly booked up indefinitely. Most of them had heard of the plight of 464J and wanted no part of it. As for Santa Marta, forget it. Santa Marta was the Siberia of the tropics in aviation circles, and no "legitimate" pilot was the least bit eager to see its sights. Especially not the infamous Santa Marta jail where a lot of legitimate pilots had found themselves incarcerated on trumped-up charges, along with the "doper" pilots on substantial ones. On top of that, all were reluctant to fly a jet that had been sitting ignored and neglected next to the ocean for over three salty years.

Even had I found an interested pilot, I wouldn't have dared show him the photos of the instrument panel, and I shuddered to think of what he would have to say about the nose full of Colombian boulders.

However, perseverance is often rewarded. About three in the afternoon, I received a call from a hardy soul, Mel Cruder. Bill Jones at Jet Care had found him for me. Mel and I talked a few minutes. After I explained the situation, he was still willing to meet me the next morning—Sunday—to discuss it. I went to find Raul to tell him the news and to ask him to call the judge so that

I could make plans with Mel.

June 29, 1980—Miami, Pilot Mel Cruder joins the crew

Sunday was June 29. I got in about eight fifteen in the morning and found Raul there still trying to remove red paint from the parts. He had spoken with Valdez. His careful attention to a stubborn patch of paint and the absence of a smile on his round face told me that he had no good news.

"What did he say?" I demanded.

"Well, he says we can't come yet. He wants us to call him Tuesday night. He says he's still working on the papers."

"Did he seem friendly? Was he any different than the last time you spoke with him?"

"*Si, si,* very friendly. The same as always."

"Shit, Raul. I think Valdez is stuck in low gear. I don't believe he knows how to write the papers. God only knows Aldo doesn't … Do you think maybe we should get him some help?"

Raul didn't know—all we could do was to wait until Tuesday and see what Valdez had to say. He shrugged, extended his hands and said helplessly, "What else can we do?"

"Are things always this *mañana* in Colombia?" I asked.

Raul tried to comfort me, telling me that what we had done in the past two months normally would take eight months or a year. It was not like the United States.

"If we did things like that here in the States, we'd still be in the eighteenth century," I fumed.

"*Si, si,* Bobby, I know," Raul said soothingly.

The intercom switched on, announcing that I was wanted in the lobby.

"Come on, Raul, let's go. That must be our pilot."

Mel Cruder was not at all the way I had pictured him. On the telephone he had sounded like a man in his thirties, but at first sight I upped the figure to fifty. Later he told me that he was actually sixty. He was a clean-cut man of medium height and weight with a silvery crew cut. After we had introduced ourselves, I explained what I needed and he handed me his resume. His qualifications were impressive: he had many thousands of hours of jet time and numerous type ratings.

"Damn, Mel, it looks like you can fly anything," I remarked. "But I have to tell you, this is no piece of cake. Juliet has been sitting there for three years without any maintenance and without being flown. Dave Pearson has …"

"Dave Pearson?" Mel interrupted. "You mean Dave at Jet Care?"

"The very same," I replied.

"Hell, Dave and I are good friends. I'm an A & P mechanic, too. I can help Dave with the repairs." Mel was excited and enthusiastic. I didn't have to sell him at all. Lady Luck was finally smiling at me.

I showed Mel my photos of 464 Juliet, telling him that we still didn't know if she would fly, but that Dave had said she would.

"So if you want the job, it pays two thousand dollars to fly her out and one hundred fifty a day while you are working. I'll be your copilot, but I must tell you now, I have never even flown in a Learjet, much less right seat. What the hell, it's an airplane and a piece of machinery—I'll master it."

Mel was realistic. He remarked, "If you're crazy enough to do that, then I'm crazy enough to fly it. You just do what I tell you and there'll be no problems."

Mel wanted to know when we would leave. I shot a look at Raul and hesitated.

"Mel, I'll be honest. I think the end of this week or perhaps a little longer. I don't know for sure, but we may be there a week or more. Dave says we need three days of ball-busting work and then she'll be ready. That's all I know yet."

Mel nodded. We spoke for an hour or so. I told Mel about Dave's inspection and gave him a rundown of what I had been doing to get the plane released.

When Mel left, he shook hands with an "I'm your man" and said he would be waiting for my call within a few days.

"What do you think, Raul?" I asked.

"Of Mel? He looks good. Of you in the right seat? Ave Maria Santisima," and he rolled his eyes heavenward, then grinned and asked, "Are you sure you can do it?"

"Refugee, you must have faith."

"I have faith. What I don't have is the wish to die."

That afternoon at home, Terry, the kids, and I were starting to barbecue in the patio when my son Jeff called from the house that Raul was on the line. When I took the call, Raul told me that Valdez had just called. His *señora* was arriving in Miami the next morning to be with a relative in a hospital in town.

June 29, 1980—Miami, Judge Valdez requests a loan

"Valdez wants us to pick up the *señora* at the airport and take her to the hospital. And he asked me to call you to see if you could let him have five or six thousand dollars. I didn't know what to say."

"That's a lot of money, Raul," I said slowly. "Did he say what he wanted it for?"

Raul supposed it was for the hospital expenses.

"What do you think, Raul? What happens if we do not get the jet released? The judge will have the money, and I'll have nothing."

"I know," Raul was distressed, "but if you say no, what happens then? You'll still have nothing."

It seemed to me that I had no choice. I was going to have to ante up before the cards were even cut. Hell, I hadn't even seen the deck yet. But I was going to have to gamble. I had gambled before in business but this was the longest shot I'd ever taken.

"OK, Raul, call the judge and tell him I'll be glad to help in any way I can. But tell him also that I had been having problems finding a suitable pilot but that now I have one. Tell him that it is urgent that we fly down this week, or at least by next weekend, since I can't hold the pilot indefinitely."

Terry looked at me questioningly when I returned to the patio. I told her.

"How much have you spent on the jet?" she asked.

"Somewhere near twenty thousand dollars so far, out of pocket," I said, scaling the figure downward fairly substantially.

"That's quite a bit, on top of the rest you'll have to put out," she remarked. "I hope you know what you're doing. It seems a little too good to be true that you can spend a month or two down there and come out with a million dollar jet for—how much?—less than one hundred thousand dollars. My woman's intuition says that something is funny. Why hasn't someone else gotten it out before if it's so easy?"

I had no truthful or even logical answer to give her. These were all questions I had been asking myself.

Raul called back that night to tell me he had transmitted my message to the judge. Valdez had been very grateful. *Señora* Valdez was to arrive the next day at eleven on Avianca and he had promised the judge we would meet her at Miami International.

"What about our going down, Raul?"

"Let me finish. He will have an answer for us Wednesday morning. We are to call him at home."

"Shit, Raul, he said Tuesday. Why Wednesday now?"

Raul didn't know, but it was only one day. I was getting sick of the one days and the one weeks and the one months but said nothing more except that I would see him the next morning.

JUNE 30, 1980—MIAMI, SRA VALDEZ'S ARRIVAL

Raul and I were talking in my office as the time grew closer to pick up *Sra.* Valdez. He had been making strong efforts to reassure me of the judge's good intentions and that we would succeed in getting the release. He reminded me that Valdez wouldn't dare screw us, especially with Alfredo in the picture. Alfredo's father, the Minister, could step on Valdez like a bug. Raul graphically illustrated how this would be done by energetically grinding his foot on an imaginary insect on the floor.

"That's why I agreed to give him the money," I said. "Valdez was happy when we brought in Alfredo, he welcomed the suggestion. If he was planning to cheat us, he wouldn't have wanted anyone else involved. That's one reason. The other is that I think he would have asked for more. And he wouldn't have involved his wife if he wanted to screw us. That isn't Colombian."

Raul was nodding vigorously. He was completely optimistic. This was a strong bond between us. We both thought positively.

We spotted *Sra.* Valdez as she came out of customs and immigration. I had met her in Santa Marta and had exchanged words of greeting with her there, but little else. She was a small, neat woman, simply dressed and looked like the good housekeeper her house had indicated she was. She was pleased and relieved to see us as she knew nobody else in Miami, was unfamiliar with the city, and spoke no English. After we had welcomed her and inquired about her husband, we drove her directly to the hospital.

As we pulled up to the entrance, Raul gave me the nod to deliver the money. I handed her six thousand dollars in one-hundred-dollar bills. The timid and awkward way she accepted it was reassuring. It was obvious that Valdez had in no way indicated to her that she should treat this transaction as anything except a friendly loan. I actually had to take her hand and fold it around the roll of bills. She murmured, "*Muchas gracias, Sr.* Wood."

We offered to help her with anything she might need during her visit, and she smiled as she thanked us again, adding that she had a brother-in-law who lived in West Palm Beach, who was already at the hospital. She would be staying with him.

When we took her bags up to the room, she introduced us to several members of the family. The patient was an old lady, *Sra.* Valdez's aunt, who seemed very fragile and weak. We stayed only a few moments, as the room was crowded, and, then, returned to the office.

We reached Valdez by telephone in the early afternoon. Raul dutifully reported the safe arrival of the *señora* and the delivery of the six thousand dollars. Raul was laughing, nodding, and interjecting pleased "*Si's*" at regular intervals, which told me the judge was happy. He reminded Valdez we would call Wednesday.

JULY 2 TO JULY 6, 1980—MIAMI, GETTING MY DUCKS IN A ROW

It was Wednesday, the day we were to call Valdez back. I paced my office, impatiently waiting for Raul to arrive. The minute he stepped through the door, I had him by the arm, dragging him to the phone to place the call. We got through immediately, as it was only a little after seven in the morning in Santa Marta. First, the rituals of inquiries about health and the expressions of gratitude for our attentions to *Sra.* Valdez. She had called her husband the day before and had apparently given us glowing references for courtesy and kindness.

When the international goodwill routine had run its course, Raul got down to business. He was smiling and nodding as he talked—not bad news, at least. When he reached "*Bueno, Sr. Juez*" and "*muchas gracias*" and "*hasta luego, Sr. Juez,*" I looked at him expectantly.

"Good news," Raul stated. "Valdez said we could start next week."

"But when next week? What day?"

"He didn't say. He said to call Monday, and he would let us know."

"Is he stalling? You talked with him. How did he sound?"

Raul thought Valdez had sounded serious. I thought we would have to push Valdez. Just a little.

"We'll make plans to leave Sunday," I announced. Raul looked doubtful.

"Well, Bobby, he said we should call."

"All I want to know is if you think he'll be mad if we show up Sunday."

Raul reluctantly guessed not.

"Fine. You make the reservations. I'll get the rest of the parts together. We're going."

After lunch, I telephoned Paul Engstrom to advise him that we had been given the go-ahead to start work on 464 Juliet. Paul seemed pleased. This was certainly more progress, he told me, than anyone else had made in the past three years.

"Paul," I said, "I know my deadline is only eight days off, but please bear with me. If all goes well, 464 Juliet should be finished next week. I don't know the exact day, but I'll call you from Colombia and keep you updated."

"Don't worry about the deadline," Paul said, and we hung up.

I flew up to Fort Lauderdale to Jet Care to make arrangements with Dave Pearson and to order some of the parts and supplies I would need.

Dave was smiling and cheerful, and his, "Shoot, I'll be ready," was reassuring. I gave Bill Jones some money on account and left.

Back at the office, my next errand was to pick up my ferry permit from FAA. Bill Everett had it ready for me and reminded me to have the mechanic sign it. He wished me a good trip and I told him I would be in touch when I returned.

Later that afternoon, Jim Hildenbrand, my insurance agent, came by. Jim is a fine-looking man, about six two, well-built and impeccably dressed at all times. He had handled all my aviation-related insurance since I had first started in the business. I had told him some time before that I would be requiring insurance for 464 Juliet and he had stopped to see when I would be needing it.

I told Jim I would be leaving for Colombia Sunday evening, adding that, hopefully, the next time he would see me, 464 Juliet would be in the States.

"Don't worry about the insurance," he told me. "When do you want it put into effect?"

"Let's say next week—let's start it on July 10."

He nodded, telling me that I was covered. "Do you really think you'll get it out?" he asked, curiously.

"Why do you ask, Jim?"

"I'm not saying you won't. But there are lots of people around who've heard what you're up to, and a lot of them don't think you're going to pull it off."

"Who, specifically? I don't think there is anyone, not even you, who knows exactly what I'm doing toward getting her released. I'm pretty sure I will."

Jim laughed.

"You know how it is in aviation here in South Florida. It's a small world. And pilots are the biggest gossips in the world. Rumors about 464 Juliet have been around for years and the word is that you aren't going to get her out. Lots of big money people have tried and failed. So everybody is watching."

"OK, let 'em watch this redneck. But you can tell them that B.W. isn't sitting around drinking mint juleps. I'll get 464 Juliet out."

Jim nodded and said he was sure that if anyone could do it, Bobby Wood would be the one.

"If you swing it," he added, "here's a list of some others." He handed me several sheets with the make and numbers of various aircraft that had been confiscated in Colombia, dozens of them.

I looked through the lists incredulously, asking where he had collected them.

"Ever since you started on 464 Juliet, I've been asking insurance companies to see if they were interested in getting any planes they are handling out of Colombia," he replied. "So, if you want to tackle these, we could have a booming business."

"OK, Jim, but I can tell you one thing, when I get 464 Juliet out, I'm going to enjoy my nervous breakdown first. I will have worked for it, and I will damn sure deserve it. Then we can talk business. After 464 Juliet, anything else would have to be a piece of cake."

CHAPTER TWENTY-NINE

We were ready to return to Barranquilla. Terry had prepared me a large carton with sixty-five dollars' worth of Pepperidge Farm Goldfish, M & Ms, Hershey Bars, salted nuts, cookies, and five pounds of Lipton's ice tea mix so that I would not be hungry during my stay. Other baggage consisted of the two reconditioned Learjet batteries, five large boxes of parts, and luggage for Raul, Mel, Dave, and me. We looked as if we were going on a safari to the Amazon when we checked our baggage at the Avianca ticket counter. I gripped my briefcase tightly for the duration of the pre-flight sit down at our departure gate. My briefcase contained the ninety-four thousand dollars I would need for this final trip. Raul had telephoned the day before to make sure that Diego, our guy in customs, would be on duty when we arrived. Diego, who would get us through without hassle, had been promised extra money not to screw it up. All of us were excited as we boarded.

"Refugee," I said to Raul, "I hope this is our last trip commercial. Next time we go to Colombia it will be in 464 Juliet to work on the oil deal."

Raul nodded happily. We sat down with our heads together to check over the list of all the things we had to do, assigning certain projects to our amigos who could take care of the local requirements. Mel, my copilot, was bending my ace mechanic Dave's ear four or five sears forward in the next seat section. I could see the intensity in their conversation reflecting a non-stop series of questions and answers for the full two-and-a-half hours of the flight. If Mel was to get up-to-speed, then Dave was the man to get him there.

As we deplaned, I handed Raul the briefcase. In case of any unexpected problems, the first person to be hit on would be the gringo. Raul accepted it reverently.

A beaming Diego, our amigo in customs, greeted us. His eyes sparkled in anticipation of his fat tip. He quickly ushered us past the other incoming passengers at customs. We waited by the luggage area. This was a thirty-foot opening in the wall where the baggage carts were pulled to for unloading.

We stood there watching. The unloading process began noisily and the other passengers were immediately galvanized into frantic action to retrieve their belongings. They scurried back and forth, waving to the porters for attention, jabbing forefingers at their pieces, elbowing each other aside to be the first taken care of. Others were up on the counter, dragging their suitcases off the cart in their impatience to be first. A new cart was brought in, and they surged toward it. They behaved like a flock of pigeons after popcorn and were a lot noisier.

I was glancing over the heads of all those passengers milling about, trying to catch sight of Donado—he had promised to be there. I asked Raul where he was, and Raul shrugged an "I don't know." We could see Toño and Aquiles outside, through the glass door. Finally, the rest of the passengers had picked through all the remains of the baggage and departed, and we pushed and shoved our assortment of packages and bags onto the customs counter.

"What is the purpose of these parts?" the customs agent asked.

"We brought them down to repair a plane for Aerocivil," Raul replied.

The agent extended his hand, requesting our papers.

"What papers?" I wanted to know. My heart was sinking.

The scenario was shaping up for another hassle, another shakedown.

We explained that the parts were not for sale or use in Colombia. They were to repair an American plane to be returned to the United States. But we were wasting our breath. The agent turned to find his supervisor. They huddled together in conference for a few minutes, casting glances our way. Raul stood holding the briefcase as if it contained a time bomb. Diego was getting nervous, too.

"Raul," he said in a whisper, "pay them. Don't make any trouble. What if they ask me about the briefcase?"

The agent and his boss had made their decisions. They returned to the counter where we waited.

"The duty on these parts is twenty-five hundred dollars," the boss announced. The *Dinero* Syndrome, in play, yet again. This time it was re-appearing in an extraordinarily egregious amount.

Raul looked to me for instructions.

"Argue them down. They don't know about the money. All their attention is on the parts," and Raul drew them aside for about twenty minutes of animated and heated bargaining.

Finally he returned.

"No deal, Bobby. They're serious. You have to give them something."

"*Señor*s," I called to them, motioning them to come over. They sprang to attention, licking their lips, eyes gleaming. I had a surprise for them.

"I'll pay the twenty-five hundred," I told them, "but I'll need a receipt so I can get our money back." Their jaws dropped at this unexpected turn. I added that I would have Mr. Luis Donado straighten it out in the morning, as he was handling the matter.

They retired to their corner to try to figure a way out of this development. I instructed Raul to join them and offer four hundred dollars, a transaction which would require no receipt. Raul conveyed my offer.

This was the signal for a new ritual. The week before I had seen a TV documentary in which a group of anthropologists were studying and filming neighboring clans of monkeys. I vividly remembered the different kinds of typical primate behavior, as they called it. And I was now getting a replay of some of the same characteristic movements and posturings I had observed in the film—the advances and retreats, the grimaces, the waving arms, the meaningless noises, all intended to intimidate the opponent rather than to signal an attack.

We had been there almost an hour and a half by this time. Raul came back. "Six hundred dollars is the best I could do," he informed me.

"Tell them to fuck off, then, Raul. Start opening the boxes and tell them that we are making a complete inventory, serial numbers and all. They then can confiscate it all. And tell them that they will have to sign the inventory list because I'll need it in the morning to make sure that nothing is missing."

I was working up to a little primate behavior by now, too, but mine was for real—I was furious. I did some stomping and arm waving for their benefit. Dave and Mel were trying to calm me down, which only egged me on.

"I don't mind getting screwed," I grated, "but I'm not going to be gangbanged this time."

Dave was already familiar with these routine occurrences, as he had been a witness to a couple of them on his first trip with me. Mel, on the other hand, was shocked and appalled that I would dare take any initiative with the Colombian officials, fearful of the consequences.

By the time I had finished blowing off my head of steam, Donado arrived.

"Raul, Bobby, *como estas* (how are you)?" Donado greeted us, apologizing for being late. I ignored the supervisor and his assistant, who were waiting in their corner for a decision. They were suddenly very quiet and were casting anxious looks at me and Donado. Finally, the supervisor could stand it no longer.

He made the Colombian grabbing gesture to Raul, which indicated a renewal of bargaining, and Raul approached them. After the exchange of a few words, Raul returned.

"He accepts your offer. He'll take the four hundred dollars."

"Like hell he'll accept the four hundred dollars," I said. The shoe was on a different foot now. Mr. Supervisor was in deep shit and I knew it. The addition of Donado to the scene had brought in a new bargaining point.

"Here, Raul," I said, extracting two hundred-dollar bills from my left rear pocket, "tell him I'm giving him two hundred dollars just to keep peace. Remind him that I wouldn't have to give him even a *centavo* now that Donado's here, but that I am willing to give him something just to get this stuff out of here right away."

Raul relayed my message. Mr. Supervisor accepted the two hundred dollars with a sheepish look and a glance at Donado. Donado saw the transaction but said nothing. For two hundred dollars he wouldn't interfere with the system. Donado had to work with these people, and it would do him no good to cut off their cash flow. The two hundred dollars was enough, but not too much. He wouldn't make waves.

As we climbed into Donado's truck, Raul remarked that I didn't need him anymore since I was turning into such a real "banana republic" Colombian. Donado joined in the laughter. But despite my act of confidence, I was still thrown into inner turmoil at these situations. Everything could be perfect one minute and within the blink of an eye, explode into a savage confrontation that demanded instant evaluation and action. I didn't deceive myself into thinking that this would be the last incident of its kind.

Donado inquired if the judge had told us when we could start work on 464 Juliet.

"No," I replied, "but we're going to see him in the morning. Actually, he doesn't even know we're here yet. He told us it would be this week, so we came down a few days early to get everything set up. I have to find some nitrogen, some oxygen, a fuel truck, some jet fuel, and a few other odds and ends we couldn't bring down with us."

Donado nodded, but his face showed some concern. He informed us that he would have to be out of town for two days—he was needed in Cali on official business. He added that, of course, he would be available to help us in any way he could when he returned to Barranquilla.

This was bad news. I had no doubts whatsoever about Donado's good will toward me, but I was going to need a good bit more than his marginal attention in the days to come. My deadline was drawing close. Every day counted.

Raul and I had discussed this problem at some length and had come to the conclusion that we would need Donado's complete attention. I was completely willing to give Donado a concrete incentive but knew it would have to be handled carefully. Donado was a proud man. He was also an honest man, exceptionally honest considering that he had a limited income and yet occupied an official position which he could easily have used to line his pockets.

However, I knew he could use the money and if I could give it to him in such a way as to keep his pride intact, I felt it would help our progress. I nudged Raul on the leg and made the money sign we had agreed on, slipping him a five thousand dollar roll of one hundred dollar bills.

"*Señor* Donado," Raul began, "Bobby wants you to have this for your help. He's very grateful for all you've done, and he feels bad about imposing so much on your time … ."

Donado interrupted him, "I don't need money to help Bobby. He's helping my boys, and that's all I want," he said and pushed away Raul's hand.

"Donado, wait," I said earnestly, "this is different. I know how you feel about your boys, and how they feel about you. There will be a lot of expenses when they are living in Miami. I could give them the money little by little there, but I think it would be better for them to receive it from you—their father. You're the one it should come from—not me. Please take it. This is how I prefer to do it. If you think it over, I'm sure you'll agree."

Donado could see the logic in my explanation and finally accepted the money in the spirit it was offered. I breathed a sigh of relief.

The hotel personnel greeted us with happy smiles, scurrying to help us with our boxes and luggage. We had to get two separate rooms as the double bedroom suite wasn't available.

Raul told me that he and Donado had spoken a few minutes in private and that Donado had been pleased with his unexpected windfall. Donado had assured Raul that he would personally see to it that 464 Juliet was given priority. This was what I wanted to hear. I had an uneasy feeling about the Air Force. It was a very hard-ass organization and Donado with his many close connections would be a perfect go between.

Raul also mentioned the pay-off at the airport that Donado had witnessed.

"He told me that he knew what was happening—he didn't interfere because he knew you had the situation under control and he enjoyed watching you outmaneuver them. If the situation had gotten out of hand, he would have stepped in."

This much I had already figured out, but I was gratified to know that Donado had brought it out in the open.

On the morning of July 7, Aquiles, Raul and I started for Santa Marta after a normal stop and a twenty dollar tip at the bridge. Mel wasn't happy about being left behind, but I knew that Dave, Toño, and the rest of our amigos would keep him amused while we were gone.

"Do you want to stop and see Aldo?" Raul asked.

"No," I said, "he'd probably want us to waste half the day waiting at the restaurant while he set up the appointment with the judge."

Aldo's officious and ridiculous negotiations of these summit meetings had long been a source of amusement to all of us. I was sure it would have been far less difficult to get an audience with the President of the republic, and I wasn't in the mood for any of Aldo's bullshit that day.

The first twenty miles from Barranquilla to Ciénaga were much worse even than the last time we had passed over it. The small potholes in the asphalt had grown to a size that could actually have ripped the tires off the car. Fortunately, by this time we knew where they were located, so Aquiles cautiously zigzagged his way to Ciénaga. After passing through the slum area of the town, the road turning northward to Santa Marta was in excellent condition. The drive along the base of the Sierra Nevada on our right and the Caribbean on our left was beautiful. The foliage was brilliantly green and the whole panorama was spectacular—like, well, like another country.

We made a ritual stop at the "shrine" of 464 Juliet to remind her that we would be back soon, and then went on to Santa Marta.

When we reached Valdez's office, Raul motioned us past the outer office staff. We now had clearance to proceed directly to Valdez's inner sanctum. Valdez was surprised to see us, but there was no trace of annoyance in his greeting. He was hospitable as he pulled up chairs for us and invited us to sit down.

We explained that we had come down early as we had a lot of preparations to make prior to starting the actual work—Raul listed a few of the important ones.

Valdez hastened to thank me again for the help and "kind attentions" we had shown *Sra.* Valdez in Miami, and I felt that his appreciation more than offset any possible concern about our unexpected appearance.

Finally we had an opportunity to return to the all-important question: When could we begin working on 464 Juliet?

"Well … I still have more work to do on your papers … But if Luis Donado is available, I think it would be safe to say this Friday."

"This Friday" would be July 11, one day past my deadline. I was also perturbed about the sudden lack of confidence that clouded his voice. I warned myself to go slowly. Our unannounced arrival was as far as I dared go at the moment. At least his verbal go-ahead was a step in the right direction.

After several minutes of conversation on other subjects, Raul hitched his chair closer to the judge and told him that I was ready to discuss the "other matter" with him.

Valdez looked at me hesitatingly, then smiled and gave a nod of confidence. The ice had been broken.

"Very good," he approved, "but not here." He was reluctant to discuss the "business" in an inappropriate locale, but eager to pursue it. "We will meet at my home one day this week. Maybe tomorrow or perhaps Wednesday." It was arranged that he would telephone us to let us know when he could see us.

"Have you had lunch yet?" Valdez asked. As it was only ten thirty in the morning, we hadn't. He asked if we would join him at noon. We were naturally happy to accept his invitation and left with "*hasta luego's*" until our return.

Raul was elated as we walked outside. We were "een like Fleent" with the judge, Raul was sure. I was not so happy about this new delay. Why the hell did he need five more days to finish his papers? I still hadn't seen page one of anything, and I was getting anxious. But what could I do?

When we returned to Valdez's office at noon he was ready to leave, and he suggested *La Seffora* for lunch. Judge Valdez was showing good faith in having us as his guests in a public place. We had hastily arranged to leave Aquiles in another restaurant as he had not been included in the invitation.

Valdez was surprised when I ordered nothing more than a double portion of French fries, and he tried vainly to tempt my appetite with lobster—or perhaps a nice beefsteak?—and I had, to assume doleful expressions of regret and hold my stomach while Raul explained that poor Bobby had a very delicate digestion. I don't know what the judge thought about French fries for a bland diet, but he was polite enough not to mention any doubts he might have had.

As we ate, Valdez indirectly skirted the edges of my participation in the "business" but did not make any concrete suggestions as we were in a public place and as we had planned to get down to brass tacks sometime during that week. I made all the right noises and even volunteered a show of eagerness to get started. I watched his eyebrows, his eyes, and his facial expressions, all of which indicated his satisfaction.

Raul and the judge worked their way through the soup, a main course with rice and fried plantains, and the side dishes. Our table, on the second-floor patio, overlooked the beach, giving a magnificent view of the picturesque bay with its large rock formations. I glanced down at the road between the hotel and the beach and noticed two small cars pulling up and parking below us.

We were about eight feet above the cars. As we watched, two men emerged from each of the cars. I was amazed to see that all of them had on long coats at that time of the year when the heat was most intense. The men looked around and noticed the three of us above them. They exchanged a few words and returned to their cars.

It was time for us to go, so we left the table and Valdez paid the check. We walked the block and a half to where we had left the car. Everything was quiet and sultry.

Suddenly the sleepy silence exploded and a burst of automatic gunfire split the air. I swung around but saw nothing. Another burst, lasting for long seconds. Valdez kept walking, unperturbed.

"Raul" I shouted, "That sounds like it's coming from the beach."

Raul nodded, and yelled back, "Let's get out of here."

Then the second of the two cars that had been parked below us at the restaurant came screeching around the corner and sped off to the south. All was quiet again, as if nothing had ever happened.

The judge hadn't even blinked.

"What happened?" I asked him.

He shrugged and said he didn't know but that "probably it was *marimberos* fighting over a deal … *quién sabe?*"

This was the second shooting in broad daylight I had been exposed to in Santa Marta, and I could see that it must be an almost daily occurrence to elicit so little response from the spectators.

"Are you in a hurry to get back to Barranquilla?" the judge wanted to know as we got near our car. We told him no.

"I am free for several hours," the judge said, "and we can continue talking about this matter today."

Raul went off to the restaurant where we had left Aquiles to tell him we would be delayed while the judge and I waited. It was evident that the judge was eager to talk concrete "business" and that he was now confident about beginning.

When we got back to Valdez's home, he took us into his den, closed the door and turned on the air conditioning. Raul and I were offered coffee and Coca-Cola.

We sat down. This was it. I'd better get all my ducks in a row and say the things Valdez wanted to hear. I had to keep control to do this.

Valdez would have to be put on the defensive. I made the opening move.

"Judge Valdez, Raul has told me a little about your operation. But before we start, you must understand several things. As you know, most of my customers that buy airplanes are in the 'business.' I have introduced them to big buyers in New York, Los Angeles, Chicago—all over—and they have done very well.

"However, there is a big problem in the United States right now—quality."

I went on. The marijuana coming from Colombia was poor. Mostly green junk and too much "shake"—seeds, stems, even dead rats. A lot of junk. It only brought $175-$200 a pound wholesale. On the retail, about $275-$300. A bad product and a bad market.

The only way we could make any money would be if the judge could supply "pure gold"—not dry, with lots of resin. I didn't expect "sinsemilla"— but close to it. If the judge's plantation could come up with the quality, we would all be rich. I kept feeding him the right language.

The judge interrupted eagerly, "We have the very best. We very carefully select our merchandise. We lay it out in the sun for four, five, six days—if it rains we gather it up and store it until the sun is out again. It is all fresh. None of it last season's crop."

He went on at length, praising the quality of his merchandise and assuring me that I would receive only the very best. He even seemed to find my skepticism a good indication of my expertise on marijuana.

He introduced the next point on the agenda for discussion—transportation—asking if I had any DC-3s or DC-6s.

"No," I told him judiciously, "and if I did, I still wouldn't use them for this type of operation. If we do 'business' together, it will be for a long time. Most of the large airplanes the *marimberos* use now get caught. There is too much exposure in the States using those old junkers. The days of the DC-3 and the DC-6 are gone. Besides, when one of them is parked at an airport, the DEA is onto it like flies. They bring lots of heat."

The judge wanted to know what we would use then. I told him that we would use Cessna 402s or Titans, or even Navajos. There were thousands of those planes around that would do the job. They were safe. They wouldn't bring the Feds pounding on our door asking questions. I explained that these smaller planes still had legal fuel systems that would carry enough fuel and a fifteen hundred pound payload from Colombia to north Florida, non-stop.

Valdez's face fell. He had been harboring illusions of doing deals of five thousand pounds and up. This didn't worry me. I then drew his attention to the virtues of doing a steady series of one thousand or fifteen-hundred pound deals as compared with a risky big deal. He became convinced that this was indeed the "safe" way of conducting the "business."

I finished my pitch by telling him earnestly, "We don't want a one-shot deal. You and I want a steady long-range 'business.' The chances of doing a big deal and getting away clean are one in a hundred. But with small deals, the chances are ninety-nine in a hundred."

Valdez was impressed with this logic.

"You are very clever, Bobby. I like your action. When can we get started?"

"Not so fast," I interrupted, "there are many things that come first. Number one, I have to see your merchandise. Number two, I have to see your airport. I can't go into this blind; I have to know about gasoline, protection from the Air Force, your runway, camouflaging … ."

The judge was emphatic in stating that everything was 100 percent efficient. I was not to worry about the Air Force. The right people would be informed so that no overflights would be made when loading was taking place; it would be arranged that certain planes would be grounded for repairs or inspections. He would take us to see everything and if something did not meet my approval, it would be changed.

Before we finished, I also had to remind Valdez of the priority of 464 Juliet.

"You must realize, Judge Valdez," I said, "that I have a considerable investment already made in getting the airplane released and that, until this happens, I am somewhat restricted as to the amount of time I can put into anything new. But if everything goes as planned, we can get down to final arrangements probably by next week." I was hoping that Valdez would appreciate this polite way of telling him to move his ass.

We spoke until about four o'clock and Raul and I left, promising to call him the next night. Raul was grinning from ear to ear as we drove off.

"We are going to be rich—I promise you," he gloated.

"Don't forget—464 Juliet comes first," I warned him, and he nodded.

After picking up Aquiles, we stopped at Aldo's in Ciénaga. Aldo was standing by the tree in front of the house, which he suddenly grabbed for support when he saw who was in the car. He waited for us and reached for Raul's arm to support him as he cautiously returned to his father's rocking chair on the porch.

It was getting harder for him to carry on his invalid act, but he was still trying.

We inquired about his convalescence and he smiled bravely and told us he was still in severe pain.

"When did you arrive?—I didn't know you were coming," he said.

We told him we had gotten in the night before. We added that we had a lot to get done before we could make our final plans.

"The doctor said I should stay in bed, but I have to get back to work and help you, so I'm trying to move around. My brother, Gomez, came down from Bogotá; he and I did some work on the papers."

Aldo's tone of voice indicated that we were truly blessed in having such dedicated counsel.

"Have you spoken to Valdez?" I asked.

"Oh, yes. He's working on your papers. I am planning to see him tomorrow to find out when you can start working."

"You mean you can travel now?" I asked incredulously.

"Oh, yes," he said, "my sister has lent me her car until she has her baby—she isn't allowed to drive now." He proudly announced that he had even driven some the day before.

"I wish I'd known," I said, in mock disappointment. "We just came from having lunch with Judge Valdez. We'd have stopped and picked you up if we had known you were able to get around." I was twisting the knife in his back and he could barely conceal the pain. He had slipped badly in his own bullshit, and I was enjoying every minute of it. He had moaned and groaned his way completely out of the picture that day, and he had no one to blame but himself. I figured, however, that by the next morning his recovery would be complete.

We told him about our plans for the next few days and that he would be needed to help us, which he acknowledged with a grateful nod and eager expressions of assent.

"Aldo, I have the seventy-five thousand dollars with me at the hotel. Make sure you and Valdez have the papers finished by this weekend. The pilot is with me, and we should have 464 Juliet finished by Saturday or Sunday."

The magic word was seventy-five thousand dollars. It brought the bright dollar signs to Aldo's eyes as he beamed and promised to see Valdez in the morning and be in Barranquilla in the afternoon. He would push very hard. That was a promise.

As we drove off, we were all sure that money had truly been just the remedy Aldo needed to put him back on his feet.

Dave, Mel, Fernando, Toño, and an unknown player were in a poker session when we walked into the room at the hotel. The first thing I noticed was that my survival kit had been broached. Wrappers and jars were all over the floor. I was furious but said nothing.

Mel wanted to know our plans.

"OK, you guys, first thing tomorrow we find a truck we can use. After that, the nitrogen and jet fuel. Then we transport them to Santa Marta."

Mel wanted to know the answers to dozens of questions, but I was too tired to get into all this after such a long day, so I put him off with a "Wait, we'll take it one step at a time" and shut him up for the night.

CHAPTER THIRTY

We got off to an early start to find a fuel truck. Aquiles, Toño, Fernando, and I drove through every street and alley in Barranquilla until one o'clock in the afternoon. There simply was not a fuel truck for hire in the city. Finally, we spotted a small trucking firm on the outskirts of town. We explained what we needed and were amazed to see a happy smile spread across the proprietor's face.

"*Si, señors,*" he said energetically. This was still another man with a gold tooth that sparkled in the sunlight. I had come to the conclusion that gold teeth were status symbols in Colombia. Anyone with money for a dentist wanted none of a porcelain repair that looked just like his own teeth—he wanted the best. The best, as any idiot would know, was gold.

We were surprised to hear that he had several trucks that could be used to transport jet fuel. He led us through a rickety fence behind his office to his lot. He waved his hand at his collection of vehicles.

"This one here will hold two thousand gallons. It's in excellent condition," he stated. He pointed out the ancient hoses. "You can put the valve right here and regulate the fuel."

I didn't know whether to laugh or cry. There sat a dilapidated and filth encrusted old "honey-dipper" wagon. From a twenty-foot distance, the stench nearly stifled us. Raul stepped into the breach.

"*No, no, señor. Usted no comprende … ,*" and he went on to explain that we needed a truck with a tank for jet fuel, not for cleaning out a cesspool.

"*Si, si, señor, comprendo … ,*" the proprietor insisted. In one hour, he claimed, he could clean out the tank and the lines. It would be *muy bueno*— very good. We would see. We could rent it very cheaply.

After six hours of seeking and not finding, I had substantially reduced my requirements. Just possibly we might be able to use it.

Mel was carrying on about filtering the fuel, leakage, etc., etc., and working himself into a nervous collapse about everything that could go wrong. Finally I told him to relax and stop putting the cart before the horse.

We had plenty of chamois cloths we could use for filters. If "ole honey" was our only solution, we would have to take it from there and then concentrate on the other problems.

"What about contamination?" he wanted to know. He wouldn't give up.

"Mel," I said patiently, "they may be able to clean it good enough; just get off my back a minute and let me think."

Raul, Dave, and I walked back a few feet and sat down on some old drums, staring glumly at our "only hope." Suddenly, I realized what I was kicking my heels against—an oil drum.

"Raul, I have it. Let's go find some drums. I f we can find some good ones, we'll rent another truck to haul the drums."

I was confident that drums would be plentiful on the market. There were dozens of clandestine airstrips nearby that must use drums. In the words of Raul, no problem.

However, I was wrong. We spent the rest of the afternoon searching for drums. The *marimberos* had apparently cornered the market long since, and we were up against a stone wall.

We returned to the hotel after dark, dejected and empty-handed. At about 7:30, Aldo knocked on the door and hobbled in on a cane. We talked a while and finally Aldo anxiously inquired about the money.

"You don't have it in the room, do you? It's not safe here." He was extremely distressed at the thought that someone might steal the money—*extremely distressed.*

"No, I wouldn't keep it here. Come with me—I'll show you that it's safe."

Aldo leaped from his chair and followed me downstairs to the area behind the front desk where the safe deposit boxes were locked up. When I checked out the box and opened it, Aldo drew close. At the sight of the packet of crisp one hundred dollar bills he extended both hands, as if hypnotized. He began to stroke them slowly, sensually over the money, as if he were caressing a beautiful woman.

"How much is here?" he crooned ecstatically.

I told him that I had eighty thousand dollars—seventy-five thousand for him and the judge and five thousand for extra expenses. I wanted him to think I was cutting it close; there was no purpose to be served in his knowing the full amount. He was just too greedy and would more than likely fabricate some last-minute "expenses." I had not shown the others the money, but with Aldo, I felt it would be an incentive to spur him on to activity. I was making his mouth water. Now it would be up to him to figure out a way to expedite 464 Juliet's release so that he could satisfy his appetite.

Aldo walked out of the room like a sleepwalker, in a daze. As we entered the elevator, I reminded him that he had forgotten his cane. He gave me a sheepish look, went back to the counter, and retrieved it without a word.

Again, Dave, Raul, and I left with Aquiles to look for drums. I sent Mel with Fernando, Aldo, and Toño to find nitrogen. Aldo was driving his sister's small imported station wagon and was full of smiles and optimism.

We blanketed the city again, looking for drums. At first we inquired about new drums, then good used drums, then drums of any size, shape, and condition.

Everywhere we went we got the same story: "*No tenemos (we have none)*."

Finally, in complete frustration, I announced that we were getting nowhere and that we would just have to go get "ole honey." When we got there, we could see that the owner had indeed worked hard on improving her appearance and that she had been fairly well cleaned up; but, nonetheless, she still had a certain "air" about her that unmistakably gave her background away. We decided, however, that we would take her to the airport to pick up the fuel anyway.

I felt like a complete buffoon as we pulled up to Esso Colombiana's fuel depot. The guards stared at us incredulously and then burst into loud and rude laughter. This did nothing to improve my mood. Raul jumped out to tip them so that we could enter and they provided the ultimate insult by refusing to accept the tip. Things were that bad. Of course, there was no question of allowing us to enter with the truck, so we left her at the gate.

We slunk into the modern office building and were told we could see Mr. Castellano. After he heard what we needed—six hundred gallons of jet fuel now and six hundred more in a few days, he shook his head sadly—No, he couldn't help us. It was a policy of Esso Colombiana.

Probably a wise policy, I was thinking. They must have run into problems in the past, due to the high demand of the dope smugglers for this necessary item. Perhaps we could convince him that he was dealing with someone legitimate.

While we were pleading with him, a clean-cut Colombian of medium height, about thirty years of age, walked into the office. "Whose tank of shit is that parked outside?" he demanded. Raul's face turned red with embarrassment as he translated the man's unflattering comment. I wanted to crawl under the desk, but spoke up bravely and claimed it as my own. He burst out laughing and I had to join him.

Our shared amusement seemed to create instant rapport. He introduced himself to us as Guillermo Sanchez, shook hands, and asked sympathetically what he could do for us. Raul explained our dilemma and I told him of our fruitless two-day search for fuel drums. When we mentioned Luis Donado, he became even friendlier, as he knew Donado quite well. He had also heard about 464 Juliet and was interested in hearing about our efforts to obtain her release.

We exchanged cards and talked a few minutes longer. Mr. Sanchez suddenly seemed to have come to a decision. He excused himself and turned to Mr. Castellano.

"Castellano," he said, "we're going to let these gentlemen have the drums. Sell them all the new ones they need. Call your friend Domingo and tell him to bring his truck over here to load them." Then he turned to me and said, "Mr. Wood, I will need a letter from Donado requesting the jet fuel. This is a legal requirement, you understand."

Raul and I sat dumbfounded. After two days of black frustration the sun had suddenly broken through. In fifteen minutes, Sanchez had solved everything. I sent up a fervent prayer of heartfelt thanks for this lightning-swift "up" that had appeared so unexpectedly. I was convinced it was "ole honey" more than anything else that had won Sanchez's support. He knew that no smuggler in their right mind would ever dream of driving up in a rig such as ours to buy fuel.

Raul and I examined Sanchez's card and realized that he was one of Esso Colombiana's highest executives. My policy of going to the top was a sound one. It worked, even when by accident, the top had come to me.

Castellano made out the invoice for twelve new fifty-five-gallon drums, which I paid for immediately. While we waited for his friend Domingo to arrive, Sanchez stayed with us to see that everything went as he had ordered.

We thanked him sincerely for his invaluable help, and he smiled, wishing us luck and telling him to call him or Castellano if we needed anything else.

In less than thirty minutes, a nearly new Dodge stake body truck was loaded with the drums. We waited outside the gate for Raul to get the letter of authorization from Donado. He finally returned, without the letter. Donado was not expected back until late that night, and we would have to come back the next morning.

I was disappointed but still, we had progressed. We arranged to meet Domingo at the hotel in the morning. He promised to be there and to guard our new drums with his life. Then we mounted "ole honey" and took her home. She had done us proud.

I was glad to be able to give Mel the good news that "ole honey" was retired from the scene, since this spared me an evening of his gloomy predictions.

Raul telephoned Valdez to tell him of our progress and to arrange our next meeting. Another poker game was set up, and liquor and snacks were ordered. It took a series of strong hints and loud yawns to break up the party, but finally, around midnight, they left. I looked at the tab and groaned inwardly—another $150.

THURSDAY, JULY 10

Up at six. Another day, another problem.

Wednesday's glow had faded a little in the face of the unhappy fact that my deadline had arrived. I knew I had to call Paul Engstrom, but what would I tell him? The truth, of course—but I had no idea of how to present it. However, priorities first—we had to take care of the letter authorizing the sale of the jet fuel. Donado was already at work at 7:45 A.M. when we walked into his office. We were all happy to see each other, and he apologized for his necessary absence of the past two days.

"How can I help you?" he wanted to know.

We told him that we had the new drums on a truck outside but could not have them filled until we had his letter of authorization. He nodded and immediately prepared the letter for us. He also told us he would give us a permit to transport the fuel to Santa Marta. This was equally important if we were to be successful, as the Air Force monitored all fuel sales, particularly its transportation. This display of control satisfied two purposes. First, it indicated to righteous citizens that the Colombian Air Force was keeping an eye on the marijuana "business". The FAC boys certainly were doing just that, but were also watching to be sure no one was operating without paying the military for the privilege.

I was pleased that Donado had taken the initiative regarding fuel transport. It would bypass needless delays and hassles.

The first part of the document was in the form of a legal request, from Raul, since he was a Colombian citizen, for purchase of the fuel and its transport to Santa Marta. The second was Donado's official granting of the request. It was typed on a legal-size sheet of paper stamped with the seal of the Republic of Colombia.

AEROCIVIL ADMINISTRATIVE DEPARTMENT (SEAL)
BY HAND | BARRANQUILLA SECTIONAL OFFICE
TECHNICAL AND SECURITY CONTROL SECTION

Through this document, I respectfully request that your office certify first, that aircraft LEARJET North American Registration N464J is grounded at Simón Bolívar Airport (Santa Marta) where repairs are currently being made to make it airworthy, and, second, it has now become necessary to transport the fuel requirements needed to make regulation tests of the airplane's motors. Upon such certification, proper authorization is requested for purchase and transport of ONE THOUSAND FIVE HUNDRED gallons of JET-A1 fuel from the ESSO plant at Simón Bolívar Airport.

> *Respectfully,*
> *(signed) Raul Soto*

AEROCIVIL ADMINISTRATIVE DEPARTMENT
AERONAUTIC SUPPLY AND SECURITY CONTROL ZONE THREE BARRANQUILLA

> *Barranquilla, July 9, 1980. In consideration of this request and the documents belonging to aircraft with American registration N-464, Learjet, that are found therein, purchase and transportation of the fuel requested for testing and moving the aircraft to the, country of origin is AUTHORIZED, upon order of the Department of Civil Aeronautics. The work being done on the aircraft in reference was authorized by this office. Vehicle license NO TR-4771.*

> *(Seal) Aerocivil Administrative Dept. Technical Control Unit, Barranquilla Office*
> *(signed) Luis Donado, Chief, Technical Control and Security Unit, Barranquilla*

"When are you going to transport the fuel?" Donado asked.

"Right away," I told him, "just as soon as we get it loaded."

I knew Donado would be busy that day catching up with work that had accumulated during his absence, so I asked casually when he thought he would be free to go to Santa Marta with us. He said that since we would be busy getting the fuel and taking it to Santa Marta, he would be able to take care of his more urgent matters during that time and could be ready to start out with us the following morning. We left with the authorization, promising Donado to pick him up at home at 8:30 A.M. the next day.

Raul and I were walking on clouds as we went down to the truck. Finally, after two months of frustration and bullshit, we could start repairs on 464 Juliet. I kept singing, over and over, "Flyin' my baby back home" to the tune of an old song.

When we arrived at the fuel depot we presented our letter and were filled up immediately. Not even ripped off on the price. Even the gateway to hell opened in welcome and we ungrudgingly gave the soldiers a normal tip as they checked our papers and waved us on. We made a happy procession with Fernando in the truck with Domingo leading the way, followed by Aldo's car and then Aquiles' vintage Chevy. I don't even remember who rode where, but the gang was all there: Mel, Dave, Toño, me, and the others.

We stopped at Aldo's place to store parts we had brought down and then sped on to the airport.

When we reached the gate, we found that our lucky streak of the past two days had played out. It was locked.

"Raul, go find the airport manager—not that old fart, Baratta." That old fart must have heard me, because he was suddenly there, waving his arms and shouting at the top of his voice.

"Damned gringos, damned *marimberos*. You have no respect for government property. Don't you see the sign?" and he jabbed a knobby finger at the "*Entrada Prohibida*" sign on the fence alongside the gate.

I whispered to Raul to slip Baratta twenty dollars to see if his bad temper responded to money. It didn't. Baratta waved Raul off with an angry gesture and renewed his insults.

"Forget Baratta, then. He's crazy. Let's go find the administrator," I said.

We left Baratta glaring in a cloud of dust and drove around to the west side of the airport. Raul went in to look for the administrator. When he returned he jumped in the truck, yelling to the rest of us that we were to return to the gate. When we got back, a slim, tall official was waiting for us. He introduced himself as *Sr*. Zapata, the Aerocivil administrator of the airport. He apologized for Baratta, explaining that Luis Donado had been in touch asking that we be taken care of. Baratta had known nothing about it, and he was notorious for sticking to all the bureaucratic procedures.

Zapata rode with us over to the compound. Learjet 464 Juliet was sitting there forlornly, still immobile in the mud. I could hardly wait to get to her, but first we had to unload the fuel.

Zapata instructed us to take the fuel to the east side of the compound, next to the grease pit. We struggled half an hour unloading the 350-pound drums. The bed of the truck was four feet off the ground and we had no "lift" tail gate. The soldiers stood around sleepily, picking their noses and scratching their rears. Baratta was over by the terminal, pacing back and forth. He would stop from time to time, hands on his hips, to glare in our direction.

Zapata was embarrassed by Baratta's antics and apologized again. He mentioned that there were always problems with the old government employees nearing retirement. No administrator was empowered to fire directly, everything had to be done through the main office in Bogotá, and by the time a complaint had been processed, the employee would already be pensioned. These old bureaucrats knew that in a "war of attrition" they would always be the victors. So, what could Zapata do?

We thanked him for his courtesy and consideration, and before we left, arranged to be there in the morning, early, to start work on 464 Juliet. We added that Luis Donado would be with us.

After paying the truck driver, we left for Santa Marta. It was almost two thirty, and I had to call Paul Engstrom. There were several Telecom offices in the town with operators to place overseas calls and I could make the call from one of them.

About two miles out of Santa Marta, smoke started billowing out of Aquiles Chevy. We pulled over and Aquiles leaped out, bellowing, "Fire! Fire!" at the top of his voice.

Flames were licking out from under the dash on the driver's side.

"Open the hood," I yelled. Aquiles had it tied down with wire, as otherwise it was prone to flip open when the car hit a pothole. He was all thumbs, but after what seemed an eternity he got it open.

I shouted for pliers and grabbed them, frantically working the battery terminals loose. Aquiles was splashing his spare radiator water on the dash to check the flames. Finally, the fire was extinguished.

We stood there dumbly for half an hour, touching the metal from time to time to see if it was cool enough for us to investigate. When I finally could get under the dash to pinpoint the trouble area I could see that "trouble" was scarcely the word for it. It was a disaster area. Never in my life had I seen such a masterpiece of jury-rigged wiring. Almost every single wire under the dash was naked and hanging down like the roots of some exuberant jungle vine. After half an hour cramped under the dash with the sweat pouring into my eyes I decided that the most serious problem was a hot wire leading to the makeshift turn indicator, which had shorted.

I managed to get power to the ignition switch, but all the wiring for lights had been burned beyond repair.

Cranked and running again, we drove to town and located a Telecom office. It took an hour and a half to get my connection with Paul Engstrom, and I was thankful for the time difference which meant he was still in his office.

I explained briefly to Paul what was going on and told him I expected to have 464 Juliet ready to fly by Sunday. Hopefully, the paperwork would be finished by Monday or Tuesday.

"Don't worry," he assured me, "I'll extend the deadline until I hear from you. Just get 464 Juliet out."

Paul cut short my thanks by remarking that he completely understood the problems I had been having from different sources and that he would be happier than I when 464 Juliet came out.

"Forget the deadline for now. Concentrate on your work. And good luck," he finished. I almost sobbed with relief at receiving Engstrom's quick and unquestioning reprieve. The July 10 deadline had been hanging like a guillotine over my head, and Paul had lifted it away.

Thursday was now almost gone by the time we returned through the gates of hell, and I was hoping we would reach the city before night had fallen. There was little chance of this, as dusk is very short in the tropics, but I still had hopes.

A few miles beyond Ciénaga, we saw Aldo's car come to a halt. It had a flat on the left rear. As was to be expected, no jack. Also par for the course, no decent spare, just an old rag of a tire worn down to the cords, half-heartedly patched with several boots.

We had no flashlight. Aldo stood by helplessly, suddenly resuming his invalid role. We assigned him the task of holding a torch of twisted newspaper, to light our labors.

When we finished putting on the spare, we were ready to resume our journey. By that time it was pitch black. I drove Aquiles' car, following close to Aldo and keeping my eyes glued on his tail lights to keep a minimum distance between the two cars. We crawled along for a few more miles. Lady Luck was still not finished with us—the left rear blew again.

There was virtually no place to pull off, so we stopped, partly on the highway, not a light to be seen except oncoming headlights from cars that flew by us as if we had the plague. To tell the truth, I would have grabbed a wrench if anyone had stopped. We were in very rough territory. A lot of people had been killed along this stretch of road, and not in automobile accidents.

"Look, Aldo," I said firmly, "there's no way in hell I'm going to spend the night here." I was sure I spoke for everybody.

I took charge, ordering everybody into Aquiles' car. I would drive Aldo's station wagon, alone, so as to keep the weight to a minimum. Aquiles' Chevy with its springs completely bottomed out was dangerously overloaded, too. But, hell, we had to take some calculated risks.

"What about the rim? It'll be ruined," Aldo shrieked.

"Tough. I'll buy you another. Just get in." Aldo sulked but obeyed.

Aquiles' poor old Chevy, without lights, groped its way behind us. It was a classic example of the lame leading the blind. I banged down the highway at ten miles an hour. The torn rubber flopped and threw off a trail of pieces all along the highway until the last shred was gone. Finally, I was riding on the bare rim.

I could see the sparks flying through the rear view mirror. Suddenly, I had a mental picture of Aldo's anguished face as he helplessly contemplated the ruin of his sister's car, and I started to laugh. I couldn't stop—I laughed until tears streamed down my face. And, then, I thought of how ridiculous I was, laughing like a hyena in the middle of the night on a godforsaken road, and broke down again. I was able to control myself only when the light of the military outpost about eighteen miles out of Barranquilla appeared ahead.

I leaned out the window and shouted for Aquiles to halt. "What do you think about stopping there? I'm afraid this rim won't take much more."

They discussed the pros and cons, and, finally, we decided that nothing could be worse than staying where we were. We limped slowly into the post. Raul was out of the car, explaining our misfortunes, and our luck reappeared as suddenly as it had departed. The men stationed there told us that we were welcome to stay the night with them—they didn't even ask to see our papers. Otherwise, there wasn't much they could do. However, they were willing to rent Raul their flashlight for ten dollars if he wanted to light Aquiles' way into town.

Raul pulled Aldo's "good" flat tire from the trunk and transferred it to Aquiles' car. We all were convulsed with laughter as Aquiles pulled off toward Barranquilla with Toño in the left rear seat holding the flashlight out the window. It was crazy and pathetic and we cheered them out of sight.

We fought a losing battle against swarms of mosquitoes until about one thirty in the morning, when Aquiles drove up in a taxi with Aldo's repaired tire. Fortunately there was just enough rim, just barely, to mount it.

It was exactly 3:00 A.M. when we got to bed. I have never felt a softer pillow.

I must have slept very fast that night, as I got twelve hours packed into three and a half hours and was up at six fifteen. My first thought was of getting to 464 Juliet, and my adrenalin was pumping as I awakened the others and told them to move.

CHAPTER THIRTY-ONE

I watched my friends gobble down a hearty Colombian breakfast and envied their appetites while I finished my bowl of French fries. Aquiles was to remain in Barranquilla while repairs were made on his Chevy. I gave him one hundred dollars and told him to meet us in Santa Marta as soon as possible.

Donado was rarin' to go. In view of our critical transportation situation, we used his truck. Again he blazed his way across the peninsula, leaving Aldo far behind. Since there was an ice house along the main road in Ciénaga, we stopped to stock up and give Aldo a chance to catch up. My stomach heaved when I saw the ice. It was filthy. Along with unidentified foreign matter, a large cockroach was frozen stiff in the block. However, we decided we could keep the cans of iced tea and bottles of soft drinks cold. It would have been instant ptomaine poisoning to use the ice in our drinks.

Aldo finally came into sight and we went straight to his house to pick up supplies and parts. Donado's truck was sagging when we had it filled completely with the parts, the tools, and the jack we had been stockpiling in the Reyes's dining room and spare bedroom. Everyone was talking and laughing with excitement as we drove to the airport. We were sharing the happy anticipation of 464 Juliet's imminent resurrection.

Surprisingly, Donado didn't stop at the gate. He drove to the southwest corner of the terminal and told us to wait with the truck, taking Raul with him. Around nine thirty they were back. Donado's stern face, clenched fists, and tense body told me that he was in a towering rage.

"What's wrong?" I asked, bewildered, looking first at Donado, than at Raul. Donado strode past me without a word. Raul gave me his "shut up" sign and motioned for Aldo to bring his car. Something was wrong, drastically wrong, if Raul would leave me open-mouthed without even a word of explanation.

The Donado boys, Toño, Dave, Mel, and I sat uneasily by the ocean, throwing rocks into the surf and wondering what had happened. It was frustrating to wait there in complete ignorance of what had happened but worse yet to listen to Mel's gloomy assumptions of the worst.

"I thought you said Donado had clout," he complained.

Dave, always tuned in to other people, sensed my growing annoyance with Mel's useless questions, nudged him to shut up, nodding meaningfully toward Fernando whose English was more than adequate to understand Mel's remark as a slur on his father.

My spirits had plunged. Another of those fiendish, inexplicable "down" moments had materialized from out of nowhere and turned our fine day into blackest night.

Aldo, Raul, and Donado finally returned at half-past noon. Not saying a word, and with serious faces, they marched past us into the terminal. Donado was still in a towering rage, but a new element had been added—purpose. He had fire in his eyes and I could see that somebody was going to get scorched.

In fifteen minutes they were back.

"Fernando," Donado commanded, "take the truck around to the gate."

Raul motioned for us to follow. I was anxious to find out what had happened, but knew it would still have to wait. Donado had to be allowed the opportunity to restore and reinforce his authority. First, with whoever had questioned it. Then, with us, his American and Colombian friends. And, finally, with his sons. A rigid code was involved, as inflexible as in a duel of bygone centuries. Donado's honor had to be satisfied. His image was precious to him.

We joined Donado and Raul alongside 464 Juliet. Donado stood immobile, watching Fernando dismount from the truck pulled up at the gate, waiting.

The opponent appeared on the scene. It was Baratta. He made the opening move, shouting at Fernando. The moment of attack had arrived. Donado surged across the asphalt toward Baratta and launched a violent verbal assault. Baratta tried to put up a show of resistance but he was no match for Donado's blistering attack. He fell back, then cowered, and with lowered eyes, slowly retreated, walking away in defeat.

Donado surveyed the field, where he had been victorious, and walked over to the truck like a champion, then driving it over to his admiring audience alongside 464 Juliet.

"OK, Bobby, we can start unloading now. I'm sorry for the delay." Renewed authority rang out in his voice. No explanation—we had seen for ourselves.

All of us set to work unloading. Several minutes had passed when Mel asked Dave if he had left the emergency window open. Dave had not, so we walked around the plane to investigate.

Dave was already there and reported that someone had been inside.

Donado had returned to the terminal, so I sent Raul to find him. When they returned, we showed him that someone had broken in. Donado's recently cooled rage rose anew. In the meantime, Dave had climbed inside to unlock the door.

I climbed into the cockpit. My fears were confirmed.

"Look at this fucking mess," I yelled in disgust. "Some son of a bitch stole the radar. Look."

Donado stuck his head inside the door as I pointed out the rack where the radar had been mounted. It had been completely severed with wire cutters. It would have taken more than one person to remove the equipment. After cutting the rack, they had ripped the radar out of the instrument panel. My fury was mounting along with Donado's.

"Don't touch anything," Donado warned, and then he marched back to the terminal to get *Sr.* Zapata. The two of them climbed into the cockpit and examined it. Zapata headed toward the compound, bringing back with him the eight or nine soldiers on duty and leading them at a trot over to 464 Juliet. Donado, as the ranking man, was now very much in command. He questioned them sternly, and they were all suddenly most military with "*Si, mi jefe*s," and "*No, mi jefe*s." None of them knew or admitted to knowing anything or had seen anything of a suspicious nature. Donado was not finished. He informed them in no uncertain terms that if anything else disappeared from the airplane or if anyone so much as touched it, he would personally see to it that all of them were court martialed.

Then he left with Zapata.

Finally, I had a minute to find out what had happened that morning. Raul and I went into a huddle while he explained. First, Raul reminded me that as chief of Aerocivil for all of the northern region of Colombia, Donado was in control of all aviation matters, including airports. When he had gone upstairs to see Zapata, Zapata had told him that orders had been received from the military post in Santa Marta—from the colonel himself—that no one was to go near 464 Juliet. Zapata had been caught in the middle of a confrontation. Donado was Zapata's superior, but since the orders had come from Bogotá, Zapata could do nothing more than wait for clarification. Donado and Raul had gone to get Judge Valdez to intervene. Valdez had been able to pull rank on the colonel—apparently he had enough clout to make it stick.

"Did Valdez find out who it was in Bogotá that issued the orders?" I wanted to know. Raul had no idea. He hadn't been inside the colonel's office during the meeting with Valdez.

Raul went on to explain that this three-way confrontation had been a serious insult to Donado. To inform the *Jefe* of Aerocivil that he could not enter an airport in his own domain was not done.

"Everything is fine, now," Raul said, adding gleefully, "Did you see him chew out old Baratta's ass?"

When Donado returned a short while later, I was happy to see that he had calmed down, although still upset about the theft of the radar. He apologized again, and then asked what our procedures would be now that we could finally get to our delayed activities.

I told him that our first priority would be to clean out the entire fuel system, change the filters and recheck the engines. Then we would crank the engines and make sure they checked out. Dave had been sure they would be all right, but if we had bad luck, we would have to stop right there. It would be useless to go any further.

Donado nodded his approval, and we got to work. First, we had to move 464 Juliet. She was mired down helplessly and we needed firm ground. We secured a long rope to the nose gear and tied it to Donado's truck. She didn't move an inch. Donado ordered a helper to bring an Avianca tug and a stronger rope. Finally, we cheered as 464 Juliet stirred her limbs and groaned into forward movement. Three long years in the grave had taken its toll. The tires were flat, the wheels and brakes completely packed with dirt, rust, and rocks.

It was a clear afternoon and the sun was unmerciful as it beat down on our heads. With all the earlier bullshit behind us, I started cleaning the tip tanks while Dave began the punishing task in the "hellhole" of changing fuel filters and servicing the hydraulics. It took me two hours to clean out the tip tanks. Mel was checking all the systems in the cockpit. Raul and Fernando worked feverishly supplying us with tools and rags and quickly doing whatever they were asked to attend to.

When Dave finished the fuel filters, he installed the batteries. Mel emerged from the cockpit and helped Dave remove the lower engine cowlings.

"Dave," I shouted, "be sure you pull the oil screens again, just to make sure nobody has put something in the oil."

Mel and Dave busied themselves with the engines while I cleaned and re-cleaned the tanks. At last, Dave was prepared for his final inspection and told me we would soon know what we had to know about the engines. "Put the juice in her, Bobby. Let's check for leaks."

Mel then spoke up, "I'm not putting the cart before the horse now, Bobby. What brainstorm do you have for filtering the jet fuel?"

"I've got a little surprise for you, Mel," I replied smugly. "Raul, open that box—the one alongside the wheel."

Raul flipped open the box and pulled out a brand new twelve-volt Gasboy pump, complete with fuel filter, twenty feet of hose with nozzle and attachments for fifty-five-gallon drums. I had fortunately been prepared in case we had to use drums.

"On occasions, I have been known to plan ahead," I remarked.

"Very nice, Bob—I apologize," Mel said.

Raul and the Donado boys rolled five drums of fuel to each tip tank and Fernando pulled Donado's truck over. We opened the hood and attached the alligator clips to the battery. I flipped on the Gas Boy switch and it purred like a kitten.

"OK, boys—pop the tops," and in less than forty-five minutes 464 Juliet had taken on five hundred gallons of jet fuel. Not a drop anywhere.

We worked delicately at the sump drains that were stuck shut with bugs, dirt dauber nests, and other unknown substances. Shortly they were in working condition. 464 Juliet was almost ready to crank.

Raul had already stretched out one hundred feet of water hose, and Dave started washing out the engines. All of us ducked our heads under the spray from time to time to cool off. The low water pressure made it difficult to flush the engines but we did the best we could.

The final job was to wedge all the wheels with large rocks. Then we shouted to everyone to clear out of the way. We were ready.

"Mel, you go on in," Dave instructed, "and Bobby and I will stand by at the right engine with the fire extinguisher."

We were all feverish with hope and anxiety. Even Donado was on tiptoe as I gave Mel the "light her up" signal. Mel hit the start switch and wound it up to 10 percent. The starters whined. Mel pushed the throttle to start position. Our ears were rewarded with a responsive "whoff." A large fireball burst out of the tail cone, followed by several pops and bangs.

At this point, Juliet impolitely relieved herself there on the asphalt strip, expelling from her inner workings large quantities of old mud dauber nests and trash that had built up inside her during the past three years. She seemed to be in the eye of a black tornado for a few seconds. However, she kept on winding up. At around 35 percent power she emitted several more loud and rude noises and expelled another accumulation of debris. But she kept winding up to 48 percent power.

Mel let her idle and leveled off. An occasional loud pop followed by clouds and brown smoke was heard but gradually she smoothed out.

Everyone cheered. Even the soldiers smiled and joined Donado as he held up his hands and applauded our lady.

Dave and I rushed under the engine to check for fuel and oil leaks. Bond dry. Grinning from ear to ear, we ran around into the cockpit to get Mel's report.

"Everything OK," he stated. "Oil pressure, fifty pounds; oil temperature, normal; generator charging 150 amps."

I clapped him on the shoulder.

"Great, we're going outside. When I give you the sign, push her all the way up to 101 percent. If she's going to blow, let's have her do it here."

After waiting a few minutes to let the temperatures come up to normal, I gave Mel the full-power sign. A great, shuddering thrill gripped me as I heard 464 Juliet triumphantly roar to life. The tall grass behind her bent down flat as heat waves poured out of the tail cone. I felt like a giant, standing as tall as the sky.

Mel ran her up several times. "Perfect. Absolutely beautiful," I shouted and gave Mel the "cut" sign.

Dave and I, together with Donado, raced over to the right engine. The heat was incredible, but we came as close as we could for a quick inspection. Everything checked out normal. Dave had a wide smile and a handshake for me as he announced, "She's perfect, Bobby."

Donado was as delighted as the rest of us, making an A-OK with his thumb and forefinger and clapping us on the back. Dave had amply proven his expertise to Colombia's chief of Aerocivil.

"OK, guys, we're halfway home." I was eager to find out what the other engine would do. "Mel, hop in, and light up the number one (the left) engine."

My stomach was full of butterflies as Mel hit the start switch. Winding it up to 10 percent, he pushed the throttle to start. This time there was no big "whoff"—464 Juliet just popped a few balls of fire and soot out of the tail cone, then hesitated and slowly started to turn up. Then came another large puff of flame and smoke that stubbornly persisted for ten or fifteen long seconds. We watched tensely with fingers crossed. Finally, she started to speed up. The flames grew longer and, after another loud pop, she crept up to 48 percent. Mel put her on idle. She was trying to clear, expelling huge clouds of brown smoke. Two eternal minutes passed. Dave ran up to the door telling Mel to shut her off.

"No, no," I interrupted, "push the throttle forward; see if she will clean herself out."

Mel inched the throttle forward gently. The tach climbed—60%—70%—80%—90%—still popping.

"Hold her there," I instructed. She cleared her throat, finally, and settled down, restlessly.

Dave and I stepped out and gave Mel the full-power sign. At last 464 Juliet was smoothing out and began to roar like a tiger ready to pounce.

I jumped into the cockpit and eased her back to "idle." It was as smooth as glass.

Mel poured the power on several more times and finally cut it off. Everyone came forward to bend down and check for fuel leaks, but none were found.

Dave was grinning in relief, "For a while there, I wasn't sure she was going to make it."

"Me, too; I must have sweated off twenty pounds."

Donado had also been alarmed. He had never seen a jet engine behave that way before and shared our relief when it finally smoothed out. Mel ran her up again and after a series of full-power bursts, 464 Juliet's left engine was running as beautifully as the right.

After a coke break we replaced the cowls. Aquiles had been gone on an errand and came racing back when he had seen the smoke and heard the noise from some distance down the road. He had raced back, fearful that he would find 464 Juliet in a state of total destruction and was vastly relieved that it had been nothing more than a noisy ritual of resurrection.

We all got busy cleaning up as it was already 6:30 and growing dark. We needed a good night's rest because the next day would also be a grueling one. Dave carefully safety-wired the emergency exit from the inside. Then he locked the door and removed the batteries. We dropped our packed-up parts off at Aldo's and sped back to Barranquilla.

We were up again at six the next morning, stopping to pick up Donado. He was in a fine mood. The sun was just coming over the mountains as we drove over to 464 Juliet. No one at the gates to hell molested us, and we were able to get set up quickly.

By ten o'clock we had Juliet up on jacks and had removed the wheels and tires. Mel had the tedious task of wire-brushing the heavy corrosion from the wheels. They were deeply pitted inside where the tire seals fitted against them. With luck, they would hold air. Mel finally finished and meticulously mounted the tires.

The left main outboard was frozen solid with rust over an eighth of an inch thick. I was sawing away for over two hours between the floater with a hacksaw, and I had already used up several blades. Donado came over to examine the jury rigging I was attempting to make.

"What's wrong with them?" he asked.

I explained that I was trying to remove enough of the rust without taking the brake assembly apart, since a few quick applications of the brakes, when rolling, would remove the rest because they were metallic brake pads. He looked at me doubtfully.

Early in the afternoon I could see that Dave was having trouble. The heat was brutal. Dave's face was deep red and he seemed dazed. "Dave, you'd better lie down in the shade under the wing and rest. I can't afford to have you collapse on us now." I realized then that no one had even stopped for lunch. Everyone was working non-stop and would have kept on until ready to drop, without complaint. We called a half-hour break which was welcome.

Then we hit it again. Dave was lubricating cables, flaps, spoilers. I helped Mel mount tires, pack wheel bearings, and begin the task of reinstalling them back on the jet.

"OK, Mel," Dave finally shouted, "hop in—let's do a retract test."

Again we crossed our fingers. Mel turned on the auxiliary hydraulic pump and selected "gear up." Everything rose as normal, except for the nose gear, which jammed and released crumbled pieces of dirt dauber nests. After we lowered the gear and cleaned out the nose wheel well, the gear worked perfectly.

Donado slapped Dave on the back and gave him an admiring smile. He was more impressed by the minute with Dave's expertise. "I have never seen anyone work so fast and so easily," he told me. "When I first saw Dave, I thought he would be inexperienced."

"I know, Little Dave fools a lot of people," I said.

Donado had a knowing grin on his face. "I've noticed. He did a wonderful job clearing the vanes."

Son of a bitch, I thought. He knew all along about the "stuck vane" trick we pulled when we first fired up the engines in front of Judge Valdez. He had been waiting for a chance to inform me that we hadn't fooled him, without saying so directly. He winked and laughed. Although nothing more was said, I knew he had adopted this way of letting me know that he was helping me with the judge, without jeopardizing himself as the head of Aerocivil. I felt that he was also amused at the gringos turning a con game around in Colombia, right in their own back yard.

"OK, Bobby, get off your ass," Dave shouted. "Let's get ready to check the brakes."

We returned to work. Raul had been inside the terminal, and when he rejoined us he drew me around to the other side of 464 Juliet.

"I have good news," he whispered. "Mario, the one who works here for Avianca, told me he had some leads on the radios. He wants us to meet him tonight in Ciénaga, at his house, at about eight thirty."

I was excited. "What does he have? Does he have all of them?"

Raul didn't know and said that we would have to wait and see. He went back to the terminal to inform Mario that we would be there.

It was close to six when we were ready to crank 464 Juliet for her "taxi" test of the brakes. I informed Donado that we were ready and requested permission to use the runway for a high-speed test. Donado was dubious.

"Let me check with the tower," he advised and then left. Several minutes later, he returned with bad news. The tower had given its approval but the military had overridden the tower. We were allowed only a few feet—right where we were parked.

"They are bringing over a truck to park in front of the jet to make sure you don't blast off," Donado told me. He was upset, but could do nothing without provoking another confrontation, which was the last thing any of us wanted.

The truck was already there and the soldiers were positioning it about thirty feet directly in front of 464 Juliet.

"Bobby," Mel barked, "how in the hell can I test anything in thirty feet? We need to run her up to at least eighty or one hundred miles per hour to burn all the shit off the brake pads."

"Just get in—crank it up and roll her as fast as you can," I barked back. "Something is better than nothing."

Everyone stood back as 464 Juliet fired to life. The soldiers in the truck were alarmed at the possibility of becoming barbecued sacrificial lambs. They scrambled out of the cab and cast fearful looks at the roaring jet as they withdrew to safer distance, out of her path.

Mel pushed 464 Juliet up to 98 percent with brakes locked, then released them. She leaped forward about ten feet and Mel applied the brakes. She stopped about five feet from the truck. Dave gave Mel the sign to cut her off.

The three of us were relieved to see that the brakes held, but Raul, Donado, and the others applauded wildly as Mel climbed out of the cockpit. All the self-appointed "experts" appeared to be convinced that 464 Juliet was now completely airworthy and that everything was conveniently as good as new.

"Look at that," I whispered to Dave, "they're acting as if we had moved a mountain. They're carrying on as if Juliet is all ready to take off, just because she moved twenty-five feet." I was concerned that they had sold themselves on the idea that we didn't need any more testing.

"Yeah, that's the trouble," Dave observed. "What's the saying? *A little knowledge is a dangerous thing?*"

"Well, let's get cleaned up. I'm going to ask Donado about a test flight; keep your fingers crossed." I immediately approached Donado to bring up this important matter for his consideration.

"Luis, we'll be finished tomorrow and then we'll need to fly her. What do you think?"

"No, it's impossible," he shook his head regretfully. "They won't even listen to such a request. They'll naturally assume that once you were airborne, you would just keep going and not come back."

I marshalled my arguments on how we could set their fears at ease regarding the possibility of us hijacking our own airplane—Donado himself could fly the test fight with an armed military guard, I myself would stay on the ground as a "hostage," and we would reduce the fuel load to only complete a local flight. We would agree to almost any terms just to be allowed to test-fly 464 Juliet.

He continued to shake his head, "Impossible, Bobby. Not until you obtain the legal release from Valdez. Even then, I am frankly worried that there will be problems with the military." He leaned closer and added in a low voice, "My advice is this, Bobby. Whenever you do get her airborne, keep going."

Donado's warning alarmed me. He was trying to tell me something. Perhaps he was merely indicating that he had little control over the decisions of the military. On the other hand, he might be hinting at the more ominous possibility that once 464 Juliet was put back into airworthy condition, the military might decide that she was too large a prize to be given away so freely. I recalled vividly that at one time 464 Juliet had been assigned to the Air Force for use as the President's standby personal airplane and it seemed only natural that the military would be reluctant to part with their claim to her once she could fly again.

This wave of doubt plunged my confidence downward. After going this far, would my efforts to get 464 Juliet out fail at the last moment? I said nothing of my fears to Donado, merely nodding and thanking him for his concern.

We finished cleaning up and secured the airplane. Completely exhausted, we arrived at Aldo's house at seven thirty. I felt guilty leaving the others the task of unloading, but Raul and I had to get rid of some of our grime to go to our meeting with Mario, our amigo at Avianca. Donado was immediately interested to hear of this appointment. His first reaction was that he, too, should be present. The matter might involve illegalities within his area of competence. On second thought, he decided that priority had to be given to getting our hands on the radios. If the matter became "official," an investigation would most certainly cause further delays.

"You and Raul handle it yourselves," he told us, "but if you find out that airport personnel are connected with stealing them, I want to know. I'll have their asses—but *after* you get the radios back."

We parted, agreeing to meet Donado again the next morning. He left with the boys for Barranquilla.

Raul, Toño, Dave, and I comprised more than enough bodies to make up a negotiating committee, which served as a great excuse to leave Mel and his interminable questions to be answered by Aldo, who was still "recuperating" from his accident.

As we drove through the streets of Ciénaga, we picked our way through deep ruts and potholes, narrowly missing straggler chickens that squawked and flapped out of our path. Neighborhood women were swiftly walking along the dirt paths, balancing large flat basins resting on twisted circles of rags on their heads. One of the women had a screaming baby in one arm, a basket of vegetables in the other, and a bucket of water balanced inside the basin on her head. All were dressed in threadbare cotton dresses, and few wore shoes. All bore signs of the thankless, backbreaking labor of trying to keep a home with very little money while lacking the convenience of running water in their miserable shacks. Survival was a marginal matter in those parts.

Mario was screaming at his mongrel dog as we pulled up. It had messed inside the house and his children, all naked, had tracked it around. His wife was bringing a bucket of water to wash their feet. She and Mario's sister were clean, but dressed no better than the women we had seen in the streets. Mario's crisp white shirt and tan cotton pants looked very elegant in these surroundings. I knew that his wife had washed them by hand, spread them in the sun to bleach away any stains, and then had painstakingly ironed them with an old flat iron heated over the primitive stove in their open kitchen, which would seem like a major undertaking to any United States housewife used to wash-and-wear apparel, automatic washing machines, and steam irons.

Mario's home was an attached section of a low-cost housing development built of gray cinder block. It consisted of a couple of rooms and a large covered patio in the back that served as kitchen, dining room, and laundry area. The windows had no glass but were equipped with shutters. The front door had apparently been furnished from a demolished house as it was splintered and blackened with age.

Raul briskly got down to business, asking Mario how many radios he had located.

Mario's hesitation indicated that he was shy and uneasy about talking in my presence. He had seen me in Donado's company and he wanted to do nothing that would endanger his job. Raul was quick to reassure him that we weren't interested in making any problems.

"All Bobby wants is to get his radios back," he urged, and I nodded in agreement.

"Don't worry about reporting this to Donado," Raul continued, "we'll pay to get them back. No police. No problems. This is just between the three of us."

Mario seemed relieved. He spoke more openly and told us that the radios had been taken out almost two and a half years ago by different people but he had connections and would try to help us.

We got in the car and drove to Santa Marta, through darkened streets toward the east side of the town. We drove down a narrow dirt road taking several turns in different directions until I had no idea where we were. This was the worst section of town, and here Mario told us to stop. There were no street lights, a few dim lights glowed weakly from the shanties.

Mario told us to remain in the car. We were happy to comply, since not too far off we heard gun shots ringing out in the muggy air.

"When Mario gets back why don't we tell him we'll come back tomorrow, in the daylight," Dave suggested. All of us were nervous and uneasy.

Mario returned in fifteen minutes.

"Let's go," he said, "but first take off your jewelry and leave your wallets here with Toño. He can stay with the car to make sure it isn't stolen, either."

This was a twilight zone where gringos, especially gringos with anything of value, were marked as easy prey. The chances of walking alone, unmolested, were slim. Any stranger foolhardy to appear here alone could easily be found dead along the road in the morning.

We walked close together alongside the dark road. Even the dark houses seemed to be crouched, ready to spring on us. Several half-drunk Colombians were stumbling and cursing as they approached us.

"Don't stare at them," Mario hissed, "look straight ahead."

As we approached them, we could see that they carried pistols which they were flourishing to underline their loud conversation.

"They're bad ones," Mario muttered. "Wait here. I know one of them. I'll calm them down."

Raul, Dave, and I huddled like babes in the wood under the shelter of a large tree. Mario's peace-making efforts were successful—he returned to us and led us to an old house about ten feet off the edge of the road.

We stood waiting. Finally, out of the alleyway emerged three Indians and a Colombian woman of around thirty years of age, plump and barefoot, in a poorly fitting handmade dress. The men carried boxes wrapped in newspapers and tied with twine. Without a word, they set them down on the stone wall and unwrapped them.

Even in the poor light I could see they weren't the Learjet radios—they were old DC-3 equipment.

"No, Mario, they're not the right radios," I said.

The three men were displeased that their merchandise wasn't suitable and began grumbling when they realized there would be no Saturday night drinking money. I quickly instructed Raul to tell them that perhaps we could use what they had, but would have to check the airplane first. For their trouble, Raul would give them fifty dollars. We figured there was little sense in giving them nothing but bad news in their own backyard, and Raul agreed that fifty dollars ought to ease their disappointment.

They were willing to accept the consolation prize and left. Raul chatted for a few minutes with the plump woman; he was a man to take advantage of every contact which might be useful on a future occasion. Apparently he had a feeling this woman might be a good person to cultivate. We were still apprehensive as we walked the endless half block back to the car and we entered it like scared rabbits leaping into their burrow. On the way back to the "safe harbor" of Ciénaga we were all very quiet.

Mario was apologetic about the false lead but assured us he had others that might be more promising the next day. We gave him a little beer money and dropped him at his favorite bar, El Cedro.

Aquiles' Chevy was humming as it took us across the moonlit peninsula. All of us were crowing about 464 Juliet's first movement in over three years. What we had done with a skeleton crew and minimum equipment in a day and a half would have taken most shops three or four days, and we were rightly proud of what we had achieved.

Aquiles wanted to know if she would be ready to fly the next day.

"Shoot, yes," Dave replied, "she'll be ready."

Even back at the hotel we were congratulating ourselves on the good work we had done and talked until past midnight. Mel asked endlessly if we were going to be able to leave on Monday. I ducked the question every time he asked it. After the radio incident in Santa Marta, the expiration of my deadline, and Donado's "no test flight" edict, I had very strong reservations about when we could leave. I also had to face up to another very disturbing matter—Valdez's ability to produce. I knew he had the authority to do this, but all signs were now indicating that he didn't know quite how to go about it. No one knew better than I that it was a highly complex legal puzzle that would demand great skill to unlock. Valdez's evasive glances and hesitations haunted my uneasy dreams that night.

CHAPTER THIRTY-TWO

The slums of Barranquilla sprawled before us, asleep in the first rays of sunlight as we headed for Santa Marta. *Maybe tomorrow*, I thought. Maybe tomorrow 464 Juliet will take us out of this godforsaken spot. The garbage-strewn streets with their mangy, starving dogs rooting in the battered cans, the matted burros, and the ramshackle huts grew more and more depressing. *Please God, let it be tomorrow*, I prayed silently.

Dave must have sensed my feelings and wanted to shake me out of my funk with a "Hey, wake up. Tomorrow we'll be gone."

"Right," I said, "and this would be the perfect time to give these dogs something to remember us by." I stuck my head out the window and barked viciously at a scrawny pair scratching their fleas on the curb. I speak canine without a trace of gringo accent and they jumped to attention with ears cocked to answer the challenge. One was so startled and ready for battle that he leaped on a third dog that had just turned the corner unexpectedly, which resulted in a snarling fight. Other neighborhood dogs came running to join the free-for-all. We had tears in our eyes from laughing as we pulled away.

When we reached Donado's house, he greeted us in his shorts.

"I'm sorry," he told us, "but I can't go with you today. There's a problem at my office I have to take care of. Fernando can go with you and take the truck. If you have any problems, call me at work."

We asked if there would be any problem with the manager about working without Donado's being with us, and he told us he had already spoken with Zapata and that everything was taken care of and in good order.

Our stop at the bridge was short and after we had given the customary tip we drove on. Aldo was sitting in the rocking chair as we drove up. His bloodshot eyes indicated that his night life was returning to normal, and he muttered that he was not feeling very well. He would join us later at the airport. He allowed us to load up what we needed without even a token offer of help. We left him nursing his hangover.

We stopped at Zapata's house, who greeted us courteously and followed us to unlock the gates. The soldiers acknowledged our presence only by lifting their sleepy eyes and returned to dozing in their chairs. Colombia was a real Saturday night country, and Sunday was the day of atonement and recuperation.

We got busy at once, ignoring the blazing sun which beat down on us without mercy. Mel sat patiently on the right wing, grinding off corrosion where the vortex generators had been knocked off. Dave relentlessly pulled more panels, checking control cable tensions and lubricating pulleys.

"Mel, Dave—look!" I pointed to the southeast where a Colombian Air Force T-33 fighter was making a sixty-degree bank to the left. We jumped up on the wings as the plane made a high-speed pass about one hundred feet east of us. We could see the pilot clearly as he stared down at us from a distance of only fifty feet overhead. Pulling the power back, he circled to the left and came back, this time even slower and closer. Then he pushed the throttle forward and sped off toward Barranquilla.

"What do you think that was all about, Raul?" I asked. "I guess he was checking us out."

Less than forty-five minutes later, I was in the cockpit when Mel shouted, "Bobby, we've got company."

A Colombian Air Force Queen Air—obviously one that had been confiscated and put to use— pulled up in front of 464 Juliet. Two distinguished-looking officers stepped off.

"Don't say anything," Raul whispered, "Let me do the talking."

"Who is in charge here?" inquired one of the officers. I knew immediately that the old T-33 fighter had been doing more than just a routine fly-by.

"I am," Raul spoke up. "I am Raul Soto. This is Fernando Donado, son of the *Jefe* of Aerocivil in Barranquilla," and they began explaining our presence, only to be interrupted by the same officer.

"This is Colombian Air Force property. You and your American friends have no authority to be here," he stated sternly. "You must leave immediately."

"Fernando, go call your father, quick. Tell him what's going on. He should call us here or come over, if he can. Just get it straightened out," I instructed hurriedly.

We were being escorted off the ramp as Fernando ran up to the control tower. Some twenty minutes passed while the Air Force personnel from the Queen Air milled around 464 Juliet and were closing her up.

Fernando appeared, rushing past us to the men by the Queen Air. After a minute of conversation they all mounted to the control tower. We waited. Finally, Raul and Fernando came back, smiling and motioning that we could return to work.

Fernando had been able to reach his father. Donado had talked with the major, informing him that we were there on orders from the Third Penal Court and Aerocivil. The officers had not been happy, but there was nothing they could do.

Now there was "no problem," according to Raul.

I was by no means sure that this would be the last we would hear from the Air Force. Their signals had already been crossed. One day the gringos were OK, the next day not.

Mel was also disturbed. "Look at them," he muttered. "Some of them are just kids—they don't look older than fifteen or sixteen. Kids that age with machine guns pointed at us—they might get trigger happy and let us have it if someone so much as sneezed."

We told Mel that it was the young recruits who got the shit details and that we were probably safer with them than with the older soldiers who were safely at home, nursing their hangovers. It was just "life in Colombia" on a Sunday afternoon.

We were close to finishing up our day's work around two fifteen when Mario came strolling across the ramp to speak with Raul. Raul called me over.

"Mario's located the radar. He wants us to go with him."

"Fine," I replied, wondering if I had enough money with me. I checked—about eighteen hundred dollars. It should be enough. I stopped only to tell Dave and Mel where I was going.

"Shoot, go ahead, Bobby," Dave said. "We'll be finished up here in another hour or two, and we'll just clean up and wait for you."

I slid behind the wheel of Aquiles' limousine and asked Mario for directions. Headed toward Santa Marta, Mario kept telling us that this was only a lead, that he didn't have anything to do with the theft, that he was only trying to help … . Raul reassured him. All we wanted was to get the equipment back. There would be no problems. We would pay. No questions asked.

When we had driven through the east side of Santa Marta, the area began to look familiar.

"This is almost where we were last night," I said. Mario nodded and motioned for me to keep going. The memory was still fresh of the encounter the night before in "no man's land"—or, rather, "no gringo's land."

We continued driving three or four miles more and were arriving at the base of the Sierra Nevada when Mario indicated that I should pull over. The plan was that Mario should wait for us there on the road. We were to continue on the road to the next dirt road where we were to turn left and proceed to the next right. We were to stop at the second house on the right and go inside.

"Wait a minute, Mario," I said, "why the hell aren't you going with us? We have no protection without, you."

"I can't," he explained. "They don't want me to know who stole the radar. If you want it back, you have to go alone. They said alone, without me."

I looked at Raul dubiously. What did he think?

Before Raul could answer, Mario interrupted, "Remember that woman last night?" Raul nodded. "Well, she'll be at the house. Everything will be OK."

The fact that Raul had done some public relations work the night before gave us a slight bit of reassurance, so we drove off. Raul was nervous, too. "They want money, not us." He whistled in the dark.

About five minutes later we pulled up to the cinder block house Mario had described. It sat alone, surrounded by trees, with little sign of life except for several Colombians and Indians outside, staring at us with immobile faces.

Raul got out and told me he would go in first. I sat in the car feeling like a fish in a bowl without water, completely out of my element and trapped.

In a moment, Raul was back to take me inside. There was a dirt floor. The large area was divided into "rooms" with dusty sheets hanging from wires. The plump woman was inside, waiting with three naked children clinging to her knees. She was nervous and kept licking her dry lips, leaning toward the door as Raul explained that I would cause no problems. All I wanted was the radar. Slowly he was persuading her to relax and to trust in us.

A young Colombian walked in who spoke briefly with Raul while he eyed me coldly. When he left, Raul told me that the young man was the advance guard, in a manner of speaking, "just checking to see if everything was all right."

Another fifteen minutes passed. I was restless and had moved to the door when I saw three men walking out of the woods toward the house with newspaper-wrapped packages in their arms. I nudged Raul.

The woman invited us to sit down. The legs of the old wooden chair were as shaky as mine—I sat down carefully.

The three men came through the door. Two of them were mestizos (mixed bloods), shirtless and barefoot, wearing long pants hitched low to accommodate their huge bellies. Sweat was running down their chests. Both had .45 automatics tucked in the front of their pants, nestled between their belt buckles and sunk into their blubber. The other, somewhat more presentable, wore a shirt and was armed with a well-honed machete. He motioned for me to unwrap the packages that they had set down on the floor. No one had yet spoken a word. I tried to break the rough twine binding the packages. The third man reached down impatiently and with a contemptuous flick of his machete, opened them.

Its edge glittered as he returned it to its scabbard. I willed my hands to be steady as I removed the paper. There they were—the AVQ 20 radar indicator that I had found in the plane, and the AVQ 20 R.T. unit, stolen two and a half years before. The two thefts had apparently been carried out at different times by the same three men. Fortunately for me, they had not found a ready market for the indicator in the meantime, as Learjets were not common in those parts.

Several other radio boxes among the rest of the packages had come from different airplanes. I picked up the two pieces and placed them on the table.

"Raul, tell them this is all we need. The rest don't belong to the Jet."

My shopping list did not meet their approval. Scowls appeared on their already sullen faces and they mumbled to each other in dissatisfied tones. Finally, the fattest of the two big-bellies spoke up.

"*Bueno, señor.* We'll take forty-five hundred dollars for these two—in American dollars." He spoke in a demanding voice and although it was in Spanish, I understood every word.

I figured that this was an asking price, another display of the *Dinero* Syndrome, and instructed Raul to tell them that one thousand dollars was my top offer. I could buy new ones in the States for twenty-five hundred dollars, and these had to be repaired. More important, I didn't have the four thousand dollars cash on me.

Raul was nervous about conveying my counteroffer. Beads of sweat sprang out on his forehead. The moment the last word left his mouth the fattest man pulled his .45 and put it to my head. The second pulled his as well, pointing it at Raul. I stood frozen as I felt the pressure of the end of the barrel boring into the side of my head, twisting the hair.

All three burst into a violent exchange, and I could feel the gun moving against my scalp as he waved his free arm in the air. The hammer was cocked, and I had visions of my brains being splashed all over the wall were his trigger finger to slip.

"Raul, what the hell is going on?" I managed to get out, holding myself rigid to avoid any sudden movements.

"They're talking about killing us. They think that if we walk out of here without buying, we'll call the police. Pay them the four thousand dollars—fast."

I reminded Raul that I didn't have it to pay. Thoughts raced through my mind at a millisecond pace. Of my life with my family, thousands of miles away. What a hell of a way for it to end. A rotting corpse in the jungle. The endless anxiety and false hopes for my wife and children. I had read about people feeling the cold barrel of a gun against their heads. Bullshit. I felt no cold steel, only the sensation of how fragile a skull would be under the impact of a high-caliber bullet.

The plump woman, who seemed to be the companion of the third man, had guts. She began to argue with them. At first, I thought it was to have them take us outside, so as not to kill us inside the house with the children present. Her man had picked up a length of rough rope that I believed would be used to tie us up.

Raul was pleading with them and with me.

"Bobby, say something, do something. I don't want to die." To be trapped in a corridor with no exit and certain death close by is a profoundly dreary and depressing experience. I had a desperate urge to vomit, stemming from the twisting knot in my stomach. Each second now drew out like an hour and I had a crazy impulse to do something, anything, to break the impasse. The return of emotion brought a glimmer of hope. There still was one last slim chance of reprieve from death.

I suddenly twisted away from my executioner, at the same time pulling a roll of large bills from my pocket. I threw it on the table and turned to face them, waving my arms and screaming defiance.

"No! I pay only fifteen hundred dollars—no more—Raul, tell them if they want more, they should keep the stuff. Or eat it. I don't care. Tell them I'm not the police. I'm not interested in them, just the radar."

My outburst was not a calculated risk, only a last desperate bid for survival, but it worked. They stared at me as if I were a mad dog, and then looked to Raul as he was frantically explaining my words and adding that I would be willing to pay more if they could produce the rest of my parts.

The woman added her arguments to Raul's, shouting, "Are you three crazy? They aren't going to go to the police. Take the money and let them go!"

The danger was not over. Death could still come at any moment, but they were giving her words some thought and began arguing violently with one another. The pistols were no longer aimed at us. By now, the weapons had become extensions of their moving arms, no longer primarily instruments of death.

Again the woman stepped in.

"They're *marimberos*—they don't want any trouble."

I silently thanked God for Raul's lying tongue. He must have volunteered this misinformation during their friendly chat the night before. The woman pulled her man by the arm into the adjoining "room." The other two remained with us, just staring hostilely. Our very lives were being decided by a kangaroo court there in that godforsaken hut in the wilds of Colombia. Still, our situation had improved vastly over that of a just few moments before, and my mind was no longer the frozen wasteland it had been.

She emerged from behind the sheet curtain, moved to the table, and picked up the money. She counted it out and then turned to us.

"There's only fourteen hundred dollars here," she said accusingly.

"Bobby, give her another hundred," Raul stuttered.

Now I was beginning to feel more optimistic. The money had been accepted. A transaction had been completed. There was still a possibility that they would kill us, but it was no longer a probability. After all, they could have killed us first and then taken the money freely, without any quibble about the missing one hundred dollars. Nevertheless, I was relieved when she told us we could go.

"But remember," she added, "don't tell anyone where you got the equipment or who sold it to you. Go, now—before they change their minds."

I grabbed the two pieces of equipment that had almost cost us our lives and started out the door. I had a ridiculous impulse to say "thank you," but a quick glance at the still smoldering trio of Colombians told me that this was no time for lingering farewells.

Praying for Aquiles' old Chevy not to fail me, we hustled inside and sped down the dirt road. Raul was still in a state of shock, and groped for words.

"You're a crazy fucking gringo," he finally blurted out. "What made you do that?"

"Do you think they were serious?" I asked?

"Hell, yes. It was just a matter of where."

I nodded, "Well, that's why I did what I did. There was just nothing else left to do. I didn't 'decide' anything; I just reacted. Something told me our only chance was to act like one of them."

It was the truth. A primitive instinct must have spurred me to the violent reaction that dissipated their deadly concentration on killing us.

"You're crazy. You're crazy," he stated, over and over. "But it was a good thing for us that you are crazy."

"Who stopped them, Raul? I didn't understand everything they said."

Raul thought that the house belonged to the one with the machete. He didn't want us killed in his house. That was why he got the rope, to tie us up and take us out somewhere. But it was the woman who stopped it. She told them we weren't police. Raul admitted he had told her that we were in the "business" the other night, as he had thought she might be able to help us locate more of the Learjet parts. So she felt it was safe for them to let us go and not get involved in a murder.

We got back to the main road and found Mario where we had left him. He jumped in.

"I see you got the radar," he remarked, grinning.

I didn't say a word, driving on as Raul explained what had happened. Mario made abject apologies, which I pointedly refused to accept. His "*Lo sientos*" in no way absolved him from responsibility, and I advised him of this in no uncertain terms.

"I know damned well you had an idea what the fuck might happen. You let us walk right into that den of killers without a word—just a lousy excuse that you weren't supposed to go in. You were scared, that's all. From now on, you're going to have to work a little harder for your money. You're going to have to persuade everybody who wants to sell us equipment to bring it either to the airport or to our hotel in Barranquilla. I'm not going through that kind of bullshit ever again."

I felt better once I had reamed Mario out, but I held my silence and prayed to God in thanksgiving for having spared us, while Mario and Raul chatted amiably, as if nothing had ever happened.

If all the things that had been happening to me over the previous two months, and especially that day, had happened to the others who had tried to get 464 Juliet out of Colombia, then it was no small wonder she was still there after three years. That day's event was no simple mind game. It was the most dangerous game of all, played with the barrel of a cocked .45 against my head, with nothing between me and oblivion but a slippery finger on the trigger.

We dropped Mario at the lobby terminal and carried our radar out to 464 Juliet. Raul proudly displayed it to our friends, and excitedly recited the particulars of our brush with death. I was too exhausted to play it anything but low-key so I sat under the shade of 464 Juliet, toasting life with a Lipton iced tea. My mouth was parched and I smoked nearly half a pack of cigarettes chain fashion.

Dave reported that 464 Juliet was now completely airworthy. This was good news, but my thoughts were still back in the concrete block even now in the shadow of the Sierra Nevada.

Mel asked if the judge had our papers ready. I told him I didn't know but that we would call him that night. All I wanted to do was rest for a short while. After a few minutes, however, I roused myself from my drowsiness and spent the next half-hour checking our list of completed squawks. It met with approval.

"Do you think she's safe?" I asked Dave.

"It would be better if we could test fly her," he answered, "but, shoot, I'm not worried. If she goes down, we go together."

"That's my Davey," I answered, "always think positive."

He just grinned. Dave's disposition had been a major factor in keeping harmony among us during the past back-breaking days of labor. The sun was dropping in the west and the heat had abated a little, giving us some relief. Raul assumed his public relations director role, gathering everyone together who had helped us in any way to pose for photos in front of 464 Juliet. After the photographing session, we secured her and left for Aldo's house.

Aldo's hangover had not responded to treatment. We found him where we had left him that morning in the old rocking chair. He explained that his back had pained him so severely that he hadn't felt up to driving. Jesus, he was still milking that wreck for all it was worth.

"Aldo, has Valdez finished the papers?" I wanted to know, adding that 464 Juliet was ready to fly.

Aldo's eyes grew bright and he sat up with animation. "You mean that you've been able to get the airplane ready in just two and a half days?—Are you sure?—Is it true?"

He was obviously impressed by the miracle we had wrought. "What about the papers?" I insisted.

"I tried to call him today, Bobby, but he wasn't home. I'll try again tonight and then call you at the hotel," he promised.

I was annoyed—Aldo wasn't producing any miracles of activity for us, that was for sure. Something was wrong, I could sense it. Mel's never-ending questions added to my concern as Raul and I tried to devise some way to get both Aldo and Valdez moving.

Back at the hotel, Raul and I took a walk outside to talk privately.

"Why doesn't Valdez ever come around to the airport, Raul?" I asked, "It seems like he wants to keep out of sight."

Raul had no explanation to offer except that the judge might have been scared of something. It occurred to me that Valdez might be trying to avoid, as much as possible, confrontations with the military. Certainly, that very afternoon, the show of hostility from the Air Force had indicated that there could be other occasions when they would be breathing down our necks. We had been able to get Valdez to use his clout as a last resort once, and possibly could do it again, but we were beginning to see that it was necessary to exhaust all other channels first.

"Do you really think we're going to get 464 Juliet out of here?"

Raul didn't know the answer to this any more than I, but I was looking for reassurance, which he was quick to give.

"Yea, yes," he insisted, "we've worked too hard to give up. We'll find a solution"

I lay awake a long time that night, reviewing carefully everything that had happened in the past two months. I re-analyzed every person I had met, every word that was said, the tone of voice, what the person had to gain—or lose—by saying it. Who could be counted on and to what extent. Why 464 Juliet was still sitting in Colombia after three years. Why we were allowed to work on her one day, and forbidden the next. And always, my thoughts returning to Valdez and his strange delays. I even got up, turned on the light, and made a list of pros and cons, trying to see which way the scales of reality tipped. I tore it up. My chances were, at best, slim. My faith and belief in myself were my only true assets—this was the reality. The people I was up against were human, like me, not supernatural. I would find a way … and I dozed off, and it wasn't until the next morning when I woke up that I realized that Aldo had not called us the night before, so I went to rouse Raul.

"Wake up, refugee," I whispered, not wanting to wake the others, "Let's call Valdez."

"What time is it?" he inquired sleepily.

I told him six thirty, and he scrambled out of bed to shower. I waited until seven fifteen, and finally dragged him to the telephone. We were not able to get a call through for half an hour, but, finally, the telephone rang. The judge was on the line.

Raul first described all the work we had accomplished and that 464 Juliet was now in airworthy condition. I crossed my fingers as he broached the subject of her papers.

"*Señor Juez*," Raul's voice was infinitely respectful, "Bobby wants to know if we can plan to leave today or tomorrow?" His face revealed nothing as he listened. I crossed my fingers tighter. My heart sank as I heard the old refrain, "*Si, señor Juez … comprendo … ,*" and "*Pues, si, señor Juez … .*" Raul's gaze was directed at the floor—no happy smiles and winks and circled thumb and forefingers. I could tell we were not receiving good news.

"Just a moment, *señor Juez*," Raul was saying, "let me explain to Bobby … ," and he turned to me to tell me that Valdez hadn't finished with the documents. It would be at least another week, two maximum. The judge felt it would be foolish for us to wait here for them. It would be advisable for us to return to Miami, and Valdez would call us.

I was sick with disappointment.

"Tell Valdez I must talk with him today. Ask if we can come over at one or two this afternoon. Tell him it's important," I instructed.

Raul relayed my request and bid Valdez goodbye. He told me that Valdez would see us at two.

"Tell me everything he said," I demanded, and Raul obediently went over what was said, as nearly word-by-word as he could remember.

I told Raul what he must say to Valdez at our coming meeting. That I needed a letter from him stating that I was going to get the release of 464 Juliet, and that no one but me would get it. That my contract expired on July 10 and that I would be a son of a bitch if I were going back empty-handed. I needed proof for Lloyd's of London and Paul Engstrom that I wasn't jerking them around. If Valdez refused to give me such a letter, I would have to have serious doubts about his good faith. We had to get him off his pompous ass and put the pressure on him.

Raul agreed. "If he's honest, he'll give you the letter. If he doesn't—well, then we'll know."

The hardest part of the morning was to wake Mel and Dave to give them the bad news. Mel was particularly unhappy. He initiated another series of unanswerable questions but finally realized that my balls were being pinched so he eased off. Dave took it in his easy stride.

"Shoot, don't worry. I'll come back as soon as Valdez gives you the OK," he assured me.

Dave and Mel packed hurriedly. They could still catch the 10:00 A.M. flight to Miami. I had a bitter taste in my mouth as I watched them leave with Toño for the airport.

CHAPTER THIRTY-THREE

Raul and I lingered outside the hotel, sitting on the low rock wall in front and discussing the afternoon meeting when a bright red Ford Bronco pulled up. It was new, equipped with all the standard accessories of a rich *marimbero*: mag wheels, over-sized tires, and a radio antenna.

Three well-dressed Colombians wearing Rolex watches and lots of gold stepped out. I barely glanced at them and continued the conversation with Raul.

"Bobby? Bobby Wood," I heard a voice call out.

I looked up.

"I'll be damned. Federico Ramirez."

Federico walked over as I got to my feet. He gave me a hearty *abrazo* (hug) and a vigorous handshake.

"What are you doing here, Bobby?" he wanted to know.

"It's a long story, Federico. Shit, I've been here long enough to take out citizenship papers. How are the wife and children?"

"Fine, fine, and yours?"

Federico introduced his two friends, and I called Raul over to meet them. We spoke together for a few minutes. A bellboy emerged from the hotel looking for Raul. He had a telephone call from the States. Raul left. Federico suggested that the rest of us go into the restaurant to talk. Federico Ramirez was a nice-looking Colombian in his early fifties. The cut of his leisure suit and his expensive jewelry spelled out that he was enjoying considerable prosperity.

I had first met Federico some four years previously when he had virtually nothing. He had come to my parts department to buy small quantities of aircraft parts for export. Soon he was visiting us regularly. At times his wife, perhaps half his age, came with him, together with their children. The children were beautiful with large liquid eyes and solemn expressions that broke into delighted smiles when I would fish sticks of chewing gum or lifesavers from my pockets to give them. The youngest was a baby in arms, and my wife had asked if the Ramirezes could use some almost-new clothing that our baby had outgrown. The gift had been accepted in the spirit it was given, and we became friendly. Another time, Federico had desperately needed two thousand dollars, which I lent him to pay his rent and buy food.

As time went by, Federico got on his feet and prospered. When he began sending friends in to buy airplanes and aviation equipment from me, I realized that he had gone into the "business." He finally told me openly that this was the case and asked if I were interested in doing some "deals" with him, which I declined. We had still remained friends. Federico never forgot a helping hand, and he appreciated my lending him money when he had needed it so badly.

As I looked across the table at my old friend, the waitress appeared with his order, a special bitter black coffee, which he laced generously with sugar. After taking a first sip, he leaned back and wanted to know all about what I was doing in Colombia.

"Would you believe me if I told you?" I asked, smiling.

"*Si*, Bobby, but don't tell me you're in the "business." That would be an insult to your old friend—I've been after you for a long time. Even so, I would forgive you if you would work with me. You could have anything you wanted—a thousand pounds, ten thousand pounds—delivery up front, no money up front—anything for an old friend."

Chuckling, I told him that if I lived in Colombia I probably would be in the "business," in which case he would most definitely be the only person I would even consider as a partner. His friends were enjoying the novelty of an encounter with a "straight" gringo and laughed at Federico's outrageous offers to set me up in style.

We finally got around to my reason for being in Barranquilla.

"Do you know anything about the Learjet over in Santa Marta?" I asked.

"*Si, si,* what about it?"

"I've been working for several months to get it her out of Colombia."

"Who told you that you could get it out?" Federico suddenly became serious.

"Do you know Judge Valdez in Santa Marta?"

Yes, Federico knew him. I explained that Valdez was handling the papers which were to be completed within a week or two, and I gave him a run-down on what had happened thus far. I told him about Donado and Alfredo in Bogotá.

Federico was listening intently. However, his friends were shaking their heads and smiling incredulously. I stopped my narrative to ask what was so funny.

"You're joking, aren't you? I know you like a good joke," Federico answered.

"No, I'm serious. I've spent over twenty-five thousand dollars so far. That's no joke."

"How much is it going to cost you, Bobby, altogether?"

I told him I would also pay out seventy-five thousand dollars to my lawyer and for the judge when the papers were completed. Federico gave me a long look and sat in silence a few moments, shaking his head sadly.

"What's wrong, Federico?" I demanded, alarmed.

"Look, Bobby, I remember a long time back when you helped me. Now I'm going to help you. Believe me, that jet isn't going anywhere. It's been here since 1977. It belongs to the Air Force and the President of the Republic. I know of at least half a dozen Americans that came down here to get it out. There were even payoffs to steal it and every single one got screwed."

My heart plummeted as Federico went on, telling me about Colombians with real connections who had attempted to get it released but had failed.

"But Federico," I protested, "Alfredo in Bogotá wouldn't scam me, and Luis Donado—the head of Aerocivil—is solidly behind me. How can you say I don't have a chance? Why would they let me work on it?"

"*Quién Sabe*," Federico shrugged. He said he was not trying to cast doubts on the good faith of Alfredo Escobar or Luis Donado. What he was trying to tell me was that in Colombia good faith was just not enough. Perhaps the Air Force was very happy to have someone appear out of the blue to make the jet airworthy and to do so for free. Perhaps there was one thing I was overlooking—perhaps the absolute top clout in Colombia was the military.

"How do you think I can run my 'business?'" he demanded. "I have friends in the Air Force, friends in the Army—even the general is a friend. Without these friends, I couldn't move a pound out of Colombia. You don't have these friends, and I am telling you, sincerely, that without them you don't have a chance. Nobody is going to walk in here and take that jet out. Don't waste any more money, Bobby, please. I beg you as a friend."

I sat there immobile, trying to withstand the deadly blow being dealt to me from the hand of a friend, knowing that he was giving it to me only to help and not to harm me. I fiddled with my glass of Coca-Cola, trying to think of one logical reason I could put forth to prove him wrong, and finding nothing to say.

Federico put his arm across my shoulders, saying, "Bobby, you are like a son. Please listen to me. They are playing games with you to screw you out of your money. People here have no mercy on Americans. Go back home. Forget the jet. I don't want to see you get hurt."

I felt like putting my head down on my arms and sobbing, but I somehow managed just to sit there, frozen. Federico's friends were in complete agreement with his advice.

I wanted desperately to be alone, but couldn't insult Federico by leaving. I could see he was pained by having to be the bearer of bad news.

I changed the subject. We talked about Federico's "business" for several minutes and any lingering doubts I might have had about his assessment and advice were dissipated when he told me he had done "business" with Valdez.

Finally Raul came in to tell me that Toño was back from the airport, and I was able to make a quick exit. "Thank you, Federico, especially for your advice. I'll take it seriously," I said. We exchanged warm goodbyes, and I started directly up to the room. Raul followed without a word, casting anxious glances at my set face.

I sat on the bed and looked out toward the Sierra Nevada. I had to acknowledge that Federico wasn't lying, that there was no reason for him to lie; he had nothing to gain by lying. Raul stood by silently, waiting to hear what was wrong.

Finally, I told him. Raul was hard pressed to accommodate my conviction that Federico had been telling the truth with his optimism that we would succeed. But he tried.

"Bobby," he said earnestly, "I know he is a friend. He wasn't lying to you. He is just making a mistake. He doesn't know what he's talking about."

"Horseshit, Raul," I interrupted rudely, "he's even in the 'business' with Valdez. He uses Valdez's airport."

We sat talking in circles, trying to weigh everything Federico had told me, and were getting nowhere. I would have gone crazy if I sat there another minute, so I rallied into action, telling Raul to go downstairs and find Aquiles and Toño to take us to see Valdez. I had to do something to shake off my acute depression.

The drive across the peninsula was spent in almost complete silence. I prayed most of the trip for God to give me the strength to keep going and the wisdom to deal with this new problem. The only time Raul opened his normally voluble mouth on this trip was to speak words of encouragement. We found a parking spot a couple of blocks away from Valdez's office and waited half an hour for him to arrive. He greeted us cheerfully when he walked in.

"Bobby, Raul, *como estas?*"

He was very pleased to hear that 464 Juliet was airworthy, repeating over and over that it was good news, very good news.

"Do you have good news for us, Judge?" I pressed, "Can you tell us yet when the airplane can be officially released?"

His face fell. No, it would be a week or two before he had all the documents together and *la providencia* finished. *La providencia* was the court's final ruling, summarizing all the salient facts concerning the confiscation of

464 Juliet and containing the legal precedents and reasoning upon which the plane's official release would be awarded.

I was well aware that this was going to be a difficult job and had suspected for some time that Valdez was having problems formulating a clear-cut summary that would answer all the highly complicated legal requirements of Colombia.

"I have another problem," I informed Valdez. "I need you to write me a letter addressed to Paul Engstrom, informing him that 464 Juliet will be released and that it will be released only to me."

"Why do you need such a letter?" Valdez hedged.

Slowly and cautiously, for at least the fifth time, Raul and I explained the July 10 deadline. We skirted around the term "conditional sales contract" which he either did not understand or refused to understand. I was also apprehensive that he might understand all too well that I could lose my ownership if Lloyd's insisted on holding me to that deadline. Valdez's reluctance and timidity concerning 464 Juliet raised a possibility that he might be glad for an excuse to wash his hands of the matter. Not matter how strongly tempted I was to point out to him that I was now in this situation only because of his endless indecision and delays, I had to hold my tongue.

I made Valdez understand that I had been granted an extension of time and that his letter would provide confirmation of the fact; it was a formality, but a critically important formality. Suddenly, out of the blue, the word "protocol" came to me. The judge's face brightened. "Protocol" was a word he understood well. It didn't rhyme with "procedures," but it was in the same column in his legal dictionary.

"Very well," he said briskly, "I will write the letter if it will help you."

I breathed a sigh of relief.

"What date do you want shown?" Now Valdez was all business. He opened his file on 464J and removed several documents, excusing himself to go to his secretary's office to dictate the letter. He asked us to wait for the few minutes he would be gone. Then he would give us the letter.

Raul was smiling and full of renewed optimism. "See, Bobby. I told you. He's serious; the letter will take care of the problem."

My eyes strayed to the file Valdez had left on the desk. Since he had let us examine its contents previously, I had no qualms about looking through the documents again. One of them caught my eye. It mentioned Jimmy Chagra, and I had not noticed it the first time Raul and I had gone through the file.

"What does this say?" I asked curiously.

Raul looked through it, a chubby finger passing under each line as he read. He appeared puzzled. Again the finger passed down the paper, more slowly this time.

"I don't understand," he said slowly. "It says here that Jimmy Chagra's case was examined again on February 20, 1979, and that he and Jerry Wilson were recharged with trafficking in narcotics and that the others had suspended charges. I don't know what that means."

I didn't either—I thought Raul had made a mistake in the date. Taking the document back from Raul, I double-checked it. Yes, it read February 20, 1979. This was very, very strange. How could Chagra be recharged for the same crime almost two years later? Hell, there was never any crime in the first instance, and those charges had been dismissed about two weeks after 464 Juliet's arrival on June 15, 1977.

Then I remembered another date from all the clippings I had been reading: Chagra had been indicted in Texas somewhere toward the end of February 1979. Those two dates at the end of February 1979, so close together, had to be more than just coincidence. As for the other two men on board 464 Juliet with Chagra, Bolling and Parada, both had been unconditionally released of all charges—violation of airspace and drug trafficking—in August of 1977.

Suddenly—or not so suddenly—charges were being "suspended" also on February 20, 1979. It sounded as though this matter had been kept on ice for quite a long time—far too long for anything so fishy not to smell very bad.

Our speculations were interrupted by Beatriz, Valdez's secretary, calling out my name.

"Your letter is finished, Mr. Wood," she announced, handing it to me. Raul and I went over it together. It was written on the usual lined, legal-size official paper with the government seal and, below, Valdez's signature and his court seal.

THE UNDERSIGNED THIRD CRIMINAL JUDGE OF THE SANTA MARTA

CIRCUIT, AT THE REQUEST OF THE INTERESTED PARTY, HEREBY STATES

To Mr. PAUL ENGSTROM, LAWYER, Representative of Lloyd's of London; that MR. ROBERT WOOD JR. appeared before this office stating that he was the only and sole owner of an airplane, LEARJET, Model 24, North American Registration N464J. This airplane has been inspected by the Colombian Aerocivil agency and at the present time is awaiting final processing of the request for its delivery (to said Robert Wood, Jr.)

Santa Marta, July 8, 1980

It sounded fine, and I nodded to Valdez, smiling and thanking him.

"We can go across the street right away to the Notary Public to legalize it," he offered. After we had finished this piece of business we returned to the office.

I was still not able to pin Valdez down about the release date. He suggested that we telephone him from Miami in about a week. Perhaps he would have more concrete news for us at that time. For the moment, I had to be content with having obtained the letter for Paul Engstrom, so we bade him farewell and departed to pick up Aquiles and Toño.

I wanted to stop at the Santa Marta airport to have a last look at 464 Juliet before leaving. Unmolested, I walked over to her while Raul remained in the lobby talking with Zapata, the airport manager, making arrangements for the airplane to be watched during our absence. I just strolled around 464 Juliet for fifteen or twenty minutes, touching her from time to time, making plans to restore her beauty, mooning like a modern-day Romeo unable to tear himself away from his beloved.

My leave taking was rudely interrupted by none other than Baratta, the old bureaucrat, who seemed to appear as regularly as a noisy bird in a cuckoo clock, waving jerking arms and shouting, "Get out."

"Your work is finished here. You have no authorization, to be here. You must leave," he cawed at me. I was too drained by the events of the last several hours to enter into another unnecessary confrontation, so I politely gave old Baratta the finger and went inside to find Raul.

He was deep, in conversation with a man I hadn't seen before. When he spotted me, he waved a beckoning arm.

"Bobby, I want you to meet Tomás—remember, I told you about him? He's the control tower supervisor."

I nodded and we shook hands. Raul whispered that Tomás had something he wanted to discuss with us, alone. We went upstairs and sat down at the far corner of the deserted restaurant.

I looked at my new acquaintance. He was a man about thirty years old, neatly dressed. His straight Indian hair was so black that it gleamed almost blue in the sunlight.

He got straight to the point: Would we be interested in doing "business" with him? He had all the marijuana we could buy. Fine quality. He assured us crisply that he had complete control over the airport for doing "business."

"What about the military?" I wanted to know. "They're right here."

"Sure they are; who do you think does our loading for us?" Tomás replied. He explained that the military was a highly important element in the operation. They transported the marijuana to the strip in official vehicles, requisitioned the fuel and did all the troubleshooting. When a shipment was scheduled, the police from Rodadero put up road blocks. Tomás, of course, controlled the runway lights. As for the Air Force, the T-33 was paid to stay on the ground during key hours. Of course, they were free to shoot down any intrepid freelancers who tried to infringe on the profitable territory they had marked as their own.

"We load a lot of planes here," Tomás said proudly, "and we've never had a problem yet. We have everything well organized."

I could see they did. I could also see that I was going to have to wear my *marimbero* face for still another eager and persuasive recruiter in Santa Marta. I would have to play along with Tomás, too, if I expected to get cooperation at the airport.

"I'll talk with you about this later, Tomás," I replied, with what I hoped sounded like sincere enthusiasm. "I'll be back here in a week or so."

Tomás left us, happy and confident that we were going to be great amigos. Raul was equally jubilant, pleased at the prospects of a new and luxurious life for both of us.

"We're lucky," he pronounced with great satisfaction. Then, suddenly, he remembered something else ... Zapata, the manager of the airport.

"What about Zapata?" I asked.

"He wants to talk to you, too—about the 'business.' He has an operation himself. He asked me to feel you out about coming in with him." Raul could scarcely contain himself at the great abundance of connections being thrust upon us.

"Tell Zapata I'll talk with him when I get back the next time," I instructed Raul. It was beginning to sound like a broken record. Zapata was still another key man at the airport who had to be kept happy. The number of people hitting on me was turning into a mob scene.

I had finally concluded that the *marimbero* plague had reached epidemic proportions here in Santa Marta and that those infected with it showed a characteristic symptom—a mania to infect the few remaining Colombians left who had not yet succumbed to the disease. What a crazy, upside-down world it was, where a man had to conceal his immunity or else be considered a freak and an enemy by those infected.

Raul ran off to Zapata's office to make his report, returning to tell me that Zapata was pleased and was looking forward to the new connection. Zapata, too, offered to front his merchandise; my credit rating there was A-1.

I gave Raul a "thumbs up" sign and we rejoined Aquiles and Toño.

We would stop at Aldo's before returning to Barranquilla. We all needed a good laugh. When we reached the house, Aldo's father was finally back in the rocking chair which Aldo had commandeered for his convalescence. Aldo was not there, but would be back shortly. Sitting on the porch with Mr. Reyes to take advantage of the shade, we sipped our iced water while we waited for Aldo's return.

Not long after, Aldo arrived, apologizing for his absence with a tale of "important business." The smell of liquor on his breath told me that his business had been conducted at his favorite bar, but we went through the polite bullshit without any mention of being aware that we knew how he spent his afternoons. Before I was fully prepared to unload on him for dragging his feet, he took Raul and me aside to ask us to go with him into his bedroom to talk privately.

"Bobby, I have good news for you. I know you stopped and saw Valdez today—I talked with him about an hour ago."

What was this? I marveled. *No reproaches and hurt feelings that we had gone to see Valdez without him?*

Aldo continued, "I'm going to save you twenty-five thousand dollars. How about that?" and he looked at us for applause.

"Tell me more Aldo," I encouraged.

Aldo was beginning to think Valdez was getting cold feet. He was therefore taking matters into his own hands. He had already made tentative arrangements with the colonel at the military headquarters in Santa Marta for us to steal the jet. He had told the colonel of all the money I had spent and how I was being jerked around. The colonel had agreed that he would have his men turn their backs, so to speak, while we took off. Aldo had assured the colonel that this would be a relatively easy and quick matter since the jet was ready to go.

"What about the civil airport personnel, Aldo?" I asked. "Who's taking care of that?"

"Don't worry. The colonel has everything under control, he assured me of that," Aldo replied.

"And what about Valdez? He'll cut off your balls, Aldo."

"Valdez won't know I had anything to do with it. He'll think it was all your idea. I've covered myself there." I was sure of that, I thought grimly. "Of course," Aldo added judiciously, "you won't ever be able to come back to Colombia. So you have to keep that in mind. But it will save you twenty-five thousand dollars."

I looked at Aldo thoughtfully. The fact that I had not yet refused to take advantage of his money-saving offer encouraged him to go on.

"There's just one thing, Bobby. If you want to do it, you will have to pay the fifty thousand dollars tomorrow. The colonel said it would take one day to set things up. You could plan to leave this Wednesday morning early, about five."

Aldo spent the next half hour describing carefully the details of the scam he was eagerly preparing to pull on Valdez. At this stage, I was becoming desperate enough to consider the merits of such a plan. My friend Federico had made it clear to me that without cooperation from the military I could not possibly get 464 Juliet out of the country. Valdez had let me down so many times that I was close to convinced that he just couldn't swing his end of the deal. The only negative aspect, at the moment, was that Aldo simply didn't have enough credibility with me to risk it. If he was willing to shoot down Valdez, who did possess some clout right in Aldo's own backyard, he would be even more likely to have the Air Force shoot me down—literally and before I took off—if I made this deal with Aldo.

I could think of only one way to test the offer—the old ploy of a counter-offer, which had worked before with Aldo.

"OK, Aldo," I said, "I like the idea, but there is one small problem."

Aldo was all ears.

"I'll take you up on your offer," I continued, "but I won't pay either you or the colonel until 5:00 A.M. Wednesday. When the jet has been cranked and running—and on the runway–I'll hand you the money alongside her as I step inside."

"Oh, no, Bobby, that won't do—the colonel would think that you planned to take off without paying. No, no."

"Look, Aldo, if I don't pay, he can still shoot me."

Aldo was protesting that things weren't done that way in Colombia. I had to show good faith. The colonel might think I didn't trust him.

"It looks to me as if the colonel doesn't trust me," I countered. "He has to show good faith, too. Tell him no deal."

Aldo's face was full of dismay as he kept insisting that the colonel was to be trusted. The dollar signs were fading from his eyes. His new scheme to pick up a fast buck was slipping away from him.

I asked Raul opinion of Aldo's plan. Raul hemmed and hawed—maybe yes, maybe no—and threw the ball right back in my lap. It was up to me.

Finally, I told Aldo I would think it over and let him know the next morning. Aldo had to be content with that answer. When it was time for goodbyes, Aldo gently tapped me for two thousand dollars to cover more of his medical expenses. I considered his request for a few seconds, and came to the conclusion that I should also cover my back with a counter offer here, as well.

"I'll tell you what I'm going to do, Aldo. You give me a check for two thousand dollars and I'll hold it until you get 464 Juliet released. When you do, I'll tear up the check. If you don't, I'll turn it in for collection," and I took out two thousand dollars.

Aldo, once again bright-eyed at the sight of money, quickly wrote out the check. Actually, this transaction was nothing more than a formality. I knew there would be little chance of collecting against the check if 464 Juliet was not released.

Back at the hotel, Raul and I called Donado to inform him of the results of our meeting with Valdez. We also had to find out whether he would help us in the morning by bringing my money to me once I was on board the flight. The soldiers would make trouble for us if we had to take it through the security check. Donado told us he would be happy to oblige, and would meet us at eleven thirty in the morning.

Again Raul and I returned to analyzing all our encounters of the past week. I was desperately searching for the realities among the unrealities, something that made sense. There was only one scrap of reality I could positively identify: the fact that Judge Valdez had not asked me for any more money. If anyone in Colombia would logically do so, it would have been Valdez. It was slim enough evidence of his good faith, but it was all I had, and I clung to it. I finally dozed off while my mind was still spinning, trying to separate what I wanted to believe from what was reality.

JULY 15, 1980—BARRANQUILLA, ON MY WAY HOME, THINKING AND PRAYING

Donado was smiling as Raul and I walked in. We talked about 464 Juliet until the Avianca flight was called. Donado was non-committal about the chances of getting her out, he offered neither encouragement nor discouragement.

We handed Donado a small package, neatly wrapped, which contained the eighty-thousand dollars. Raul and I went through security, submitted to body and hand luggage search and boarded the airplane. When we were inside, Donado came on board and handed Raul the packet. This was one of the few pleasurable aspects about Colombia, having someone like Donado we could trust.

Never in my life have I been so depressed as when we were taking off. Clouds completely hid the Sierra Nevada, matching my dismal mood. After our original high spirits at finishing our restoration work on 464 Juliet with such good results and so quickly, everything that could have gone wrong had done so in the past day. All I wanted was to be back home, away from that hellhole.

Raul went to sleep almost immediately, snoring gently in his seat. I didn't begrudge him his easy mind—he didn't have at stake what I did so I let him enjoy his rest, while I stared blankly out the window, praying and thinking.

CHAPTER THIRTY-FOUR

JULY 15, 1980—GESTAPO, UNITED STATES STYLE

We landed in Miami at five in the afternoon. After going through immigration we went downstairs to customs, picked up our luggage and moved to the check-out counters. Raul and I automatically took places in different lines. We had standing bets of a dollar on who would clear customs first. Each time one of us moved ahead we would exchange cheerful grins.

Within minutes I found there was little to be cheerful about. When the customs agent took my passport, I requested a 4790 form to declare my money. He immediately gave me a sidewise and knowing look, shooting a rapid fire of questions at me—What was I doing in Colombia? Who did I go there to see? What business was I in?

"Let me finish this form, please," I suggested. I handed it to him in a few seconds and looked him over. He was an unattractive specimen around thirty years of age, over six feet tall with a lumpy physique and wearing a scruffy-looking, untended black beard.

After examining the completed form, he turned and raked me over with an insolent gaze.

"Just where did you get the eighty-thousand dollars, Mr. Wood?" he sneered.

"From my bank here in Florida, the First State … ," I began, but he didn't even let me finish.

"Wait here," he ordered and left me standing. I waited for several minutes, wondering what the problem could be and becoming more uneasy as each minute passed. He had punched my name into the computer when I had requested the form; I wondered why. I knew my name wasn't in the computer. I had never been arrested in my life, nor had I ever been stopped or questioned concerning my recent travels to Colombia. I looked around and over to the left, about thirty feet away, spotted him with two other agents. They were talking and glancing my way. Finally, he advanced toward me with one of the men.

"Come with us," the bearded one ordered. I was escorted to one of the small identical cubicles, which I assumed were interrogation rooms, at the far end of the room. The cubicle was only about eight by ten feet, furnished with a small table and two chairs.

Pointing to the table, he said curtly, "Set your briefcase down here and open it."

The other agent, younger and clean-shaven, removed the packet of money. He glanced at me curiously. I was conservatively dressed in a summer suit and apparently did not match the profile they normally looked for. Something was wrong. Why had they stopped me? The first agent, then the second, counted the money.

"Exactly eighty thousand dollars," said the agent with the beard.

"That's right," I said, "eighty thousand dollars is what I declared on the 4790 form."

He ignored my statement and snarled, "Empty your pockets on the table."

"What for?" I wanted to know.

"You are being detained," he threw back at me.

"What for? I haven't broken any law."

"Shut up and empty your pockets," he insisted, contemptuously.

I was becoming angry at his completely uncalled for insolence. "I'll be damned if I'll empty my pockets," I gave back. "You are violating my civil rights. I demand to see a supervisor. Right now."

Goon No. 1, the bearded agent, threw me a murderous look and slammed out of the little room. He returned shortly, without a word, and stood alongside Goon No. 2, glaring at me. There were five long minutes of silence, broken by the opening of the door to admit a pockmarked face of a man in his late fifties.

"I'm the supervisor," he informed me impatiently. "What the hell do you want me for?"

I could see that I had really screwed up by demanding to see him. He was no reasonable man of authority who would straighten out subordinates who had gotten out of line. His entire attitude made it loud and clear that he would back them up and that ranks had been closed against me. Nevertheless, I made an attempt.

"Sir, my civil rights are being violated. I filled out the 4790 form required by law. Now they want to search me."

"They ain't violatin' nothin'," he informed me, contemptuously, and slammed the door shut.

Goon No. 1's face showed great satisfaction that his authority had been established. He was going to rub my nose in it for daring to go over his head. He hitched up his pants in anticipation and brought his hairy face within a few inches from mine.

"Now," he gloated, "you empty your pockets."

"I want to call my lawyer," I was still fighting back, still angry.

"No phone calls. Empty your pockets."

I was seething as I took everything out and placed billfold, keys, cigarettes, papers, cards, and miscellaneous items on the table.

They examined everything. As they pawed through my belongings, two Secret Service Agents entered the room, interested, evidently, only in the money. After carefully thumbing through the bills, one of them announced that the money looked all right, it wasn't counterfeit. They left as quickly as they had appeared.

Like most people, I have always been revolted by what I knew and heard about the Gestapo of Nazi Germany. Not just for the vicious and murderous cruelty of their agents, but equally for their complete disregard of human dignity which stripped its victims of personal identity and basic rights. I was appalled to learn that here in my own country, in the year 1980, a new variety of Gestapo was firmly entrenched under another name.

I was being detained, incommunicado, being searched without just cause, had broken no laws, and was being treated with insolence and contempt by a pair of government officials that my tax dollars helped to pay. It was truly Gestapo—United States Style.

Goon No. 1 left, and Goon No. 2 settled down to examine the quantities of papers in my briefcase. He scrutinized each scrap, both sides, as if expecting to find highly classified plans to our most secret missiles. After he had screened each paper, he set it aside on a "finished" pile and proceeded to the next.

Goon No. 1 returned and began his own screening of the "finished" papers. After all of these were done, they tore my billfold apart, thrusting fingers inside to see if it had hidden compartments. This went on for an hour. The pile of papers was about five inches high. Then they unsnapped the straps of the rear compartment of the briefcase which contained all the documents of the Tubara oil deal, the geological reports on a new nickel-mining project *La Comunidad* had just given to me for consideration, the 464 Juliet papers, and the file I had been compiling for Red Garglay at FAA on all of the planes with United States registry I had seen in the Guajira. This file showed tail numbers, dates, and special information I had obtained piecemeal. Some of the material contained notes on aircraft that even the Colombian authorities knew nothing about, as I had gotten it from other sources on the ground.

"Well, look at what we have here," Goon No. 1 said with an oily expression in his voice. "I see you've been to Riohacha, Mr. Wood."

"And look at this," Goon No. 2 echoed, pointing out some notes I had scribbled on my Air Unlimited stationery.

"It looks like we found ourselves a real big-timer," observed Goon No. 1 in a satisfied voice. "Are these airplanes yours?" he asked, pointing meaningfully to my list of over thirty aircraft I had spotted for Riohacha and surrounding areas.

He was eagerly pulling out the other lists and giving me the same nasty, mock-pitying smiles as he examined them and handed them to the other agent.

"Why don't you call Red Garglay at the FAA in Opa-Locka? He'll tell you what it's all about. You'll see that it's information he asked me to find and turn over to him each time I return from Colombia."

"Yeah, sure, Mr. Wood, I bet," scoffed Goon No. 1, openly incredulous to think I would take him for such a fool. "And I believe in fairy tales, too."

Goon No. 2 had laid his hands on the Tubara documents including the geological report on the new *La Comunidad* nickel-mining operation. "Hmm, I see you're building an airstrip," he said.

"What for, Mr. Wood?" Goon No. 1 chimed in, enjoying the cat-and-mouse game. "To send your planes down there for some more drugs?"

"You're both crazy; I'm not building anything in Colombia."

I had no idea what either of them was getting at. He thrust the document under my nose and pointed to a notation that said a two-thousand-foot airstrip could be prepared in a few weeks to give access to the remote area.

I looked at it.

"Don't you see where this is? It's in a mountain area between Medellin and Bogotá—it's part of the report on the terrain close to a nickel mine. The proposed strip would be for moving personnel in and out in light planes. If you knew anything at all about aviation, you'd realize that taking off in a mountainous area over eight thousand feet high from a two-thousand-foot strip could be done only with a small, high-lift type of plane. You certainly couldn't carry any kind of a heavy load and actually take off there. Why don't you read *all* of the report?"

Goons 1 and 2 merely smiled at each other, getting a kick out of hearing more of Mr. Wood's "fairytales."

Next, they were examining the photographs we had taken on our oil expedition in Tubara. One of them was of me standing in a wooded area along one of the trails we had used to reach the wells.

"Isn't this, you, Mr. Wood?" they wanted to know. "Is this your marijuana plantation?"

More exchanges of derisive looks. I finally shut up completely. If they were such assholes as to believe that trees over one hundred feet tall were marijuana plants, they wouldn't recognize anything that was true. I shrugged, walked over to one of the chairs and sat down, calmly ignoring them. This seemed to infuriate Goon No. 1.

"Stand up," he suddenly snarled. "Take off your pants."

Knowing it would do no good to argue, I stood up and dropped my trousers to my ankles.

"Would you look at that," he exclaimed in delight to his friend. "He doesn't have any underwear on. Where's your underwear, Mr. Wood?" His voice was sly and slimy.

I just stood there, letting him stare at my bare lower half with my pants crumpled around my ankles.

"I was in a fire in a race car in 1971," I said calmly, "and after that I never wore any. I was badly burned by the rubber in the waistband. Anything else?"

The way they stared at my crotch made me wonder if they were perverts as well as bullies. This would not have surprised me in the least. By this time my loathing had reached a pitch that had plunged me into an icy fury. They allowed me to stand before them for a time longer but as my failure to show humiliation disappointed them, I was finally told I could pull up the pants, which I did, slowly and deliberately, staring them full in the eye to show my contempt.

I sat down again and waited. They again got busy, removing papers and files. Goon No. 1 picked up the 464 Juliet file and the Riohacha file and started out.

"Just a minute," I interrupted, "you can't remove those files."

"Like hell I can't," he retorted. "Just sit down and shut up." He was back in fifteen minutes and replaced the files in my briefcase. I was sure he had removed them for photocopying, as I had heard Goon No. 2 whisper something about " … that one, too?" as Goon No. 2 had been picking up the papers before leaving.

Next I was told that a special agent was coming down from Fort Lauderdale to question me. What could that be all about?

Miami International Airport was fully staffed with agents from customs, the DEA and the FBI. Why, then, would they have to "import" a special agent to interrogate me? There had to be a very special investigation going on, shrouded in secrecy. Despite the baiting I had received from the goon squad, this must have nothing to do with drugs, nor with counterfeiting, nor with illegal currency transactions and manipulation.

I had been there for two and a half hours. The special agent was finally announced, and Goon No. 1 took him to another office, I assumed, to give him a playback of what had already happened and to hand over the copies he had made from the papers he had taken out of the room. These, I was sure, contained the clue.

They were the files on 464 Juliet and Riohacha. Things were beginning to come together. Harry Gilbert, the American Consul in Barranquilla, had knowledge of my trip to Riohacha and had questioned me at some length when I visited the Consulate there. There was also the mysterious American official from some unidentified agency who had been inquiring about me at the Barranquilla airport. Although I was sure my name did not appear on the computers of the "routine" agencies, I was beginning to wonder if other computer lists existed for different purposes. One fact was clear—464 Juliet was most certainly on a computer. My friend at the FAA, Red Garglay, had told me that the jet and its passenger list were on file with a great deal of classified information. Even though Bobby Wood's entrance on the scene had been a recent one, I might have gained access through the back door, so to speak, by association.

The special agent entered the room where I was waiting, ushered in by Goon No. 1. He was a trim man, well-dressed and businesslike, highly profession in bearing.

"I'm Special Agent Jim Horst," he said, flashing his badge. The brief glance I was given was not enough to tell if he was from the FBI, the Justice Department, or the Treasury Department. Pulling up a chair, he sat down and addressed me.

"Tell me about the money you're carrying, Mr. Wood," he said courteously.

"Mr. Horst, I've already told the others, but I'll start over. It's money I borrowed here in the States, from the First State Bank. The total loan was one hundred thousand dollars. If you call Jack Wood—no relation—he will verify this. He's the vice president. I'm sure he's home right now. Why don't you call him?"

Horst asked if I had my loan papers with me. No, I told him, they were in my office. Again I urged him to call Jack Wood.

"What were you doing with eighty thousand dollars in Colombia?" Horst next wanted to know.

Goon No. 1 stood in the doorway, thumbing through my passport. "Look at this, Mr. Horst," he interrupted, "he's been to Colombia five or six times this year." His tone of voice clearly implied that so many trips indicated only one thing—illegal activities. His face fell when Horst showed nothing more than polite interest.

I explained briefly that I was working with the authorization of Lloyd's of London to get the release of 464J and that the eighty thousand dollars was for legal fees and other expenses. Since the release had been delayed, I had been forced to bring the money back with me. I also mentioned that I had previously carried a considerable sum down to Colombia which I had also had to bring back again—that I had filled out the 4790 form at that time and had never even been asked to show the money. So why now? Horst steered me away from the money problem and back to Riohacha and 464 Juliet. Again, I suggested that Red Garglay be contacted; he could vouch for me.

"Why do you keep mentioning Red Garglay?" Horst asked.

"Because he works for the government and knows me well. If you talk with him, I'm sure you'll know what I'm saying is true."

He nodded. Then back to 464 Juliet. Who were my connections in Colombia. I told him I had a lawyer who was working through the courts.

"But you must have some connections ... ." Horst dangled the statement like a question.

"Sure, some connections. If I had connections, do you think I'd be dragging all this money back and forth? This is purely a business and legal matter that is not working out so simply. Can't you see that?"

Goon No. 1 was more interested in the money, so he got back into the act. Besides the packet containing the $80,000, I also had $5,697 in my pockets. Why hadn't I declared the total of $85,697?

I explained that, first of all, $2,000 was a check that wasn't even signed, and therefore not legal tender. There was $3,000 left in my coat pocket and $697 in my wallet. As I was permitted $5,000 that did not have to be declared, I felt that I had been completely in compliance with the regulations.

"How much did you declare when you left the United States?" Horst asked.

"Nothing," I shrugged, "I went commercial—on Avianca. Why?"

"What? You didn't declare anything?" he asked, incredulous. "No, sir, I didn't. I didn't the first time, either. I always thought that it was a requirement to declare money over five thousand dollars only if a person went private."

Horst, was shaking his head, completely nonplussed by my reply. "Mr. Wood are you aware of the penalty for not declaring money, either entering or leaving the country?" he asked seriously.

I told him I was not, and he went on, stating that it was five years in prison, a fine of five hundred thousand dollars, and loss of the money. I was stunned. This was real trouble and they had me cold—not for deliberately breaking the law but from ignorance of it.

"Look, Mr. Horst, I declared the money coming back in. I was never trying to hide anything."

The goons were watching me avidly, enjoying my predicament thoroughly, anticipating the pleasure of throwing the book at me and receiving a bonus for nailing me.

Finally, Horst got up and walked out.

Goon No. 1 smirked and said, "Now we've got you, big boy," and also left.

Again I was alone. My mind was in turmoil. I was the one who had thought the Colombian mind games were tough. Those games were nothing but amateur night compared with these. I was in bad trouble.

Finally, Mr. Horst returned with Goon No. 1. Both of them wore disgruntled looks.

"Well, Mr. Wood, do you want to go to jail?" Horst asked in a strange tone of voice. His question and tone were just slightly off-key. Both contained an element of something. Was it bluff?

"No, sir," I replied seriously, "not if I have a choice. But I have told you the truth, and I don't have anything more to tell you. As for jail, that's up to you."

He looked at me non-committal and said merely, "OK, Mr. Wood. You may leave now."

I was dumbfounded, and somehow convinced that this reprieve had been none of his doing.

"What about the fine?" Goon No. 1 demanded.

"The fine for what?" I wanted to know.

"The fine on the $5,697 you didn't declare. It's $290," he informed me.

Aside from the obvious reason I was unwilling to argue with a pig who would stare at a naked man, I walked over to the table to pick up the mess they had left of my briefcase. When I finished, I walked out the door. Goon No. 1 was waiting. He grabbed my arm and again brought his face close to mine.

"Listen, big boy. I bet you won't call a supervisor the next time I stop you."

I shook my arm free and went over to the counter where I was to pay the $290 fine. Then I went outside and caught a cab. It was 8:45 P.M. I had been detained three hours and fifteen minutes. The fact that Special Agent Horst had not put me in jail and confiscated my money disturbed me almost as much as it would have had he actually done so. Certainly my ignorance of the law was no excuse. Had he wanted to throw the book at me, he most assuredly had me by the balls and could have charged me.

Why was I allowed to walk out with a token fine? The only logical explanation was that Horst had received orders from higher up when he had left the room. I was being monitored to lead someone to something. If I were in jail, the trail would be wiped out. If I were in jail, I would make a lot of waves and a lot of things might be made public that were embarrassing to someone. That was the only way I could figure it out. Since I was connected with 464 Juliet, someone may have thought that I had some connection with Jimmy Chagra and the murder of Judge Wood.

There was an even more logical possibility. I was discovering, little by little, something that no one else outside the "inner circles" knew. I now understood how it was clearly possible that the United States government had set up Chagra in Colombia, let Bruce Allen die there, and had been in collusion with the Colombian government to plant cocaine on 464 Juliet.

In all fairness, I must say that Special Agent Horst behaved in a completely professional and objective way with me. He never once tried to intimidate or harass me, nor had he even once stepped over the line of strictly official behavior. He was doing his job and doing it well. I have no doubt that most of the United States federal agents are like Horst.

As for the two goons—these Gestapo types do exist. Their behavior with me, the harassment, intimidation, and violation of my human dignity and human rights do not represent a single, isolated case of abuse of petty power. I will never forget nor ever forgive my experience with them.

On the cab ride home I tried to clear the confusion from my addled mind and to put aside the events of the past two days in Colombia and in Florida. I had been too close to the edge, and I had to draw back.

My wife's face showed her relief as I walked through the door.

"Bobby, what happened? Raul called and said you were being held at customs. I've been going crazy."

I hugged and kissed her and the children like a man home from the wars. We sat together in the living room while I told Terry briefly what had happened. She was frightened at all the dangerous and strange elements that had entered our lives. My baby, Jaime, too young to understand, was showering me with kisses and patting my face with her tiny hands as I talked. Slowly, the tension abated as she gave me her innocent comfort.

CHAPTER THIRTY-FIVE

After several days of Spartan rations in Colombia, I was happy to sit down to a heroic breakfast with the family. Amply fortified, I set off to the office. My first order of business was to see Red Garglay to find out if he could shed any light on my interrogation by customs and Special Agent Horst, at Miami International the night before.

Red was busy with his staff meeting until 8:45, so I lined up all pending matters waiting on my desk in their order of importance and had already begun assigning jobs to be taken care of that were most pressing.

Raul had been informed the night before that I had finally cleared customs, but he wanted to hear all about it. I told him he would just have to wait, so he trotted off to attend to work that had piled up in his department, saying that he would be back when I had time for him.

I arrived at Red's office just as he returned from the meeting. We went inside and I quickly described what had happened. He was as astounded as I had been and couldn't even guess why there had been any problem other than the one connected with declaration of money. The fact that this, finally, had been dismissed with a small fine was even more mystifying.

"Red, you know and I know that there isn't a reason in the world for me to be in the United States government computers—so I just don't understand what all the hullabaloo could have been with a special agent. Could you check your connections for me? If for some reason I'm on somebody's list, I sure as hell want to know," I asked.

"Sure thing, Bobby," and Red picked up his phone to place the call. He gave his friend my name and was told he would have the information he wanted within a few minutes.

The last time we had met, I had been happy and confident that I would be returning with 464 Juliet. He was genuinely disappointed that this was not the case, especially when I told him that she was now ready to fly and needed only the elusive and long-delayed papers to let her leave. We had chatted only about five minutes when his call was returned.

"Yes, that's right—Robert E. Wood, Jr.," he smiled at me and added, "also known as Bobby Wood. Nothing? You're sure? Would it by any chance show up somewhere else? No? OK, my friend. Thanks a lot," and he hung up.

"No, Bobby, you're clean," Red told me. "There's not a word on you. I know it's a big blow to learn that you're not on the Top Ten, not even the Top Thousand."

Then he became serious.

"You know, Bobby, it occurs to me that it's not you at all. It could be that tail number N464 Juliet. Remember when I ran that check on the people it carried down to Santa Marta? Damn near everything turned up classified on that input. Maybe somebody got clever—maybe they punched in Bobby Wood and when nothing came up, they punched in N464 Juliet. They could have got pretty excited then. What do you think?"

That was precisely what I did think and what I had already been thinking, I told Red.

"I'm relieved in one way, Red, to know I'm not on their lists. But if the problem is with 464 Juliet, I'm worried. Because that may be the reason I keep running into all these brick walls and delays in getting her out."

Red agreed that this very well could be the case, but could come up with no concrete suggestions for pinpointing the specific problem—he had no idea at all who might help me. " … Unless … ," he began.

"Unless … ," I began, at the same moment, "I get in touch with somebody who could give me some first-hand information, somebody who was there."

We looked at each other with broad smiles. I had the list of names Red had checked out for me! Somehow, I might be able to track down the pilot, Tony Gekakis, the copilot, Steve Bolling, or the two paramedics, Miguel Parada and Jeff Ellis through Jet Avia in Las Vegas. We both thought that this idea, which had struck us simultaneously, was a fine one, and I resolved to get busy on it at soon as possible.

My next item of priority was to see Jack Wood at the bank. First, I wanted to report on progress (464 Juliet was airworthy) and lack of progress (still no clearance papers). I also wanted to ask him for a letter stating that I was a customer in good standing with his bank, which had granted me a loan in the amount of one hundred thousand dollars. I just might need it to establish my credentials in case—God forbid—there should be a recurrence of any problem concerning the "464 Juliet money."

As any and every banker worthy of the name would be, he was visibly shaken by the near-calamity of my having the loan proceeds temporarily confiscated and was equally upset that a good businessman like Bobby Wood would have been so unaware of the regulations concerning a citizen's obligation to declare certain monies leaving and entering the country. As a former member of Air Force Intelligence, he delivered me a short lecture in best military style that left me feeling like a real "sad sack."

"OK, Jack," I pleaded, "go ahead and break me to private."

He laughed, and told me that that's exactly what he would have done, if not having court-martialed me.

"Seriously, Bobby," he returned to the delays in the release of 464 Juliet, "I am more than a little worried that she's still there. I know, first-hand, all about the *mañanas*—we're having the same problem with aircraft confiscated there that the bank is handling. And then, too, I know some of these Latin military and Air Force types. What if the generals gang up on you and decide that an operating Learjet is just too good to slip out of their hands? Have you given that any thought?"

Yes, I have—a lot of thought.

"Jack, just keep the faith. I still think I can do it," I said. "I know a lot of people are skeptical, but I just won't give up."

"I know that, Bobby. All I'm trying to do is to say that you're in a very vulnerable position right now and that you're going to have to be careful."

I left Jack armed with the letter he had provided but considerably downhearted by his realistic concerns.

I returned to the office around noon. Paul Engstrom would be in his Los Angeles office by that time, so I placed a call to report on the new delays and the letter from Valdez. I knew I would have to talk with Paul with more optimism than I was actually feeling. Jack's assessment of my chances had cast longer shadows of doubt on the ones that were already nagging me mercilessly. On the other hand, I had to be completely honest with Paul. I owed him respect and gratitude for the great help he was giving me, and he was out on a limb for me with a very important client, Lloyd's of London.

His first words confirmed to me his quality as a gentleman and a professional.

"Have you heard anything more about Ortiz, the lawyer from Cartagena, and the American who was with him?" he wanted to know.

I was able to report, thankfully, that nothing more had been heard of them, which he was glad to hear. Then I described the work we had done on the Learjet and that 464 Juliet was now ready to go. We had been able to locate some of the missing equipment and might be able to track down more when we returned. He was pleased that we had been able to complete this work which represented real progress.

I also read him the translation of the letter Judge Valdez had prepared which would serve as official recognition of the fact that Learjet N464J would be delivered to Robert E. Wood, Jr. upon completion of the necessary formalities which were now in process.

We discussed the extension he had given me on the deadline, now almost a week gone by. He thought the letter would be helpful in justifying the extension, but was somewhat disturbed that I still could not give him a definite date on the release.

I was in a dilemma, trying to give some logical explanation of the judge's illogical delays regarding the release, without unduly alarming Paul of my own concern.

"Paul," I said frankly, "I honestly don't know why it's taking so long. I do know that it's complicated."

Paul could relate to that—no one was more aware than he that Lloyd's and a regiment of experts had put three fruitless years into the complications.

"I am convinced, however, that Judge Valdez is acting in good faith," I continued, "and that there are dozens of signs that he's being honest with me."

Naturally, I couldn't give Paul the examples of Valdez's "business" offer or his judicious consideration in not squeezing me for up-front money other than hospital expenses for his wife's relative. Paul certainly would not have understood or approved, I'm sure.

Our talk lasted for almost an hour. I promised to send the judge's letter immediately by courier service, and to call Paul the following week, hopefully with definite news.

Before getting back into my Air Unlimited harness completely, there was another thing I wanted to do: Track down someone, anyone who had been aboard 464 Juliet on her flight to Colombia on June 15, 1977.

Jet Avia in Las Vegas would be the logical starting point, so I called Las Vegas information, only to be told that Jet Avia was no longer in business. On a long shot, I asked the operator if a Steven C. Bolling was listed. He was. It was as easy as that. She gave me the number and I dialed it as soon as I got a clear signal.

A woman answered, her voice soft. Yes, she was Mrs. Bolling. No, her husband wasn't at home. He was out of town on a trip. She expected him back over the weekend.

I told Mrs. Bolling that I was very anxious to speak with Steve. There was no purpose in dragging out my long and complicated story. I merely told her I was working with Lloyd's of London concerning the Learjet Steve had copiloted to Colombia in June of 1977, and that I wanted to talk with him as he might have information useful in obtaining its release from that country.

As was to be expected, she remembered it well, and was completely interested and helpful. She said she was sure Steve would be glad to talk with me, and I gave her my office and home telephone numbers so that he could return the call when he got back home.

I would have to wait a couple of days, but I was looking forward to hearing what Steve might have to tell me.

I plowed into my backlog of work for the rest of the week and was able to look forward to a well-earned Sunday, swimming, barbecuing, and just being lazy with the family.

Around noon on Sunday, Steve telephoned me. I gave him a more detailed account of my reason for contacting him. When I told him of my efforts to get 464 Juliet released, he was sympathetic but dubious.

"Are you getting anywhere with it?" he asked curiously.

"Well, Steve, that's one of the reasons I'm calling you. I keep running into problems—just coming at me from out of nowhere."

"I'm not surprised. We ran into all kinds of problems down there, too. And they were not 'normal' problems. Hell, they kept me and another guy down there, in jail for fifty-two days, for investigation. And we hadn't done a damned thing. The whole thing stunk."

I listened carefully. Steve's words confirmed what I had been suspecting and discovering.

"That's the way I've figured it," I remarked, "and I'm sure what you can tell me would help."

"You know, some time ago I heard the government was using the jet for their president. But then, later, someone told me she was still sitting there … What kind of condition is she in now? … Bad, I suppose."

"No, not bad at all—we finished working on her last week, and she's ready to fly. But still no papers saying we can go," I replied.

"Well," Steve said reluctantly, "I'm a very optimistic guy, but I'm sure as hell pessimistic about that. It took Jet Avia over a quarter of a million dollars and God knows how much other pressure just to get me and the other guy out. And Chagra—you know about him, I suppose?"

"Yes, I'm assuming he was the main problem," I began.

"Oh, absolutely, but it didn't seem like that at the time. You know he and Wilson walked after three weeks. Anyway, as I was saying, I don't know how much it cost him to walk, but it wasn't peanuts. But what I'm saying is that if they only got us out after putting up that kind of money three years ago, I just don't see how it can be pulled off by anybody. They sure knew how to shove it to you down there, take it from a guy who knows."

"You're talking to another one of those guys," I concurred.

"Look, Steve, there's just too much to cover over the telephone. I'd like to come out to Vegas sometime soon whenever you have some time to spend with me. The only thing is, I may be returning to Colombia this week, but I'll know for certain by the middle of the week. If I don't go there, I'll definitely fly out to Vegas over next week end."

MONDAY, JULY 21, 1980—

Raul walked into my office around eight thirty with his usual, "*Qué pasa,* Bobby?"

I absent-mindedly asked how his weekend had gone, and he shook his head sadly, "Bad, Bobby, very bad. I had problems … ."

His oldest daughter, eighteen, had gone to a movie with some friends without asking permission. He had quarreled with his wife about her frivolous lack of discipline with the girls. She had quarreled with him about never being home. He had grounded the two oldest girls for two weeks. The next to the oldest had quarreled with the oldest for involving their innocent younger sister in wrongdoing. The baby of the family had been frightened by all the commotion and had tripped on the stairs and cut her lip. All in all, a bad weekend—what was the world coming to?

I listened patiently, marveling, as always, at Raul's strict, sanctimonious attitude about his family in the face of his own double-standard moral behavior. When he finished, I told him to sit down and listen to an account of my conversation with Steve Bolling.

"I don't want to make definite plans to go out to Las Vegas until we've talked with Valdez to find out when we can go back to Colombia. So get on the phone, Raul."

He was able to get through almost immediately. I waited through the usual preliminaries of greetings, inquiries about the health of the judge and the judge's *señora.* Finally, Raul got down to business. How were the papers coming along? When did the judge think we could come down?

No smiles, no eye contact—no good news.

"What's his excuse now?" I asked wearily as he hung up. "The same … Valdez says we should call him again next week. He says he's working on *la providencia.*"

"Raul, he's stuck in low gear," I shouted. "Why the fuck is he dragging his feet?"

"Bobby, take it easy … Valdez is being very careful … I guess."

Even Raul seemed depressed; he was becoming as unhappy as I was about Valdez's snail's pace. At any rate, I could at least make the trip to Las Vegas to talk with Steve Bolling. On Friday night, July 18, when I knew he would be back, I telephoned. We made plans to meet the next day.

JULY 19, 1980—LAS VEGAS, MEETING 464 JULIET COPILOT, STEVE BOLLING

Steve Bolling met me Saturday afternoon at Maxim's on the Las Vegas Strip. He was a tall, well-built man in his late thirties with a fair complexion and a ready smile. An easy walk, an unhurried drawl, and a hearty laugh all indicated an even temperament and a good sense of humor. I liked him at first glance.

He was interested in hearing all the latest news in the saga of 464 Juliet. The fact that he had played a key role in the opening "chapters" and that I was now very much on the scene and in the thick of things gave us an immediate rapport.

I told him again that I was sure his first-hand account of the complications that had developed in Colombia as a result of his trip might give me some insights into resolving the strange and inexplicable delays I had been experiencing in obtaining release of the jet. He readily agreed to tell me everything that had happened to him and to the others, but was still doubtful about whether I would be successful.

He showed me a small, battered tablet with lined paper and a scrapbook.

"This is the diary I told you about that I kept in Colombia. It wouldn't be much help to you alone, but I brought it along to jog my memory and be sure of what happened when," he laughed. "Fifty-two days is a long time."

The tablet was full of the notations Steve had made almost daily, giving the highlights of the long days he had spent in Colombia from June 15 to August 5 of 1977.

As we talked, he would glance at it, stop to recollect details, and then launch into his account.

CHAPTER THIRTY-SIX

Depart Las Vegas.

We first dropped off a passenger at Phoenix. Then we stopped at El Paso. Jerry Wilson's wife met us there. She brought a packet to the airplane. It was for Jimmy Chagra—his passport and some other papers. Then on to Atlanta to pick up Chagra. He was the person who initially chartered the airplane to go to Santa Marta; we were headed to Columbia to pick up Jerry Wilson.

Jerry Wilson was a former employee of Jet Avia. He was well thought of and we were under the impression that we were going to Colombia to try to save his life—we had been told Jerry had been burned in a car accident.

We stayed overnight in Fort Lauderdale so as to arrive in Santa Marta in the daytime, on the morning of the fifteenth of July, 1977.

Q. WHEN DID YOU DISCOVER IT WASN'T JERRY WILSON YOU WERE TO FLY OUT?

I found out about it that same night, June 14, in Fort Lauderdale. Jimmy Chagra told me it wasn't Jerry, it was Bruce Allen. He had lied, saying he had said it was Jerry Wilson because he wasn't sure he could get the plane or that we would go if it was a mere stranger. We all knew of Jerry Wilson. You know Colombia's reputation for problems; Colombia is bad news. I don't know who else knew the truth. I told no one because I didn't care who it was—all I knew was there was a man, seriously burned, whose life we could possibly save. I didn't want to do anything to spoil his chances.

JUNE 15, 1977—DEPARTURE FROM FORT LAUDERDALE

Q. WHAT ABOUT FILING YOUR FLIGHT PLANS?

We filed a flight plan from Fort Lauderdale to Port-au-Prince, Haiti, where we planned to stop for fuel. And we filed another from Haiti to Santa Marta. Both of these were filed in Fort Lauderdale. We were to leave early in the morning. After getting into the airplane, we contacted the Fort Lauderdale tower and received clearance, which meant that Haiti had our flight plan on file.

I personally filed the flight plans, both of them, both legs. We had received our clearance for the first leg, which is normal procedure. You ask for clearance step-by-step, as you finish a leg—you know all this.

Anyway, we proceeded to Port-au-Prince. I checked there to find out if they had our flight plan to Santa Marta. They didn't, for what reason I don't know, so I re-filed it. A two-hour advance notice is required for Santa Marta, but we were refueling, which took some time. And the time to Santa Marta would be an hour and twenty, twenty-five minutes. Also, we were delayed in leaving the runway. So we would be arriving well over the two-hour period. When we were ready to go, we called the tower and were given our clearance for Santa Marta, which meant that Barranquilla, which is the control center for Santa Marta, had received one, or both, of our plans.

Q. I ASKED ABOUT THE FLIGHT PLANS BECAUSE PART OF THE PROBLEM IN SANTA MARTA WAS THAT THEY CLAIMED YOU HAD VIOLATED COLOMBIAN AIRSPACE AND THIS WAS ONE OF THE REASONS THE PLANE WAS DETAINED.

Steve laughed, "Don't I know it … ," and got on with his story.

"Anyway, when we got to the fix where we were entering Colombian airspace, we changed radio frequencies and reported our position. We identified ourselves as N464 Juliet and were given our clearance for Santa Marta. At no time were we refused entry into Colombian airspace. We were cleared by the tower, by approach control, to Santa Marta tower for landing. And we landed.

We were met by customs and immigration personnel. Jimmy Chagra left, first going up to the tower, then returning to go into town. His stated purpose was to bring back the patient. The rest of us waited. The immigration officer came back and wanted our passports. He said he would take them to get our visas for us. We asked if we needed visas. He told us no, but that he would get them for us anyway.

After an hour or so, some other officers came over and said they wanted to search the plane. We said fine and took them over. They were from DAS (Administrative Department of Security), which is like the FBI. They made a thorough search, about twenty minutes. They opened up everything—briefcases, luggage, medical equipment, boxes. And when they were finished they said, "OK, nothing there, it's fine."

About this time, the ambulance arrived.

Tony, the pilot, said he would go up to the tower to file a VFR flight plan to go to Barranquilla to refuel. Anyway, the ambulance was there now, with Bruce Allen. However, before the paramedics could take him out, the DAS agents stopped them.

The ambulance sat there for better than a half an hour in the broiling sun—no air conditioning—with Bruce Allen in it. Then it headed back to town taking Bruce Allen back to the hospital. When Tony got back from the tower, he also told us we were having a problem.

Q. DID YOU SEE BRUCE ALLEN? HOW SEVERELY WAS HE BURNED?

From what I could see of him, he was extremely burned … He was propped upright on a cot, terribly burned. His arms were swollen to about twice normal size, sticking out from his body. He could hardly bend them. He could see us and could talk, but he was barely lucid. He was thrilled about going home, almost crying and so happy to see us. I can't describe how badly he was burned, but it was very bad. I didn't speak to him, but I heard him talking—apparently he knew what was happening. He was not completely coherent, but he knew.

Q. DID IT SEEM TO YOU THAT HE HAD BEEN PROPERLY TAKEN CARE OF?

That's hard to speculate since I don't know much about what has to be done for burn victims. But I assume that he hadn't been, because the Colombian doctors at the hospital had reported that they simply didn't have the proper facilities for that kind of treatment and that he would die unless he were taken to a burn center.

After the ambulance left, the four of us—Tony Gekakis, the two paramedics, Jeffrey Ellis and Miguel Parada, and I were detained, forcibly detained, and put in a Jeep. We were not handcuffed, but there was an armed guard with us.

They took us to DAS headquarters in downtown Santa Marta. We weren't told why or what was happening. A little later, Jimmy Chagra was brought in, along with Jerry Wilson. Wilson had apparently been with Bruce Allen in the airplane that crashed. He had escaped without any injuries.

Q. WHAT DID THE PILOT, TONY GEKAKIS, SAY TO THIS? HAD HE KNOWN IT WASN'T WILSON THAT WAS BURNED?

When he saw Jerry at DAS headquarters, he acted surprised and glad to see him. He later told me he had had some doubts about whether it was Wilson early on who had been burned. When he had seen Jerry's wife at the airport in El Paso she hadn't seemed upset and he thought she was very calm for a woman whose husband was in critical condition. Maybe everyone knew—I don't know.

At any rate, now we were six. The five who had come on the Learjet, and Jerry Wilson, who had already been in the country.

That afternoon a local lawyer came in who was representing Chagra. His name was Jose Pinedo. They called him Don Jose. Don Jose was straight out of *Casablanca*, He looked like Peter Lorre in a white linen suit with a panama hat. He was obviously well known and respected. All the officials kowtowed to him and called him Don Jose. By that time, we were realizing that all was not right, but we had no reason to think that we wouldn't be allowed to leave the next morning. Of course it was too late to leave that day, but we were still counting on going the next day. However, things got really grim that evening when they loaded us in a truck and took us to the military stockade on the outskirts of Santa Marta.

We had to take everything out of our pockets. They searched us, but we kept our clothes and shoes. Then they put us into six-by eight-foot cells, two to a cell. There were four cells on each side of an open concrete courtyard. At one end was a wall. At the opposite end was a large dormitory. Fifteen, twenty, or more inmates were in there together, in the big room, with bunk beds. There was nothing in the cells but concrete floors and walls. It had a roof. We spent the night trying to sleep on the floor.

About midnight, I looked outside. There, in the middle of the courtyard—it slopes to the center with a drain in it and had a couple of dim lights shining—I saw a rat coming up out of the sewer hole. He looked around and started to crawl out. Someone else saw it, too, and threw a tin can. The rat went back into its hole.

Q. WHO SHARED THE CELL WITH YOU?

Jimmy Chagra. There was old Jimmy sitting there, telling me he couldn't understand what had gone wrong, that everything was supposed to have been taken care of. That it would all be over by the next day. That we'd pick up Bruce Allen and get out of there—go back to the States. He kept saying how much he appreciated our doing this for him. He would make sure that Tony and I each got a five thousand dollar toke when we got home. So, of course, I spent the rest of the night figuring what I'd do with my money.

Q. DID YOU HAVE ANY IDEA THEN OF WHAT WAS REALLY FIXING TO GO DOWN?

No, but I wasn't putting too much faith into going back the next day. And I wasn't putting too much faith in the five thousand dollars either.

Q. WHAT WERE YOU MAINLY CONCERNED ABOUT?

My main concern was that I knew Chagra was a dope dealer. I was afraid—and I think it was true—that the Colombian government or the United States government, or both, wanted Chagra. Now they had him—but how were they going to hold him? Because we didn't break any laws coming into the country. There was no dope deal. This was strictly an air ambulance operation. So how could they?

Q. FROM WHAT YOU'VE TOLD ME, IT LOOKS AS IF CHAGRA HAD EVERYBODY PAID OFF AT THE SANTA MARTA LEVEL. OTHERWISE, HE WOULD'NT HAVE HAD THE CONFIDENCE TO GO DOWN THERE, EVEN ON A LEGITIMATE FLIGHT. AND NO LAWS HAD BEEN BROKEN. SO WHERE WAS THE PRESSURE COMING FROM TO HOLD HIM AND THE REST OF YOU?

I'm pretty sure not from Santa Marta. It very likely could have come from Bogotá. Or from our own government.

Q. AT THIS TIME DID YOU KNOW WHETHER THE UNITED STATES EMBASSY IN BOGOTÁ WAS AWARE THAT YOU WERE THERE? OR THAT YOU WERE GOING THERE?

Oh, yeah, certainly. Chris Karamanos, our boss, had told Tony Gekakis, our pilot, on the phone the night before that he had spoken with Sergeant Brown at the Embassy in Bogotá and with the United States Consulate in Barranquilla, and to the doctor in the Santa Marta hospital. Santa Marta doesn't have a United States Consulate.

Q. SO ON THE NIGHT OF JUNE 14 THE CONSULATE IN BARRANQUILLA AND THE EMBASSY IN BOGOTÁ KNEW THAT YOU PEOPLE WOULD BE IN SANTA MARTA ON THE 15TH TO PICK UP THE BURN VICTIM?

Absolutely.

JUNE 16, 1977

That morning we were released from the stockade and given back our belongings. They took our pictures outside the jail, profile-type pictures, and we returned to DAS headquarters in Santa Marta. We were questioned again there.

That same day a woman named Bonnie Frank from the American Consulate in Barranquilla showed up while we were there. There was also a United States Drug Enforcement Agent named Paul Provencio who came to see us. He was based out of Santa Marta. Provencio said he knew Chris Karamanos, they had served on the same police force in Newport Beach, California.

We were running into a problem, though. On this day, Chagra and Jerry Wilson decided to try to get Jerry out of the country expeditiously. What they wanted us, the crew, to do, was to tell the Colombians that Jerry had flown in with us. Then, when we were released, all six of us would go out together. We were supposed to pretend that Jerry had been with us all along. So we thought, well, what the hell—being friends and all—we would be out that afternoon, anyway—that we'd go along with it. And we did. That was our initial story. I don't know if it contributed to what turned out to be the overall problem or not. What decided it for me was that I thought we could get Bruce Allen out. I was sure by then that it was his only chance.

Q. DID BONNIE FRANK OR THE DEA AGENT SAY ANYTHING ABOUT GETTING BRUCE ALLEN OUT OF THE COUNTRY?

No, they never showed any concern at all about Bruce Allen. They never even mentioned his name. There was old Bruce, over there dying, and all they were concerned about—it sounded like to me and I thus assumed—was building a case against Chagra.

Q. WAS BRUCE ALLEN STILL ALIVE? WHEN DID HE DIE?

He was still alive. To the best of my knowledge, he lived six days. I don't think I heard about his death until the following Tuesday.

Q. DID ANYONE MAKE AN EFFORT TO GET HIM OUT OF THERE DURING THAT PERIOD?

I have no idea what efforts were being made. We were held pretty much incommunicado. But nothing was said about Bruce Allen when Bonnie Frank and Paul Provencio were there.

About Provencio, the DEA, it seemed like he could pretty much see through the story about Wilson. He had previous knowledge, as it turned out. He said, "Well, you guys had better get your story straight. Whatever it is, get together and stick to it." I found out later that Jeff Ellis hadn't been willing to go along with the story. Since we had been individually interrogated, Ellis had given it away, so Provencio knew.

That night we stayed at DAS headquarters. Someone brought in some mattresses and we slept on the floor.

JUNE 17, 1977

The next day was Friday.

We were taken to Bogota on Avianca airline. Captain Acevedo accompanied us. He was armed—he didn't have to pull the gun. We weren't handcuffed and were treated quite well.

Bogota was cold, because of the elevation. We were taken to the national headquarters of DAS and checked in. A representative from the

United States Embassy, Richard Henry Morefield and his wife visited us. They were nice and polite. He was with the Consulate. They came in the evening and brought some clothing for us—we only had the clothes on our backs—and food and books. They told us they could not help us in our legal problems. Their job was simply to inform us that our government knew we were there and to make sure we were treated humanely and to let us know we could have lawyers if we needed them.

Q. HAD ANYBODY FROM OUR GOVERNMENT EXPRESSED ANY CONCERN ABOUT BRUCE ALLEN?

No. Absolutely not. They knew about him, but no one was concerned. We tried to impress on people over and over and over again that the man would die if we couldn't carry out our mission. They merely told us that they could do nothing, that we were being detained for investigation, with no explanation even of what we were being held for.

Both in Santa Marta and Bogotá, we insisted that Bruce Allen would die unless we got him out. All they would say was that it was beyond their control. In the hands of higher-ups. That our Consulate could not help. They knew how bad his condition was.

JUNE 18, 1977

This day, Saturday, we were fingerprinted and they took more photographs. I forgot to mention that the night before they had taken our money and all of our personal belongings.

JUNE 19, 1977

Sunday. Nothing eventful. I noted here that some nuns came by and brought some hot tea. It was good, the cells were very cold. There was no heat and the temperature was in the fifties. The cells were open. Ours didn't face the outside, but the hallway windows were open and it was very cold.

Q. WHAT WAS HAPPENING NOW ABOUT THE FACT THAT WILSON HAD NOT BEEN ON THE LEAR JET?

Throughout the whole time, we were in individual cells, but mine was alongside Wilson's. We talked back and forth and by that time, we had all pretty much decided that we'd better tell the truth. That was the next day or so, so let's go on to Monday … I'll get to that later.

JUNE 20, 1977

> *There was an American, a fellow named John, in the cell on the other side of mine. I didn't know what he was there for, I assumed it was drugs. He was very despondent. On Monday he cut his wrists. I looked out the window and saw blood running across the floor into the hall. I called the guards and they opened the door. He didn't die, but he slashed both wrists. They took him to the hospital. I never heard anything more of him.*

JUNE 21, 1977

> *On Tuesday they questioned both of the paramedics and Tony Gekakis, Fingerprints again—they took nine sets of fingerprints in all. I guess they had enough to put in every post office in Colombia. That's all I have for Tuesday.*

JUNE 22, 1977

> *On Wednesday Jerry Wilson and Jim Chagra were interrogated most of the day. It was about this time that the truth came out about Wilson. We had managed to get messages back and forth amongst us, and decided to tell the truth.*
>
> *Initially Wilson was unhappy about this. But he began to see that we were not going to go along with him, so he devised another story that worked out even better. The new story he gave them was that when he heard about his friend Bruce Allen being burned, he borrowed a Cessna 210, flew to the Colombian coast in the vicinity of Riohacha and found his way across the country to the hospital in Santa Marta. That explained his purpose in the country. The worst they could do to him would be to deport him. Which is ultimately exactly what happened.*

Q. WHEN DID THAT HAPPEN?

Later on. He was released when Chagra got out. Also, on June 22, they assembled us and had a local television news cameramen there to shoot some footage. None of us had been allowed to shave. We had showered a couple of times, but we looked like desperados. This was eventually shown in the States.

I know it was shown in Las Vegas. We had been in the country for eight days by then.

JUNE 23, 1977

> *On Thursday, we had a visit from a lawyer. It was an attorney from the States who explained that Colombian lawyers had to represent us since we were under Colombian law. Mike Levitt, Jet Avia's attorney came, together with another lawyer from Phoenix who came because he spoke Spanish. Also, that day, Pablo Salah visited us. He was our Colombian counselor. He was very optimistic about getting us released quickly. He gave us some Colombian money—in a Colombian jail you have to buy anything you want. If you want a meal, you have to buy it, have it sent in …*

Q. YOU MEAN IF YOU DON'T PAY, YOU DON'T GET FED?

Right. (Steve laughed)—but it's not a joking matter. In the jail at Bogotá, at national headquarters of DAS, a trustee would come by and take orders. About all you could get was sandwiches. But if you didn't have money, there was no food. Water, yes. We had water in the cells.

JUNE 24, 1977

> *On that day, Friday, we were escorted back to Santa Marta. No handcuffs. When we got there, we were taken again to the DAS headquarters where we had spent our second night in the country. Then on to the prison—the Carcel Judicial de Santa Marta. They checked us in and assigned a room. All six of us were assigned to the room in a kind of trustee area of the prison, apart from the general inmates. It was an unused storeroom, with nothing in it. No beds. Chagra had brought several thousand dollars with him and he still had it. They gave it back to him when we left Bogota. So he tipped one of the DAS agents to go out and buy mattresses, sheets, pillows. We put them on the floor, but it was better than sleeping on the concrete. There were no real bathroom facilities. We were allowed access to a garden area behind, about 100 feet away. It was just an open field. We had to buy toilet paper. They sold it to us there. If you didn't have money for toilet paper, I guess you would just have to use your hands …*
> *The open area was about forty acres, all within the walls of the prison. A series of small farm plots. An irrigation pipe close to our building fed into a small reservoir about ten feet wide. From there it led into an irrigation*

ditch that crisscrossed the forty acres. Individual inmates could rent these little plots of land, about twenty by twenty feet, and grow food. We used the irrigation ditches for our toilet facilities. We had water inside.

Q. WHAT ELSE COULD YOU PURCHASE IN THE JAIL?

Just about everything except booze. I never saw any alcohol. Drugs, yes. I saw cocaine and marijuana being used in the jail, By Chagra and Wilson. They bought it from the inmates. I have no idea where the inmates got it— either from visitors or from the guards. I wouldn't be surprised if it came through the guards because it would have been a good source of income. And for sure, it boils down to money there.

Anyway, that same day, Jim Chagra's lawyer, Don Jose, the Casablanca lawyer, came to visit us. Just a visit, not to report anything new …

JUNE 25, 1977

Saturday. Nothing much happened. We were settling down and adjusting to our little dormitory. We had our meals sent in. This had been arranged by Jet Avia through our attorneys, to send meals in to us from a local restaurant. The food was good—mostly rice, chicken, bread—but not bad.

Except for having to pay for necessities, the treatment was fairly humane throughout the whole stay. There was never any physical abuse. If we hadn't had any money it might have been different. We probably would have ended up in the main prison. There were some pretty rough people in there.

Q. DID YOU PAY TO BE KEPT SEPARATED FROM THE REST OF THE INMATES?

The arrangement suited us, but we didn't pay for it. I think it suited the government to have us separate from the others. They didn't want us in with the others. There was too much controversy about the matter. They obviously didn't have a case. We were never charged, just "held for investigation." All I could figure out was that they were still trying to find some way to hold Chagra.

Q. DID THEY EVER FIND A REASON TO HOLD HIM?

No, they released him after three weeks.

JUNE 26, 1977

> *Sunday. A Colombian girl named Carmen Regina visited us. She was an employee at the Santa Marta hospital. She had been concerned about Bruce Allen and had met Jerry Wilson there. She kind of liked Jerry, so she came and visited him in jail. They seemed to develop a little thing for each other …*
>
> *But a strange thing happened that day. Two American girls came in to see us. Their story was this—and it's peculiar: They were from California, just bumming around the country, staying high. That was their terminology. They were either dopers or wanted us to believe they were dopers. They came into our room and talked with us … .*

Q. THEY WERE ALLOWED IN TO SEE YOU?

Yes, they rapped with us, as they said, for about an hour. They asked a lot of questions—What are you guys doing? What are you doing here?—etc., etc., etc.

Q. HOW DID THEY KNOW YOU WERE THERE?

Their story was that since they knew a lot of people in the dope trade, they would go to the jails of any town they visited to see if there were any Americans or people they knew, just to see if they could help in any way. Real social workers. I don't know—I couldn't buy it. I believe they were sent in by the United States Government to try to get some information, to try to find out something that would incriminate us. I don't remember everything they asked, but I recall there weren't any personal questions. It was all "What are you guys doing here?" "Why are you in jail?" "What did you really do?" "Are there any drugs involved?" "Were you trying to smuggle?"—questions like that. When they first came in, we were all glad to see some new faces, but after they left I got to thinking and now, looking back on it, I think they were put there to get information.

JUNE 27, 1977

Monday. We got some phone calls. Jim Chagra got a call from the States from his brother Lee, an attorney. Chris Karamanos called and Tony and I talked with him. Chris had a recorder ready so that we could tape messages for our families.

Don Jose visited again. He visited us almost every day for about a week.

JUNE 28, 1977

Tuesday. We had a visit from Bonnie Frank, the American lady from the Consulate in Barranquilla. She brought another lady, Nancy, with her. Bonnie Frank had visited me on June 16.

Also on that day Dr. Pablo Salah, our Colombian attorney from Bogotá, came. He said a decision would be made by the next Monday or Tuesday by a judge who would determine our fate.

JUNE 29, 1977

On the following day we got more phone calls. I talked with my wife Barbara. It was the first contact I had had with her since the day I left Las Vegas—two weeks. She was quite concerned. It made me feel better to talk with her.

JUNE 30, 1977

I don't remember what happened' during that day, but in the evening there was a shooting. Some of the inmates had lost their visiting privileges and they were complaining about the food. They got into a riot and a guard shot one of them.

JULY 1, 1977

We went to F-2, the criminal investigation section of DAS. We were taken there to identify our personal belongings that had been taken out of the airplane. They showed me the box of Prist, the fuel additive I had bought. It comes in aerosol cans, six to a box, the box being about a cubic foot in size. The box had two or three cans left in it and some other odds and ends—scissors and stuff from the paramedics.

I identified my things, a briefcase and some other items; then we were taken back to jail. Salah came by later, showing us tickets he had already purchased, saying it looked as if we would get out on Monday or Tuesday.

JULY 2, 1977

Saturday—laundry day for me. I washed a pair of corduroy pants and hung *them* up outside our little room. They were stolen. I tried to ransom them back—put out word that I would buy them back for five dollars with no questions asked. I just had one other pair of pants that the Consulate people in Bogotá had given me. Apparently the guy that stole my pants ended up stabbing someone and was sent to the hole—solitary confinement. I wrote here that I could probably barter them back when he got out, but I never got them back. Maybe the guy never got out of the hole.

JULY 3, 1977

Carmen Regina, Jerry's friend, visited. And on that day, Picasso started painting a picture of Jeff and Parada. Picasso was a character. An inmate, a trustee—he lived in the room next to us. He painted pictures of the other inmates to make some money. He was charging Jeff and Parada twenty dollars for their portraits. Later I had him paint a picture of me. Still have it. With my mustache ...

JULY 4, 1977

Independence Day. Lots of speculation about our release. It wasn't a holiday in Colombia, for a change. Since it was a working day, and a Monday, and we had already been told that possibly Monday or Tuesday we would be out, we hoped that we could celebrate the Fourth of July. It didn't work out that way.

JULY 5, 1977

Tense all day, waiting for word. Late that afternoon Don Jose, Chagra's lawyer, came and advised us that Jim Chagra, Jerry Wilson, Tony Gekakis and Jeff Ellis were being released the next day. Miguel and I must stay. Bad news.

They took us all into a room and read us the judge's verdict. We were informed that since our landing and the initial inspection of the airplane, it had been inspected again. This time cocaine had been found on the plane—I think 50 grams. This cocaine, they said, had been found in the Prist box, the box I had put on the airplane. There were also the pair of scissors that Miguel Parada had identified as his. Therefore, both of us were tied to the cocaine.

The judge's decision was worded to sound like the cocaine was also ours since we had identified as ours the articles it was with.

Here's a side note: Earlier that day Miguel had his ashes read—there was an old guy in the jail that read ashes. You drop cigarette ashes in a cup of tea. When they settle to the bottom he reads them. And the old guy told us we wouldn't be leaving that day. It turned out to be true. Miguel didn't smoke, he had to borrow somebody elses cigarette ...

JULY 6, 1977

Wilson, Chagra, Gekakis and Ellis went downtown to DAS for outp rocessing. Miguel and I were left alone. That day Picasso started a portrait of me. The others still had to come back that afternoon, but we already felt lonely.

Antonio, a trustee who was always helpful—he'd get us Cokes and clean, and we would tip him—helped us rearrange the room for just two people. For a penitentiary it was pretty nice. We gave him one of the mattresses we had left over ...

That day a local attorney, Donado Rebelledo, came by. He was to be our liaison, supposed to keep daily contact with us. He told us he had a master plan for our release and guaranteed that we would be there no longer than ten more days. Then he left. The other four came back around six in the evening. They were on

their way out of the country the next day. We were very sad. They brought more conflicting stories about our release, mostly rumors.

Miguel was in pretty good shape. His sister called that evening to tell us there was a lot of public sentiment for us in the States and that apparently most of the people were on our side. We had heard through Karamanos and other phone calls that the news had been spread all across the country. Also, I knew that Chris had spoken with the Governor of Nevada, a friend of his. Jet Avia flew the governor often. Chris had also spoken with Senator Howard Cannon, señior Senator from Nevada, trying to get help through the Embassy to get us released. But so far, nothing.

JULY 7, 1977

Miguel had another call from his sister. She said that he was on the front page of the Las Vegas Sun for two days. Chris Crystal, a local reporter in Las Vegas, had said she might come down to Santa Marta for a human interest story. We were feeling pretty good because it sounded to us as if we were getting a lot of public support.

JULY, 8, 1977

The director of the prison heard on the news broadcast that we would be leaving. He told us that the newspaper the day before said that the cocaine was going to be reanalyzed. I didn't put a lot of faith in any of this. My diary says that Picasso was working on my portrait ...

Chris Karamanos called that day. Tony was on the line with him—he was home by then. This was Friday. They tell me that we will be released Sunday or Monday ...

That afternoon we met two men from Florida. Mark J. Hines and Skip Mann. They had come down in a twin-engine—an Aztec or a Navajo—on a drug pick-up. They couldn't find the little airstrip in the jungle, *so they landed in Santa Marta with the airplane, an empty airplane,, First they threw away their guns. They missed the strip and were running low on fuel, so they thought they'd just go in to Santa Marta, fill up and go *back home. That didn't do too good. They were arrested.,*

They told us they would be there for a few hours and then probably be deported. I told them I didn't think so … As it turned out, they were not too far wrong. At that time they had been in the country for four days, mostly at DAS headquarters. The following day, they left.

JULY 9, 1977

Spoke with my wife Barbara. Saturdays and Sundays they have conjugal visits there at the jail. I made a note that I sure wished she had been here.

Skip and Jeff, the two would-be drug runners, left that afternoon for Barranquilla to be deported and go home. Picasso finished my portrait that day. Pablo Salah came by with Rebelledo. They said fourteen days. My, little sister Linda called. She's very cool-headed. Our lawyers say the search the Colombians Made was full of holes and that's the way we're going to get out.

JULY 10, 1977

Jerry Wilson's friend Carmen still came by to visit us. She told us that she'd gone to the party the other four who got out had at Puerto Galleon the night before they left. That night Miguel told me that Jeff had told the truth about Wilson the first time he was questioned by Captain Acevedo at DAS. So they knew all along that the rest of us were lying. But, as I said, it really didn't make any difference.

I also talked with Chris Karamanos and Tony Gekakis and asked them to see about getting Don Jose, Chagra's local attorney for us. He seemed to know everybody and probably could get more done here than Salah and Rebelledo. No matter how famous Salah was in Bogotá, he wasn't getting much done in Santa Marta.

My other sister, Suzi, called. My brother and some of my in-laws were beginning to doubt my honesty and were wondering if I had truly been involved in some kind of drug thing. But at least my wife and my sisters all trusted me.

JULY 11, 1977

The lawyers came in again, talking about the following Monday or Tuesday. Quote, unquote. It's getting to be like a placebo. Tomorrow, tomorrow, tomorrow …

Q. THE MANANA SYNDROME?

Yeah. That day a new director was installed in the prison. The other one was quite a nice guy. Before the others left, Chagra had given him a good bit of money. That was one of the reasons we were allowed to get phone calls. I didn't have the money to pay him off, but he still allowed us the calls.

The old director had been fired because there had been an escape. The new director was a hard ass. He called a formation of the prisoners to the assembly room that day and told everybody that he was a hard ass. He made a little speech, introducing himself as the new director.

JULY 12, 1977

This was our twenty-eighth day in jail. I note here that the new director set a time limit for the families that brought meals to their kin in jail. Up to then, it didn't matter if the food was delivered after nine o'clock, it was allowed in. But the new director wouldn't allow it. They fed the prisoners, but the food was bad. The Colombians who could afford it or who had families there had it sent in. We bought it because it was a matter of eating slop or buying.

We started to wonder about getting phone calls. We got one from Bonnie Frank, but the director told me there would be no other calls and no visits except from the attorney.

Q. WHAT DID BONNIE HAVE TO SAY? WAS SHE CONCERNED ABOUT YOU OR JUST DOING HER JOB?

She just was checking on how we were being treated. My wife had spoken with her a few times and Bonnie told me about Barbara's calls. As for anything else, she was very bleak, very grim. She told us stories about people sitting in jail in Barranquilla for three years. From the day we got there, Bonnie Frank always acted as if she believed us guilty of something. She never had the slightest doubt that we weren't down there running dope. I don't know what she based it on, maybe because she had not seen too many Americans down there flying airplanes legitimately, she hadn't been exposed to many legitimate operations. But her attitude was, "Well, you guys had better get used to staying around here for a long time." It was a case of being guilty until proven innocent, even among our own people.

JULY 13, 1977

Apparently the new rule about phone calls didn't always apply because

Barbara called. I found out that Miguel had promised the guard we would send him some money. But other calls were refused that day.

Our local attorney, Rebelledo, came by. He hadn't shaved and was reeking of booze. I have nothing against drinking, but when I'd been in that jail for a month and this guy representing me shows up and I can see he's been up all night drinking—I didn't like it.

JULY 14, 1977

Two inmates were thrown into the hole for fighting. Also, I wrote a letter to F-2 which Miguel translated for me. I'm petitioning the F-2 to take us out to the airplane so that we can put the control locks on it.

Q. YOU MEAN THE PLANE WAS UNLOCKED? THAT IT HAD NOT BEEN LOCKED SINCE THE FIRST DAY?

Yes. The control locks were off it, the intake plugs weren't in the engine, the fuel covers weren't on. I wanted to secure the airplane. Since the first day, when they took us away, we weren't even allowed to go near the plane. So it was unlocked from the first day.

That afternoon, Pablo Salah came in and took the letter to deliver to F;2. He also brought new tickets, first-class tickets this time.—back to the world.

JULY 15, 1977

Miguel got a call in the morning, but it was cut off—not by the guards, just a bad connection. I have a note here about the guards. They used their sticks very handily when they were putting someone in the hole. Usually it was a young kid. The guards just beat the shit out of the kids with their sticks. I'm glad I never got on their bad side …

Salah came by again and said it looked good for the Friday coming up. I wrote a note saying, "Christ, I'm losing patience with these people. Mañana, mañana, mañana." I also have a note here saying that I think Salah spends most of his time covering Rebelledo's fuck-ups, and "What an asshole Rebelledo is."

Q. HOW WERE YOU MENTALLY, THEN, ABOUT THESE HEAD GAMES?

Pretty good. I was taking it out in my little diary here. I would get over it by writing it down. It helped me relax. I took the whole thing pretty good. If they'd told me I was going to be there a year, I could have lived with it. Or that I would get out the next day. But the uncertainty was getting to me. The ups and down's of faith one minute and despair the next.

Q. THAT'S HOW IT MS WITH ME. ONE MINUTE THE SUN SHINES BRIGHT AND THE NEXT MINUTE IT'S PITCH BLACK.

That was what got to me, too.

My wife called that day. The new hard ass said it would be the last call. But we'd had about four or five "last calls" already. I talked as long as possible. She sounded good, and I told her I would write her a letter, which I did.

JULY 16, 1977

Nothing except a call from Salah saying he would be by on Tuesday

JULY 17, 1977

Carmen came by and the new director allowed her to visit us.

JULY 18, 1977

Bonnie Frank came in and brought us some United States magazines and newspapers. We were happy to get some reading material. She was still the same, doing her duty and paying the required visit. Also a DEA agent, Bob somebody came in with a DAS agent. I wouldn't talk with him. I met him but told him I didn't think I should discuss anything with him because Salah had told us not to, without him. I caught hell about this later, from a United States attorney in Midland, Texas. It was when they were trying to indict Chagra on the drug charges some time later. I was called before a Grand Jury to testify about the trip to Colombia. The United States attorney had all the information in front of him. He started getting on my ass about why I wouldn't talk to a DEA agent—one of my own countrymen ... And I said, "Shit, you're a lawyer. If you tell your client not to talk with anybody unless you're there, you'd expect him to do the same." Nothing ever came of that ...

Anyway, the DEA didn't tell me why he was there, but I assumed it was because of the ongoing investigation into Chagra.

JULY 19, 1977

Salah came in. We were going to get out on Saturday. Never heard that before—I wrote—ha,ha.

JULY 20, 1977

Colombian Independence Day.

JULY 21, 1977

Another lost day. One third of the summer was gone.

JULY 22, 1977

Bonnie Frank called. She had talked to Barbara the night before. Bonnie reported that Barbara had told her to tell me that the lawyer for the airplane insurance company had said a decision would be made on Tuesday the twenty-sixth. I wrote here—"What else is new??"

JULY 23, 1977

Same old Salah trick. He didn't show up. Carmen brought me a letter Barbara had mailed to her. Carmen had smuggled out the letter I had written to Barbara and Carmen enclosed it with a note that Barbara could write to me through her.

I have a note here that the sub-director was going to bring me a bottle of whiskey and that the son of a bitch didn't do it. It was Saturday night. I was looking forward to a little snort. I gave him ten bucks in advance, and he didn't show up. I wrote here, "These Indian assholes are the biggest liars in the world."

JULY 24, 1977

Sunday. Miguel's brother called to say that there are problems with immigration in the States and that they're not going to let him back into the country.

JULY 25, 1977

We're looking forward to Tuesday the 26th. We've had no word. My mind was like a piece of silly putty. I never really lost faith that I would get out. From hindsight, I realize that I should have been more worried than I was. But all my life I've been an optimist, and I was optimistic then. I got mad at petty little things, whereas I should have been worried about spending years down there.

JULY 26, 1977

Nothing.

JULY 27, 1977

Good news and bad news. Salah came by and said the judge ruled in our behalf.

There were actually no charges. But the investigation was over and Miguel and I were cleared of trafficking. However, another judge from another court had charged us with contraband—the contraband being the airplane. By flying it in, we brought contraband into the country. It never ended, the shit didn't … We were cleared of drug charges, now our airplane was contraband. How in God's name can this be? My hat goes off to this country.

Our Country gives them money and helicopters and God knows what else, but when they want a Learjet, they will stop at nothing.

JULY 28, 1977

Visit from Salah and Rebelledo before they went to see the judge. Rebelledo said he would ask the judge's permission to take us into town Saturday for some shopping. Salah returned before leaving for Bogotá to say he thought he could deal with the judge satisfactorily.

Barbara called. We were still getting some calls, without even paying off.

JULY 29, 1977

Colombian holiday.

JULY 30 AND 31, 1977

Nothing.

AUGUST 1, 1977

Pablo Salah came in and took Miguel and me to make statements to the judge. We bought the guards lunch and I had three beers. They tasted good. It was my first time out of jail. After we had been to see the judge, the guards let us buy some clothes. I didn't have much money but I had enough for a pair of pants and a shirt. Then I bought the guards the lunch and the beers. I have noted here that Salah was supposed to be wining and dining the judge that night, and that I was supposed to see Salah in the morning.

AUGUST 2, 1977

Now things are starting to happen. They took us to the airport. The jurisdiction over the airplane was to be transferred from one judge to another, are we were supposed to be there. The judge didn't show up, so we went back, the airplane still hadn't been secured, as far as I knew.

AUGUST 3, 1977

Salah came and said we could leave in the morning. He was waiting for the judge to sign the papers. I could foresee waiting all the next day. I write that I hoped I could get over my bitterness before I got home because I didn't want to burden Barbara with it. I was getting bitter, yes.

It had been one stupid thing piled on another for seven weeks. The barbaric system, or lack of system, of justice was beyond imagination. Besides, I had developed a bad case of hemorrhoids from defecating au naturel—squatting. That was one of the small things that was upsetting me. The only good thing about it was that I was shitting on Colombia. But still, I wrote I was thankful to be there rather than in a hospital with cancer, or something.

AUGUST 4, 1977

We were released at 10:00 A.M. Spent the day clearing at DAS and taking care of other paperwork. Miguel and I got drunk that night. We spent the night at the hotel right there on the beach. The one with the restaurant on the second floor. I still have the key at home, but I don't remember the name …

AUGUST 5, 1977 WE FLEW TO MIAMI ON AEROCONDOR.

We flew to Miami on Aerocondor.

It was a good flight, good service, good meals. Miguel had a problem in Miami with the immigration people, but we outfoxed them. I had a passport. Miguel didn't and we knew it would be a problem. I cleared customs first and called Karamanos and asked, "What about Miguel?" He said to have Miguel go ahead and try to clear. All he had was a Chilean passport, but Karamanos said he should try and we would take it from there.

They stopped him and hauled him into a little office. I called Karamanos back and told him what was going on. Karamanos got on the phone to Washington, to Senator Howard Cannon from Nevada and asked him to intercede on Miguel's behalf. So either Cannon or someone from his staff called the Miami immigration people. For that reason he wasn't immediately deported. Originally they were going to put him on the first flight to Chile. Miguel didn't want to go back to his country because of the political situation there. But with the help of Cannon's office, they were going to allow him to proceed through the United States. He was to have to go to Canada. Canada was going to allow him to stay there until he got accepted back into the United States

Q. HAD SENATOR CANNON KNOWN THE SITUATION FROM DAY ONE? HAD HE BEEN WORKING ON IT?

Oh, yes, he knew about it. Chris had told me several times that Cannon was working on it. Anyone in politics in Nevada is a friend of Chris's.

So they allowed Miguel to go, and we bought him a ticket from Miami to Los Angeles and then to Vancouver. The airplane stopped in Las Vegas, so we got him off there. He stayed undercover for several days and after talking with the attorneys, he turned himself in. He was allowed to stay. He was already there, and it didn't hurt anything to let him stay. Eventually he was able to get permission to stay, his green card. And he's still in the country.

We had a connecting flight to Houston, so it ended up being quite late, around ten at night, by the time we got to Las Vegas. Only Chris was at the airport, because with Miguel, we were afraid others might lead reporters out there. But Chris had a restaurant then, and my wife was there with Miguel's family, so we had a good reunion.

CHAPTER THIRTY-SEVEN

JULY 19, 1980—LAS VEGAS TO MIAMI, REMOVING THE COBWEBS

Steve Boiling's log of his fifty-two days in Colombia cleared up some of the nagging questions about the events surrounding the flight of 464 Juliet to Colombia on June 25, 1977. It went a long way toward piecing together a complex jigsaw puzzle with a random collection of scraps of information having no special significance when viewed singly but, when fit together, revealed a nearly complete picture. We sat down together to analyze our pooled knowledge of this strange story.

It had been established, without a shadow of doubt, through depositions in the United States and Colombia and evidence on public record, that the flight to Santa Marta was legitimate in every way. The flight plan was properly filed and approved; clearance had been given for landing. Colombian court records showed that nothing unusual was found on the airplane in the search made upon its arrival. The two paramedics had no passports, but the Colombian authorities never treated this as a problem. The U. S. Embassy in Bogotá had, in fact, informed Jet Avia officials that passports were not required provided the passengers in question remained in the airport until departure. Additionally, the flight was an air rescue, internationally acknowledged as a life or death mission and normally given special courtesy and consideration.

Why, then, were the passengers and airplane detained? I asked Steve to speculate on the most logical explanation.

From the first day, Steve had felt their problems were directly related to Jimmy Chagra. For years the United States Justice Department, the DEA and the FBI had been engaged in an ongoing investigation of the whole Chagra family. The fact that Jimmy Chagra was under surveillance became public knowledge. Later, Steve had been called to appear before the grand jury to testify against Chagra concerning the flight of 464 Juliet.

It made no sense to suppose that the Colombians in Santa Marta were interested in nailing Chagra. Drugs are a big business in that part of Colombia. Chagra's participation created a huge influx of American dollars for the powers-that-be. His fixes were "in." He had gone there before on "deals"—certainly he had no misgivings about going again on a rescue mission to airlift to the United States a gravely injured "employee," whom he could not simply ignore and leave to die there. He was not in a position to take any heat; he had to go. He couldn't delegate a responsibility of these proportions. In short, he was actually safer in Santa Marta than on the streets of El Paso or Las Vegas, as later events ultimately proved.

It had to be the United States agencies that wanted Chagra. The United States government has its documented, and undocumented, ways to lean on foreign governments to cooperate through their law enforcement and criminal investigation agencies. However, in this case, there were complications that had to be overcome: Jimmy Chagra's excellent protection in Santa Marta and the fact that he had broken no law in entering Colombia. No legitimate cause existed for charging him with anything. Nevertheless, a highly convenient circumstance existed that could be used. This was the Colombian legal system, based on Napoleonic Law. A person can be held for an indefinite period of time, just for "investigation." The old story of being guilty until proven innocent. If Chagra could be held there long enough for satisfactory details of a "deal" to be negotiated and set up, the United States agencies would have something of value to use in preparing the indictment against him.

The essence of any deal is quid pro quo. The "something of value" the Colombian Government would receive was to be the gift of an airplane worth over a million dollars. Aircraft confiscated for any illegality in Colombia revert to the government and are either kept there for use or are ransomed back to the owners.

Colombia has built up a considerable fleet, gratis, in this manner over the past several years; public coffers and private pockets have both been enriched.

However, there had to be some semblance of legality to do all this. If the Colombian government was to confiscate the plane, they would have to cooperate by producing evidence of violation of the law by the crew in general and by Chagra in particular. By holding these people for "investigation," the machinery for fabricating the evidence of an indictable offense could be assembled, given a little time.

The convenient and customary offense, "violation of Colombian airspace," was first charged. The validity of a flight plan, which indeed was filed for 464 Juliet, can be corroborated in official flight records, but this takes time. In the interim, time was gained to create convincing scenarios for other offenses.

United States and Colombian agencies in Bogotá were undoubtedly aware that it would be difficult to stage anything in Santa Marta where Chagra had made many powerful amigos. In Santa Marta, records could mysteriously disappear—they often had.

Santa Marta, with its corruption orientation and its completely pro-organized crime posture, was too risky: However, it would be feasible—although highly unusual—to transfer the suspects in a matter of purely local jurisdiction to another jurisdiction. So a decision was rapidly made to send the detained Americans to Bogotá. It was much more expedient to interrogate them in DAS national headquarters under the eyes of the American counterpart agencies. In this way, the record would be inviolate. This procedure may have served, as well, to remove Chagra from Santa Marta where he had the connections to buy his way out before details of the deal were completely worked out.

After spending a week in Bogotá, the six men were returned to Santa Marta, still in custody. As was to be expected, the charge of violation of Colombian air space was dismissed. So it was time to bring forth the new charge. This time, a decision was made somewhere to produce evidence of narcotics smuggling. This would be especially appropriate for Chagra. Two weeks after the airplane had been searched and pronounced clean, three separate Colombian law enforcement agencies were assembled to re-inspect it jointly and report their findings severally. Quite the overkill. Still, it would establish the legal bases for three different "investigations," if they were needed, for present and future use.

Lo and behold, this delegation found fifty grams of cocaine on top of an open box of fuel additive and surgical items, sitting in the middle of the aisle of the plane.

As evidence, it was pitiful. Fifty grams of cocaine brought *into* Colombia by a kingpin of narcotics traffic in a million-dollar Learjet was highly suspect. But fifty grams was sufficient cause for confiscation of the plane and would serve as well as a more "commercial" quantity which could disappear as mysteriously as it had appeared.

Possibly, other evidence was found linking Chagra to the crash of the marijuana plane in the Guajira which later cost Bruce Allen his life. He had other drug traffic activities in Colombia that may also have been under surveillance.

Certainly Chagra's "business" in Colombia formed an integral part of the "continuing criminal enterprise" charge that eventually lead to his indictment and ensuing conviction.

The United States and Colombian agencies apparently knew what they were doing by removing Chagra from Santa Marta before his amigos there could mobilize to help him. Even after the cocaine was "found" inside the Learjet, Chagra and Wilson were able to buy their freedom, given, as they were, "unconditional liberty" to return to the United States from Santa Marta.

Chagra and Wilson may have been allowed to walk for other reasons, too. Perhaps the United States agencies were even desirous of having Chagra and Wilson free to return to the States, once criminal enterprise charges had been firmly established in different jurisdictions. Perhaps they didn't want Chagra sitting in a jail down in Colombia—better to have him back in the States, thereby eliminating time-consuming and complicated procedures of extradition when they had enough solid material for preparing their indictment.

A similar line of reasoning would apply to Wilson, who was scheduled to be tried in Ardmore, Oklahoma in August of 1977. It would not have served the best interests of the United States Justice Department to have Wilson absent from the proceedings. (The Justice Department was exceedingly eager to bring in a conviction at Ardmore, as was shown by their over-zealousness in producing testimonies so obviously false that Lee Chagra was able to disprove them and obtain release of the group of which Wilson was a member. But this was after the fact, in the fall of 1977, not before it.)

A very strange set of facts that I had learned recently from my examination of the 464 Juliet file in Judge Valdez's office also strongly indicated that everybody had been thinking ahead. It was July 4, 1977, when the Ninth Court of Criminal Proceedings of Santa Marta dismissed the charges of narcotics trafficking against Jimmy Chagra and Jerry Lee Wilson and two other of the detained Americans, who all returned to the States. But on February 20, 1979, a year and seven months down the road, the Second Penal Court of the Circuit of Santa Marta charged Jamiel Alexander Chagra and Jerry Lee Wilson anew with the crime of narcotics trafficking. How convenient for the United States Justice Department. A judge in a town in Colombia had suddenly recalled a supposedly closed file on Jimmy Chagra sitting on his desk for over a year and a half, just in time to help indict Chagra on February 27, 1979 on his criminal activities in Texas, Florida, and Colombia.

Pilot Tony Gekakis and paramedic Jeff Ellis were released along with Chagra and Wilson. The crew member normally to be held should have been the pilot, but Steve, the copilot was elected, along with Miguel Parada, the other paramedic. Steve felt that one employee from Jet Avia and one from Mercy Ambulance were held as part of the "confiscation deal" unfinished business, since these were established companies that could afford to ransom the plane and personnel. Ellis and Gekakis were both high-strung and nervous and Gekakis was also in poor health. Bolling, along with Parada, who spoke Spanish, had better survival potential, so they were the logical choices to be kept until the Colombians had secured their "something of value."

Following this line of reasoning, decisions had to have been made previously by the authorities to set the scenario in which Steve Bolling, the copilot, would identify the box of fuel additive and Miguel, the paramedic, would identify the medical implement. Their admission of ownership of these tied them neatly to the cocaine so that they could be held longer for renewed "investigations" into narcotics smuggling and as "hostages" for forthcoming negotiations to get them and the plane released for a price. Basically, Steve Bolling and Miguel Parada, both innocent Americans, were being kept there as capital assets by the Colombian government.

I was also interested to hear Steve's thoughts about how much the United States government knew about the flight of 464 Juliet, its purpose and its passengers prior to going to Colombia.

His opinion was that they had to be most definitely aware of all these. First of all, Chris Karamanos, owner of Jet Avia, had spoken twice with the American Embassy in Bogotá. In the first call, made on June 11, he described the nature of the mission and gave Jerry Wilson's name as the patient (as he had been informed by Chagra). He also inquired then about the telephone number of the hospital in Santa Marta.

The officer in charge informed Karamanos that he would report the matter to his superior. The second call was to inquire about the need for passports. It cannot be claimed with certainty that United States officials in Bogotá knew Wilson was under indictment in the United States, but it is possible. What would have been highly suspicious was the fact that an American had been burned in Santa Marta, information sufficient to have alerted the DEA to look into particulars of the rescue mission and to monitor its arrival. A DEA agent and a representative of the United States Consulate in Barranquilla were on the scene the day following arrival of 464 Juliet.

Chagra's name would have appeared on the United States Customs General Declaration filed in Ft. Lauderdale on June 14. Once in the computer, it almost surely would have been flagged as he was under surveillance and investigation, and this information would have been relayed to the proper agencies.

Another indicator may have been the tail number N464J. Jet Avia, it was later learned, had also been under investigation, so the number also could have been flagged.

There was still another possibility. An informant may have been with the DC-6 when it crashed on takeoff. Wilson had not, as first reported, flown in on 464 Juliet. The second and "official" version was that Wilson borrowed a Cessna 210 and flew to Bruce Allen's rescue when he heard of the accident. Steve Bolling, however, supplied the third and true version: Jerry Wilson had actually been on the DC-6, escaping without injuries. He had brought Bruce Allen to the Santa Marta hospital and phoned Chagra to make the necessary arrangements.

Steve told me that there had been a third member of the crew of the DC-6 who escaped with a broken arm and left the country. According to

Steve, he was never heard of again.

Later, I was to see a translation from an article in Bogotá's *El Tiempo* of June 23, 1977, which may—or may not—have been the truth about the third man. The article contained many incorrect statements but the excerpt below is included as a matter of interest.

> "It is possible that Warren Edward Walden, the other American arrested in the Ernesto Cortissoz Airport in Barranquilla, has connections with the case being investigated here.
>
> As was reported in EL TIEMPO, authorities believe that Edward Walden is the same person who brought his countryman Bruce Allen to the Santa Marta hospital from Riohacha, together with a Peace Corps nurse in the Guajira. However, Walden told a different story when he was arrested, saying that his plane crashed in the sea in the Cienaga Grande area, north of Magdalena. He said he managed to survive in a boat in which he drifted for fourteen hours.
>
> Sources close to the examining magistrate, Enrique Gardia, say that the Edward Walden case will be incorporated into the proceedings against the dead American in this capital city (Santa Marta)."

Even later, I learned that there was a mysterious fourth man, the pilot or copilot of the DC-6, who was an informant for the DEA. He had been detained at Miami International Airport in the middle of June 1977. I could not find out whether his drug activities were superseded by his employment with the DEA before or after that date, which is really immaterial. He could have provided the DEA with valuable testimony either before or after the crash.

There was one last piece to the puzzle: Bruce Allen. Ironically, although his lingering death made him the key piece, it also made him a pawn in a game that proved to be too big for him.

Steve Bolling's compassion in undertaking the mission of mercy with full knowledge of its hazards had touched me deeply. Steve was no soldier of fortune. He was a professional, an average American "family man." Knowing that 464 Juliet was chartered by an important member of organized crime to airlift a man seriously burned while smuggling narcotics, he was still willing to put his liberty and reputation on the line to save that man, even after he learned he was a stranger.

Had Bruce Allen died in the crash everything would have been different. Because he lived, Jimmy Chagra was forced to make a move which ultimately provided the authorities with important evidence of his Colombian drug smuggling activities named in his indictment.

Bruce Allen, regardless of his involvement in a crime, was denied a basic human right. He was a man who had a chance to live and the American right to do so. He was denied his chance to live because our government wanted Jimmy Chagra ... and the Colombian government wanted a Learjet. It was as simple as that.

The United States government could have agreed to extradite Bruce Allen if he recovered. It would have cost them nothing to let him be taken back to be treated in the best facilities in the world. But this would have ruined the game plan. It was known that he would be doomed to death if he was left there. Their complete callousness to his fate was even more appalling than their cynical lack of morality in attaining what they wanted by manipulation of the law. Allowing a man to die to suit their own purposes, officials made their deal with the devil.

If our law enforcement agencies place themselves above the law and are free to create their own laws, cynically and extemporaneously, we are perilously approaching the situation of Nazi Germany where the state could preempt the law for its own convenience, even to taking the life of anyone standing in its way. After decades we are still tracking down the few remaining Nazi criminals that transgressed basic codes of morality governing human behavior. It is unspeakable that we should allow our agencies to be guilty of the same practice.

There are those of us who live within the law that merely shrug and ask who gives a damn about a criminal like Chagra or a man suspected of running dope like Bruce Allen. This is only one side of the coin. No one can condone criminal activity. Criminals must be brought to justice and punished. But when the ends begin to justify the means in prosecuting criminal activities, a line has been crossed. The first step, no matter how small, is too far. When this step has been taken, any law-abiding citizen can equally be hunted down, trapped, and live in fear of a knock on the door in the night. This is the other side of the coin. Then life becomes existence in a jungle where the beasts with the sharpest fangs and the strongest claws rule.

I was still pondering on the conclusions Steve and I had drawn from our shared knowledge as I relaxed in my seat on the 727 taxiing onto the Las Vegas runway. The surface shimmered in the hot desert air. My mind was finally satisfied as to what had happened as a result of 464 Juliet's flight to Santa Marta, Colombia. I felt it would help me, although I was not entirely sure of how.

I had tried unsuccessfully to catch any inconsistencies in the key points of Steve's account of his fifty-two days in Colombia. There was no doubt whatsoever in my mind that he had told the truth about everything he knew. Every single piece of information he provided fit perfectly into mine. Putting them together had cleared up almost all of the mysteries and shown me where the sleeping giants were lying.

The most appalling part of his story was what was revealed concerning the complete and callous lack of concern for Bruce Allen. No one—saint or sinner—should have been allowed to die the slow, lingering, agonizing death he met with when present and immediate alternatives existed to possibly save him and to certainly ease his pain. Deliberate torture of an enemy was understandable. Deliberate indifference to the suffering of an ally was not. His only value had been that he had served as bait in a trap for Chagra. When Chagra had been caught, the bait was thrown away. Bruce Allen became a victim of an atrocity in the vicious war the United States Justice Department was waging against the Chagras.

How had I been caught up in this long-unsolved mystery?

Pure circumstance, I knew. But even more to the point, how was I going to do what no one could do in the past three years? In spite of the skepticism of many of the people whose judgment I respected, I felt that there were some grounds for believing that I could get 464 Juliet out of Colombia. I took out a piece of paper and listed every negative and every positive consideration based on what had happened thus far. I finally had boiled down the "positive" list to three realities that I could relate to.

The first item on the "positive" list was Judge Valdez. I was convinced that with regard to the release of 464 Juliet, he was dealing with me honestly. If anyone could have conned me out of seventy thousand dollars, it was Valdez. I would have given him the money at almost any recent time if he had asked me for it, and he knew it. Yet he hadn't requested any advance payment other than the sum I had given his wife. He had made an irrevocable commitment to me the moment he had accepted Alfredo Escobar's intervention. He would not dare dishonor our agreement under the very nose of the Minister of Justice who held supreme authority over him. By accepting this powerful protection in Bogotá, he had incurred the responsibility of following through. Valdez was also motivated strongly by the possibility of our future "business" relationship, a further guarantee that he would fulfill his part of the bargain if humanly possible. The only gray area was the matter of the strange delays, which I was becoming certain stemmed from his inability to prepare the document in such a way as to satisfy the Ministry of Justice. He was fearful of the consequences, despite the fact that he had the authority to sign such a document. It was almost as if he were waiting for something to take him off the horns of his dilemma.

My second positive asset was Luis Donado. Donado, always the gentleman, had never fed me any bullshit nor had he been any less than 100 percent honest with me. He had never tried to minimize problems nor optimize chances for success. In every area within his competence he had helped me greatly. His love for his sons was real—I had seen the tears in his eyes when he spoke of Fernando's problem. I knew he deeply appreciated my help in furthering their flying careers.

My third positive item was 464 Juliet herself. She was now basically airworthy, but another six months on the ground would cripple her permanently. My legal position was strong. Documented proof of ownership had been recognized in Colombian courts on the basis of legal documentation from the States. I could tie up any attempts to contest such ownership. There would be no justification for the Colombian legal system to invest the time and money in fighting over what would become a pile of scrap metal by the time it had ended. In my particular situation, I could turn her into an asset. They obviously couldn't, even three years before. I therefore felt that the legal authorities of Colombia would present no serious problems once the proper authorization was filed for her release. This, of course, revolved around Valdez.

These three points were my realities. They were my "handle." My greatest problem initially was that no handle had existed to gain control of the situation, or if one had existed, it had been lost. I now had something that I had created out of confusion and chaos, and I would hold onto it, firmly.

Aside from the one negative item concerning Valdez's indecision, there was another, more ominous one I had to acknowledge. This was a real giant, and not sleeping—the military. I could not dismiss Federico's warnings that they could and would stop me. They were powerful enough to do it. The military in Colombia in no way resembles the light opera contingent of buffoons so often seen in movies and on TV. They wield very real power within the country. 464 Juliet had at one time been assigned to Colombian Presidential use, which had been rejected due to lack of qualified technical personnel to service and fly her. Their condemning her as unairworthy had been, at that time, a ploy to save face. In the interim, of course, she had deteriorated to such a condition; but, we had worked miracles on her, and she was now restored. I was fearful that the powers-that-be were now having second thoughts. The Air Force was certainly aware that she could fly. Otherwise, why would they have insisted on the truck parked in her path to prevent us from making a suitable brake test on the runway?

Another disturbing aspect: both Luis Donado and Alfredo Escobar had made it clear that any official body with even the slightest claim to possession of the plane had turned into a dog in the manger whenever interest had been shown in ransoming or purchasing the Learjet. Their unyielding greed had produced a situation whereby not one of them had been able to profit. In other words, no one in Colombia had been able to cash in on the deal with the United States agencies concerning Chagra. This could prove to be a serious stumbling block, which the military might very well place in my path before all is said and done.

I resolved to keep these two problems fully in mind and to search for their solution. If I could resolve the problem of the judge's delays, I might be able to circumvent the one with the military by finding some way to take advantage of the fact that they were at odds with all the other Colombian official bodies concerning jurisdiction over 464 Juliet.

I deplaned back in South Florida late that evening, grabbed a cab, and was home in a few minutes. The trip had revealed new information and resolutions, and it had been a rewarding one.

CHAPTER THIRTY-EIGHT

Raul was late.

I paced back and forth in my office; I paced back and forth to the interior shop; I picked up the interior shop-extension half a dozen times.

He finally arrived at 9:15.

"Raul, where the hell have you been?" I barked. "We're supposed to call the judge this morning and it's getting late."

Raul was apologetic. He was still fighting with his defiant womenfolk. Although outnumbered seven to one, he was stubbornly determined to establish himself as the head of the household.

He immediately got busy on the phone but, as feared, the circuits were now overloaded. While we waited and dialed, I told Raul of the wealth of information I had gotten from Steve Bolling. He was interested to find out that most of our deductions about 464 Juliet's flight had been confirmed, and that we had not been imagining the full scope of complications it had caused.

Valdez was finally on the line at 10:45. The invariable ritual of salutations and exchange of health information finally turned to business. Raul's fading smile, downcast eyes and weary slump told me immediately that he was getting the invariable "not yet" answers from Judge Valdez. I sat in my chair and studied the ceiling. These procrastinations were making my anxiety intolerable, frustration was clawing at me without mercy.

"What's the problem now?" I asked as he hung up.

"The same one. He says he's still working on *la providencia*."

"How long can a *providencia* be?" I wanted to know, "It seems to me he's had time to write a whole book."

"Take it easy, Bobby," Raul tried to calm me. "I'm no lawyer—I don't know why it's taking so long. He keeps telling me that it is very complicated, that it has to conform to the law—like he's scared of doing something wrong. That's all I know."

"Raul, did he say anything at all except the same old things?"

Raul was beginning to look trapped, torn between his desire to give me some small scrap of optimism, and his sure knowledge that I could smell out a lie before it was even out of his mouth, just by the look in his eyes and his expression.

"No, Bobby, nothing at all," he said reluctantly, "but I still think he's serious, honest."

He was alternately mumbling, shuffling and casting pleading looks at me to take him off a painful hook. At the height of the impasse, Terry walked into the office.

"What's wrong now?" she asked, and sat down to wait for an answer, crossing her arms firmly to indicate that she intended to get it. I tried to sidestep, too angry and depressed to find an answer that would satisfy without alarming her.

"Just another six or seven days more," I said morosely, "Valdez isn't finished with the papers yet."

"What's taking so long?"

"I don't know what's taking so long," I snapped.

"I think you're getting the runaround," she began hotly.

"Look, Terry," I shot back impatiently, "You don't know what's going on. It's only a minor problem—I'll solve it."

"Well, Bobby, I've been hearing that for three months now. It looks to me as if you're no closer now than you were at the beginning. If you're smart, you'll forget it." And then, in a superior tone of voice, "Let's just say it's my woman's intuition: you aren't going to get that jet out of Colombia."

This was the last straw.

"You, you and your woman's intuition," I sputtered. "You don't know what you're talking about. All I get is crap, so don't let me hear it from you."

Raul was folding and refolding a small sheet of paper he had in his hands, concentrating on his task with bent head and serious attention. Terry averted what was shaping up to be a real battle by shutting up and leaving the office. Raul shot an apprehensive look at her retreating back and then at my face to see if he dared offer a word of commiseration. He seemed to think better of it and tried to resume our former conversation.

"Valdez said we should call him back in a week," he said in a subdued voice.

"Sure," I said bitterly.

Raul and I continued to talk for a good while longer, round and round, going over the same old ground to see if we had missed any clues concerning the delay. Nothing new emerged and Raul returned to his department.

He was back in half an hour, telling me that he had just received a call from his brother, Toño. Toño had been over to Santa Marta to see the captain of the Rodadero police station in the hope that he might get some new leads on the radios.

I sat forward. Maybe Toño had good news.

No, there was nothing new about the radios. But Toño had learned something I should know about. The captain had told him that four Americans had been there about three months before, trying to negotiate the purchase of 464 Juliet.

My immediate thought was that it had been Gordon.

"What were their names?" I wanted to know.

"He didn't know their names. All he knew was that one was a lawyer, one a businessman in the export-import business from the States, and the other two were just young guys. They were all from Tampa," said Raul.

The four men had first talked with Zapata at the Santa Marta airport. Zapata reported their interest and everybody turned out to talk with them— the army, the air force, customs, and the police. The Americans made an offer of seventy thousand dollars to dismantle the Learjet and even had a ship available to take her back to the States. The army, air force, customs, and police had agreed only upon one point: that the offer was not adequate. After a series of negotiation meetings that lasted two weeks, the main point of discussion was between the Colombians and concerned which one had the right to receive payment. Finally, the meetings terminated with a Colombian counteroffer of $370,000. Nothing had been learned about which group was to receive it; possibly it was to be split four ways.

"Anyway, the delegation from Tampa left with a promise to return," Raul concluded.

I was not surprised that they had left. The Colombians had greedily priced themselves right out of the ball park. But surely the Colombian appetites had been teased by the prospect of $370,000? This created new complications. First, I had never given even the slightest indication that I would contribute to their unofficial "United Way" fund. Second, although the $370,000 price tag the Colombians had indicated as their "final price" on an airplane unable to fly out of Colombia was grandiose, now, three months later, she could leave Colombia under her own power, thanks to non-bidder Bobby Wood. I had provided the military and their compatriots with an unexpected bonus: a new bargaining chip. Now, if the group from Tampa were still interested, they would not have to front-end load the costs of tearing down 464 Juliet to have her shipped back to the United States.

Raul said that Toño had added that these people were apparently serious, at least in the opening negotiations, as they had paid a Colombian attorney a five thousand dollar fee just for the initial stages of their efforts.

I had already dismissed the idea that this group was involved with Gordon, but I knew from many sources that others had attempted to get 464

Juliet released, and here was a new threat I couldn't ignore.

After Raul left, I considered this new information in the light of Federico's warning and Terry's "woman's intuition." A new element of reality had been introduced on the negative side of the balance which could tip the scales. I had to grant that a possibility of failure truly existed, and I would be a fool not to acknowledge it. Like most highly competitive people, I am in total agreement with the old saying that winning isn't everything, it's the only thing. I could handle defeat if I were competing with clearly defined rules, but this had become far more than a game. It had been a series of savage encounters with no rules at all. Now I knew who the adversaries were. I would beat them at their own no-rules game. If I were not the winner, there would be no winner at all. The other face of Bobby Wood could accept nothing less than a "scorched earth" policy if given no other choice.

I had an idea of how to put the policy into action but needed help with it, so I decided to have a talk with my friend and investigator, Jim Burkett. When I got him on the phone, he arranged to meet me the next morning.

July 29, 1980

Jim arrived at my office the next morning with his usual friendly smile.

"Sit down, Jim. I need your expert advice and help."

Jim settled down with a Coca-Cola in hand, waiting to hear what I had to discuss with him.

"Look, Jim, I know I can trust you. So listen to what I have to say and just answer yes or no. Don't patronize me."

"Dragon, you know me better than that," Jim assured me.

"First, I still believe I'm going to get 464 Juliet released. I know you can't look into my head. But you do know that I never kid myself. I'm a winner at heart and have no time for bullshit. That's why I am saying that there is, and always has been a remote possibility, that I might fail in my attempts to get 464 Juliet released. God forbid it happens, but if it does, I'm going to make damn sure no one else gets her."

Jim nodded and I went on.

"I've just put too much into this—not money—too much of my identity, or spiritual juices—or whatever you might call it—to let anyone else have her. Or even to let her sit there and rot away. Does this make any sense to you so far?

Jim nodded again.

"So what I have decided to do, as a last-ditch effort, if there is absolutely no hope, is to steal 464 Juliet out of Colombia. I already have a plan. The big problem is that the Colombian who set it up is an asshole with a capital *A*, and I don't have too much faith in what he can do. He's not really what you'd call an ace in the hole."

"Then what happens if that doesn't work out?" Jim was curious.

"You're my ace in the hole, Jim."

"How's that?"

"If I can't steal her, I want to destroy her. You're the expert in explosives and underwater operations. I need you to help. 464 Juliet is parked right on the beach, about 150 feet from the water. We could anchor a small boat a quarter mile or so out, swim to the beach and work through the tall grass to 464 Juliet. It would be easy to plant some charges under her and blow her to bits."

Jim sat back staring at me wide-eyed.

"You're serious, aren't you." This was a statement, not a question.

"Deadly serious. If I don't win, nobody wins. As they say, it's not the money, it's the principle. I don't know if it's a moral principle, or an emotional principle, or what. But I know this much. It's the only way I could write the ending to this chapter of my life … and still live with myself."

Jim was studying me as I talked. He understood that this was a decision I had not made lightly.

"Jim, I don't think it will come to this. But just in case—I have to make plans for the worst. I've got to face reality. There is one more idea I have to explore before I make any final decisions. I'll know what to do by Monday, and if I find I can't pull it all together, I need you."

"You've got me, Bobby," Jim said. "We'll blow that mother fucker off the face of the earth. They'll be picking up the pieces in Bogotá. We'll give those Colombians something to cry about. If you have the balls to do it, I'll be right beside you."

Jim immediately got down to the logistics of the prospective demolition foray, explaining different types of charges, where to plant them, how to set them off, underwater gear we would need—even the size of the hole I wanted to leave in the ground.

I then spent some time explaining to Jim everything that had really been going on in Colombia. Jim was the only person besides Raul who knew about the judge's "business" offer.

"With all this plotting," said Jim, "I almost forgot—I had my contact run you through the computer and you came up clean. I don't have any idea why the customs people said you were on the government's watch list. It must be 464 Juliet and not you. That mercy flight leads to the connection with the Chagra gang and the murder of the federal judge."

When I arrived home that night, family relations were strained. Terry and I weren't on speaking terms over our spat at the office that morning.

I found the unaccustomed silence uncomfortable, but anything was better than her spoken criticism and negative opinions in my overburdened state of mind. I was deeply frustrated with the whole situation, and now I was angry at myself for having taken my frustrations out on Terry. It was simply because I was shouldering the whole burden of Juliet—the risk, the hope, the challenge—alone, and I desperately wanted Terry to understand but didn't know how to make her understand. I said a quiet prayer, asking for guidance and forgiveness and the strength to carry on.

The next six days dragged slowly toward Monday, August 4, when we were to call Valdez once more. Raul got there on time, and immediately reported to my office.

"*Buenos dias*, refugee," I greeted him. "Is today the day?"

"I hope so, Bobby. I'll call Valdez right away."

While he placed the call, I racked my brains to try to come up with some new approach to obtaining the right answers from the judge but could think of nothing. Raul finally got a connection.

My eyes were glued to his face and after a couple of minutes my heart sank. Raul was now, yet again, into the "*si's*" and "*comprendo's*," and his every word hit me like a blow in the solar plexus.

When he had finished, he turned to me like a school boy expecting a whipping, waiting for me to yell at him. I was past even that point.

"Bobby, Valdez promised—ten more days, more or less."

"Horseshit, Raul. I can't go to the bank on that. Has he done anything? Has he made any progress?"

"Bobby, you have to understand. It's Colombia. They don't do things the way we do them in the United States. It's slower. The airplane has been there three years."

"Look, Raul," I snapped, "I'm tired of fucking around. Valdez doesn't need a push, he needs a shove—forwards or backwards, whatever. Nothing in my life was ever given to me. If I wanted something, I had to make it happen. And believe me, I'm going to make something happen in Colombia. Good or bad. And now … listen very carefully, Raul … it's time to get Valdez some help. You remember the friend of Dr. Plada—the Supreme Court Justice?"

Yes, Raul remembered, nodding as he said, "Dr. Salgado."

"Right. Get on the phone right now and call Dr. Plada. Ask him to get in touch with Salgado and set up a meeting. As soon as possible."

Raul was alarmed, "What about Judge Valdez? What will he say? What about Aldo? He wouldn't go along with that."

I brushed off Aldo's reaction with a rude "Screw Aldo." As for Valdez, if he had any brains at all, he would welcome Dr. Salgado's intervention.

"Dr. Salgado is considered the smartest, most respected legal expert in

Colombia. If the judge doesn't want him that will answer our question and tell us that he never intended to release the jet."

Raul's concern about what Valdez would say was disappearing rapidly, and soon his round face was beaming.

"*Si, si,* Bobby," he was now agreeing, eagerly. He heartily approved of this new strategy. The only problem he could foresee was that since Salgado was such an important man, he might not be interested in helping us.

"Look, Raul, he's a man, just like we are. He puts his pants on one leg at a time. Even if he used to be a Supreme Court Justice, he has a private law practice now. That's how he earns his living. He has to work, just like we do. Besides, Dr. Plada is a friend of Salgado's, and he'll give us a good recommendation."

"What about money? I'm sure Salgado will be very expensive."

Raul was falling into his bad trait of failing to look ahead. I explained that since 464 Juliet was sitting in Colombia and was ready to fly, every passing day made it easier for someone down there to screw up the works. I was sure there were still some unknown sleeping giants in Bogotá that might awaken and reach out their hands to snatch 464 Juliet away.

"Let's consider Salgado's fee as an investment," I went on, ""and we'll offer him five hundred dollars just to meet with me—that should get his attention. Then, if we still have his attention, I'll give him ten thousand dollars in cash to come down to Santa Marta to straighten out the mess for Valdez. I don't care if it takes a month or a week or a day or an hour—the less time, the better—the fee is the same. Raul, if this doesn't get his attention, nothing will. With what I already have invested, it won't make any difference one way or another. We ain't got shit now, so there's nothing to lose."

Raul had followed my reasoning step by step and had not lost his way. He was becoming exuberantly optimistic, even to the extent of offering a suggestion of his own.

"You know, Bobby, it might be a good idea to have Gustavo get in touch with Salgado. He knows him, too, and he mentioned that he's been to Salgado's office in Barranquilla."

"He has an office in Barranquilla? Great. Call Gustavo now."

Gustavo wasn't at home; he would be in that night.

I was galvanized into action now. I had a feeling we were getting somewhere and that if all went well, it would produce a powerful reinforcement to my "handle" on the release of 464 Juliet.

"Let's call Alfredo Escobar and ask what he thinks of the idea," but Alfredo couldn't be reached either.

I elaborated on this new plan to Raul to make him understand why the time element was so critical. Raul, with his own version of the *Mañana*

Syndrome, had completely forgotten about my deadline with Paul Engstrom and Lloyd's of London.

Thinking about Paul made me realize that I had promised to call him that day, which considerably dampened my revived spirits. It was premature to tell him of my new strategy, so I would still have to relate the old story of delays, delays, delays.

When I reported to Paul that the judge had still not finished *la providencia*, he merely said that he didn't think another week would be a problem. He had received Judge Valdez's letter, which was completely in order.

He even was optimistic, saying, "You've done more in the past month than anyone else could've done in the three years 464 Juliet has been down there. Just concentrate on getting her out. And don't worry about the deadline. The letter is still good enough for now."

I sat back with a feeling I had been given a reprieve. Even the telephone conversation I had absolutely dreaded turned out well.

AUGUST 5, 1980

Raul had spoken to Gustavo, who had been enthusiastic about the idea. He was sure it would speed up the snail's pace if Salgado came into the picture.

AUGUST 6, 1980

Raul burst into the office without even pausing to knock, with a broad smile on his excited face. "Good news, Bobby—Great news, in fact. You are one smart gringo."

Gustavo had called back that morning, after trying unsuccessfully the night before, to say that he had talked with Dr. Salgado and explained the problem with the jet. Dr. Salgado was very interested in meeting with me. When Gustavo had conveyed my offer of ten thousand dollars for a solution, Salgado had asked several times if Gustavo was sure of the amount. He had given Gustavo his office number in Bogotá for us to call him there at nine o'clock, Bogotá time. Gustavo was very pleased, Raul told me, because he knew Dr. Salgado is one very smart lawyer.

We waited impatiently for the hour to arrive—ten o'clock, our time, was nine in Bogotá. When the large hand hit the twelve I picked up the phone. We got the call through almost immediately.

Raul meticulously dusted off his best manners and eloquence for conversational openers. It would have been abrupt and rude to get down to the business at hand with too great haste.

"Tell him about Alfredo," I prompted when I heard him mention our oil deal with Dr. Plada.

He nodded and smoothly dropped Alfredo Escobar's name after they had discussed my connection with Dr. Plada. Yes, Dr. Salgado knew the Minister and his son well. Finally, they turned to my problem. Raul outlined it briefly—briefly for Raul—and Dr. Salgado agreed to meet with us and Judge Valdez. The conversation then turned to money.

"*Si, Doctor*," Raul was urbanely assuring Salgado, "$10,000 *correcto*, $10,000 *en efectivo* (in cash)."

"*Mucho gusto, Doctor*," Raul was now reaching the closing ceremonial remarks, "*Igualmente, Doctor*," and "*Muy agradecido, Doctor*," and, finally, the conversation was concluded.

"You were right, Bobby. Salgado said he would help you. He asked if all your papers were documented in Bogotá. I told him that Alfredo took you there himself and had them authenticated. He said to forget the five hundred dollars you offered for the first meeting." Raul told me this in an awed voice, as if Salgado had produced a miracle by declining the extra money.

"He said that ten thousand dollars would be more than enough if he succeeds," Raul was babbling in a delirium of joy at all these new developments.

"OK, Raul, stop there. Let's go for the big one. Let's call Judge Valdez now and break the news. You have to be careful—tell Valdez that Aldo's accident has unfortunately delayed matters and that I felt Dr. Salgado might be able to provide him with more help than Aldo can. Don't act as if I think the delay is Valdez's fault—put it on Aldo's condition. The last thing I want to do is to give Valdez the idea we think he's a dummy. If Valdez says OK, we're home free. If he doesn't like it, we've got problems. So let's sit down and figure out exactly what you should say—even answers to questions he might ask."

We discussed every possible angle for several minutes to be sure that everything was covered.

As I had just cut Raul off short, he had not yet been able to tell me a few other important matters Salgado had brought up. Raul, now calmer and more controlled, said that Salgado had recommended that we meet him in Barranquilla rather than in Bogotá, as he would be on the coast Friday, August 15, to make a speech. Dr. Salgado had also added that there wasn't much he could do in Bogotá anyway, as he would need to be in Santa Marta to talk with Valdez to carefully examine the documentation of the case.

I was disappointed at having to delay the meeting more than another Week, but could see that this arrangement would be convenient.

"Before we start celebrating, let's get hold of Valdez. And Raul, remember, be very, very tactful."

It was almost noon before we got through to Judge Valdez. I was sitting forward and listened impatiently to the preliminaries, waiting for Raul to sound Valdez out on my suggestion about Dr. Salgado. Raul first apologized for calling so soon after our first phone call that week. Then he took a breath and plunged in.

He first stated that Mr. Wood was quite unhappy because of Aldo's problems, especially since we knew how very busy the judge must be and since Aldo was in no condition to provide proper assistance. Mr. Wood wanted to find out if the judge would be willing to have the further assistance of Dr. Julio Salgado, who would additionally represent Mr. Wood on the Learjet matter.

A silence. Raul was nodding his head, "*Si, señor Juez—el mismo*—the very same—Dr. Julio Salgado—the Supreme Court Justice from Bogotá."

Raul was still nodding happily as he told Valdez that we had spoken with Dr. Salgado that very day, that Dr. Salgado would go with us to Santa Marta as soon as possible. And, finally, that we would call Valdez back as soon as we had confirmed our meeting with Dr. Salgado.

Raul could hardly contain himself as he hung up.

"You're one smart SOB gringo. You must be Colombian," he shouted.

"Calm down, tell me what he said."

"Bobby, now you're going to get the Learjet for sure."

"How do you know?"

Raul explained that Valdez had been very excited, asking several times to be sure it was the right Dr. Salgado. Valdez had commented that Salgado was the most able and most respected lawyer of the entire country. A former Supreme Court Justice! Valdez would be honored to meet him. Dr. Salgado would be a tremendous help.

"You were right all along, Bobby," Raul continued, "Valdez said that if Dr. Salgado looked over the papers and said they were all legal, this would be all the protection he needed from the officials in Bogotá. He has been worried about the ones in Bogotá, the higher-ups."

With Dr. Salgado's legal expertise, no one could contest his credentials or the legality of what would be prepared. Also, Valdez had remarked that Dr. Salgado had tremendous power in the Colombian government—that he was often called on to interpret fine points of Colombian law when disputes arise. His word was law.

After digesting all these new developments, we called Dr. Salgado again. He was agreeable to an early Saturday morning meeting on August 16.

"Raul," I whispered, "Ask Salgado to phone Valdez now and confirm the meeting and tell him that we will be happy to pick Dr. Salgado up at the Barranquilla airport when he arrives on the fifteenth."

We spent the rest of the afternoon discussing our new plans and finally decided to telephone Valdez again to find out if Dr. Salgado had called. It was significant that Raul got down to business almost immediately without a single preliminary.

Valdez was highly pleased to inform us that Salgado had indeed called, and seemed impressed at the speed with which everything had been arranged. The meeting was set for 9:00 A.M. at Valdez's home on Saturday morning of August 16. I had a mental picture of the frenzy of housecleaning that would be taking place on Friday at the Valdez residence in preparation for the visit of such an important personage as Dr. Julio Salgado.

Raul was again nodding, "*No, señor Juez,* I will say nothing to Aldo," and he winked at me wickedly when he saw that I understood.

"Valdez is tickled shitless about Salgado," Raul said. "And you heard me—he doesn't want Aldo to know about the meeting. He wants to talk with Salgado alone. If Alfredo comes, that would be all right, but no one else."

Both of us were full of hope and elation about our new found amigo and could scarcely wait to meet him in Colombia. After Raul left, I sat alone for a couple of hours, trying to refine the new game plan and to envision any possible thing that could go wrong in my upcoming meeting with Salgado and Valdez.

Although Air Unlimited kept me busy for the next few days, time seemed to be set on a slow-motion clock. I had gone to see Bill Everett at the Miami International FAA for a new ferry permit. I had also paid a short visit to Red Garglay, who wished me luck this time. Paul Engstrom had been informed of my plans to go to Colombia, hopefully for the last time.

Late afternoon of August 13, I went to Jet Care and met with Dave Pearson. We got together the few last-minute parts still needed. I got back to my office around 6:30 and tried for almost two hours to run down Mel Cruder. As luck would have it, Mel was gone on a charter until the following week.

Raul and I scoured my list of Learjet pilots. All the people Bill Jones and other friends had suggested wanted no part of the operation. Rumors of my delays in Colombia had, evidently, spread quickly, and it seemed as if every pilot in South Florida knew the story of 464 Juliet and was interested only in avoiding any contact with her.

Finally, I picked up the folder with employment applications. Thanks be, there was one "possible"—Sam Jenkins. Fortunately, he had written down his home telephone. A few minutes later I had him on the line.

Sam informed me that he was working as a flight instructor at Aviation Flying Club at the Opa-Locka airport and that he was not thinking of making a change.

"No, Sam, you misunderstood me. I'm not looking for any more flight instructors. What I need is a Learjet pilot. I see on your application that you have a type-rating for Lears?"

Sam's polite interest suddenly changed to cheerful enthusiasm. Was I kidding?

"No, I'm not. I'm in a jam—my regular pilot, Mel Cruder, is out of town, and I need someone right away to fly a Learjet out of Colombia."

"Don't call anyone else," he interrupted eagerly. "I'm your man. I've been trying for some time to get a job flying Learjets."

"First, Sam, let me explain a little more about the job. I …"

"Never mind, Bob, I'll meet you in the morning, as early as you say. I'll take the job."

We arranged to meet at eight in the morning, and I cautioned him that we would have to leave that same night. Raul had been listening avidly to the conversation, and he immediately wanted to know who the pilot was and why he hadn't even let me explain the details of the job.

"Yes, I know—very odd, but he sounded happy about doing it. He really wants the job," I replied.

AUGUST 14, 1980

Raul was already at the office when I arrived at 7:30 A.M.

"*Qué pasa*, refugee?" I greeted him cheerfully. "Did your wife kick you out of the house when you told her you were going to Colombia today?"

"No, no—she's not mad at me any more," he said confidently. "I came in to see this new pilot. It's my ass, too. You know?"

I was laughing at Raul's assumption that he could automatically assess a man's flying qualifications on the strength of a handshake and a glance at his face. We walked together into my office to wait for Sam.

He appeared a little before eight, knocking on the open door frame.

"Come on in. You must be Sam," and I got up to greet him.

Sam was a tall, well-built man about 225 pounds, which included not an ounce of fat. He had short, jet-black hair. His well-pressed pants and shirt were immaculate. Even his briefcase seemed polished as he placed it on the desk. He dwarfed Raul who stood up to shake hands with him.

We sat a while and chatted about Sam's flying background. Besides being a flight instructor for his last one thousand hours, he had also flown in the Air Force for a short period as copilot on a B-52. What about Learjet time?

"Well, Bob, it's been a year since I flew one, but I have almost 950 hours in Lears. Don't worry; five minutes in the flight manual and I'll be up to snuff."

Sam was very enthusiastic—almost too enthusiastic in the light of the almost uniform lack of enthusiasm I had been running into recently. I still wanted him to have the particulars which I had tried to give him the night before, and I asked him if he had heard of Learjet N464J that had been captured in Santa Marta, Colombia, about three years before.

"Yes, Bob, I'll be honest with you and you don't have to explain. Rumors and tales have been heavy in South Florida on what you're doing in Colombia. That's why I didn't want you to go into all the details last night. I do want a chance to get into flying Learjets again—full time—so whatever the story is, I'm willing."

I was curious to know who had told him what and asked about it.

"Everybody knows, Bob. You know how much scuttlebutt there is in aviation circles. Most everybody who's talked to me about you and 464 Juliet don't think you're going to pull it off. But just in case you do, I want to be there."

"OK, Sam, the job is yours," I told him. "It pays twenty-nine hundred dollars to fly her back. I'll be your copilot, but let me tell you right now, I have never flown a jet. The only ratings I have are for single- and multi-engine aircraft, and I am also type-rated in a Douglas B-26, that's it."

We sat for an hour telling Sam everything we could think of concerning the condition of 464 Juliet and what had been done on maintenance. Sam finally was ready to go. We were all smiling and optimistic as we arranged for him to return at four that afternoon to leave on the six o'clock flight.

"Well, refugee, what do you think?" I asked Raul.

"He talks good … What do you think? You're a pilot," Raul hedged.

"I liked his attitude. He seems like my kind of man. And at least he's got balls. Besides, we're in no position to be real choosy at this late date. We'll just stand back and listen to what he has to say when he sees the nose full of rocks in the jet," I remarked.

Raul and I both burst out laughing, as we remembered the shrieks of horror Mel Cruder had uttered when he had first seen the boulders. And I, at least, knew how crazy people would think we were to attempt to fly 464 Juliet out in that condition.

Terry walked in at about 12:30, offering me a cold Coca-Cola and a warm smile.

"I'm sorry for what I said before, Bobby," she said, "but all this has been hard on me, too. With you gone so much, taking care of things here, and with the children and running the house, it gets too much for me … ."

I was happy and relieved that Terry and I were making peace before my departure.

"I know, honey. But right now, I need all your support. Just believe in me. It's hard enough down in Colombia dealing with all the insanity. I need a clear head. Peace of mind with you is what I need to deal with it. It won't be much longer, I promise you."

"I do understand, Bobby—I'm sorry," she said wholeheartedly. We sat there quietly for a few moments, silently enjoying the satisfaction of restoring domestic peace and tranquility.

Terry broke the silence hesitatingly, choosing her words with care.

"Do you have any idea how long you'll be gone?"

"Honestly, I don't, but I promise you one thing, it won't be until I'm back with 464 Juliet," I answered. I mentioned not a word about the plan Jim and I had made to scuttle 464 Juliet if all else failed.

"Bobby, all I can say is I love you. I know you have to do what you have to do. Just remember us here and hurry home."

My mind was at rest. Terry's words of understanding and sympathy were like a draft of pure oxygen that cleared my brain of the clouds that had been obscuring my attitude toward finishing up this difficult endeavor.

"Look, I have a surprise for you," she suddenly exclaimed, breaking up the seriousness of our talk. "Come … ," and she led me out to where the cars were parked. "Open the trunk," she instructed, and then, "Open the blue suitcase."

I obeyed, and when I lifted the lid, I could see that Terry had performed a labor of love. It was completely packed with all my favorite crackers, nuts, candy, ice tea, cookies, even Vienna Sausages.

"Damn, Terry," I joked, "I thought you wanted me back soon. You've provisioned me for months."

Raul, Dave, Sam, and I climbed out of my seriously overloaded car when we arrived at the airport around four fifteen. I kissed Terry goodbye, and she watched me with a loving smile as I went into customs. I made sure they gave me a stamped copy of the 4790 form I filled out. I had ninety-three thousand dollars in cash in my briefcase, and I sure as hell wanted no more problems on this front.

CHAPTER THIRTY-NINE

Diego had been alerted to our arrival and was on hand to provide us with the usual "special treatment" through customs and immigration in Barranquilla. When we got outside, we were greeted by the largest reception committee we had ever had: Aquiles, Aldo, Toño, Gustavo, Fernando, Donado Jr with girlfriend plus two additional friends. Only two people had known of our arrival time, Gustavo and Toño. But news travels fast in Colombia, especially concerning free food and drinks.

After depositing my money in the safe deposit box, where I had been lovingly conveyed by Aldo, who couldn't take his eyes from the packets of one hundred dollar bills, we returned to our hotel and all straggled up the stairs, which gave me a chance to pull Raul aside.

"How the hell did Aldo know we were coming?" I whispered.

"I have no idea—perhaps it was through Gustavo," Raul said.

"I wonder if he knows about Dr. Salgado yet," I said.

Raul didn't know the answer to this, either.

"I'm going to tell him now," I decided. "This way he won't be able to say I went behind his back, and it will show him that I'm in charge now. He certainly won't say anything bad about Dr. Salgado."

While the boys were bringing in the luggage, I took Aldo over to the side window. I had made up my mind to let Aldo save a little face, so I gave him substantially the same story we had given the judge, naturally dressing it up a little in Aldo's favor.

"Aldo," I began sympathetically, "I know you've had a bad time of it with all your injuries from the accident," Aldo's face quickly assumed a piteous look, "and after talking with Judge Valdez several times, I realized that he needed some help, since it was so difficult for you. So, in short, I decided to call in Dr. Julio Salgado."

Aldo's invalid look rapidly changed to one of alarm.

"Why did you do that? What's wrong with my brother, Gomez? I told you he was working on this."

Aldo was refusing to pick up the cue and was ignoring the face-saving "out" being offered. I had to be a little rougher.

"Just a minute, Aldo. Let's get something straight. I pay the bills. Your brother, Gomez, hasn't done a single thing I can see. And, frankly, I'd rather have an ex-Supreme Court judge helping Valdez."

Aldo's eyes opened wide.

"You mean *that* Salgado? Dr. Julio Salgado of the Supreme Court?"

I nodded.

Aldo had finally responded to the cue and made an attempt to recover by mumbling that he hadn't known who I meant at first.

"How did you get him?" he asked inquisitively. "He's a very important man."

"Connections, Aldo," I said smugly. "You remember Alfredo Escobar? His father arranged it."

I imparted this piece of false information deliberately to keep him off Gustavo's back, adding, "Just to make sure no one here gets out of line and tries to screw me."

Aldo's initial dismay was giving way to something resembling satisfaction as he could foresee certain advantages for himself in being able to say that he was associated (never mind how remotely) in an important case with Dr. Julio Salgado, ex-Justice of the Supreme Court.

When Gustavo arrived, full of a hearty and free meal, I first pulled him aside to tell him of my talk with Aldo. He listened with a satisfied smile as Aldo sang Salgado's praises and recounted his legal exploits as if he had just been hired as the attorney's press agent.

AUGUST 15, 1980

Raul, Aldo, Gustavo, and I stood on the second floor at the Barranquilla airport waiting for Dr. Salgado's flight to arrive. It was almost two thirty in the afternoon when Gustavo pointed to a group of passengers deplaning.

"There he is just stepping down."

I tried to catch a glimpse of this important man. We were over three hundred feet away, and all I could see was an older man, walking slowly and deliberately toward the baggage area.

We waited outside while Gustavo went in to help Dr. Salgado with his bags. When they emerged, he was not at all what I had expected. He was a short, slim man, about sixty-five years of age, with receding silvered hair and a fair but rough complexion. He was dressed in a neat and plain shirt and pants, without a tie, and he had a coat folded over his arm. As he came closer, I looked down and saw a completely incongruous element in his otherwise conservative dress—he had no shoes. His feet were inside a pair of sandals, the kind a person would wear to the beach. I wanted to ask Raul about it but didn't dare risk the question.

Gustavo made the introductions ceremoniously, very unlike his usual loud and bluff manner. There was no time for conversation, as Dr. Salgado had to hurry to his meeting where he was the honored guest and principal speaker.

"Raul," I said, making arrangements on the fly, "you go with Gustavo and Dr. Salgado. I'll ride with Aldo. Feel Salgado out. If he brings up the subject of 464 Juliet, fine. If not, make sure he can spend a few minutes with us after the meeting."

"Don't worry. I'll take care of Salgado. You take care of Aldo."

Aldo was clearly displeased at not being chosen to escort Dr. Salgado into the city. He sulked as we climbed into his car. I paid no attention to his surly answers to my few remarks.

He finally reopened a conversation. "Bobby, I guess you brought all the money—I didn't see how much you had."

I suspected that Aldo was on a fishing expedition to see if the new arrangements with Dr. Salgado were going to alter the old arrangements with him and Judge Valdez.

"Sure, Aldo, I brought twenty-five thousand dollars," I said cheerfully. Aldo was dismayed.

"How is that? It's supposed to be seventy-five thousand," he squawked.

"Take it easy, Aldo. I'm only kidding."

He calmed down.

"Look, Aldo, I don't have the jet released yet, so you still have to get off your ass and go to work to earn the money."

"Bobby, about the money. When Valdez releases the jet, be sure you pay me. I'm your lawyer here in Colombia. Valdez doesn't want you to pay him—he told me several times to be sure you never mention the money to him."

I was almost choking on the guffaws I was holding inside, and would have given a good sum to have Aldo on film when he went into his song and dance.

"Sure, sure, Aldo, I understand," I assured him, trying to pacify him by reminding him that I would never be so stupid as to even think of trying to bribe a judge.

Raul and Gustavo joined us about twenty minutes after our arrival at the hotel. Raul reported that Dr. Salgado had his speech on his mind and didn't want to discuss anything until later. He was to speak at an auditorium about two blocks from the hotel, and after the meeting would be attending a cocktail party downstairs. Salgado had suggested we meet with him before the party started.

Eight of us were sitting around in the room. It was stuffy and noisy, so Gustavo, Raul, and I decided to walk over to the auditorium to see Dr. Salgado in action. He was just being introduced as we walked in and took seats at the rear. He was speaking on several new laws that had been passed in Colombia and how these laws should be interpreted by the lawyers of the country, many of whom comprised his audience today. Although my Spanish was not sufficient to understand the meaning of his speech, I could immediately see that he had full command of his material and spoke with the complete assurance and authority of an expert. He held his audience spellbound for forty-five minutes. I was thoroughly impressed.

We slipped out after his speech and walked back to the hotel to wait in the lobby. The meeting had apparently broken up shortly after we had left; soon the lobby and cocktail area were filled with forty or fifty lawyers, judges, and magistrates, forming and reforming into groups, holding drinks and nibbling on snacks being passed around by white-coated waiters. Everyone was formally dressed, bowing at acquaintances and embracing old friends. These men were clearly from Barranquilla's top drawer.

Dr. Salgado entered with several other high-ranking officials around five forty-five. He was also well-dressed for the occasion, and I managed to get a look at his feet to see if by any chance he still had on the sandals. No, his footwear was as immaculate as his suit.

Finally, he spotted me and Raul standing a little apart from the gathering. He held up a hand to us, turned to his companions to excuse himself and approached to the spot where we were standing.

He inquired if we had a room in the hotel and when we told him we did, he suggested we go upstairs to talk. I had carefully instructed Raul on how Salgado should be approached, and felt that I should let Raul act completely as an interpreter so that I could watch, listen, and obtain some preliminary clues on what type of a man he was in a face-to-face encounter. My initial impressions of Salgado before an audience were excellent, and I was eager to see if they would be reconfirmed.

Salgado was bringing out the best in Raul, who spoke professionally and with great dignity when giving Dr. Salgado information on my background and my connections with *La Comunidad* and Alfredo Escobar. Raul did a fine job of explaining my dilemma briefly and simply. On the few occasions that he had a tendency to digress, Dr. Salgado would firmly steer him back to the main line. Every word that he uttered was firm, to the point, and without any trace of unnecessary embroidery.

When Raul had finished, Dr. Salgado turned to me.

It was Dr. Salgado who first brought up the legal matters to be discussed.

He seemed completely satisfied with my credentials and with the information Raul had relayed to him.

"Mr. Wood," he began, "I have talked several times with Judge Valdez since your first call. I believe this matter can be resolved fairly soon. Tomorrow morning, you and Raul can pick me up at *El Presidente*—here is the address. It's only a kilometer or two from here. I will be ready at seven."

He was courteous, but strictly no-nonsense.

"Fine, Dr. Salgado, we'll be there."

He rose and prepared to leave. He had said everything he had to say and was wasting no further time in useless conversation. Completely courteous, but finished—therefore, leaving.

"Dr. Salgado," I interjected, "regarding your fee—would you like to have it now? It will take me only a moment to get it from the safe deposit box downstairs."

"No, no, Mr. Wood. When I finish. You are apparently an honest man. You have made good friends here who are also good friends of mine. They speak very highly of you."

I was trying to think of some way to impress on him how important this matter was to me, but since he was obviously ready to say goodbye, I thought it wise only to tell him I was happy to meet him and hoped he could help me. I reminded myself that I had been over-exposed to bullshit artists too long; if a man of Dr. Salgado's obvious intelligence couldn't figure out how important the matter was to me, then all was lost.

We escorted him back downstairs, and then went back to the room for our customary post-mortem. It was a jubilant one. Both Raul and I felt that we had finally retained competent counsel, help that could finally get 464 Juliet released.

About an hour later, we went back to the lobby to find that the party was still in full swing. Dr. Salgado was sitting on a large couch facing a similar couch across a coffee table. He was surrounded by at least two dozen lawyers and judges, each hanging eagerly onto every word Salgado uttered, trying to gain his attention. New admirers would drift in and out, presenting compliments on his brilliant speech. It was like a reception in the court of Louis XVI with only the eighteenth century costumes lacking.

"Look, Raul, they're kissing his ass from one end to the other," I marveled.

"Bobby, you have to understand. He's as important as the President of the Republic. To be a Justice of the Supreme Court is the highest and most respected position in the country. Besides, he is the very best; he is the one the Colombian Government calls in to straighten out the law." Raul looked as though he was about to genuflect in the face of such majesty.

Sam and Dave joined us to watch the drooling throng, and shortly thereafter, we all went for dinner.

Up at 5:30 the next morning, I munched on a few crackers while Raul went below to make sure our almost-new 1977 Dodge taxicab was there. We had made arrangements to hire the cab the night before as we felt it would be undignified to haul Dr. Salgado across the peninsula in Aguiles' 1953 Chevy. Sam was up studying the Learjet flight manual and Dave sat alongside him giving some "ground school" on the systems. Aldo had stayed the night at the hotel but had not yet made an appearance as he was shacked up with a woman we had seen him with. Raul made a few lewdly judicious remarks about Aldo's lack of discrimination in bed partners. He was right—the woman was at least fifty years old, scrawny, dirty looking, and incredibly ugly.

Even Dave and Sam chimed in with a few remarks—they were going to be very cautious about future contacts with Aldo, as they didn't want to risk exposure to Colombian "bugs." Dave told Raul he'd rather screw a rattlesnake than the dame he saw Aldo with the night before.

After a few more laughs at Aldo's expense we went downstairs. Ramon, our taxi driver, was waiting. His car was polished to perfection and sparkled in the sun.

"*El Presidente*," I ordered. "*Vamanos.*"

As we pulled up to park, it could be seen immediately that Salgado was well-off. It was a deluxe condominium complex, about fifteen stories high, complete with security guards. We were allowed access only to the front desk where our names were requested. They telephoned Dr. Salgado's apartment, saying he would be down shortly. We waited for him at the desk.

Dr. Salgado stepped off the elevator in a tropical shirt worn over his slacks. He again had on his sandals. I hoped that Judge Valdez would not be too formally attired. I knew that Salgado would be unruffled, but Valdez might be embarrassed.

Raul and Dr. Salgado did most of the talking as we sped along the road smoothly with Ramon at the wheel. I had learned that the doctor was an early riser, usually up at six and early to bed, seldom later than eight in the evening.

He was a strange man. He never spoke merely to fill gaps in the conversation. If he had something to say, he said it and then shut up. He would often pick up his newspaper and read while others talked around him. He was not being rude, just uninterested in idle chatter.

We pulled up to Judge Valdez's house at about eight forty-five. There is another Colombian syndrome not yet mentioned—the Late Syndrome. A guest arriving for dinner at eight is more than likely to find the hostess still in curlers. Nine would be the more likely hour to arrive for an eight o'clock appointment. Salgado was completely unperturbed, and we certainly would not dare suggest a fifteen-minute sightseeing tour of Rodadero to time our arrival at the hour fixed.

Valdez must have been watching behind the crisp, white curtains, because he was at the door to meet us with open arms. His beaming face and bright eyes told me that this was a red letter day in the judge's life. He greeted Salgado as if he were the President of the Republic.

As I had expected, the house gleamed and sparkled. There was not a wrinkle in the cushions, not a speck of dust, even the leaves of the houseplants had been wiped and seemed to be glazed. We were ushered into the judge's den. He turned on the air conditioning, invited us to sit down, drawing up the best chair for Salgado. He rang for a servant who brought in coffee and special cakes, fresh out of the oven. He even remembered a Coca-Cola for me.

Raul and I sat back and listened as Salgado and Valdez established diplomatic relations with "shop talk." I whispered to Raul to ask if they would prefer that we leave them to themselves and return later. Perhaps they would be more comfortable talking business privately.

Valdez immediately accepted our offer; clearly he, at least, wanted to discuss the matter alone with Salgado.

"We should be finished around four or five this afternoon," he told us, "and then we can all have a drink together."

"OK, Ramon," I said as we returned to the taxi, "Let's go to the airport."

"Why didn't you want to stay?" Raul asked me.

I laughed and said, "Where's that one smart Colombian called Raul Soto?"

He looked at me in puzzlement.

"Look, refugee," I went on, "Valdez needs help—right?"

Raul nodded.

"I thought it would be a good move to let Valdez have a free hand. It would put him in an awkward situation, trying to tell Salgado about his inability to write *la providencia* with us sitting there breathing down his neck. He would look like a dummy—this way he can save face. Didn't you see how happy he was when I suggested that we leave? I was taking him off the hook."

"*Si, si*, Bobby," Raul said, comprehension finally dawning on his face, and, enviously, "I wish I'd thought of that."

The airport terminal was almost deserted. We walked through the building and across the ramp without challenge. No Baratta, no soldiers, very quiet. I walked around 464 Juliet daydreaming that she just possibly might be glad to see me. This pleasant excursion into fantasy was cut short by the appearance of several young soldiers with machine guns at their sides who trotted over. They had apparently been sleeping and were not pleased that we caught them "off duty." In the States, we call it sleeping on the job. We were politely but firmly escorted out.

As we walked up the stairs to the restaurant, Raul spotted a fellow he had met during our last trip. His name was Pedro. Pedro had been working for Avianca at the Santa Marta airport for several years, and Raul had talked with him about helping recover the radios. After a brief introduction we invited him to join us for a Coca-Cola. While we chatted, Pedro informed us that he had just been laid off the week before.

"What about the radios?" Raul asked, "Any news?"

"Not from outside the airport," Pedro replied, "but I do have something from inside. You know that old fart, Baratta?"

Raul and I both acknowledged, wearily, that indeed we did. Pedro told us that he had been in Baratta's office two weeks before and had spotted three or four radio boxes that belonged to the Learjet.

I came to immediate attention, interrupting Pedro, "Did you say anything to him? That I wanted to buy the Learjet radios?"

"*Si, señor* , but he said they belong to the government. He's a crazy old man, *muy estupido*."

I was furious at that officious old windbag whose sanctimonious interference in matters completely outside his authority had constantly caused us unnecessary problems.

"Fuck Baratta," I shouted. "Let's go tell the airport manager, Zapata. He'll get them back. They shouldn't have been taken out in the first place."

"Bobby, take it easy," Raul interrupted. "If you do that, Zapata will have to make an investigation. Then you'll never see them again."

Raul was right. I was letting my anger and loathing for Baratta obscure my judgment.

"*Señor* Wood," Pedro suggested, "I think I can get the radios for you. Just give me a few days."

"How?" I asked.

Pedro's plan was to get into Baratta's office through the side window on the following night and simply steal them back. I was against it. I had too much to lose to get involved in breaking into the office of an Aerocivil official. Pedro argued that he knew everything about the layout and operation of the airport and could be in and out without anyone even knowing he was there, except that the radios would be gone. He could make it look like an inside job or an outside job, whichever was better.

"Look, Pedro," I finally said, "I really need those radios, and I'd prefer to buy them back, not steal them, but, hell, I don't see anything wrong with stealing back something that was stolen from me in the first place. My only concern is that I'm not going to get myself involved in any break-in here."

Raul nudged me.

"Bobby, relax. Let him do it the Colombian way."

I was still unconvinced. It seemed like an unnecessary risk. If Pedro was caught and implicated me in a petty crime, it could ruin everything. Even though those radios were legally my property, the powers-that-be could bust my ass if they found out I had anything to do with an illegal entry into government property.

Pedro continued talking. He earnestly assured me of his desire to do this because he wanted my help for something very important to him. He was burning to go to the states—he had studied English and spoke it quite well, and even had a visa. His thought was that if he could help me in Colombia, I would be willing to help him find a job in the States.

"You can see, *Señor* Wood, that I would be a stupid man to connect you if I got caught. But I won't get caught—I can do it, I promise you."

Pedro's motives were putting the risk into new perspective. It was now greatly reduced and worth taking, so I consented. Raul was nodding approval and Pedro was excitedly envisioning a new and better life in the States. Promising to call us Monday, he left.

Raul and I sat together speculating about 464 Juliet's future. By this time, we were getting more curious and anxious to know the outcome of the meeting between Salgado and Valdez and whether we would hear the good news we wanted when it was finished. I was almost afraid to hope, but hope was stronger than fear. I was confident we now had a strong possibility of obtaining release of 464 Juliet.

Raul's attention was suddenly distracted by the appearance of yet another *amigo*, and he pointed, saying, "Look, here comes Tomás."

Tomás walked over to greet us, surprised that he hadn't known we were back.

"Did you come here to talk about the 'business,'" he was interested to know.

"Maybe so," I extemporized.

Tomás quickly launched into the progress he had made since our last visit. He had established several connections that might give important leads on the radios.

"Tomás," I said, "if everything goes as planned, we'll be leaving with the jet next week. So, if anyone here has any of the radios, pass the word around that they'd better step forward with them, or they'll be eating them for supper after I'm gone. Now's the time. If they're holding out for top dollar, they'll be stuck with them."

Tomás eventually got back to the subject of the marijuana connection. I was given the same old sales pitch: no problems, top quality, no problems, all I wanted, no problems, no front money. Boasts of total control of the airport, who flies in and how, an airtight deal with the military, the air force, the police department. No problems.

I put on a good show of great interest, slapping him on the back in praise of his organizing ability and intelligence in controlling such a large operation.

At three forty-five, I was finally able to break off the flow of conversation by announcing to Raul that it was time to go. Tomás was still making his pitch as he walked us out to the taxi. He even stuck his head through the window when we were inside, reluctant to have us leave.

We were in front of Valdez's home in Rodadero a little after four. No, we weren't too early. They had already finished. Dr. Salgado was ready to leave. I was burning to burst into questions, but sensed that it would be prudent to wait for a proper opening.

Dr. Salgado bade the judge goodbye courteously but quickly and we left in the taxi. When we had settled down, Dr. Salgado turned to me with an enigmatic smile.

"Mr. Wood, I am surprised to hear no questions. Aren't you interested?"

"Of course, Dr. Salgado, extremely interested. But I am certainly not qualified to ask specific questions about the legal aspect of the Learjet. Operational or technical aspects, yes. Legal? You're the expert there. The only question I would dare ask you is if everything is all right. And I am dying to know the answer to that one."

Dr. Salgado seemed pleased with my answer as his smile grew broader.

"I like your style, Mr. Wood. Your patience is incredible and commendable. I was merely testing you; everything is going to be fine. I need to spend this evening and tomorrow, possibly tomorrow evening, in doing some paperwork for Judge Valdez. I will have it ready for you to take to him on Monday."

"When will it all be over?" I asked.

"Everything should be finished by Tuesday or Wednesday. I believe by Wednesday the airplane will be legally free."

I was unprepared for the force of the wave of elation that surged through me. My throat was constricted as I tried vainly to express my satisfaction and I had to fight for self-control. I shot a sidelong look at Raul. He was grinning from ear to ear.

Dr. Salgado ventured no further details. I interpreted this as a signal not to ask anything further, which, I believe, was the case, because he immediately dropped off into a light sleep. He awoke when we stopped at the bridge. The soldiers spotted a familiar face of someone known to distribute tips, so they ordered us out. I was confident that there would be no bullshit as Salgado was eyeing the soldiers. Raul stepped out and whispered to the soldier, by now searching me, that a Supreme Court Justice, Dr. Julio Salgado, was in the cab and was watching them, so they should be careful. One of the soldiers glanced cautiously toward the cab and then back to Raul.

"If you don't believe me, go and ask for his I.D. card," Raul warned him.

This apparently convinced them, and their surly faces became more friendly. They waved us on. Salgado hadn't opened his mouth, either during the encounter or as we drove off. As far as he was concerned, this was an incident not even worth commenting on, and, he settled his head back on the headrest and dozed off once more.

When we dropped Dr. Salgado at *El Presidente*, he left us with instructions to telephone him the following evening at 6:30.

As soon as Dr. Salgado disappeared from sight, Raul and I were able to remove the reins from our jubilance. The lid blew off all the pent-up pressure that had built up from the endless delays Valdez had subjected us to for so many weeks.

"Raul, it's almost too good to be true. I can't believe it," I exulted.

"*Si, si*—believe it. It's true. I told you. I told you," Raul babbled.

Dave and Sam knew it was good news just by the way we burst through the door. In no time at all, they were up and around us, shaking hands and pounding me on the back.

"I knew you could do it," Dave shouted.

We settled down, finally, to give them what details we had, which actually were few. The jet was to be released legally by the middle of the week. Dr. Salgado said it was definite.

Once the euphoria had dissipated and I had got my feet back on earth, I began to realize that although we were almost in the clear on the legal aspects of 464 Juliet's release, we still had another high hurdle in front of us.

I called Raul into another of our "question and answer" sessions.

"You know, Raul, I want to believe this is all over, and you want to believe it is, too. But we still have a problem."

Raul looked puzzled.

"I think we're celebrating too soon," I continued. "What about the Air Force and the military? I can't believe that one man can sit down with the judge for six hours and produce more than one miracle. Legal release, yes; but, I can't believe that we're going to get out of here without any problems from the Air Force and the military."

Raul was unwilling to climb down from his cloud.

"*Si*, Bobby, maybe so. But Salgado is such an important man, important enough to take care of all the problems."

"I hope you're right, but I'm not going to let my guard down yet. I still don't think we're in the clear."

We returned to the others. Sam was lying on his bed reading the flight manual. Dave and the others were playing poker and drinking. Finally, around two in the morning, I was ready to turn in. Raul and I returned to our room and got in our beds.

"Bobby," Raul inquired, "why is Sam always with his nose in the flight manual?"

"Shit, Raul," I said, looking up, sleepily, "I don't know. Maybe he forgot how to fly?"

I turned over on my bed, but now my mind began sorting through all the events of the day. I tried to recapture my excitement at hearing Dr. Salgado's words that everything was all right, but could feel nothing. The highs and lows were taking their toll. I suppose the mind and body can build up tolerance to all life's ups and downs, but I knew mine was reaching its outer limits—I couldn't take too many more of these punishing mood variations that were caused by factors beyond my control.

We were up at seven the next morning, ready to get back to matters concerned with necessary equipment for 464 Juliet. Raul, Toño, Aquiles, and I left for Santa Marta to search for some leads on the radios. Sam, Dave, and the Donado boys were planning to attend the bullfights later that day.

First, we stopped to see Mario, our contact at Avianca airlines. He had a couple of leads, but not very promising. We then went to the airport. For a change, the soldiers were at their posts, alert and watchful; so, we couldn't visit 464 Juliet. The trip was a complete waste of time.

Back at the hotel, we found the others back from the bullfight. Sam was engrossed in his flight manual, and Dave was entertaining the Colombians with his bird imitations.

Dave cut off a fine, trilling "Coo-coo," upon our entrance, to give us the latest news.

"Guess who's in jail," he shouted.

"Who? What happened?" I asked.

"Fernando," he answered.

Dave told us that they had parked Donado's truck too close to one of the exits at the arena. The bull ring was not a conventional arena structure, it was more like a Greek theater in an area cut away between two small hills. The audience sat on dirt terraces on either side of the arena below. A heavy storm suddenly blew up and they had all left to get to the truck. Sam wasn't with them, he had gone to a bar on the hill for a drink. When the others reached the truck the police were preparing to tow it away. When Fernando tried to stop them, the officers grabbed him and took him off to jail.

"Where is he now?" I asked.

"I guess still in jail," Dave answered. "Donado Jr. took off to find Donado; I guess they're trying to get him out now."

I wasn't worried about Fernando. His father would be able to get him out easily. What did upset me, however, was the thought of finding our mechanic and pilot in jail. I quickly read them the riot act.

"OK, Dave, you and Aquiles go to Donado's house and see if everything is all right. But look, Sam, you and Dave—from now on, don't go off anywhere where you might find yourselves in a jam. You got me?! This *is* Colombia; you're both lucky they didn't nab you just on general principles so that you'd have to be ransomed out."

I glared at both of them, and they nodded in understanding.

As arranged, at 6:30 we telephoned Salgado. Raul got him on the line immediately, and I watched for telltale signs, but found none. Salgado was not a man to waste words on preliminaries, nor even on the meat of a conversation. Raul was merely listening carefully, not beaming and not downcast. At the end of the conversation he turned to me with a deadpan look seldom seen on his expressive face.

"Bad news?" I inquired anxiously.

Raul laughed triumphantly.

"No, no, Bobby. I was just playing a joke on you because you always hang over me when I make these calls for you. Everything is good. Salgado said he would be finished later tonight. He wants us to come to El Presidente to pick up the papers tomorrow morning at nine. We can hand carry them to Judge Valdez. It looks real good, Bobby."

"Great. Let's call Valdez and make an appointment to meet him at 11:30."

Valdez was happy to hear from us and asked us to meet him at his home, not the office.

Raul turned to me, saying, "Bobby, that's the best Valdez has sounded since we started all this. He's one happy man."

Dave and Aquiles had returned to tell us that Fernando was safely at home, and they resumed the poker game as I ate out of the giant lunch box Terry had prepared. Sam sat at the desk all evening reading the flight manual.

"Damn, Dave," I whispered, "he's reading that manual like a mystery novel."

We treated it like a joke, but I was beginning to wonder.

CHAPTER FORTY

We picked up the papers from Dr. Salgado, promptly at nine, and departed for Santa Marta in Ramon's taxi. I was taking no chances on Aquiles' Chevy for carrying these important documents. Today was no time to get stranded on that God-forsaken stretch of road. As we sped along, I couldn't keep my hands off the thick sealed envelope, shaking and squeezing it like a kid with a Christmas package waiting under the tree, labeled "Do Not Open Until December 25."

"Raul, my curiosity is eating me up. What do you think is in here?"

Raul took the envelope from me, also shaking and squeezing and holding it up to the light.

"Papers, Bobby," was his unimaginative reply.

"I know that, but doesn't it feel important?"

I knew it contained the key to unlocking 464 Juliet's prison here in Colombia. Later, when I finally opened its contents, I would find that it held other keys, too, keys to secrets that had been locked away for over three years. I would learn that the key to my full understanding of Juliet's story had been forged from the complex circumstances surrounding the death of an American citizen named Bruce Allen and the vendetta against the notorious drug kingpin Jimmy Chagra.

We arrived a few minutes early for our appointment and were prepared to wait, but Valdez sent a servant to ask us to enter. Valdez was waiting, and he ushered us inside with great hospitality. He poured me a Coca-Cola and served coffee to Raul and himself. This day, I figured, we would be returning to the old routine of several minutes of preliminary formalities; as it turned out, however, the meeting was all formalities, no business.

I was at a complete loss to understand Valdez's failure to snatch up the envelope and rip it open to see its contents. How could he stand the suspense? I wondered, but there it sat unopened, before him on the desk. He would fondle it gently and unconsciously from time to time but made not a move to do more than that. Valdez was a real Hitchcock at suspense.

Finally he looked at his watch.

"I must go to the office now," he said, "I must work on your papers."

I had to make a strong effort to keep from puckering up like a kid who had just dropped his ice-cream cone in a sand pile. I felt cheated of a treat that had been promised, delayed, and finally was in my hands, only to be snatched away once more. We rose to leave, disappointed but without protest.

"Call me at ten tomorrow morning," Valdez said, and with handshakes, sent us away.

Again we told Ramon to take us to the airport.

"Raul, I bet he had that envelope open before we were around the block," I remarked.

"*Si*, Bobby—but one good thing, he seemed anxious to get to work."

Pedro was the first person we saw at the terminal.

"*Señor* Wood, I need to talk to you and Raul," he greeted us.

We walked up to the vacant restaurant and took a table at the far west end, overlooking the ocean. I was as anxious to hear what Pedro had to say as he was to tell us.

"Did you get the radios?" I asked.

Pedro had tried, but they were gone. He looked everywhere, but he guessed Baratta had taken them home.

"But I did find the telephone, the stereo, and a part of the radios," he reported.

"Where? Who's got them?" I wanted to know.

"Someone I know who used to work here. He has them in a house outside Santa Marta in the mountains. He promised to bring them here in a day or two."

I asked how much he wanted for them. Pedro didn't know, but he felt the price would be fair. He promised to find out.

"I found something else, in Baratta's office," he added. "It's probably not important, but you are always taking pictures so I thought you might want it," and he pulled out a photograph of 464 Juliet.

Raul and I looked at the photo. Suddenly my inner alarm systems sounded. I looked at it closer.

"Where did you say you got this?" I demanded.

"I told you, in Baratta's office."

"Were there any more?"

"No, only this one. It was on a shelf in his closet."

"Raul, look at this again, closely." I held it under his nose. "What do you see?"

"Just 464 Juliet." He was bewildered.

"Look again. Where was it taken from?"

"I see now, Bobby. From upstairs, somewhere up high."

"Look again. Do you notice how close the jet looks. And the curved shadow on the right?"

"*Si, si,*" he said.

"This photo was taken from something like a porthole on the second floor with a telephoto lens. Someone is spying on us." There were two indistinct figures standing at the nose of the plane. I thought they might be Gustavo and me, but I couldn't quite make them out.

Suddenly, it hit me. The American Consul, Harry Gilbert, who knew all the places I had been; the American agent at Barranquilla, who had asked Diego questions about me; and the incident in Miami, where the special agent had questioned me.

"Someone here is watching us, Raul. Baratta is working with him, I'm sure. Why else would he be such an asshole with us? Everybody we've run into in Santa Marta loves money, but Baratta won't take a cent. I don't believe it's because he's honest; it's just that he's on someone else's payroll. Someone must definitely be paying him to watch us. I can assure you he's not snapping shots of 464 Juliet as a hobby—not with a telephoto lens through some kind of a porthole."

We studied the photograph several minutes longer to see if we had missed any small detail.

"Let's walk over to the balcony near Baratta's office, Raul. Maybe we can figure out exactly where the photo was taken."

When we arrived at the area outside Baratta's office, we could see that this location created precisely the angle that the photo was taken from. We were standing by a section of decorative concrete wall pierced with holes, taking the place of a standard balcony railing. The holes formed a repeated pattern of figure-eight openings, and I could immediately see that with a camera held close to one of these openings and pointed to 464 Juliet across the way, the curvature in one of the figure-eight openings in front in the lens could create precisely such a shadow as that found on the right side of the original photo. Someone had either stepped out of Baratta's office or had stopped there, and, while partially concealed by the wall, had taken the photo with the camera inserted in one of the halves of a figure-eight hole.

We returned to the restaurant, as we didn't want to be found doing our detective work in the vicinity of Baratta's office. Pedro wasn't aware of the significance of his find, but both Raul and I knew it could be a serious threat to us. I am not a person who sees international spies lurking on my doorstep, but neither do I take kindly to being spied on or monitored, and someone clearly had more than a casual interest in 464 Juliet.

Soon after Raul and I left for Ciénaga, we stopped at Aldo's house. His father informed us that Aldo had not been home for several days and that he had been under the impression Aldo was with us in Barranquilla. At least, that was what Aldo had told his wife.

When we got back to the hotel, we had the usual contingent of guests plus a couple of new ones. Dave was entertaining them on my behalf, and he rolled his eyes upward as I walked through the door. Sam was lying on the bed with the flight manual.

"Damn, Sam," I joked, "did you forget how to fly?"

"No, Bob, just brushing up … ," and immediately he stuck his nose back into his studies.

There was no point in alarming everybody about the strange photograph Pedro had given me, but everyone was clamoring to know when we would be leaving. Everyone was disappointed that I still couldn't tell them the date we would leave.

Our "guests" were calling down for room service, and I dug into my suitcase of provisions. I still wasn't able to stomach the food sent up on the trays, so, I dipped into my own personal "CARE Package" for Vienna Sausages and saltines and washed them down with ice tea and cookies for dessert.

About nine o'clock there was a loud knock on the door. Little Dave opened it and gasped. I looked up to see Aldo, flanked by a pair of the most unappetizing women I ever laid eyes on. All three were happily drunk. They all squeezed through the door as a single unit, the women clinging to Aldo's arms, wobbling on four-inch spike-heeled shoes. Aldo was peacock proud to be escorting two such "beauty queens." Both giggled as he paused to nuzzle the short fat one with the gold tooth that sparkled as she laughed. She wore a sleeveless low-cut dress of red satin generously adorned with sequins. It dipped under her ample rear and spanned her stomach to show the indentation of her navel. Bushy tufts of black hair peeped out at her armpits.

The other was taller, also chubby, with greasy, straight hair hanging down her shoulders. Her dress was of similar cut, also shiny, printed with enormous and garish tropical flowers. Her shapeless legs were hairy. Her face and neck had the texture of alligator hide, which she tried to conceal with heavy layers of dark make-up. Both girls wore stiff, false eyelashes reinforced with heavy black mascara that had smeared around their eyes, giving them the appearance of raccoons. The reek of Aldo's Florida Water, their perfume, stale liquor, and perspiration quickly blanketed the room.

"Bobby, come here!" Aldo called to me genially. "I've brought you a girlfriend—both if you like."

That Aldo was all heart. He spoke with the expansive air of a sultan giving me the pick of his harem.

He staggered over to introduce his *señor*itas, which was a signal for more giggles.

"I've never seen you with a girl here, and I know you must be lonely," he said. "Aren't they pretty?"

I managed a sickly grin and nodded, but I wanted to choke the whoremongering pissant who was weaving in front of me.

"Come on with us, down to my room," he was insisting, his tongue twisting over his words.

I shot a murderous look at the others in the room, whose faces were almost purple from pent-up hilarity.

"Thank you, Aldo. You don't know how much I appreciate it, but I'm waiting for a very important call from the States. My wife has a problem … But you go on ahead to the bar. I'll join you in an hour or two," I said lamely.

After a few more minutes of pimping, posing, and posturing, Aldo and the *señor*itas were resigned to hit the road. I edged them toward the door and watched them make their zigzag way down the hall just to be sure they were gone. Then I turned back manfully to face the others who, I knew, had been busily thinking up remarks to kid me for passing up such a glorious evening.

They were all laughing too hard to be able to say a word. It took about ten minutes for everyone to calm down, but even afterwards, one of us would suddenly burst out laughing, having recalled the look on Aldo's face and his generous offer.

August 19, 1980

All of us were up early, sitting around the room and wondering what our phone call to Valdez would bring. Sam was studying the flight manual and Dave played solitaire.

Finally, it was eleven o'clock. Raul placed the call to Santa Marta. While speaking with Valdez, his "*sí's*" and "*muy bien's*" sounded like good news on the line. I could understand most of the conversation on Raul's end. In succession he had asked "What time?" and then said, "Yes, he has it here," and then, "We'll be waiting." Then he hung up and turned to me.

"OK, Bobby," he said, "the jet is yours."

I wanted to be cautious and not to over-react and jump the gun.

"Slow down, Raul; tell me everything, from the beginning."

Raul gleefully recounted the conversation. Valdez had finished the paperwork. The *providencia* was ready. Valdez was coming to Barranquilla that night to collect the money.

"Does that mean we can leave, tomorrow?" I asked.

"No, not yet. Valdez said he would explain tonight what the next steps are."

"What do you mean 'next steps'?"

"Take it easy, Bobby. Valdez will explain. I don't know."

"I don't understand. If *la providencia* is finished, what's the problem?"

Raul simply didn't know. In his eagerness to give me good news, he had jumped the gun. I was still in the dark. Either Raul hadn't understood the judge or the judge had not given him the information I wanted.

"What did he say about the money?" I asked.

"Just that everything was finished and that he was coming here to be paid," Raul replied.

"What about Aldo? He said we were to pay him, not the judge."

"Bobby, all we can do is wait until tonight. Valdez will explain everything. What's the matter? Aren't you happy?"

I told Raul I was, but inwardly I had some reservations. What next steps could there be? Not knowing this was bothering me, and nothing was clear enough to make any sense.

The day dragged by. All of us were on edge. We were still making plans to leave, perhaps Thursday or Friday at the latest. At six thirty, I went downstairs to the safe deposit box and counted out seventy-five thousand dollars.

Returning to the room, I asked everybody to leave.

"Look, guys, just stay downstairs until I come and get you. Valdez wants this to be private," I explained.

It was seven thirty and the judge had not yet appeared. Where could he be? I fumed to Raul.

"Take it easy, Bobby," Raul said, giving me his stock advice, "this is Colombia."

At seven forty-five, there was a knock on the door. Raul opened it and there was Valdez.

"Raul, Bobby, *como estas*? I apologize for being late. You know how the buses are."

I couldn't believe my ears. Here was an important dignitary coming to collect seventy-five thousand dollars, riding a bus. I wondered if he planned to take it home later tonight in a shopping bag, hidden under a bunch of bananas.

Valdez didn't waste any time getting down to business.

"Raul," he asked, "did you tell Bobby about *la providencia*?"

"*No, Señor Juez*," Raul answered, "I wasn't exactly sure what you meant, so I waited for you to explain."

Valdez nodded and turned to me. He told me that *la providencia* was indeed finished. However, for its legality to be complete, the law required that it be published three successive days in the newspaper. If unchallenged, it then became law. The notice would appear this Wednesday, Thursday, and Friday. By six o'clock Friday evening, then, the stipulated time period would end. This was the first step.

The second step would be taken on Saturday, August 23, at the Santa Marta airport. Judge Valdez, his secretary Beatriz, Dr. Salgado, Luis Donado, Zapata (the airport manager), and I would meet for performance of the *diligencia*—the formal and material delivery of the Learjet.

I was disappointed to hear of these delays, but at least I now knew what the "steps" were.

Valdez continued. Besides publication of *la providencia*, Colombian law also required that copies be sent to all interested officials and agencies, in this case the National Council of Narcotics, the Command of the Magdalena Police Department, the Barranquilla-based Air Force Command, the Aerocivil authorities and Administrative Officer at the Simón Bolívar Airport in Santa Marta.

This last piece of information made me highly uneasy. The giants that would receive copies of *la providencia* were far from asleep at this stage of the game. The *providencia* would most certainly remind them all that Bobby Wood would be flying N464J out of Colombia under their very noses without leaving anything in their pockets. I was sure they had no intention of standing around waving me a cheerful farewell. I felt like a sitting duck. I was going to have to give this some serious thought. However, Valdez was now moving on to financial matters.

"Do you have the money?" he asked politely.

"Yes, sir, I do. Just a minute," and I opened my brief case, pulling out fifteen stacks of onehundred-dollar bills, totaling up to seventy-five thousand dollars.

"Judge Valdez," I continued, hopefully with some degree of delicacy, "I have a question."

He looked at me inquiringly.

"It's about Aldo. He told me he was to get twenty-five thousand dollars. Since you requested me not to tell him that I should give the money to you, will you see that he gets it?"

Valdez's face was impassive, his voice polite but firm as he answered. "I told Aldo, from the beginning, I wanted fifty thousand. If Aldo asks you how much you gave me, I want you to tell him it was that amount, fifty thousand. I don't want him to know I got seventy-five thousand dollars. His twenty-five thousand dollars is his problem, not mine." Instantly, I saw that someone was fixing to get a first-class shaft, complete with kisses, and that someone was not only Aldo; I would have to absorb the missing twenty-five thousand dollars or come up with a good excuse for why I didn't have it, which was going to be very hard. Aldo could call on a lot of amigos as unprincipled as he was himself to do me a lot of harm if he got nothing. Nor could I tell him the judge was appropriating Aldo's share of the seventy-five thousand dollars. This was not just a delicate situation; it was one hell of a mess.

There was nothing I could do at the moment, so I laid the money down in front of Valdez.

"There's $75,000 here, Judge Valdez. I believe I have given you $8,000 thus far: $2,000 in June and $6,000 to *señora* Valdez in July. So I believe the total to you is $67,000."

"Yes," he nodded, "that is correct," and he picked up the money, slowly counting each stack of fifty one-hundred-dollar bills.

I sat and watched him, uncomfortably aware that I was doing exactly what Alfredo had warned me not to do. I also thought of Federico's words of advice. It was getting hard to keep track of who was screwing whom. Aldo had tried twice to screw Valdez—first with his phony judge and then with the proposed fifty thousand dollar discount price with the military to steal 464 Juliet. And now, Aldo was getting the screwing of his life. The judge was giving him the shaft.

Fine, I thought, *let them screw each other all they want. The only thing was it was interfering with my cash flow.*

I would have to give Aldo something. I had enough money to pay Dr. Salgado his $10,000 and probably $8,000 more to pay Aldo and his brother, Gomez. That was all. I needed at least five or ten thousand reserve to buy fuel, take care of other pay-offs, and for the flight home.

I was in one hell of a spot. I knew what Valdez was pulling, but I couldn't say anything. Since he was not ashamed to reveal his lack of ethics, I could scarcely remind him of the old saying about honor among thieves. I had come a long way, I couldn't blow it.

Valdez had finally counted the money, twice, and had returned the $8,000 to me, stating in a tone of deep satisfaction, "$67,000 exactly. Very good, Bobby." There was only one thing I could do—convince Valdez that I liked his idea, but that it had some problems with it.

"Judge Valdez," I began, "I have a problem, and I need your help."

"*Si*, Bobby, what is it?"

"It's Aldo. As I told you, Aldo explained the finances differently to me. I don't have enough money to pay him now. I have to pay Dr. Salgado and that leaves me with almost nothing to get home with."

Valdez raised his eyebrows and stared at me sternly.

"Look, Judge, I know that Aldo's getting the shaft in this deal, which is fine by me. You probably have your reasons, and I've got my reasons, too. What I would like you to do is tell Aldo that I'm borrowing ten thousand dollars from you, which you are holding in escrow for him until the plane takes off. If he asks any questions, just say that something could go wrong if the jet doesn't get released—perhaps 'the military might interfere'—and then you'd have to give me back the money. If he asks more questions, just say, 'Don't you trust me, Aldo?' I'll convince Aldo either to come along to Miami to get paid—he'll think—or I'll tell him I'll bring his money down next week when I come back to pay you."

Valdez did not spring immediately to my rescue; he sat there considering the matter like a banker evaluating the assets of a loan applicant. I knew he wouldn't give Aldo a dime of "his" seventy-five thousand.

"Look, sir," I argued, realizing that I had perhaps made the deal too complicated, "when I've left and Aldo asks for his money, just simply tell him I changed my mind about the loan and that I'll be bringing him his money next week."

Valdez well understood that, until I was gone, an Aldo empty-handed would be an Aldo with a very big mouth. Aldo could harm me and possibly, but not likely, expose Valdez. Furthermore, if Valdez refused to help me (I had helped him in a family matter), he would be losing face, which was not a very propitious beginning for our budding "business" relationship.

He finally made his decision.

"*Si*, Bobby, I will do it for you," he nodded.

"Thank you, sir, I appreciate your help." I delivered my thanks in a normal tone of voice as if this were a normal accommodation that I had expected to be forthcoming, adding that I was sure we would have a good "business" future.

Valdez got busy packing his stacks of money in his briefcase, first pulling out a folder with legal papers inside. He handed me several sheets, saying it was my copy of *la providencia*. I was intensely curious to see it, but contained my impatience and set it aside until he left.

"Well, Bobby, I must leave now. The last bus is at ten o'clock."

"You're not going to ride the bus to Santa Marta carrying all that money, are you?" I blurted out.

"*Si, como no*? (Why not?)" Valdez couldn't understand my concern.

Raul and I both protested that it could be dangerous and that he should be careful, but he shrugged off our fears and assured us that he would have no problems.

Before he left, he asked me to call him the following night. He wanted to take me to his airstrip and to show me his merchandise.

"We must get started very soon," he urged.

"Yes, sir, I would like that," and I promised to call him at his home the next evening.

As soon as Valdez was gone, I turned to Raul and he turned to me. Both of us opened our mouths at the same time to say the same thing.

"Valdez is screwing Aldo."

"Aldo's going to have a fucking heart attack."

Raul was in a state of shock. He couldn't believe it. This was too much, even for him.

"What are you going to do, Bobby?" he finally asked practically.

"Shit, Raul, I don't know. I have to explain the missing twenty-five thousand dollars somehow. Aldo knows I brought all the money with me."

Raul was aware that, along with Aldo, I had also been maneuvered by the judge into the line for the shaft. He was loyally indignant.

"I'll have to think, Raul. Maybe I can come up with something. But right now, let's take a look at Valdez's *providencia*."

"Bobby," he shot me a conspiratorial look, "You know whose *providencia* it is, don't you? It's Salgado's. You were right: Valdez didn't know how to do it. But Salgado said we should pretend Valdez did it."

This was no news to me. I assured Raul I would keep it to myself. I noticed also that the document was dated August 16, 1980, the day I took Salgado to the judge's house. It had been backdated—now that Salgado was in the picture we were gaining days, not losing them.

We sat down on the couch and opened up the long-awaited *providencia* on the coffee table. Raul laboriously translated the parts I didn't understand. The fully translated text is given below.

> *THIRD PENAL CIRCUIT COURT SANTA MARTA*
> *Santa Marta, August 16, 1980 WHEREAS:*
> *DR. JULIO SALGADO VASQUEZ, holder of Professional Card No. 4475, acting as attorney for Mr. Robert E. Wood, has petitioned release of aircraft Model 24 Gates Learjet No. 24-164, Registration N464J issued by the Federal Aviation Administration of the U.S.A., as it is the property of his client and has been detained at this Court's orders. The antecedents shown in the official records are given in the following FINDINGS:*
> *FIRST: Members of the Rodadero police post seized an airplane, jet class, registration number 464J, that landed at Simón Bolívar Airport around 9:30 A.M. on June 15, 1977. Its occupants were arrested. They identified themselves as Jamiel Alexander Chagra (gambler), Jerry Lee Wilson (businessman), Jose Miguel Parada Benitez (paramedic), Jeffrey Lee Ellis (paramedic), Stephen Bolling, (pilot) and Anthony Gekakis (pilot).*
> *SECOND: The plane was seized because it allegedly entered the country in violation of Colombian air space without the necessary documents to land at Simón Bolívar Airport at Santa Marta. However,*

this allegation was disproven by presentation of such documents.

THIRD: *After the plane had been carefully inspected with nothing out of the ordinary having been discovered aboard, inasmuch as all items were related to the medical and hospital field as shown in folios 3 to 6 of the original records, these items were turned over in accordance with the inventory included in the transcript of folio 227.*

FOURTH: *The persons detained were questioned by Santa Marta police officials and the DAS immigration section of Bogota to which city they were transferred.*

FIFTH: *In a decision Of July 4, 1977, the Ninth Court of Criminal Proceedings (in session) stated: "Due to the foregoing circumstances, not only the commandant of the Magdalena Police Department and the Director of the Judicial Police, but also several police officers and the commander of the police post at Rodadero, who had all been informed of the matter, went to Simón Bolívar Airport and initiated a (new) search of the plane, finding inside fifty grams of a white powder, which was shown to be cocaine after testing for narcotics. They proceeded to inventory the contents of the airplane in the presence of the Regional Attorney General of Santa Marta, thereupon confiscating all items found in the plane and listed in the official inventory contained in folios 3 to 8. The plane was also detained at Simón Bolívar Airport and placed under this Court." (Folio 182)*

SIXTH: *The Prosecutor of the Circuit Court, in his opinion of July 22, 1977, stated his agreement with the petition to revoke the arrest order against Jose Miguel Parada and Stephen Bolling. This document gives an argument intended to establish that the presence of a bag of cocaine inside the plane could have been a maneuver of one of the individuals who later searched the plane subsequent to the first search in which no element considered criminal had been found. To that effect, the Prosecutor states: "The circumstantial evidence was the basis for the order to arrest Parada and Bolling and consisted in the fact that the carton where the cocaine had allegedly been found also contained medical equipment belonging to Parada and items belonging to Bolling, since the latter had bought the Prist, an additive for jet fuel, and it was he who put it in the plane.*

Steven Bolling explained during his interrogation that the box of Prist had been purchased by him before departure and that it had originally contained six tubes. They used three in the plane and one was lost at Port-au-Prince. The box was small and rectangular. It was stored in the baggage compartment behind the last seat. It had originally contained only the tubes with the additive. However, according to the police, when they found said box, it was not behind the last seat but in the aisle of the airplane. In addition to the Prist tubes, it also contained a music cassette, a black leather box with surgical scissors, a blue plastic spatula, a pair of socks, and a black box with no markings. This circumstantial evidence loses all validity with the testimony of Major Granados who states: "I believe I was very clear in the reply I just made to the Court's question, to the effect that I am listing the items which I felt were unimportant and included only for purpose of noting them together with everything else found inside the plane. I saw no importance whatsoever in a pair of socks, a case for scissors or surgical clamps, a knife, and a music cassette. As I said, the socks had been on the floor of the airplane and the scissors and other implements were in the back of the first folding seat of the airplane, since the seat was reversed—they are swivel chairs that are movable. The items I named were in the pouch for hand luggage and the cassette was inside the tape deck in the plane. I was the one who put those objects inside the carton ... ."

"This is why the surgical implements owned by Parada were found in the box in which cocaine allegedly was found. This circumstantial evidence was invalidated by Major Granados when, by his own admission, he told us that he himself had placed the items in the carton, which facts had served as cause for the judge to take preventive measures (make arrests).

"This is also sustained by Sergeant Jaime Lamprea: "Actually, as I remember, some of the items listed by the paramedic were not originally inside the box; they were over the chairs and the floor, and since there was no bags to use we put things into the carton—the socks, for instance, were found on the floor, the cassette was with the sound equipment, the scissors and knife were in the back of a seat, in the pouch there ... ."

"I repeat, this circumstantial evidence was certainly the basis for issuing the arrest order which the attorneys of Parada and Bolling have petitioned to be dismissed and the validity of such evidence has been discredited by the testimony of Major Carlos Ernesto Granados and Sub-Lt. Jaime Lamprea Duarte." (Folios 280-282)

SEVENTH: The Ninth Court of Criminal Proceedings (in session) dismissed the arrest of Jose Miguel Parada Benitez and Stephen Bolling by decision of July 27, 1977 (folios 285 to 287) and with this decision, all of those who had been implicated were set free, as in a verdict of July 4, 1977, the same court had dismissed the charges against Anthony Gekakis, Jamiel Alexander Chagra, Jeffrey Lee Ellis, and Jerry Lee Wilson (Folios 182-193).

EIGHTH: The Second Penal Court of the Circuit of Santa Marta, on February 20, 1979, considered the merits of the summary thereupon calling for trial of Jamiel Alexander Chagra and Jerry Lee Wilson for the crime of narcotics traffic, according to Article 38 of Decree 1188 of 1974, temporarily staying charges against Anthony Gekakis and Stephen Bolling *and paramedics Jose Miguel Parada Benitez and Jeffrey Lee Ellis.*

The court recognizes that the purpose of the flight from the United States to Santa Marta had been to take back to an American hospital the American Bruce Allen, who was in the San Juan de Dios Hospital of Santa Marta as a patient with serious burns resulting from the crash of the plane he was piloting in the region of Las Tetas in the Guajira. The burned pilot was taken in a Red Cross ambulance to the Simón Bolívar Airport, but the aircraft was forced to remain there under the orders of the investigating officer. The patient was returned to the hospital where he later died.

The order to prosecute makes no mention of the plane and is limited to calling to trial two of its occupants, because, according to the facts shown, such persons had known of the drug-trafficking background of the patient and of the presence of the confiscated drug. But these are only assumptions, since no evidence of such statements appears in the records of the proceedings.

NINTH: The two pilots of the airplane, Anthony Gekakis and Stephen Bolling, both state that the president of Jet Avia Airlines, Chris Karamanos, had ordered them to go to Santa Marta to pick up a burn patient and take him back to the United States; that they made the trip in one of the company's airplanes, first taking aboard other passengers; that they landed in Simón Bolívar Airport in Santa Marta, giving the authorities all the documents required for landing; that they loaded the airplane with medical equipment for the patient; and that they did not know who could have placed the bag of cocaine in the carton containing fuel additive.

TENTH: The medical personnel, a paramedic and a medical aide, Jose Miguel Parada and Jeffrey Lee Ellis, gave the same versions of having been informed that they should go to Santa Marta to take care of a wounded person for his trip back to the United States, for which purpose they brought medical equipment with them.

ELEVENTH: Jamiel Alexander Chagra was one of the passengers. Since he knew Spanish, he was to be the interpreter.

TWELFTH: Jerry Lee Wilson had not come in that airplane. He had arrived earlier, in the Guajira, in another plane on the morning of June 15, 1977, and after having ordered his pilot to take the plane back to the United States of America, he went on to Santa Marta with the purpose of getting his friend Bruce Allen taken back to a hospital in San Antonio (Texas).

THIRTEENTH: Extensive documentation has been submitted to the court records, such documents showing clearly the following:

a) Jet Associates, Inc., a corporation of Arkansas, appears as the owner of the airplane registered under Number 464J, Model 24 Learjet, Serial

Number 247164.

b) On June 1, 1977, Jet Associates, Inc. leased the plane subject of this investigation to Jet Avia Ltd., with main offices in Las Vegas, Nevada.

c) Jet Avia took out an insurance policy against physical damage and loss of the plane, the insurer being Cravens Dargan & Company, which issued insurance policy HAVO 85608.

d) According to the statement of Paul W. Engstrom, legal consultant for the insurance company: "On June 15, 1977, the airplane flew to Santa Marta, Colombia, as Jet Avia. Jet Associates had no knowledge of this flight and is not implicated in it. The craft was confiscated by the authorities pending an investigation, and it is still detained."

e) The insurance company paid the First National City Bank of Little Rock, Arkansas, $617,891.49 on December 29, 1978, for the lien against the plane, which was declared lost for insurance purposes, since the Colombian authorities had detained it as part of a criminal investigation.

f) On January 31, 1980, the insurance company paid Jet Associates, Inc. and Jet Avia Ltd. the balance of the price of the plane, the same insurance company thus becoming owners of the plane which they sold, according to Jet Associates, to Air Unlimited, Inc., a corporation of Florida, and to Robert E. Wood.

g) All the transactions noted on the preceding report are proven by the documents annexed by the petitioner, legally translated into Spanish, notarized by the Colombian Consul and her signature authenticated by the Foreign Ministry of Colombia, in accordance with Record Nos. 259 and 260 of the Civil Procedure Code.

FOURTEENTH: No proof has been established in the records to show that Jet Associates, Inc. had knowledge of the trip their airplane made to Santa Marta on June 15, 1977 that had been chartered to Jet Avia Ltd., and even had they known this, it has not been demonstrated that they had knowledge that such a plane was transporting fifty grams of cocaine.

WHEREAS: Article 59 of the Penal Code establishes the general standard that weapons, instruments, and articles which may have been used to commit a crime or whereby a crime is committed by their use, may be returned to whomever such articles were taken from or to a third party not adjudged guilty of their use. Such standard is justified, since punishment of third persons or owners of instruments used for such crimes, who have not participated in their commission or planning nor given their consent to them, would lead to legal punishment of innocent persons. Sanctions are amply justified when passed against the authors and accessories to crime by means of fraud and with malice aforethought. But when the vehicles or instruments of a third-party owner are used where the owner has not given consent to the crimes or about which they have no knowledge, it would be wrong to punish such third parties. This same principle is found in Paragraph 2 of Article 52, Decree 1188 of 1974, upon establishing that: "Exceptionally, return of vehicles and other means of transportation can be ordered to third parties who prove that, in spite of proper maintenance and care of such vehicles, they could not know the criminal use to which their property was subjected."

The interpretation of this precedent requires us to study, although summarily, the concept of guilt in civil and in criminal matters, since it appears that guilt or non-existence of guilt constitutes the legal bases for such goods to be turned over to the State and not returned to the third parties. We know that in civil matters, guilt is based on an ideal pattern of behavior while in penal matters, where guilt is mainly subjective, such guilt has its psychological point of departure in the imprudence or audacity of the agent. In the civil, there is guilt only when the person does not act as any other person would in the same external circumstances. In the other, the criminal, guilt is, as aforesaid, and in accordance to Article 12 of the Penal Code, apparent, when the agent does not foresee the damaging effects of his acts or, when knowing them, mistakenly believes he can avoid them. Using these presumed doctrines as premises, we must analyze the behavior of the owner of the airplane in the face of the facts under investigation in these proceedings. We know, because evidence has already been introduced in the record, that the American firm Jet Associates, Inc. leased the plane to Jet Avia Ltd. and, according to the nature of that contract, the lessor or person who hands over such article for use, is not required to have knowledge of the form or circumstance of its use by the lessee. However, in this case, the lessee, Jet Avia Ltd., could not even know or suspect that, once the plane was chartered, some of the passengers might transport the cocaine with them. Furthermore, if we accept the opposite argument, we must arrive at the ridiculous conclusion that the owner of an interstate bus could lose his vehicle because some of its passengers carried marijuana or cocaine or, even worse, that Avianca could lose a jet because one of its passengers was caught with cocaine. The absurdities given as examples will lead us, logically, to a negative reply in the sense that neither the owner of the bus, nor Avianca, nor Jet Associates, Inc. nor Jet Avia Ltd., as legitimate owners, can lose their ownership rights to the bus, to the jet or to the plane as a result of any of the circumstances described.

It cannot be shown that the behavior of Jet Associates Inc. or the behavior of Jet Avia Ltd. was careless, negligent, or remiss in assigning to any of them civil responsibility in their behavior in regard to the flight that such plane, owned by the first and leased to the second, made on

June 15, 1977, made to Simón Bolívar Airport of Santa Marta, because this, as compared with the other, cannot lead us to conclude that they had acted without due care and diligence. Nor in the penal aspect can we assign to said firms any lack of due care since the normal operation of such business frequently includes the lease of planes and their charter for commercial purposes. Carrying out those legal acts does not constitute any daring or risky act aimed at placing such conduct within the framework of criminality. In other words, it has not been demonstrated in the proceedings that the owner company of the plane, nor the leasing company nor, in consequence, the legitimate owners of the plane, could be guilty in either civil or penal aspects and therefore, they are supported and protected in their rights by Article 59 of the Penal Code and the last part of Article 52 of Decree No. 1188 of 1974.

In the case under investigation, we see that the owner corporation of the jet class plane with registration number 464J was leased to another corporation providing transportation services to the public and that this corporation chartered the plane to travel from the United States to Santa Marta to bring back a severely burned patient. The plane carried a considerable amount of medical equipment and also two paramedics to help the patient who, by reason of not having been taken back immediately to an American hospital, had to be readmitted to San Juan de Dios Hospital of this city, where he later died.

As the airplane has been proven to be the property of an American corporation, as well as it has been shown that another corporation had chartered it for a patient to be taken from Santa Marta to the United States, it follows that no possibility exists for the owner corporation to have been able to participate in any of the stages of alleged narcotics traffic, in the amount of fifty grams of cocaine.

Furthermore, since no proof was established in the proceedings whereby it could be shown that the owner corporation of the airplane or the leasing corporation participated in the commission of the alleged narcotics traffic from the United States to Colombia, and in a small quantity of only fifty grams of cocaine, it would be a miscarriage of justice to order confiscation of the plane owned by the first party, leased by the second party, and chartered to the third party for purposes other than transporting narcotics, in this case for taking a patient from Santa Marta back to the United States.

As it has been amply demonstrated that the owner corporation of the airplane not only did not participate in the commission of the alleged crime of narcotics trafficking in the quantity of fifty grams of cocaine and, equally, that it had not even had knowledge of the plane with registration number 464J making its way to Santa Marta since, by leasing it to Jet Avia, Ltd., it thereby authorized the latter corporation to charter it, the Court disposes and so orders return of the airplane to its rightful owner, Mr. Robert E. Wood, who obtained such rights to the property in the manner already described, or to his attorney, Dr. Julio Salgado Vasquez, who is authorized to receive the airplane.

As a result of the foregoing substantiating facts, the Third Penal Court of the Circuit of Santa Marta, administering justice in the name of the Republic and by authority of the Law

SO DECREES:

FIRST: To order, as in effect it is now being so ordered, to turn over to Mr. Robert E. Wood, or to his attorney, DR. JULIO SALGADO VASQUEZ, aircraft jet class, Model 24, Gates Learjet, Serial Number 24, 164, registration number 464 J, issued by the Federal Aviation Administration of the United States of America, which was confiscated at the order of this office at Simón Bolívar Airport of this city, in accordance with cause shown in the foregoing.

SECOND: In carrying out the dispositions of Decree 1188 of 1974, Article 52, and in concordance with Decree 1514 of 1975, Article 1, this decision shall be transmitted to the National Council of Narcotics and also be officially communicated in writing to the Command of the Magdalena Police Department, to the FAC Command based in Barranquilla, to the Aerocivil authorities and to the Administrative Officer of Simón Bolívar Airport in this city.

THIRD: Since this document has been legally executed,

LET IT BE COPIED, COMMUNICATED AND CARRIED OUT.

The Judge(signature)
JORGE VALDEZ

Raul's English version of *la providencia* was much simpler than the one shown. At times he did not have the English equivalent for words, but could "talk around" many of them—"alleged" became "they said so," "persons detained" was "guys they arrested," "interrogation" came out "they asked a lot of questions," and so forth—but we managed. I learned enough to reconfirm Steve Bolling's story as 99 percent correct and to upgrade many of my own speculations from mere conjecture to likely certitude. We carefully examined the "Findings" of the Third Penal Circuit Court of Santa Marta. These were the facts that Valdez had for so long unsuccessfully tried to piece together and that Salgado had finally accomplished on his behalf.

The second finding legally established in court records that 464 Juliet had entered Colombian airspace legally. The third established that nothing illegal had been found on the jet upon her entry into Colombia. We had known this, but it now had been officially stated.

Raul pointed out that the items found in the initial search of the airplane on June 15, 1977, had been turned over to the officials.

"That means," he concluded, "that they must have kept them somewhere until the next time they searched the plane."

"Then they must have brought them back when the Magdalena Police Department, the Director of Judicial Police, the commander of the Police post from Rodadero, and the other policemen were ordered to search it again on July 4, 1977," I agreed, which brought us into finding five. "They brought everything back, plus the fifty grams of cocaine, and arranged it into that nice picture we saw in Valdez's office—remember?—the box with the fuel additive and socks and scissors in it, sitting there in the middle of the aisle?"

Raul nodded, "*Si*—the bag of cocaine was right on top. Even a blind man could have found it, if it was there the first time."

I noticed something else in item five.

"Hey, Raul, look who was on the scene during the second search: the *procurador general*, the regional attorney general of Santa Marta. He's the one I met with the phony judge who Aldo tried to pass off on me at first, when he tried to pull the eighty-thousand-dollar scam. That attorney general is also in the "business"—Valdez told us the *procurador* was his partner in the cocaine end. Remember?"

"I told you Bobby. I told you," he reminded me virtuously. "Everybody in Santa Marta's a crook."

We moved on to lengthy finding number six, where two officials, Granados and Lamprea, had testified on the record that it was they who had put Bolling and Parada's belongings inside the Prist carton on the initial search and that nothing suspicious had been found at that time. Finding seven indicated that the Ninth Court had dismissed the charges against these two on July 27, 1977. The same court had dismissed the others, including Chagra and Wilson, earlier, on July 4, 1977. Steve's surmise had probably been true: He and Parada had been chosen to remain as hostages to give the Colombians bargaining power. After all, their "ransom" alone cost Jet Avia over a quarter of a million dollars. It had probably cost Chagra and Wilson a bundle to get out just under the wire, or even a little time after the cocaine had been "found."

When we examined finding eight, we discussed the information we had found previously among the papers in Judge Valdez's office: that on February 20, 1979, the Second Penal Court had charged Chagra and Wilson for the crime of "narcotics traffic," and had "temporarily suspended" charges against the other four. This had aroused my suspicions the first time I had seen it.

It had been just too conveniently close in time—seven days—to the date of Chagra's indictment on February 27, 1979, for "continuing criminal enterprise" in Colombia and the United States.

Now I was beginning to wonder. Did this new charge, brought over a year and a half later, refer to the fifty grams of cocaine? Not likely. The court record showed that the cocaine had been planted. However, since all six of the men were mentioned, it still had something to do with 464 Juliet. But now, it could no longer be the flight itself and the cocaine. It had to be the events preceding the flight and the reason for making it. Specifically, the crash of the DC-6, and, very possibly, since the "enterprise" was "continuing," other operations of Chagra's in Colombia as well; but, it most definitely had something to do with the DC-6 marijuana operation, which gave the United States agencies their first breakthrough in getting something concrete on Chagra's Colombian activities.

"Look, Raul," I said, pointing to finding twelve, "they bit hook, line, and sinker on Wilson's story about flying down to the Guajira in a private plane when he heard of the DC-6 crash. Then, by all rights, since this is the official version, Wilson should have been off the hook for the DC-6. How could they charge him for anything? They accepted that he wasn't on 464 Juliet. They accepted that he wasn't on the DC-6, at least on record in Colombia. The only thing that makes sense is that our government wanted the Colombian government to have on record somewhere an unspecific charge of narcotics trafficking against Chagra and Wilson, keeping the other four "suspended"— on ice—just in case it was eventually discovered these men had been involved in Chagra's criminal operations. For Wilson and Chagra, they could fill in the blanks as needed with specific details—possibly from the people they persuaded to be informants. That's the only way it makes sense to me."

Raul was giving close attention to my line of reasoning and nodding his head.

"What I think, Bobby, is that Chagra was *Numero Uno* on their shit list."

"He was high," I agreed, "high enough for them to condemn Bruce Allen to sure death. They traded Allen's life against the time they needed to plant evidence so the Colombians would hold the men and get something for their trouble. And for time to find out what they could about the DC-6. The SOBs didn't even do a good job of it."

We also discussed the sure skill Dr. Salgado had shown in his presentation and clear reasoning using legal precedents to justify release of 464 Juliet, which he had miraculously constructed from what he had found in the jumble of papers Valdez had in his file. Salgado had proven, in short order, from existing legal records that none of the persons detained had been guilty of bringing cocaine into Colombia or illegally entering its airspace. Also, in the event any doubt remained concerning still unresolved criminal guilt (the February 20, 1979, charges still hanging fire) he had shown that none of those in the line of ownership could be held civilly responsible for criminal use of the Learjet.

Dr. Salgado had covered every possible loophole.

We sat back in satisfaction. He had done a masterful piece of work.

"Raul, it just occurred to me, we might have another problem. Do you think they'll charge us for three years of parking for 464 Juliet?"

Raul considered this only for brief second, and answered with a vigorous "*Si.*"

We made a note to telephone Dr. Salgado about this matter first thing in the morning to see what could be done. Then we went downstairs to collect the others we had kicked out quite a bit earlier. Dave was planted in front of the television set listening as if he understood every word. Sam was deep in the flight manual.

I sat down and told them that we would still be delayed, explaining about the three-day required public notice of *la providencia*. "We'll all go to the airport on Saturday the twenty-third for the delivery of the plane to me."

Dave nodded peacefully, but Sam was not happy.

"You mean we can't leave until Saturday?" he complained.

"Sam, I made it clear before we left that I couldn't give an exact day for leaving. What's the problem?"

"It's my wife," he said, "I told her we would be back by Wednesday or Thursday. She's not going to like it."

I told him to join the club—mine wasn't going to like it either—and then I suggested that he'd better get on the phone and give her the bad news.

CHAPTER FORTY-ONE

Raul and I got up early to get moving on the problem concerning the three years of parking fees that would undoubtedly have to be resolved to avoid unpleasant last-minute surprises. We decided we would first talk with Luis Donado before we approached Dr. Salgado. Donado would know how to approach the matter.

He greeted us warmly when we arrived at his office at the airport.

"Look what I have," and I handed him my copy of *la providencia*.

He looked through it, nodding with satisfaction as he read.

"So, my friend, it's all over—the Learjet is now yours."

"Practically," I beamed, "after 6:00 P.M. Friday—and of course, the *diligencia*—you're supposed to be there—that's Saturday morning."

Donado wrung my hand and congratulated me that the end was now tantalizingly close.

"Donado, I have a question. I'm sure there might be a problem at the airport about parking fees for the last three years. What should I do about this?"

Donado sat in thought for a minute.

"Is Dr. Salgado still in town?" he finally asked.

When we told him this was the case, he suggested that we call him to arrange a meeting between the two of them. I was pleased at Donado's eagerness to help me. Raul immediately got busy on the telephone and when Salgado was on the line, he handed the instrument to Donado. Salgado's presence, even on the telephone, seemed to bring out everybody's party manners, and Donado was no exception. He was visibly impressed with Salgado and eager to meet this important man. Raul had told him the past Friday that Salgado would be representing me.

"Very good, Doctor Salgado," Donado was saying, "I'll send them over to get you right away," and, after our "goodbye's," he turned to us to say that we should pick up Salgado right away and that he would wait for us.

"He wants to speak to me personally," he said in a pleased tone of voice.

Forty-five minutes later, we returned to Donado's office with Dr. Salgado.

Donado had straightened up his desk and had someone dust it and empty the wastebasket in our absence. He was at his military best as he greeted Salgado.

Raul and I left them to converse privately, saying that we would be in the restaurant. Some thirty minutes later, they joined us for lunch. Neither of them made any reference to their meeting, and I asked no questions, since I figured that this was "my style," which Salgado had liked.

However, I did ask Donado about buying jet fuel; I needed about 350 gallons more.

"No problem, Bobby," he assured me, "you can use my original letter of authorization. Just call if you have any problems."

When we finished lunch, Salgado was ready to return home, where we drove him with little conversation. He seemed drowsy and probably was looking forward to a siesta.

"Why didn't he say anything about the meeting?" I asked Raul on the way back to the hotel.

"I don't know—but he said we should call him tonight. He'll probably tell us then."

Toño looked relieved to see us when we walked in. Valdez had telephoned Raul half an hour earlier and had left instructions for him to call immediately. I sat down on the bed as Raul talked with Valdez. The conversation was short.

Raul was not his usual voluble self on the telephone.

"What did he want?" I asked when he had finished.

"I don't know, Bobby—just that he wants to see me this afternoon, right away. I'll take the bus over. If I need you, I'll call and Aquiles can bring you …"

"Wait—what for? Why does he want to see you alone?"

"I don't know."

"Is everything all right?" I was still puzzled that only Raul was to go see Valdez.

"Sure, no problems. Relax, Bobby. Take it easy. I'll be back tonight."

"OK, Raul, just as long as you're back early enough to call Salgado. You know he goes to bed with the chickens."

The rest of us spent the afternoon around the hotel. Dave played solitaire. Sam studied, and I wondered what Valdez wanted to see Raul about. I was also worrying about the repercussions the knowledge of *la providencia* would be creating in the various offices of those officials who had received copies.

By nine thirty, I was beginning to get anxious. Raul was not back yet. I sat playing solitaire unenthusiastically to kill time. Finally, Raul walked in.

"Where the hell have you been?" I jumped on him, other anxious questions crowding into my mind.

"Where are the guys?" he wanted to know. He sounded like a conspirator.

"They're out—to eat or somewhere," I replied impatiently, "Come on, don't keep me in suspense. What did the judge want?"

Raul merely smiled mysteriously and walked over to the bed where he sat down. I looked curiously at him as he silently removed his left shoe. Then his sock. He straightened up and held up a small clear cellophane packet. Carefully opening it, he held it out to me, beaming, as if it were the Hope Diamond.

"Pure, Bobby," he gloated. "Valdez said this is the purest cocaine in Colombia."

A chill of pure horror streaked through my body.

"Are you fucking crazy?" I screamed at Raul. The smile froze on his face at my words.

I grabbed the packet from his hand, darted across the room to fasten the safety chain of the entrance door and then tore open the bathroom door and threw the packet into the toilet and flushed it. I cursed the low water pressure as the little packet floated lazily in circles and prayed that it would go down when it sped up slightly as it neared the center. No such luck. The packet slowly re-appeared and bobbed on the surface, as if to mock me. I reached in, picked it up, shook off the water and tore it open, carefully shaking it to get rid of all the powdery substance, then tearing it into small bits. I flushed it again. Then again. Finally, all traces had disappeared.

Raul sat in bewilderment during my frantic activity. I was still breathing hard.

"What the fuck is the matter with you?" I grated out.

"What's the matter Bobby?" Raul's voice sounded hurt, "What did I do wrong?"

Realizing that Raul's thought processes were obviously completely fogged in and that he was flying IFR (Instrument Flight Rules), I calmed down a little and ordered him to listen.

"Where did you get the coke, Raul?"

"I told you, Bobby," he wailed, "from the judge."

"And how did you get it here?"

"On the bus. Inside my sock. You saw me."

My temper flared up again.

"You crazy, dumb son of a bitch. You rode all the way here from Santa Marta with the cocaine?"

He nodded dumbly. I clutched my head in my hands and stared at the floor as if to find an explanation for his utter stupidity. Finally, I looked up and held his eyes.

"Look, Raul. Don't you see how serious this is; I've put my ass on the line, my reputation, the well-being of my family, over one hundred thousand in cash, guns stuck to my head, and 464 Juliet is still here in this hellhole. And you … ," I choked trying to find a word strong enough to describe him, "and you, you come strolling in here, full of smiles, with a gram of cocaine that could put me in jail for years. How could you be so fucking stupid."

"Bobby, this is Colombia. Nothing will happen here," he was protesting.

"I know this is Colombia. And you can bet your sweet ass that this is just where something could happen. You're not thinking, Raul. You know we're being watched here, right?"

Raul nodded as I continued, "Just possibly, Raul, just possibly, someone could have followed you up the stairs. Right?"

He nodded again and started to explain optimistically that no one had; I cut him off.

"Listen, Raul, don't talk. The *providencia* is finished, right?" He nodded again.

"Everybody's been paid, right?"

Another nod.

"And the judge screwed Aldo. Right? "

I was giving it to him slowly, line by line, to make sure he understood every word.

"If you agree with everything I've said so far, then you ought to be smart enough to figure out that the finish to the perfect fucking con would be the 'sting.' Anyone could have followed you here, right to the room."

I shuddered to think of the possible headlines. "Bobby Wood, Busted in Colombia" or, perhaps, "Florida Man Nabbed in Narcotics Trafficking."

"It didn't happen, Raul—but it damn well could have. If I go down for something, I want to be the one who caused it, not you. And sure as hell not for some piddling little packet of cocaine you dragged across from Santa Marta on a bus. Do you understand?"

"*Si, si*, Bobby," Raul said, hanging his head apologetically, "I never thought of that. I just didn't think."

My relief that none of this had happened was enormous, but I only had myself to blame. I had effectively created this complication by not telling Raul that I had been wearing one of my "faces" for Valdez's benefit. Several times I had been on the point of revealing to Raul what I was doing but had drawn back. I was fearful that he did not have the skill to carry off such deception. I hadn't taken into consideration his inborn greed for money and my plan had backfired. Still, if Raul hadn't seen through it, as close as we were to each other, Valdez certainly hadn't either. My anger subsided. My con game was working perfectly and I realized I could still keep Raul in the dark, but he had to be given some additional instructions.

"Raul, I'm sorry I yelled at you," I apologized, "but I thought you understood …"

Raul perked up. Like most people who are anxious to please others, he became deeply dejected by disapproval and visibly happy when he was told he was forgiven.

" … but listen to me," I went on, "We'll do our deals with Valdez *after*—not before—we get 464 Juliet out. It's very important that we take one step at a time. I know I can count on you to help me."

Raul puffed out his chest to hear that he was being restored to grace.

"*Si*, Bobby. I'm sorry. I see now how it is. Just tell me what you want me to do."

"Fine. Now just forget it. Let's get down to business," I began. "What about tomorrow?"

"Valdez wants us to meet him at his house at eleven," he answered.

"OK, we'll be there. But I'll do the talking. You just stay in the background and tell me what he says and the tell Valdez exactly what I say. Don't offer any other information. And if he pulls you off to the side and asks about the cocaine, tell him I liked it, nothing more. Don't bring up the subject—I'll do it."

Raul nodded agreement, and then he got back to the subject of the call to Salgado that he had been too late to make. Had I been in touch with the doctor?

"Yes, Dr. Salgado told me he had arranged a meeting with Donado at ten o'clock in the morning, and that we were to call back tomorrow evening."

Before the evening was completely shot, Sam, Dave, Toño, Aquiles, and Fernando had all drifted back to the hotel; it was around eleven thirty.

"*Qué pasa*," Toño asked.

We told them that Valdez had more papers for Salgado, important ones. Everyone seemed satisfied, and no one asked questions about Raul's trip alone in the bus to see the judge.

THURSDAY, AUGUST 21

Telling Sam and Dave that they should find something to amuse themselves, Raul and I left for Santa Marta with Aquiles and Toño for our meeting with Judge Valdez. Sam was curious, asking a lot of questions about why he and Dave were being left behind. Sam was beginning to get edgy at sitting around doing nothing and was anxious to get going.

Raul and I had Aquiles drop us off at Valdez's house and then sent him and Toño off on a search for leads on the radios. They were to return for us at four thirty.

Valdez was dressed neatly but casually, the image of a Latin tropical country squire ready to visit his holdings. He first took us into his den. When we were seated with drinks, he looked at Raul meaningfully. He first wanted to hear my reaction to the packet he had sent me.

"Well, Raul," he said inquiringly, "Did you show Bobby?" Raul, as per instructions, forwarded the question to me for reply.

I didn't know shit from Shinola about cocaine, but I assumed an air of confidence that I was far from feeling.

"Yes, it looks good, really good. I don't use it myself, but when we're ready I'll bring my chemist down here to check the purity," I said, speaking as one prudent businessman to another. "I'm sure you understand; there is a tremendous amount of cocaine coming into the States that has been cut down to nothing. My contacts want only pure—uncut."

"*Si, si,* Bobby," Valdez was nodding sympathetically, "I know. I don't blame you. Bring your man down. He will confirm that my product is the best—never, never cut."

Valdez was on the defensive, interested in assuring me of quality. I was relieved that he was too engrossed in this aspect to ask me any technical questions because he would have discovered my ignorance immediately.

He was believing what he wanted to believe and had sold himself on my appearance of professionalism. He rose, smiling, and beckoned Raul and me to follow him. He took us through the back door of his den, through a covered patio, and over to an open-roofed shed in the garden. A large sheet of black plastic material covered a hidden pile.

Valdez pulled off the sheet to reveal half a dozen bales of marijuana that had been broken open. He reached down and ran his hands through it. He invited me to join him in the examination. My sixth sense told me that this was a test. He was still not sure of my expertise. The moment of truth was upon me—I couldn't falter now, it was a case of chicken salad or chicken shit.

I squatted down beside him and picked up a handful. I squeezed it hard, then smelled it, rubbed a few leaves between my fingers, and dropped it. It smelled dry and musty, not grassy and aromatic. I was damned sure nobody who had a choice would smoke it, and equally sure that these bales sitting in Valdez's garden shed were rejects.

"I don't want you to take offense, Judge Valdez," I said politely, but in a tone of disappointment, "but this green shit is just garbage. I couldn't give this stuff away."

I looked him full in the face, shaking my head vigorously, searching for a clue as to whether I had interpreted the purpose of the examination correctly. I thought I detected a gleam of satisfaction in his eyes, so I went on, picking up another handful and again squeezed it.

"It's dry as hell, either last season's crop or improperly dried," I ventured.

"Besides, the only quality my connections will even look at is gold. Pure gold and fresh."

Valdez was smiling broadly and patting me on the back.

"I just wanted to be sure, Bobby. You and I will do very good business. I can see you know what you're talking about." Valdez was nothing if not cautious, but I had passed his test with flying colors.

"*Vamanos*," he said briskly, "let's go to my airport," and he led us to his Jeep where his driver was waiting. I concentrated on acting normally as we strolled over to the Jeep. Any visible signs of relief on my part would arouse Valdez's suspicions, and I could see he was still being very, very careful.

"You were right, Bobby," he was explaining casually, "and that's exactly where those bales are going: into the garbage. It's some that was confiscated. It belonged to Raul," and he made a gesture with his head toward the waiting driver.

His matter-of-fact attitude indicated only amused superiority over Raul's poor judgment of quality and that only his worth as an excellent chauffeur had made it worth Valdez's while to extend a protective legal wing over an invaluable employee.

Valdez climbed into the front with Raul. Raul and I were in the rear. Valdez gave Raul instructions and we headed south past the airport. At the crossroads where the right fork led to Ciénaga and the left to Riohacha, we headed south toward a place called Fundacion.

The road was terrible, full of enormous holes, ruts and bumps. At one point we left the main road and took off to ford a small river, returning to our route after crossing. We drove an hour and a half longer on the road, which became progressively worse. Then we turned to the right, in an east by northeasterly direction. After twenty minutes, we reached a dirt road and very shortly drew up to a makeshift wire gate. We had arrived at the shipping depot of Valdez's growing operation.

Directly in front of the gate was a large "shade shed" which consisted of large round poles holding up a steeply pitched thatched roof. It was about thirty feet wide and sixty feet deep. As we came closer, I could see several roughly-made tables and chairs. Three or four men were sitting idly at the tables, others sprawled open-mouthed, asleep in hammocks strung from the rafters. The far end of the structure contained the kitchen area, which consisted only of rickety open shelves and a stove. The stove was a primitive waist-high adobe trough covered with iron grating. Several cut tree branches protruded from one end. The wood under the grate burned and as new fuel was needed, the branches would be shoved farther inside. A slim, young country girl was tending two huge blackened and battered pots that bubbled and steamed over the fire.

Everyone turned to stare at us. Even the sleepers rolled out of their hammocks to see who the visitors were. The men were dressed in torn, stained trousers, without shirts. For the most part, they were barefoot.

"Bobby Wood!" I heard someone shout. I looked around to see who possibly knew me here at this marijuana plantation in the middle of nowhere. Someone was approaching from the left, waving and again calling my name. "Bobby Wood, *qué pasa?*"

He rushed over and was shaking my hand vigorously. I finally recognized him. He was Jose, a friend of Federico Ramirez's. He had come to my charter business, Air Unlimited, in Miami several times with Federico. When I had seen him in Miami, he had always been as taciturn and impassive as a cigar store Indian. Here in Colombia he was voluble, excited to see me and bubbling over with questions.

"What are you doing here?" he wanted to know immediately.

"Just here on business," I answered, smiling.

"*Qué sorpresa* (What a surprise)," he kept repeating, and all I could do was agree that, yes, it was indeed a small world.

Jose told me he was working as the "crew chief" for Valdez now. Federico had recommended him to Valdez. The judge was surprised but pleased to find out that I knew Jose, and when Federico's name was mentioned his delight grew even more. Bobby Wood was producing better and better credentials as time went on, definitely one of the "in" crowd.

He ushered us to one of the tables, motioning the kitchen girl to clear away the battered coffee cups. She brought coffee for all, and the judge sent her to the Jeep for a Coca-Cola for *Señor* Wood. Valdez listened attentively as Jose described what a "giant" airplane operation I had in Miami. I was the center of attention, all eyes were on such an important man—a new gringo amigo whose presence unmistakably signified money.

I played it to the hilt. I had been recognized as a man of substance and had to show initiative.

"Let's check the runway," I requested with authority. "I want to see every foot of it."

We entered the Jeep and drove about two hundred feet to a strip that I could see had recently been cleared from the underbrush. To the right sat a brand-new Caterpillar bulldozer. Jose had leaped out of the Jeep and was stamping his booted foot into the packed soil with embedded crushed rock.

"See," he said, arms extended wide, "it's very hard."

I dropped to my knees and poked around with a stick to show my interest in every detail of this important element of the operation.

"Good," I pronounced, "we won't have to worry about the rainy season."

Jose and Valdez beamed as I praised the strip.

I paced toward the edge of the runway.

"About a hundred feet wide—that's good. How long is it?"

"Fifteen hundred meters," Jose answered.

Valdez and Raul stood by silently while I made my inspection. Then I said I would like to see the other end. They were all in the Jeep in a moment, and I called Raul back.

"I want to walk the full length," I explained. "I want to check for any soft spots or holes."

Valdez was impressed at my attention to details, and urged Raul to help me so that I would be completely satisfied with the construction of the airstrip. While in front of the judge, I had to be a professional to the fingertips in anything related to aviation.

The Jeep was waiting at the end when we reached it.

"Do you have a windsock?" I wanted to know, "We need some way to check wind direction to land." Raul was busy explaining the function of a windsock to a mystified Valdez, who didn't know exactly what it was. I promised that I would bring one for him the following week, when I returned to take care of the "balance." Valdez nodded. He caught the cue and dropped the subject, as he obviously was not anxious to discuss this completely different matter in front of Aldo.

We went back to the shed to discuss the logistics of the "business." The workers crowded around as I passed out cigarettes. Store-bought smokes were a real treat for them, especially American brands.

"We have a plane coming in today at five thirty," Jose was saying, pointing to a large pile of bales stacked apart, near the kitchen area. I eyed them casually, "How many bales? Twelve? Fifteen? Must be a small one." I was now playing Mr. Big.

The cook was serving up huge bowls of the stew she had been preparing for the past few hours. The chunks of meat floated together with chunks of plantain and starchy vegetables and smelled of unfamiliar herbs. I politely declined and sat back while the others pitched in with good appetite, bringing up the all-important subject of quality. Jose motioned to one of the workers, who disappeared to return with a bale that he placed on the table. With a flick of his machete, he opened one end.

Valdez supervised the operation, his hand immediately reaching into the contents to take up a handful for me to examine.

"How's that?" he asked proudly, sitting back to see what I thought of this batch.

His pride was justified. It was almost pure "gold"—fresh and sticky. I nodded in approval after smelling it, inhaling the aroma deeply.

"Very fresh—beautiful. This is exactly what I'm looking for."

Valdez and Jose sat back and looked at each other triumphantly. Now it was their turn to play Mr. Big.

"You can see, Bobby, it's just as I said. My, plantation grows only the best," he boasted.

We continued talking after the plates were removed until the arrival of an old stake body truck drew our collective attention. A shipment of newly cured marijuana had just been sent to the shipping depot from the plantation. The workers immediately got busy hauling the bales over to the shed.

"Business is good," Jose remarked, "We have a DC-4 coming in tomorrow."

I was amazed at how brisk and businesslike everything seemed. There was not the slightest indication of criminality or illegality about this clandestine operation. It was all just a day's work. A day on a construction job would have been more exciting. The glimpse behind the scenes I was getting gave no hint of fears of jail or capture by the Air Force or by any kind of Hollywood-type police procedural dramatics. Nevertheless, I knew that behind this afternoon of calm was a deadly and dangerous game. And I had to see it through; it had been and still was a part of my master plan to get Valdez to cooperate. I could see why 464 Juliet had been in Colombia for three years. If a person did not belong to the "in" crowd, he could get nowhere. All the past efforts to get 464 Juliet released had failed, because no one else had had the patience to see it through or knew how to wade through all the bullshit to get it done.

It was time to leave. We shook hands all around and promised we would see each other soon. Valdez was full of cheerful plans and boasted about his operation on the way back, and I encouraged him with a show of eagerness to get started.

We declined Valdez's invitation to come in when we arrived at his home as Toño and Aquiles were already waiting. The judge reminded us that the *diligencia* would take place at 11:00 A.M. on Saturday and that we should meet him and his secretary at the airport. Of all people, I assured him, Bobby Wood would be on time.

Toño and Aquiles reported that they had spent the entire afternoon following up lots of leads that had led to nowhere. Toño had spoken with Pedro, but Pedro's friend with the radios had not yet shown up.

Back in the hotel, Sam was reading the flight manual. Dave and Fernando were playing cards. The room was untidy; no one had picked up the trays although the beds were made.

Fernando reported that Dr. Salgado had called around five to say that he was coming over the following morning around eight thirty. We elected not to return his call to confirm the appointment since he was more than likely already retired for the evening.

Everyone wanted to know what we had done in Santa Marta. We were non-committal, just seeing about some missing equipment.

I wasn't very good company to my elated crew at this time because I was coming smack up against my next problem—Aldo. It wasn't an enormous problem, but I would have to satisfy him in some way. All the remaining unresolved problems were complicated by the fact that I had to keep Sam, Dave, and all the others, even Raul to a certain extent, from knowing exactly what I was doing. Tomorrow was Friday. It was supposed to be *the* day. At six o'clock in the afternoon, precisely, if no objections had been lodged by those who had received *la providencia*, Juliet would be mine. What else could go wrong? All the planning and scheming, in Colombia, in America—had I put it together right? Did I overlook something?

At the end of a long, exhausting day, I prayed long into an even longer night.

CHAPTER FORTY-TWO

Dr. Salgado arrived for his appointment at the precise time of 8:30 A.M. on the dot. We hustled the others out of the room and offered him coffee. It was not Dr. Salgado's style to be bothered with a briefcase; all he had in his hands was the usual manila folder, which he lost no time in opening to take out the standard officially-sealed paper on which all Colombian legal documents are submitted.

"Here are the papers about the matter of parking, *Señor* Wood," he said in a matter-of-fact tone of voice, "I have taken care of everything."

As I glanced over the document, he elaborated, "There will be no parking fees for the last three years. Only from tomorrow until you leave."

I looked at Dr. Salgado in undisguised admiration. He was a magician. No one would believe it from his quiet manner and his bare toes sticking out of his worn sandals. He sits down over a weekend to write a brief and, bingo, it's law. I mention a problem concerning "over three years of parking fees," and, presto, the problem disappears into thin air.

Donado had signed the document; it was complete.

I walked over to my briefcase and removed ten thousand dollars and brought it back to where Salgado was sitting.

"Here is the money for your fee, Dr. Salgado," I began. Since Valdez had spent half an hour counting and then double-checking his count, I wondered if I should ask Dr. Salgado to do the same, but decided not to. I had an uneasy feeling that it would be an indelicate suggestion, something like asking my children if they had washed their hands after using the bathroom.

Dr. Salgado merely raised his eyebrows politely and murmured that payment could wait until everything was finished, after the required time period had been completed.

"No, Dr. Salgado, I am very pleased with what you have done. Please, take it now," I said, adding, "The thing is I would like to ask you a favor."

I had thought of a plan that had three parts to it. First, and foremost, was to make sure that Dr. Salgado received his full fee. If anyone was satisfied, it had to be Dr. Salgado, who had performed to perfection. To make sure Dr.

Salgado was not cheated, I had paid him.

"Let me explain; I would like to ask you to pretend to Aldo that you haven't been paid yet. Tonight, I will give Aldo an additional $10,000, with instructions to pay you your fee. If he does, you can just return it to me. If he pays you less than the $10,000, I would like to know. You see, I have a lot of reasons I don't want to bother you with that make me believe Aldo has never been honest with me."

Dr. Salgado smiled dryly and gave me a knowing look. He was a highly intelligent man, fully aware of the kind of games Aldo and others like him were capable of playing.

"Of course," he assented, "I'll be happy to do that."

He pocketed the $10,000 casually without counting it, and left with his usual lack of delay.

The rest of my plan was this: Since Valdez had maneuvered me into having to tell Aldo I had paid him (Valdez) $50,000, Aldo would now have his hand out for "his" $25,000 (minus a few deductions). My problem was I simply didn't have it to give to him, but I still had to account for it.

Aldo was great at basic arithmetic, but he was stupid. The judge had cleaned me out, but Aldo was not supposed to know this. So I had to come up with something for him, plus some promissory notes. I had borrowed $10,000 from Valdez for Aldo, and had about $18,000 left. From the total of $28,000, Aldo was to pay $10,000 to Salgado, pay his brother, Gomez, and trust me for whatever was left owing.

If he short changed the doctor, and I was certain he would, I had some leverage for clipping his wings if he tried to get ugly. This, the third part of my plan, was insurance, necessary to keep him in line if it came to problems with him. Raul was clamoring to know what was going on.

"I think, Raul, that the judge must have found out about Aldo's plan to steal 464 Juliet and bypass him. If Aldo wasn't bullshitting me that he set up a deal with the military, the colonel probably told the judge all about it. I think that's why Valdez doesn't want Aldo to know he got $75,000. I think the figure—$50,000—he said I should tell Aldo was a pointed reminder. Like the Godfather—and I think that's why he screwed Aldo out of the $25,000. It was a matter of face as much as the money. He is showing Aldo that Aldo can't fuck around with Judge Jorge Valdez. So, I want to see if Aldo's going to try to screw me again, and screw Salgado, too. Don't worry. It's complicated. Just back me up. I know what I'm doing."

"Call Aldo now," I told him, "Ask him to come over. Just mention I have money for him—he'll drop everything."

While we waited, Raul and I went over Dr. Salgado's brief legally justifying the waiver of parking fees for the three years 464 Juliet had been sitting on

Colombian soil. He had done no shilly-shallying. The owner was not at fault; it had been *force majeure*, unforeseen circumstances, sometimes called an Act of God. I am too religious a man to blame any part of it on Him, and I knew full well that it had been the acts of mortals who fell far short of heavenly perfection that were to blame.

Official Paper AD03125965
SEAL OF REPUBLIC OF COLOMBIA AND $6 STAMP
DIRECTOR OF AEROCIVIL *OF COLOMBIA*
BY HAND
Ref: Plane. Jet class, Model 24, Gates Learjet, Series No. 24-164, Registration 464J of United States.

I, JULIO SALGADO VASQUEZ, with ID Card No. 3,675,484 of Barranquilla, holder of lawyer's professional card number 4475, as Attorney for MR. ROBERT E. WOOD, with due respect do petition you, after presentation of the following ANTECEDENTS :

1. Aircraft, jet class, registration number 464J, issued by the American authorities, landed on June 15, 1977, around 9:00 A.M. at Simón Bolívar airport of the city of Santa Marta, from the United States.

2. The purpose of this trip was to transport to a hospital in San Antonio, State of Texas, American citizen Bruce Allen who was in the Hospital San Juan de Dios of Santa Marta, as a result of extensive and serious burns sustained in an airplane crash.

3. The police authorities patrolling Simón Bolívar Airport, notwithstanding the fact that the airplane pilots showed all the necessary landing documents, and despite the fact that the customs officers inspected the plane finding no traces of smuggled or prohibited articles, later took advantage of the fact that all passengers had been arrested by DAS officers and again had a search made of the aircraft by the Judicial Police, at which time they found a plastic bag with fifty grams of cocaine. This led to confiscation of the plane that has been grounded on orders of Santa Marta judges from June 15, 1977, up to the present date.

4. On August 16, 1980, the Third Penal Court of the Circuit of Santa Marta decreed:

First:

To order, as in effect, it is now being so ordered, to release to Mr. Robert E. Wood, or to his attorney, Dr. JULIO SALGADO VASQUEZ, aircraft class jet, model 124, Gates Learjet, Serial Number 14-164, registration number 464 J, issued by the Federal Aviation Administration of the United States of America, which had been confiscated by orders of these chambers at Simón Bolívar Airport of this city, in accordance with cause shown in the foregoing.

Second:

In carrying out the dispositions of Decree 1188 of 1974, Article 52, and in concordance with Decree 1514 of 1975, Article 1, this decision shall be transmitted to the National Council of Narcotics and also be officially communicated in writing to the Command Of the Magdalena Police Department, to the Air Force Command based in Barranquilla, to the Aerocivil authorities and to the Administrative Officer of Simón Bolívar Airport of this city.

Third:

Since this document has been duly executed, the procedure for release of the plane may commence.

5. In the first point for consideration of the decision of August 16 handed down by the Third Penal Court of the Circuit of Santa Marta, copy attached, it is attested that confiscation of the plane was made on June 15, 1977.

6. Since such plane will be released to its owner, Mr. Robert E. Wood, only next Saturday, August 23, the order for its return will be executed on Friday, August 22, after which time Mr. Wood may make use of said plane.

7. The period of the time the plane registered as 464J of the United States—June 15, 1977 to the coming August 22, 1980—remained at the Simón Bolívar Airport of Santa Marta was a result of the order given by the judges of Santa Marta, as they considered that the plane had been used to transport fifty grams of cocaine from the United States to Santa Marta. The decree of the Third Penal Court of the Circuit of Santa Marta ordering that such plane must be returned to its rightful owner, Mr. Robert E. Wood, would give rise to the problem of payments for parking fees at the airport.

Article 1604, second paragraph, of the Civil Code, states that: "The debtor is not responsible for unforeseen circumstances, and the first article of law 95 of 1980, which replaces article 64 of the Civil Code, gives the following definition: "Force majeure or Act of God is the unforeseen circumstance that cannot be overcome, such as shipwreck, an earthquake, the capture by enemies, the proceedings of authority executed by a public official, etc."

Therefore, as the plane registered as 464J has been grounded from June 15, 1977 until today, following a legal order that had to be executed and could not be circumvented, we conclude that it is force majeure, unforeseen circumstance, that carries with it the consequence that the owner of the plane is not obliged to pay duties, taxes or tolls for the stay of said plane in Simón Bolívar airport of the city of Santa Marta.

PETITION: To exonerate Mr. Robert E. Wood from payment of fees that Aerocivil charges for parking at Simón Bolívar Airport for the period between June 15, 1977 and August 22, 1980, of airplane jet class, Model 24, Gates Learjet, Serial Number 164, registration 464J, issued by the United States Federal Aviation Administration, such stay of said plane being the result of force majeure and a result of orders issued by the judges of Santa Marta.

I enclose copy of the decision of August 16 from the Third Penal Court of the Circuit of Santa Marta ordering delivery of the plane in reference to Mr. Robert E. Wood, who, to indicate acceptance, hereby signs this petition.

Very truly yours,

(signature) Julio Salgado Vasquez

(signature) Robert E. Wood

The reply from the Aerocivil is shown below.

ADMINISTRATIVE DEPARTMENT OF AEROCIVIL, Technical Control Section, Barranquilla

Barranquilla, August 21, 1980.

In consideration of the contents of the above petition, I hereby state that in compliance, with Resolution. No. 4899 of July 31, 1980, issued by the Director of the Administrative Department of Civil-Aeronautics, Article II, Paragraph III, any aircraft with foreign registration detained by a Colombian authority and which has been released by judicial order or order of any other competent authority, will pay the fee for the initial landing and such fees for parking rights as may have been incurred will be applicable as of date of issuance of the verdict or court ruling releasing said aircraft.

Very truly yours,

(signature) Luis E. Donado, Chief, Technical Control Unit

(Seal) Administrative Dept. of Aerocivil, Technical Control Unit

At one o'clock in the afternoon, Aldo finally knocked on the door. He was bouncing with anticipation. We sent our friends away to leave us to our "summit" meeting.

"Sit down, Aldo. I have to talk with you. I have a problem."

"What's wrong?" he asked suspiciously.

"You can help me—just listen. I brought down seventy-five thousand dollars, as you know. All these extra trips and the delays, your accident—well, they've been eating into my money," I whined a little. "And last Tuesday, I paid Valdez fifty thousand dollars. I was facing ..."

"What?" Aldo screamed, "You paid the judge? I told you not to! Valdez said you weren't …"

"Wait, Aldo. Calm down. Let me explain."

Aldo's eyes were shooting sparks, which he was fanning into flames with his rapid breathing.

"I had no choice. Valdez ordered me to pay him. He didn't say why he had changed his mind, but he was very firm."

Let Aldo suck on that, I thought to myself. Let him worry that maybe the judge had heard of Aldo's plan to cut him out and steal 464 Juliet. I could see the moment this possibility occurred to Aldo by the very real apprehension that shot across his face.

"Maybe he didn't want you to see him take the money. Maybe he was afraid you'd get mad at him some day and blackmail him. I just don't know why he changed his mind, but you know how cautious he is."

This also made sense to Aldo, naturally. He was now in a more receptive mood to listen to the rest of what I had to say

I told Aldo that I had arranged a loan from Valdez for $10,000 that he, Aldo, would get the next day. I then explained to Aldo that, in addition, I was giving him another $18,000—$10,000 for Dr. Salgado and $5,000 for his brother, the lawyer, Gomez. That would leave $3,000 for Aldo, plus the $10,000 that he would collect from the judge. I had already advanced Aldo $2,000 (plus a little extra, which I was willing to forget), so I still owed him $10,000.

Right?

Aldo nodded. He wasn't happy, but my addition and subtraction met with his approval.

"Go on," he invited.

"Well, I have to come down here next week to pay Valdez the ten thousand dollars I owe him, and I can bring your ten thousand at the same time. Or, if you prefer, you can fly back to Miami with us, and I'll give you your money then."

Aldo was still sulking.

"You have to be reasonable, Aldo. None of this is my fault. Originally you told me it was going to cost me seventy-five thousand dollars total. Your brother, Gomez, was not in the deal then—he was called in when you had your accident, and by all rights, you should be the one paying him, not me. And I never figured on having to bring in another lawyer. Without Salgado, I'd still be waiting, and you know it. Between the two of them, that's fifteen thousand dollars extra I never figured on. And none of it's my fault. However, I'm willing to do all this, but you've got to help."

He was slowly realizing that he had no choice. Raul was joining in with inducements to put Aldo in a better mood.

"Hey, Aldo, come on back with us," he said enticingly. "You'll have a ball in Miami—all those pretty blondes."

Aldo was warming up to the idea. He knew it was his own incompetence that had caused me the money problem I had just explained to him. And, after all, a vacation in Miami … . In very short order, he was making excited plans.

"Bobby, we'll have to go right away to the American Consulate for my visa. It's Friday and they're closed on weekends."

I was not about to accompany Aldo to the Consulate where Harry Gilbert would surely be more than curious about my latest activities. I had been going out of my way to keep these unknown to Gilbert.

"It's better if you go alone, Aldo. I don't want the Consulate to know I'm in Colombia."

Aldo knew nothing of the problems I had encountered with the United States officials nor of the photo Pedro had found in Baratta's office at the Santa Marta airport, nor did I want to tell him.

"No, no, Bobby," Aldo insisted, "they won't give me a visa unless you come with me. You have to tell them that I'm your lawyer. That I'm going to Miami with you to work with your lawyers there on some documents."

There was no way out, so I finally agreed, hoping Gilbert would be out of the office, or not spot me.

No such luck. As Aldo, Raul, and I waited in line, I saw no trace of Gilbert and was breathing easily. However, when we handed over the passport, the clerk at the window walked away with it and entered the door to Gilbert's office. In a few moments, Gilbert emerged, looking toward us inquiringly. He spotted me immediately and my heart sank.

"Mr. Wood, how have you been?" Gilbert asked. "I thought you would be stopping by to visit us sooner than this."

"Well, I've been busy," I said lamely, "but I'm here now."

"Could I speak with you privately, Mr. Wood?"

I nodded, and he stepped over to admit me through the side door.

"Who is this Aldo Reyes?" was his first question.

"He's my lawyer. Why?"

"Reyes is a well-known name here. The Reyes family is one of the big names in narcotics traffic. But aside from that, Mr. Wood, when the agent gave me Reyes's passport, I noticed that he has been to Czechoslovakia. We have a suspicion he may be friendly with the enemy."

"Mr. Gilbert, there must be some mistake. He's not in narcotics, nor is he a communist."

"I'm sorry, Mr. Wood," he said firmly, "that may or may not be the case, however, we definitely can't issue him a visa without running an investigation on him. Just to be sure."

I asked how long it would take and Gilbert informed me that it would be about a week.

"Well, send a man to Ciénaga and do a background check on him, then," I said, as I had to go along with my protestations that it was all a mistake.

"What's your connection with him?" Gilbert wanted to know.

"He's my lawyer. Negotiating and translating with me on the oil deal I mentioned to you before. I need him in Miami."

Gilbert insisted that he couldn't help me until a check was made and that I would have to inform Aldo of this fact. I balked.

"You're saying he's a communist—you tell him."

Gilbert shrugged and walked out to advise Aldo of the problem.

"What do you mean?" Aldo shouted indignantly, "I'm a professional man. I'm no *marimbero*. I'm no communist. I just went to school in Czechoslovakia."

Gilbert's indifference to Aldo's protests maddened Aldo even more, but he got nowhere. He finally stalked off, his face mottled with rage, muttering nebulous threats about *corbatudos*—petty bureaucrats, who, in Colombia, usually wore neckties.

Raul and I tried to sooth Aldo's ruffled feathers as we walked out and returned to the hotel. We took him to the bar, where he had a few drinks in rapid succession to calm his nerves, and eventually he cheered up. Later, in the room, after I handed him the eighteen thousand dollars, his cure was complete.

"I trust you, Bobby," he confided in a maudlin voice, "I understand how it is but"—anxiously—"you will be back next week, no?"

"Give me four days after we've left here with the jet," I promised, "and I'll be back. Don't forget, I have to pay Valdez, too."

Aldo was reassured in the knowledge that I was also in debt to the judge for another ten thousand dollars. It was, after all, only a small delay.

Raul, Sam, Dave, and I sat by the bed, making a ceremony of watching the large hand on the clock reach 6:00 P.M., and we set up a cheer as it crossed the line on twelve, standing in a straight line with the six.

I could hardly wait as Raul placed a call to Valdez. He got to the point immediately, asking if everything was legal. He was nodding cheerfully and smiling with satisfaction. When he hung up, he reported that everything was fine. No problems. Valdez was glad to hear from us, but it hadn't been necessary to call.

All of us set up another loud cheer. The *providencia* was now law. Still, I had some small, nagging doubts. *After all the problems, how could it possibly have been this easy*, I kept thinking. I knew, down to the very marrow of my bones, that something was missing. The military, I was sure, was saving something, some unpleasant surprises for Juliet. I knew there would be more.

That night, Gustavo threw a large party, an event memorable in that it was the first time Bobby Wood wasn't picking up the tab. Alfredo arrived about nine thirty from Bogotá. All my gofers attended. Several members of *La Comunidad*, Aldo—even the Mayor of Ciénaga, who was a friend of Aldo's, showed up. The Donado boys were there. A few brought girls; Aldo invited two. Gustavo rented the outside patio. Everybody drank, ate, and danced. It was a gala occasion.

I left the party early and went upstairs. I couldn't afford to have a clouded head the next day—it was too important. Besides, I couldn't shake off my apprehensions. Was it really over? I kept asking myself. I lay awake a long time, unable to overcome my anxieties.

Saturday, August 23, 1980

I was up at six, making the rounds of the beds and couches of the crowded suite to wake up my "crew" and the visitors who had chosen to stay the night. Everyone moaned and groaned with hangovers, but eventually I was able to get them on their feet. Aldo had apparently not scored with either of his two *señor*itas the night before. I found him snoring on one of the couches. He was the first to leave, as he was stopping off in Ciénaga to pick up his brother, Gomez.

Ramon was waiting below in his sparkling cab. Alfredo, Raul, and I were going to escort Dr. Salgado in style. The rest of the group crowded into Aquiles' Chevy. We picked up Dr. Salgado at eight, dressed in his usual costume of slacks, loose shirt, and sandals. He was unusually animated with Alfredo, asking about the Minister and showing unusual interest in what Alfredo had to say.

We stopped at Donado's house. Fernando told us his father was at the office working, but would join us at the airport at 11:00 A.M., as arranged. I was happy to see that Salgado and Alfredo's mutual interests left me free to sit quietly. I was still nursing my anxieties along with the hope that today would be the last time I would have to make the dreary drive through the misery and poverty along the road.

When we reached the Reyes's home, a porch-side delegation rose to greet us—Aldo, Gomez, Aldo's sister (the lady judge), and Aldo's father had been waiting for us in a battery of rocking chairs, all dressed in unusual finery. Not often did a Supreme Court Justice visit Ciénaga. They had risen to the occasion.

I had already told Alfredo Escobar about the eighteen thousand dollars I had given Aldo and the ten thousand dollars I had secretly paid Dr. Salgado. He understood my game and was going to watch Aldo closely. He winked at me as we walked through the gate to greet the committee of Reyeses, who all had their eyes glued to Salgado, silently rehearsing their eloquent words of welcome. There was quite a flurry of activity when introductions were made and as Salgado shook hands with them, murmuring appropriate acknowledgments.

When the preliminaries had run a suitable course, I took Aldo aside.

"Aldo, now's the time to pay Salgado and your brother, Gomez. It's already ten o'clock, and we have to be at the airport at eleven."

"In a minute," he whispered back. He was enjoying these moments too thoroughly to be rushed. However, I urged him again, so he reluctantly asked his brother to step inside. A few minutes passed. Then he returned and invited Dr. Salgado to enter.

Raul and I were craning our necks to try to see through the semi-sheer white curtains. We could see Aldo standing, gesturing, and talking earnestly to Salgado and Gomez, sitting on the bed. He was appeared powerful and eloquent, tossing his head and waving his arms, Fidel Castro-style.

After about ten minutes, Dr. Salgado emerged. His demeanor was completely calm and normal. I was intensely curious to know what had happened inside and examined his face closely for a clue. Nothing. Nothing at all. He wore his usual inscrutable look. I would have to wait.

Finally, Aldo and Gomez emerged. I was still in the dark about what was getting to look like a game of "post office," but the smug satisfied expression on Aldo's face indicated that he had screwed someone behind those closed doors.

It was time to leave for the airport. We loaded everyone into our assortment of vehicles and departed. The airport was almost abandoned; no Avianca flights were due. We sat around the outdoor area of the terminal waiting for Donado and the judge to arrive. I glanced several times at 464 Juliet, sitting proudly by herself, poised and eager to go.

Donado finally arrived close to eleven thirty. Zapata, the airport manager, was waiting. I kept glancing at my watch, chafing. At eleven forty-five, Valdez and Beatriz pulled up. Dr. Salgado had waited patiently for almost an hour, showing no annoyance, either at his tardy countrymen or at the ridiculous gringo haste of Bobby Wood, who had hustled everyone unmercifully to be there promptly at eleven.

Baratta, the fussy old fart, was standing by the gate, trying to get a glimpse of Dr. Salgado as we all walked out to 464 Juliet. The soldiers, observing the ceremonious nature of our progress, stood at attention, unusually military and correct. I no longer felt like an intruder and was enjoying the feeling thoroughly, hoping they all saw me.

We stood around 464 Juliet a few minutes, chatting in small groups, like a congregation outside a church waiting for the services to begin. Finally, Judge Valdez motioned for Beatriz to hand him the papers. He gave her instructions to pass it around, and to have all the interested parties sign the six copies, which we quickly finished. I watched everyone sign with a feeling of joy. It was really happening. 464 Juliet was mine. Free and clear.

The *diligencia* had been performed.

COURT ORDER FOR RELEASE OF A JET AIRPLANE TO MR. ROBERT E. WOOD AND HIS ATTORNEY, DR. JULIO SALGADO VASQUEZ

In Santa Marta, on August 23, at eleven o'clock in the morning were present the judge and secretary from the Third Penal Court of the Circuit, with the purpose of making physical, real, and material delivery of a jet plane, so ordered in a decree issued August 16, 1980. At Simón Bolívar Airport of this city were also present MR. ROBERT E. WOOD, DR. JULIO SALGADO VASQUEZ, the Representative of Aerocivil, Mr. LUIS DONADO, and the Administrative Officer of the aforementioned airport. The procedure was carried out as follows: An airplane of American Registration, jet class, model 24 Gates Learjet, Serial Number 24-164, N464J, is being delivered to the parties concerned and is accepted to complete satisfaction. With no further business to conduct, the order is thus carried out, and this document signed by the parties concerned.

The Judge: (signature)

JORGE VALDEZ
Parties Concerned:
(signatures)
JULIO SALGADO VASQUEZ
LUIS DONADO, *Representative, Aerocivil*
ROBERT WOOD

It was a simple ceremony, but for me, history making.

Raul beamed at me and all of us shook hands happily. The group broke up and we headed for the shade and the breezes of the open air restaurant to get out of the blazing midday heat of the tropics. I turned around for another look at 464 Juliet, still waiting and poised as if for flight.

I feverishly wanted to ask Donado when we could leave. I felt I couldn't wait another moment to get 464 Juliet out of Colombia and had a crazy impulse to grab my "crew" and race them over to the cockpit and leave without even a goodbye. However, I had to sit through an hour or so of political talk until, finally, Beatriz and Valdez left, taking Dr. Salgado with them and saying they would be back later. At the same time, Aldo, Gomez, and Alfredo left with Zapata. Donado, Raul, and I were alone. Now was my chance.

"Bobby," Donado said hesitatingly, "are you going to take the aircraft jacks back in the jet?"

Donado was politely giving me an "out," but I could see that he wanted the jacks.

"No," I responded, "they are for you if you can use them."

"I'd like to have them, but, of course, I want to pay you for them," he offered.

"No, Donado, I wouldn't think of it. You've helped me, and I'd like you to have them."

He accepted my offer with pleased gratitude.

Finally, I could stand it no longer.

"Donado," I began, "It's almost one thirty now. I'd like to leave today or early in the morning. Do we file our flight plan here or in Barranquilla?"

My heart sank as I saw a regretful look appear on his face. He was saying, "Bobby, I'm afraid you can't leave just yet. I already sent a telex to Aerocivil in Bogotá, but you have to wait until we have their reply."

He was upset by my disappointment, and went on to explain that due to all the prior problems, and the seriousness of the entire matter, authorization would have to come from Bogotá. Then, as soon as Donado received the telex, the Air Force would have to stamp the flight plan.

I knew it!—I thought in a panic—I fucking knew it! I knew there had to have been a catch. Here it was just as I expected. "But, Donado," I protested, "the jet is mine now. Why can't I leave when I want to?"

"Bobby, I'm sorry. But again, this jet is not the average plane that leaves here. You know that."

I tried to contain myself to speak again in a reasonable tone of voice to ask how soon.

"I'll see if the answer is there when I go back to the office. If not, maybe I'll have an answer in the morning, perhaps not until Monday," he promised.

I knew I had to get off the subject as I was up to my ears in the Colombian *Mañana* Syndrome. I saw Donado's hands were tied, and that he would do whatever he could to help me. So we chatted a few minutes and then walked Donado out to his truck for his return to Barranquilla.

When he had gone, I gave vent to my frustrations. "Raul," I fumed, "I don't like it. Juliet's mine now. How can they keep me from leaving with her?"

"Relax, Bobby. We won't have any problems," Raul was saying optimistically.

However, I was not in the least optimistic. There was the Aerocivil in Bogotá, the Air Force … it just wasn't normal procedure, I argued. "Besides, Salgado is going back to Bogotá tomorrow. I can't rely on that asshole Aldo for any help … ."

Alfredo was approaching, and immediately noticed my scowling face.

"*Qué pasa?* What's wrong, Bobby?" he asked in concern.

I explained the situation to Alfredo, who partially calmed me by assuring me that if I did have any further problem, Salgado, he knew, would take care of them. He was absolutely sure I could still count on Salgado.

"By the way," Alfredo interjected, "you were really right about Aldo. He really was out to con everybody this morning."

"Who? How?" I wanted to know. I had been so preoccupied about departure that I had forgotten about my game with Aldo.

"Well, out of the $18,000 you gave him, he paid Dr. Salgado $5,000. His brother, Gomez, got $2,000. Aldo kept $11,000 for himself."

"That mother fucker. He even screwed Salgado. How did he dare? I can't believe he would be so stupid."

Raul and Alfredo were equally amazed at how short-sighted Aldo was. He had just cut himself off at the pockets with what could have been a very important connection for himself.

Alfredo handed me the packet of $5,000 that Salgado had returned to me. I immediately returned $4,000 of it to Alfredo. He had already received a $1,000 advance on the fee of $5,000 I had promised him.

"No, Bobby, you keep it," he demurred.

"No, Alfredo, I insist," I stated firmly. "Friends are friends, and I hope you and I will always be friends; but business is business, and we made a deal." I pressed the money on him, which he finally accepted reluctantly.

We sat around, still fuming about Aldo's complete lack of scruples with Salgado, when he walked back in with Gomez and Zapata. Motioning for Alfredo, they left to go with Zapata, who had invited them to have a drink with him at his home. Sam and Dave, who had been sitting alone, finally joined us now that Raul and I were free.

I plowed right into my distasteful task of informing them about the new delays.

"OK, you guys, here's the plan. Juliet is mine now, everything is legal." I showed them my copy of the diligencia. "But we have another problem. Donado has to have a telex of authorization from Bogotá approving the flight plan. He sent them the request this morning but doesn't have a reply yet. He's gone back to the airport in Barranquilla to see. Let's keep our fingers crossed that it's already there."

"You mean the jet is yours legally, but you can't leave yet?" Sam snorted.

I nodded my head in disgust, saying, "That's it. This is Colombia, my friends."

Sam was preparing to go into the same tirade I had just gone through with Raul, but I cut him off; so, he sat and sulked while Dave and I talked about all the fuck-ups we had experienced in the short time he had spent in Colombia.

Raul had been sitting quietly listening to us gripe, but suddenly he came to attention and poked me in the ribs.

"Look, Bobby … ," and he rolled his eyes sidewise to show me what he wanted me to see.

It was Harry Gilbert, the American Consul, together with another man, apparently an American. He had spotted me and headed our way.

"Look, all of you," I rapidly instructed Sam, Dave and Raul, "when he gets here, you all get up and leave. Don't go near the jet," I warned them.

"Hello, Mr. Wood," Gilbert was calling out, "What brings you to Santa Marta. I understood your business was in Barranquilla."

"That's the oil business, Mr. Gilbert. I'm also investigating that Learjet here," I offered coldly.

The false expressions of sympathetic interest from an official of the Consulate jarred me. I was reminded of their complete lack of interest in Bruce Allen, who had lain dying here in Santa Marta when a mere word from them, one word, would have allowed him to return to the States where his life might have been saved. Their only interest, in my opinion, was self-interest.

I was almost sure that his visit had been the result of a telephone call Baratta had made informing them of our presence here. What else would have brought him on a sweltering drive to Santa Marta on a Saturday afternoon? He possibly could have learned that 464 Juliet was now legally mine, if Zapata had told Baratta. However, I was not going to volunteer the information.

And what brings you to Santa Marta?" I returned his question.

He was here on business, he told me.

"What kind of business?" I insisted. I was determined to be as inquisitive as he had always been with me, and I plagued him with a series of questions that he was evading as best he could. I was viciously determined not to let him subject me to any interrogation; my episode at United States Customs in Miami had been more than enough, thank you.

He finally left; I wondered why he had never introduced his companion. I watched them as they reached the bottom of the steps, where Raul was on his way up from a trip to the washroom. Gilbert stopped Raul and engaged him in conversation. Some twenty minutes passed before Raul returned.

"What did you say to him, Bobby?" Raul immediately wanted to know, "He wasn't happy about you."

"Never mind that, Raul—what did he talk to you about?"

"He's one slick gringo. He asked me all about you: What my connection was with you; if I had anything to do with the Learjet; and about my connections here in Colombia—who they are, are they political … He's interested in us, Bobby. Another thing, he asked if I wanted to do some work here in Colombia for a lawyer friend of his in California."

I urged him to continue, but he suddenly stopped in his tracks, thought a minute, and announced that this was all.

"He gave me his card, though, and told me to call him," and Raul fished it out of his pocket to show me.

"That SOB," I fumed, "I know who his friend is in California. It's Gordon, you can go to the bank on that."

I was also curious to find out if Raul thought Gilbert knew that 464 Juliet had been released. Raul thought not; he had said nothing to Gilbert, and Gilbert had not brought up the subject. We nevertheless sat there considering this possible threat until Alfredo and his group appeared. Finally Dr. Salgado returned with the judge. Again there was general conversation among us all, with the exception of Dr. Salgado. He had withdrawn to a bench with a newspaper in hand, where he stretched out, covered his face with the Bogotá *El Tiempo* and promptly fell asleep. I chuckled as I thought of a good caption for such a scene: "Prominent Supreme Court Judge at the Bench." Salgado snored there gently, then awoke quietly, and rejoined us without comment.

We finally made plans to leave. Alfredo and Gomez were staying at the airport to take the evening flight back to Bogotá. Aldo was returning to Ciénaga; we promised to telephone him the next day.

As we dropped Dr. Salgado at *El Presidente* in Barranquilla, I asked him for one moment of his time. I needed advice.

"Dr. Salgado," I got right to the point, "What about Aerocivil and the Air Force? Will they make problems for me? Luis Donado told me I needed their permission to leave."

"*Señor* Wood, the matter is closed here in Colombia. Officially. Don't worry. If anyone here gives you any problems, please feel free to call me at my home or at my office in Bogotá. You have my telephone numbers. I will take care of anything that might arise."

He spoke calmly and confidently. It was beneath his dignity to bluster at the possibility of anyone daring to question the legality of the release of 464 Juliet.

I thanked him, again mentioning my gratitude and admiration for all he had done. He merely smiled.

"*Señor* Wood," he returned, "It was also a pleasure for me to meet you and to work with you. I would be most happy to represent you if you should need me any time in the future," and he shook hands and walked away, into the entrance.

Later that night, Raul called Donado at home, to learn that no telex had arrived. Donado told Raul he would check again first thing in the morning.

At nine thirty that evening, Dave received a telephone call from his wife. She was in a screaming fury with him. She was leaving unless he got his ass back to the States right away. Dave was hunched over the phone, a picture of embarrassment and misery. He turned his back to the rest of us. This was no telephone conversation. The only contributions he was permitted were, "Yes, but," "I know, but," and "I can't do that." According to her, he was a no-good son of a bitch. She had gone down to Jet Care and spent an hour telling everybody off. She had called Bobby Wood's wife and reamed her out good about her no-good husband. She was going to call the police.

The only thing Mrs. Pearson was not going to do, we could see, was to shut up. Dave stood there for close to an hour under her tirade. Now I understood fully his great fund of patience. Had it been my wife, I would have told her where to shove it and hung up.

When the conversation finally ended, Dave turned to us with the look of a man who had just recovered from a long and debilitating illness, smiled weakly and even tried to make a joke by saying, "Shoot, the little woman was kinda upset," then he went to the bathroom where I heard him showering.

Sunday, August 24, 1980

I spent all day by the telephone playing solitaire. Morale was at its lowest ebb. Sam was at his eternal study of the flight manual. Dave played solitaire across the room. I finally put away the cards and stared out the window toward Santa Marta.

Donado called late in the afternoon. No telex. Maybe Monday morning. Noon at the latest. *Mañana* and *mañana* and *mañana*.

Sam and Dave left to take a walk and were back at seven.

"Bobby," Dave said in a low voice, "I need to see you alone."

I nodded, stood up, and walked out of the room and downstairs with Dave. Dave was worried. He was afraid we were running into a problem with Sam. Sam didn't think we were going to be getting 464J out of Colombia. He had talked with Dave about it that afternoon, after I had told them about the telex and the Air Force stamp. Sam was sure I was being screwed now that everybody had been paid off. He had heard a lot of stories and Colombia was bad news in Sam's book. Sam was wanting to pull out.

This was all I needed. I was already ready to pull out my hair waiting for the clearance to leave, and now, this. I was, at the same time, deeply touched that Dave, with his domestic problems and the harrowing marathon telephone conversation he had just been through, should push his own problems aside to try to help me resolve mine. Dave was indeed a man for all seasons.

"OK, Dave," I said with a calm I didn't feel, "let's call Mel Cruder. Maybe he can fly, down here."

We caught a taxi over to the Telecom office, as we couldn't make the call from the room. Eventually we got a connection. Mel's wife answered. No luck. Mel was out of town and would not be back until the next week. Dave and I silently returned to the hotel. We sat down in the lobby, as there were still some things I wanted to discuss privately with him.

"Dave," I began, "have you ever flown a Learjet?"

"No. But I've ridden in the right seat some."

We sat there, again, in silence. Dave finally spoke up.

"You know, Bobby, I hate to bring this up," he apologized, "but we may have another problem." I looked at him warily. "You know, Sam's had his nose in that flight manual every waking hour of the day and night since we've been here. How many hours did you say he has?"

"Nine hundred fifty in Lears is what he told me. Shit, Dave, I've been wondering the same thing. For a 950-hour Learjet pilot, he ought to know it by heart."

"That's what I think, too," Dave said with concern, "and he's been asking me a lot of questions about the jet systems. More than he should. He ought to know the answers to the questions he's been asking."

Neither one of us wanted to voice the concern, so we sat there, once again quiet.

"Dave," I opened a new line of thought, "I know what I'm going to do. I'm a damned good pilot. A lot better than my four hundred hours of time indicate. If you sit in the right seat, work the flaps and the gear, I'll fly that baby. I've never been in a jet except for commercial airlines. But I know I can do it. It's got engines and wings, I can fly it. You know the systems better than anyone else I've ever seen."

"You're serious, aren't you?" he asked.

"Dave, I've got no choice. I know damned well I can take it off and land it. I'm not going to fly it forty thousand feet or in weather. Shit, I've got a *little* sense. But I have a WAC chart. I'll fly her low, below the clouds, and I can find my way home."

"You crazy son of a bitch," Dave cried. "Hell, yes, I'll fly with you."

"Just one thing, Dave," I warned, "and I'm deadly serious. If we run into a problem, any problem at all, and we see we have to set her down, I'm going to put her in the water. Once she breaks ground, 464 Juliet will never touch Colombian soil again. I mean it, Dave."

"OK, Bobby. Agreed. We're on. And if we die together, shoot, we're in good company."

This conversation with Dave revealed even more than I already knew about his quality as a man. Like me, he was willing to accept a challenge, even a highly dangerous one. He had no patience with those who believed only that something was impossible. He, too, believed that a person had to make things possible, make things happen. He believed in me, and I believed in him.

We shook hands and walked upstairs purposefully. Sam was there, still with his nose in the manual. Dave and I exchanged meaningful glances. Raul was on the phone. I motioned for Sam to join me on the bed by the telephone, and Raul, sensing that something important was brewing, hung up.

"Sam," I said, "I'll get right to the point. Dave told me about your talk with him. I understand how you feel. If you want, you can leave in the morning."

Sam was caught off guard by my abrupt introduction of the matter of the doubts he was harboring.

"Look, Bobby," he said apologetically, "This is nothing personal. The thing is, we've already been here eleven days and I still haven't been able even to get inside 464 Juliet. I've been watching you every day—running here, running there, putting out fires, making deals—now Aerocivil, next the Air Force. I just don't think you're going to get her out. That's my honest opinion."

I was controlling my mounting rage with difficulty. The mind games had been eroding at my self-control. To come so far, to be so close, and then to hear this negative thinking from somebody who was supposed to be all-in and on my team.

"Sam, don't you worry about Bob Wood," I managed to speak evenly, "You go on home. I'll get her out."

"What about Mel Cruder? Could he come down?"

"No," Dave answered, "we already called him. He's gone for a week or so."

"Who are you going to get to fly her, then?" Sam asked.

"I'm going to do it, Sam. I'm going to fly her, with Dave."

"I thought you never flew a Learjet," he protested.

"No, sir, I ain't never, but every one of those beauties has two engines and a pair of wings. I might not be as good as you are or some other jet jockey, but I'll get her off the ground, and back down again, alive."

Sam didn't know which way to turn. I looked at him levelly and we both were thinking, I was sure, of his big spiel at my office about how badly he wanted to fly Learjets. And now, he was abandoning me. He was feeling guilty, and I was happy to know it.

"Don't worry, Sam," I finished off in a low key, "I'll get by," and I picked up a magazine to punctuate the end of the conversation.

Sam and Dave walked into the other room. In about a half an hour they returned.

"Bob," Sam began, "I'd like to talk with you. I'm sorry for what I said. I'll stick it out. I just can't leave you here to do it alone. Dave showed me what an asshole I've been; so, I figure it this way: if you've got the balls to fly a jet alone, I respect you for it and I ain't going nowhere."

After a few moments of silence, I answered, picking my words carefully.

"Sam, thanks, I appreciate this; but let's get one thing clear—be sure you know, what you're saying. I can't have you with cold feet. If this is your decision, you'll just have to take it all the way. Win or lose."

"Bob, say no more. I'm your man."

Raul had watched us all the time in a state of nervous agitation. He was no bird man, and I was sure he would have been ready to swim back to Florida before he would have set foot in a jet flown by Bobby Wood.

Sam's decision was good news to all of us, but to Raul it was like a reprieve from certain death.

CHAPTER FORTY-THREE

We got off to our usual early start, to meet Domingo, the Esso Colombiana truck driver, at the fuel depot. Raul had called and arranged for him to meet us there. We first bought seven more drums, which were no problem, thanks to our amigo, Guillermo Sanchez, who had originally authorized their sale to us by the company. After they had been filled, we were on our way. No problems at the gateway to hell. Donado's letter of authorization was still good as gold. A stop in Ciénaga to pick up Aldo and then on to the airport.

After making us wait fifteen minutes, Baratta grudgingly opened the gate and let us enter. He had been informed by his boss, Zapata, that *señor* Wood was not to be subjected to any more of Baratta's bullshit. He had to let us in, but he was not rushing to do so.

Rather than unload the drums, we pumped the fuel directly from the truck which saved us from sweating them off in the hot sun. After we finished the fuel transfer, I made my customary inspection of 464 Juliet.

"Raul, take a look at this," I hollered. He came around to the left rear of 464 Juliet where I stood, shaking my head, cursing at a series of dents in the fuselage. Dave and Sam joined us.

"Somebody made those with a rifle butt," Sam observed. There were several large and deep dents in the aluminum fuselage. Several soldiers were staring at us warily, so I just walked away. There was no sense in starting any new problems. They would probably burn her if I made trouble.

I handed Raul two hundred dollars and told him to give it to the soldiers. I knew what the dents were—a forceful hint that they had received nothing for the protection of my property. I had to go along with it in the meantime. But I had to get 464 Juliet out of there soon.

Sam was thinking positively again after our talk of the night before, busying himself in the cockpit and checking everything carefully. He just shook his head when we opened the nose cowls.

"You weren't exaggerating a bit, Bob," he said, "This sure as hell isn't standard equipment," and he pointed to the rocks.

Dave and I took meticulous care to seal the tanks of the Lear jet, melting wax and dripping it on the sides of the fuel caps and the retaining rings. If someone tampered with the fuel system, we would know it on the ground, not aloft. We then methodically took the further precautions of applying almost half a roll of two-hundred-mile-per-hour silver duct tape to double-seal the fuel caps. Dave secured 464 Juliet when we were finished, removing the batteries.

We immediately left to get back to Barranquilla to find out if there was any news about the telex and for me to place a call to Paul Engstrom. I made the call from Telecom, and when I had Engstrom on the phone, I kept him in suspense with the old Colombian routine which I had been learning since the very first day I had arrived and had finally decided to adopt as my own—"the polite preliminaries."

Finally, I made the announcement I had been dying to make and which Paul had been waiting to hear.

"Paul," I said proudly, "*la providencia* is finished. Signed, sealed, and official. This past Saturday we had the 'material delivery' ceremony at the airport. Juliet is released, unconditionally, and fueled; all we are waiting for now is the authorization from Bogotá to leave."

Paul was excited and thrilled. He sounded like a kid with a new toy as he exulted and congratulated me on the fulfillment of my "mission impossible."

We spoke for several minutes.

"Paul, I want to ask you about the deadline. Is it still extended?" I asked.

"Don't worry about that," he assured me, "just get her out and let me know when you're back home."

I promised he would be the first to know, and we said our goodbyes. I had a fine feeling as I walked out of the booth.

We went directly to Donado's office. It was almost two thirty in the afternoon. Donado was clearly not looking forward to our arrival, as he still had no news for us. He had even sent another telex that morning and had called his superior in Bogotá. No answer.

This was the first concrete indication that someone in Bogotá did not want 464 Juliet to leave. We left in a downcast mood to return to the hotel to wait.

At six thirty, Raul telephoned Donado. Still no reply from Bogotá.

"OK, Raul," I decided abruptly, "Call Salgado. Right away. Then call Alfredo. Tell Salgado that Donado sent a telex on Saturday and another this morning. That we're stuck here."

Raul reached Salgado almost immediately and explained our dilemma. Salgado told Raul to call again the next morning, at his office, at nine in the morning. If we still had no telex, he would go directly to Aerocivil and handle the matter personally. Heads would roll in Bogotá, he implied strongly.

We then spoke with Alfredo, who said he would get in touch with Dr. Salgado to help him in any way Salgado thought fitting.

Another sleepless night. Another "*mañana*" in a treadmill of "*mañana*s."

Tuesday, August 26, 1980

Raul was on the telephone talking with Salgado at nine o'clock. Donado had told us that he had received nothing from Bogotá. He had spoken again with his superior, who had informed Donado that the delays were being caused by "higher-ups" in Bogotá. Raul was telling Salgado that no authorization had been sent and repeated Donado's information that the delays were emanating from someone "higher up."

Salgado instructed Raul to wait, that he would go to Aerocivil headquarters immediately.

"I must show them how to administer Colombian law," Salgado had told Raul. We were to stay in the room to wait for his call. He would settle the matter.

Raul was wide-eyed when he finished the conversation. It was the first time he had ever seen Salgado display anything but the mildest of emotions.

"Salgado is furious," he told me. "He's plenty pissed—I never heard him like this."

The suspense was intolerable as we sat by the phone, willing it to ring. We knew that the "push" had come to the "shove" in Bogotá. It was a showdown of power in the capital city—Salgado against the "higher-ups" in the government.

We jumped as if stung when the telephone rang at eleven thirty-five. It was Donado. Still no telex. Raul quickly explained that we were keeping the line open for Salgado's call and rushed Donado, who hurried to tell us that he knew Salgado was already at the Aerocivil office in Bogotá.

At 12:09 p.m., the phone rang again. It was Salgado. We huddled around Raul with our eyes glued to his face, listening to his "*sí*'s" and waiting for the telltale smile to appear. Finally, we saw it breaking across his face, like the sun after a storm.

"Good news, Bobby," he exulted as he hung up, "Dr. Salgado was at the office of the *Jefe* of Aerocivil. He said the telex of authorization would definitely be sent today—before six in the evening."

We all leaped to our feet with war whoops and stamping feet.

"Wait, Bobby, there's one thing more," Raul stopped me in my tracks.

"The problem has been with the Air Force all along," he went on, "they wanted the Learjet to be flown to Barranquilla first—not Aruba."

Why?" I asked, puzzled.

"I don't know; Salgado didn't say. But I think it might be that they still wanted the jet. They're not happy. They must be afraid of looking bad; remember, their mechanics examined the airplane and declared that she was not airworthy. And that the President had wanted 464 Juliet for himself. So I guess somebody is in trouble over that. Anyway, Salgado said to relax, he straightened them out."

We immediately called Donado to tell him the news. After we had finished talking with him, we were suddenly left with empty hands and at loose ends after the excitement had died down.

We sat around impatiently for the rest of the afternoon, waiting for the long-delayed telex. I was happy with Salgado's news, but would not really be fully content until we had it in our hands.

By five thirty, I was again staring at my watch, counting off the slow minutes. At five forty-five, the phone rang. Raul answered.

It was Donado. The telex had arrived. We would be right over.

We rushed downstairs and hurriedly hailed a cab, telling the driver we wanted to go to the airport, pronto. We raced into Donado's office; he was standing there waiting for us, his chest thrust out, delighted to be the bearer of good tidings.

"I'm very happy for you, Bobby," he chuckled gleefully, and then, more seriously, "Now, I'll tell you—I really didn't think it could be done. I didn't think you could pull it off. I still don't know how you did it, but you succeeded. That airplane has been a thorn in my side for three long years. I will kiss her goodbye without regret. My congratulations," and he shook my hand formally in best military fashion.

"When can we leave?" was my first question.

"In the morning, if you like. All that is left to do is for the Air Force to stamp the flight plan. I don't anticipate any problems—not after this authorization from Bogotá. They are closed now—the major has gone home. He'll be in his office between eight and eight thirty tomorrow morning."

I nodded eagerly.

"Just one thing, Bobby," Donado said, "I honestly wish you would reconsider going directly to Aruba. You really should have a test flight, and Barranquilla is only fifty miles away. It will be much safer than going out right away over the water, almost 275 miles. If you have any problems, you know what will happen."

"Donado, I thank you for your concern. But once we have the gear up, 464 Juliet will never again touch Colombian soil."

Donado took no offense; he merely smiled, as he was fully aware that I was in a burning haste to write a finish to this terribly frustrating and mind-destroying period of my life.

"What I would like to do, Donado, is to go to Santa Marta early in the morning to get the jet ready. I will have Gustavo come back here to pick up the flight plan after it is stamped. He will bring it to me in Santa Marta."

We sat together with Donado for a while longer, relaxing and thanking each other. A true bond had been made between us, and we were taking a little time to savor it. Of all the Colombians I had met, he was the one I best related to, and I admired his sincerity and honesty and complete lack of bullshit.

When we returned to the hotel and walked into the room, I held up the telex wordlessly. I had a tear in my eye and a lump in my throat and couldn't have said a word without my voice breaking.

> PROCEED FLIGHT SANTA MARTA/ARUBA MIAMI
> PROVIDED LEGAL REQUIREMENTS OF COMPETENT LOCAL
> AUTHORITIES ARE MET IN THAT LOCALITY. REGARDS.
> COLONEL GUILLERMO FERRERO ASSISTANT CHIEF
> AEROCIVIL

Again we launched into shouts and cheers and slaps on the back. It was midnight before we calmed down.

I prayed long into the night, thanking God for providing me with unknown strength and wisdom to finish my task. I wasn't yet out, but it was clear I had won. And I had not fallen victim to the Colombian scams, which was no small accomplishment in itself.

WEDNESDAY, AUGUST 27, 1980

Raul telephoned Valdez again. We had spoken with him the night before to tell him the good news. I had asked Raul to call again as a precautionary measure, just in case ... .

"*Señor Juez*," Raul said, "Bobby asked me to ask you to do him a favor. He would like you to stay close to a telephone today, just in case we have any problems."

Valdez assured Raul he would be standing by should we need him. I was somewhat surprised that he had not offered to come to the airport to see us off, but at least we could reach him if this were necessary. As a matter of fact, I was even a little worried about Valdez's "no show" for the occasion. I had an uneasy feeling that he was lying low, fearful of having a confrontation that he could possibly handle from the safe haven of his home or office, but not publicly where he might not be able to impose his authority.

We already had our bags packed and were ready to leave by seven. Spirits were feverishly high and adrenalin was pumping through tense bodies. Gustavo was on time. I gave him last-minute instructions on those who had to stamp the flight plan besides the Air Force. I was sure Donado would make no mistakes, but I was covering every possible eventuality.

7:20 A.M.

Raul, Sam, Dave, and I bade farewell to the clerks at the desk of the Hotel Royal and left with Aquiles, Toño, and the Donado boys. Fernando drove his father's truck and followed the rest of us who were taking Ramon's taxi.

8:30 A.M.

We pulled up to Aldo's house. He was putting mileage on his rocking chair, waiting for us. Within twenty minutes, we had Donado's truck packed and then bade the Reyes family goodbye, thanking them for their kindness and promising to return.

9:20 A.M.

Baratta, with a particularly surly air, stomped over to unlock the gate for us. I cut him a spiteful look as we pulled through in our truck. My mind was on Gustavo and the flight plan, and I racked my brains to think if I had left anything undone. My stomach was in a nervous turmoil as we unloaded our baggage and the equipment and parts we were taking back to the United States. The soldiers scarcely glanced at us, half asleep in a lazy torpor, while Dave installed the batteries and opened the jet. Dave proceeded with his last-minute inspection, while I carefully removed the silver duct tape sealing the fuel caps.

"Dave," I observed, "No one has messed with the fuel: the wax is intact."

We were all relieved to know that this possible trouble had been avoided.

Then I started the slow trial-and-error job of stowing our luggage, parts, tools, and bundles. Every inch of space was needed, so our load had to be fitted in precisely without wasting a square inch.

I had just finished and was stepping out of the door when I heard Toño yelling to Aldo and pointing to the entrance gates. Two large military stake body trucks roared through the gate, right toward us.

"Oh, shit, Raul," I groaned, "we have company."

Raul stared speechless as they squealed to a halt in front of us. Soldiers swarmed out and surrounded us, motioning with their guns. We were to get away from the jet—it was government property, they ordered us. Their guns were urging us to go to the terminal.

Raul and Fernando began arguing violently with the officer in charge.

Aldo, remained true to his cowardly form and never once opened his mouth. There he stood, the bastard, with twenty-one thousand dollars of my money in his pockets, doing nothing.

"Aldo, what the hell's going on?" I demanded. "Get your finger out of your ass and do something. Act like a lawyer. This is my airplane. Read them my fuckin' rights."

"But they're military, Bobby," he quavered in terror, "I can't do anything."

"Raul, call Valdez," I shouted. "Right now!"

Raul sped to find a telephone. Dave, Sam, and the others were speechless, and then everyone, it seemed, at once, burst into questions that I could not answer.

"Look, relax a minute. Give me some time to figure this out." They obediently found a bench.

After an eternally long fifteen minutes, Raul and Fernando came down the stairs at a trot. Raul the diplomat had turned into Raul the tiger. He had fire in his eyes.

He marched up purposefully and motioned me to follow.

"What's going on, Raul?" I wanted to know, mystified by his new and commanding bearing. "These bastards can't do this."

"I know, I know," he said, tight-lipped, as we rapidly approached the compound, "I just spoke to Valdez. He's calling the colonel now."

The soldiers signaled for us to stop, pulling together into formation to block us.

"Who's in charge here?" Raul demanded in a clipped voice.

One of the soldiers stepped forward smartly and pointed to a sergeant standing in the compound door. Raul imperiously pushed through the formation of soldiers and planted himself squarely in front of the sergeant.

"Sergeant, I have just spoken with Judge Valdez. He's calling your colonel at this very moment. You have no authority to prevent us from leaving. The release of the jet is now law in the Republic of Colombia. You are exceeding your authority."

Even at the height of my anxiety and fury, I was marveling at this new side of my old smiling amigo Raul. He glared at the sergeant when he had delivered his information.

The sergeant was protesting that he had been given orders—no one was to go near the jet.

This added to my alarm. Was I being screwed, or was this merely a reappearance of the ever-present *Dinero* Syndrome? I again leaped into the argument, unable to remain quiet. At its loudest, the sergeant was suddenly distracted by one of the soldiers emerging from the compound and clamoring for his attention.

"*Venga, pronto.* The colonel is on the radio," he was shouting at the sergeant, who rushed into the radio room, with Raul and me close on his heels.

The colonel's voice crackled over the speaker. The conversation was short, over almost as soon as it started, and I didn't understand a word. The sergeant said nothing to us. He left the compound and we followed. Motioning to his men, they jumped back in the truck and departed as suddenly as they had arrived.

"What was that all about, Raul?" I asked.

"It was their colonel. He told them to leave. Valdez must have got hold of him right away."

He nodded in satisfaction and took Fernando to find the others to give them the "all clear" signal. I walked over to the jet, completely drained. The mind games were still being played. I was reeling from this latest dizzying sequence of randomly programmed "up's" and "down's." Every time I thought I was coming up to the wire, a new set of complications would appear from nowhere, new obstacles between me and the goal, leaving me disoriented and confused.

10:45 A.M.

Raul was still pissed off, as much as I, at Aldo the asshole. I pointedly ignored that spineless excuse of a man, who hovered around us, mumbling defensively that there was nothing he could have done. Sam was sitting in the cockpit, pre-flighting the Learjet. Dave worked feverishly at his last-minute details.

I paced back and forth, waiting for Gustavo. It was almost eleven fifteen, and he was still not there. Was he having problems with the Air Force? There could be no other reason for his delay. Where the hell was he.

"Bobby," Sam called, "Come here."

Dave and I both stepped into the cockpit to see what was wrong.

"I tried the flaps," Sam told us with a worried look, "They're not working."

Dave rapidly chose some tools and positioned himself under Juliet near the flaps. After several minutes he stood up to tell us that we had a bad switch.

"Can you hot-wire it?" I suggested. "You know—bypass the switch?"

"Shoot, I guess so—I'll try," he responded.

Dave worked deftly for about fifteen minutes, and then he told Sam to hit the flap switch again. This time it worked. Dave and I exchanged relieved smiles as he stood up.

"No problem ... ," he said calmly.

Sam and Dave checked the flaps several more times and were finally satisfied that the repair would hold up.

Raul and I stood at the nose of 464 Juliet worrying silently and out loud about Gustavo. We were standing on tiptoe to try to see down the road. Finally, a taxicab pulled around to the rear of the terminal. Shortly after, we could see Gustavo. He was walking with confidence, I was happy to see.

"Do you have it?" I shouted when he was within earshot. He was still fifty feet away, but he reached into his shirt and triumphantly flourished a piece of light blue paper. It was the flight plan.

"Bobby," Gustavo was saying, as he walked up to us, "It was really a bad scene in Barranquilla."

I almost snatched it from his hand when he was beside us and scanned it with loving eyes.

"What happened? What took you so long?" I wanted to know.

"Wait, I'll tell you everything. Before I do, though, I want to tell you how lucky you are to have a friend like Luis Donado. If it weren't for Donado, you'd never be able to leave here."

Gustavo related that he had been with Donado at eight fifteen and that they had gone to see the major at Air Force headquarters. The major refused to sign or stamp the flight plan. The major told Donado that he had orders, received direct from his general, that 464J was not to leave Colombia. It was to be flown only to Barranquilla. Why? He wouldn't say. The men had argued and talked for almost an hour. Donado was being very reasonable at first, talking about *la providencia,* which had, in effect, now become law, establishing *señor* Wood's legal possession of the Learjet, and don't forget the *diligencia*, also law, which had given *señor* Wood "material delivery" of the airplane. Calls were made to Bogotá.

Donado and the major were friends as well as closely associated officials of the Colombian government, but the major had remained unyielding, inflexible in the face of Donado's reasoned and compelling arguments. Donado's temper had risen, but he was restraining himself from speaking rashly. He had finally resorted to pleading, calling in favors, reminding the major that he "owed" a few to Donado.

Finally, the major had received a telephone call. Either Donado's pleading or the telephone call, or both, had turned the tide. Perhaps Salgado had exerted pressure on someone in Bogotá—Gustavo didn't know—anyway, the major had finally stamped and signed it.

"You were lucky, really lucky," he concluded, "to have Donado on your side."

This was the pure, unadulterated truth. I was infinitely touched by

Donado's loyalty and support. I knew it ran against every fiber of his proud temperament to beg, which was what he had done to help me.

I again read through the flight plan which had cost my good friend Donado so dearly. It was, to me, a document of significance, a modern-day "Declaration of Independence" representing the struggle, sacrifice, and dedication to purpose all my team had put to the effort.

The three stamps and signatures on the flight plan were all in order. Two were from Aerocivil, one being from the Technical Control Unit (Donado's) and the second from the Air Transit Unit. The third was from the Command of FAC, the Colombian Air Force in Barranquilla. Still a fourth stamp was needed, which I was to obtain at the Simón Bolívar Airport.

"Let's go, Raul," I said, grabbing his arm, "we've got to go up to the tower and have them stamp the flight plan. Then we'll haul ass out of here."

Breathless, Raul, Gustavo, and I reached the top step to the control tower. It was sparsely equipped with the bare minimum of furnishings and equipment—several chairs, a radio, several wind direction and wind speed instruments, an altimeter, and several other outmoded instruments. The baseline necessities.

A young Colombian, barely in his twenties, sat in front of an oscillating fan, which languidly stirred the hot air. He was wiping the sweat from his forehead as we entered.

"Is Tomás around?" Raul asked.

"No, Tomás is off duty," said the young man.

Next, Raul handed him the flight plan, saying, "It has to be stamped and signed."

Finally, Raul brought out the telex of authorization, for which we had waited so many anxious hours, concluding, "Here is our confirmation for departure from Bogata, and if you will look right there," pointing to the flight plan, "you'll see the required Air Force seal."

The young man looked it over and handed it back to Raul. "I'm sorry," he stated, "I can't sign or stamp this. The flight plan is a forgery."

"What are you talking about?" Raul screamed. "Not only the Air Force signed this—can't you see that the Technical Unit and the Air Transit Section of Aerocivil have also stamped it and signed it?"

"*No, señor* . The documents are false. So is your telex," the boy stated nervously, licking his lips.

I couldn't believe that this young boy, scarcely out of his teens, could be acting on his own initiative in questioning documents that were obviously authentic. I suggested that Raul question him to get some answers. It was just as I had figured it.

"*Señor* , I have orders from the Commandant at FAC headquarters," he finally disclosed. "This flight plan is a forgery. The order is supposed to read that 464J is to be flown to Barranquilla—not Aruba."

We were almost ready to throw the kid out of the window. Fernando had appeared during our exchange and entered into the argument.

"You're going to be in big trouble," he assured the boy, "My father is *Jefe* of Aerocivil in Barranquilla. That's his signature and seal. Call him on the radio … or call the major in Barranquilla. Do it now."

The boy mumbled that the radio was not working, it was weak, and the Barranquilla frequency was out. He was suddenly defiant.

"Anyway, my orders come from the Air Force. I'm doing what I'm told to do."

"I've had enough of this bullshit," I told Raul. "Make this little bastard put it in writing—his exact orders—and remind him that his ass is going to be reamed out, but good."

Raul handed the boy the flight plan and the telex and ordered him to take out a piece of paper and pen. The only official paper he had were the Communication forms of Aerocivil in a pad on the desk. Raul watched over his shoulder as he wrote the following:

> *Santa Marta, August 27, 1980*
> *This is to explain the delay in the takeoff of N464J due to the fact that the flight plan presented is for Aruba, and this tower received an order from the Commandant of CACOM 3 in Barranquilla specifying that said aircraft cannot present a flight plan for outside the country.*
> *The seal of the Control Tower and the young man's signature were affixed at the bottom, together with a stamped date.*

Raul took the paper from him and we left the tower, reminding him of what was going to happen soon to his ass. Down on the ground once more, we returned to 464 Juliet. Another "down" had plunged me yet again into deep depression after my short-lived "up" due to Donado's invaluable support. I kicked at the pebbly soil, wondering what would happen next.

Raul perked up suddenly, and I followed his gaze. Tomás, the control tower supervisor, had returned.

"Tomás," Raul was shouting, "We got a problem … ."

He hurriedly explained what had taken place a few minutes before, up in the control tower. Tomás was shown the flight plan and the telex.

"Come with me," he said, "I'll take care of this."

We charged back up the stairs behind him. Tomás stepped into the room, curtly ordering the young man off duty. The boy snatched up a few personal belongings and left.

"Relax, Bobby," Tomás reassured me, "he was just following orders. I talked with Zapata and I know all your paperwork is legal."

I watched as Tomás stamped and signed the flight plan, wondering what else could happen. When he finished, I gave him a hundred dollar bill, and thanked him warmly. He acted surprised and gratified at the unexpected tip.

"Don't forget, *señor* Wood," he reminded me, "the next time you come back we'll talk about the 'business.'"

I winked and nodded as we descended the stairs once more. He called after me, shouting *hasta luego* in a cheerful voice and then asking me to be sure to call the tower's frequency when we were ready to leave.

1:30 P.M.

A sizable crowd was beginning to gather as news of 464 Juliet's flight spread across the grapevine. Raul went in to immigration and customs to attend to the stamping of our passports, which was routine procedure. He was back shortly, informing me that the passports wouldn't be stamped inside, the customs official was coming out to us.

"She wants a couple of hundred dollars—I guess she doesn't want anyone to see," he whispered.

Five minutes later, a neatly dressed young woman was gliding out to 464 Juliet, holding her clipboard and smiling brightly. At least the people screwing us were getting prettier, I thought to myself. She gathered up our passports and left for her office. Ten minutes later she returned. Raul slipped her the two hundred dollars, and she flashed him a coquettish smile and left. Even the ladies were subject to the *Dinero* Syndrome.

"OK, all of you," I shouted, "let's go."

As they made a move to get on board, I heard someone shouting at us. It was a short, neatly-dressed Colombian, already halfway across the ramp.

"Who is he?" I asked, "What the hell does he want?"

Raul didn't know—we would have to see. We met the man in the middle of the ramp.

"I am *señor* Meisel, of DAS," he introduced himself, showing a badge. "Where do you think you're going?"

Raul told him we were cleared to leave and were doing just that. All our papers were in order—and we showed them to *señor* Meisel.

"Sorry," he snapped, "you haven't been cleared by DAS."

Raul jumped in immediately, telling the DAS agent that Dr. Salgado, the Supreme Court Justice of Bogotá, had assured us that if 464J was not allowed to leave Colombia that very day, heads would roll in Santa Marta. He told Meisel that the head of DAS in Bogotá was an intimate friend and next-door neighbor of Salgado's. Meisel would be in real trouble if he tried to stop us, against the orders of two such important men.

Meisel was upset, but stuck to his guns.

"Why are you making problems?" he asked Raul accusingly. "You are Colombian. This Americano has been paying everybody here at the airport. Why not me? Has he forgotten about me?"

I was at my wits' end. These chiseling Colombians literally had to be scraped off the door while we were closing it, ready to warm up for takeoff.

I reached into my pocket and took out five hundred dollars.

"Raul, I'm giving this Johnny-come-lately mother fucker five hundred. That's it. No more. He can either take us to jail or let us the hell out of here."

Meisel took the five hundred with a mollified look, quickly checking the amount. He was satisfied that at the last possible minute he had been able to snatch some of the wealth that had almost slipped from his grasp.

Raul was surprised that he had been displaced from his role as intermediary in our pay-off transactions. As Meisel left, Raul was patting me on the shoulder and telling me to relax.

"Let's get out of here before someone else crawls out of the woodwork," I fumed. "There's no such word as 'end' here."

We turned and walked back once again to 464 Juliet.

2:25 P.M.

Clouds were scattered across the blue sky as the sun shone down on us. The crowd of curiosity seekers eyed us avidly. I was almost afraid to set foot into 464 Juliet for fear of something else going wrong. I was in far from a sociable mood, but my amigos were here and they deserved a pat on the back for their help. I shook hands and smiled, repeating my thanks. I didn't want even to look at Aldo. Throughout that entire day, as always, he had never said a single word to anyone who was hassling me. Several Avianca pilots and employees came over and looked inside 464 Juliet. I had a feeling they were taking bets as to whether we would make it. They shook their heads in disbelief—464 Juliet was so loaded I didn't blame them.

Checking some last minute details, I pulled Sam over to the right side of 464 Juliet.

"Sam, this is it—we're down to the wire. I know you're not happy about the way we're overloaded."

"That's for sure. We're twenty-five hundred pounds over gross, but I'm not worried about that. It's the engines—if we have a problem, you know what's going to happen. Do the guys know?"

"Yes, Sam, I told them. But let me finish. If we lose one on takeoff—well, let's say goodbye now. But if we make it to any kind of altitude and have a problem, I want you to understand one thing: We are not, repeat, not going to set her back down in Colombia. Never. We'll put her in the water first. I'll never give these sons of bitches here the pleasure of her company'."

Sam was listening carefully.

"Bobby, after what I've seen here, I don't blame you. I can only imagine what you've been through here for the last three or four months. To tell you the truth, I can't handle another day here, either."

Sam and I left many things unsaid that we understood by mutual and unspoken consent now that the chips were down.

Fernando was taking pictures of this momentous day, and he snapped another as I pulled the door of 464 Juliet closed. I climbed into the cockpit with Sam and fastened my seat belt. I was moving as if in a dream, not able to believe it was happening. I tried to erase all the events of the day from my mind. At that very moment, Juliet needed my complete attention.

I pulled out the checklist and glanced over at Sam to my left. Sweat was pouring from his forehead, both from the heat and from nerves. I started calling out the checklist. Sam replied to each item.

Control locks—OK.
Jet pumps—OK.
Circuit breakers—in.
Gear switch—down.
Batteries—on.
Parking brake—set.
Emergency pitch trim—OK.
Trim—set.
Standby fuel pumps—OK.
I continued down the checklist.

"Bob, set your VI (velocity indicator) bug on 128 knots. Remember, call wheel master as soon as we reach sixty knots—or as soon as your airspeed indicator moves. Call VI at 128 knots and rotate at 135 knots."

I went on with the checklist.

"Sam, Dave, look at the voltage," I called. "We're down to twenty-two volts." Twenty-three volts is the minimum requirement; I knew if she tried to "hang up" or "hot start" we would be in trouble.

"Well, Bobby," said Dave, "all we can do is pray."

"OK, Sam—ready?" I asked.

Sam, the sweat pouring down his face, nodded.

I grabbed the right generator start switch and put it in the start position, shouting, "Come on, baby."

The tachometer climbed: 8 percent—9 percent—10 percent, and

Sam placed the throttle in idle position. We heard a small "woof" as the jet fuel ignited. Slowly, now the engine started to wind up: 15 percent—20 percent—25 percent. The tachometer slowed down and slowly crept to 27 percent—28 percent—30 percent—35 percent—38 percent. We were holding our breath. Our one minute had elapsed when she finally reached 48 percent—idle speed.

With a tremendous sigh of relief, I put the switch in generator position. Sam was mopping the sweat from his face. Dave was beaming and giving us the "thumbs up" sign. We pushed the throttle forward to 70 percent and let her charge up the batteries for about five minutes.

We were on pins and needles as I put the left engine gen-start switch in the start position. I let her wind up for ten seconds or so. The left tachometer was inoperable, so we had, to estimate the 10 percent required RPM before putting the throttle in the idle position. We heard a faint "woof" as the left engine started to wind up. Finally, after about forty-five seconds, I flipped the switch to gen position. The amp meter jumped to almost two hundred amps. Dave gave us another "thumbs up" sign.

Inverts on—check: I went on down the checklist very cautiously.

Oil pressure—good.

Hydraulic pressure—OK.

Yaw dampener—check.

Anti-skid—Inop.

Spoilers—check.

Flaps—takeoff.

OK, set. Checklist complete.

Sam looked at me and Dave.

"Shit," I said, "It's now or never."

I glanced at Raul, whose lips were trembling as he made the sign of the Cross.

"Relax, refugee," I comforted him, "it'll soon be over."

Dave handed me the microphone from the portable radio I had brought down. Dave had wired the portable radio antenna into the aircraft antenna so we would have better range. The portable had only a five-watt output and it needed all the help it could be given.

"Santa Marta tower—Learjet 464 Juliet requests permission to taxi to runway three six."

I waited in frozen silence for a response. Would they stop me now? Would they shoot the tires out? God only knew—it was in His hands, after all.

I repeated the request to the tower. There were several seconds of screaming silence. Finally, "Learjet 464 Juliet … taxi to runway three six."

I could feel tears scalding my eyeballs and was shaken with a shudder of total elation. Life or death held no more fears for me. Just leaving here, nothing else mattered.

The crowd outside had stepped back, holding protective hands over their ears as Sam pushed the throttles forward. There was no doubt about it, 464 Juliet was really loaded. Sam pushed the throttles forward farther as she was refusing to budge. Finally, she moved forward.

"Sam," I pointed out, "We have to taxi down the runway. There's no taxiway here. As soon as we get on it, run her, fairly fast, and apply the brakes—hard. We have to burn off the rust on those floater plates."

Slowly 464 Juliet crept forward. We turned right, headed north across the ramp. Turning right again, we pulled onto the runway and headed south.

"Come on, Sam, faster," I urged. "Get some speed up. We've got to clean the brakes off."

Sam pushed the throttle up to 90 percent and after several applications of the brakes we came to the end of the runway and turned around.

We went through the checklist once again, praying we hadn't overlooked anything. Sam was wringing wet as he grabbed a rag to wipe his forehead.

"Remember, Bob, you work the throttles. Use 101 percent power."

I knew what he meant. I was worried only about the left engine. There was no way of telling how much power she was making as the tachometer was broken. The EPRS (Exhaust Pressure Ratio) was also inoperable. All I could do was to push the throttle forward, leading the right throttle ahead of the left. Setting the power by the right tachometer and then easing the left throttle to a position equal to the right—and praying hard.

"Ready?" I asked Sam, who nodded in the affirmative. "Santa Marta Tower … Learjet 464 Juliet ready for takeoff."

My nerves were vibrating as we waited. The seconds seemed like hours.

Finally, the radio gave us the magic words, "Learjet 464 Juliet … cleared to take off."

It was happening.

"Ready, Sam?" I pushed the throttles forward; right slightly leading the left, to 100 percent. Several seconds later, after stabilizing, I inched the right throttle to 101 percent and then matched the left throttle to it.

Juliet moved forward as her engines roared. I scanned the instrument panel for indications of any malfunction. Oil pressure, OK, and so on. We were now accelerating rapidly, and I glued my eyes to the airspeed indicator. No movement. Sam had his eyes glued on the runway.

Something was wrong. I knew we were moving faster than sixty knots. I quickly gave my airspeed indicator a sharp rap. It instantly responded by jumping to eighty knots.

"Wheel master," I shouted.

Sam released the steering button and was on rudder control. The airspeed was accelerating, "90—100—115—125—128 knots," I shouted. "130—135—140 knots."

"Rotate," I sang out.

Sam eased back on the yoke. We were really eating up the runway. Juliet proudly lifted her nose. I heard a "thump" and knew we had broken ground. I hadn't even seen her leave Colombian soil, but I was too busy for such ceremonies. I had my left hand on the throttles while I meticulously scanned the instrument panel. The left wing jerked a little as a cross wind caught us.

"Gear up," Sam was shouting as he leveled her up.

I raised the gear selector to the "up" position and monitored the hydraulic pressure—OK. Finally, three green lights.

"Gears secured," I called out.

Several seconds later Sam called, "Flaps up."

"Flaps up," I repeated.

"Ninety-eight percent power," Sam said.

Slowly I pulled the throttles back to 98 percent and matched the left with the right. Over and over, I scanned the instrument panel for any sign of trouble.

"Everything in green," I shouted.

Dave had his head inserted between mine and Sam's. He sure as hell was keeping us both honest.

"Beautiful, Sam—Bob," he breathed as he gave us his sign of approval.

Airspeed 260 knots. The checklist was complete. For the first time since we had moved forward, I raised my head and looked out the windshield. We were already at six thousand feet and climbing. We had been whisked high into the sky while Sam and I had been sweating out the backstage mechanics of the magical transformation. Off to my right was the magnificent range of the Sierra Nevada, taking my breath away with their beauty. The snowfields on the peaks sparkled liked diamonds in the sun.

In the cockpit there was silence, only the whispering of our flight. I broke it rudely but jubilantly.

"We're gone, you mother fuckers. We did it."

Sam, still solemn with concentration, even broke into a smile.

Never before or since in my life have I experienced the feelings I had inside that quietly whispering Learjet. I felt victorious, vindicated, master of my world. We had done the impossible. Juliet seemed to share the elation as she soared proudly on her way. She had her freedom, she would not falter.

"Sam," I suggested, "Let's take a short-cut." I was looking at the map on my knees. "There's no sense going any farther north to the coast. Turn right to 070 and go between those two mountain tops. We'll clear them easily and save thirty miles or so."

Sam turned right and leveled off at 11,500 feet.

"Ninety-one percent power, Bob," he instructed.

I eased the power back slowly. We were indicating 290 knots which gave us a ground speed of about 405 miles per hour. This was slow for a Learjet, but we had the power pulled back and were now in no hurry. I kept my WAC chart on my lap, checking carefully for landmarks along the coastline to make sure of our position.

Dave leaned forward and started working on the pressurization. It was not operating at all well; the cabin altitude was jumping from eight to eleven thousand feet.

"This could be a problem," he remarked, "when we go higher. We'll have to keep an eye on it."

Sam was now more relaxed. He cautiously leaned back and took a deep breath.

"Great, Sam," we all cheered.

"We fuckin' made it," I screamed again.

Sam beamed as he stuck out his chest and cleared his throat. "Piece of cake, Bob," he said, trying for a casual tone.

Raul had recovered sufficiently to join into the praise, a little shakily but heartfelt and enormously relieved. He was wringing wet, and I knew he must have felt like an experimental primate in a spacecraft. He had guts, though. Never once had he balked at getting aboard 464 Juliet, although I was certain he would rather happily have spent his own money to have returned home on a commercial flight even though he was never happy, even on the big airliners.

I pointed ahead to a large cloud build-up ahead.

"Sam, we need to turn right some. I think Riohacha is directly below those clouds."

Sam nodded and banked 464 Juliet to the right. The giant Sierra Nevada were still on my right but were beginning to diminish in height as they ran their way east. They seemed to be slowly melting into the terrain below.

As we passed about fifteen miles south of Riohacha, the skies opened up to welcome 464 Juliet. There was not a cloud in sight; the air was crystal clear with visibility at least eighty to a hundred miles.

It was as though the heavens were helping this mortal crew take 464 Juliet safely home.

"What time did we get off?" Sam was asking.

"Precisely 2:46," I said. "We should be at the northeast coast of the Guajira in about nineteen minutes. Then another twelve or fourteen minutes to Aruba … we should be in Aruba at about three forty … Sam, let's turn left now to zero six five or zero seven zero. We'd better get back on course. Look, everybody," I pointed to the ground below us. It was literally covered with hundreds of dirt strips, like stripes on a zebra.

There was one group of six or seven strips, running parallel to each other less than half a mile apart, as if they had been scored in the earth by a giant harrow.

Sam peered out of his window.

"Damn," was his comment, "I'm sure glad I don't have to land there. I wouldn't know which one to take. It would sure be hell for someone with astigmatism."

Our aerial panorama of the multitude of clandestine landing strips removed any lingering doubts in anyone's mind about the scope of the "business" operations in Colombia. If the inhabitants had worked as hard at farming their land as they had in building landing strips, Colombia would have been a place of milk and honey instead of poverty and misery.

"Please, Lord," I prayed as I looked out the windshield and saw about thirty miles ahead of us an irregular line that marked the coast of Colombia and the beginning of open water, "please just give us a few more minutes." My eyes scanned the sky for any sign of the Air Force.

My prayer had been answered. Not a plane in sight.

Finally, precisely at 3:23 P.M., we passed over the northern most part of Colombia, the head of the Guajira Peninsula. This split second seemed to hang paused as if time stood still. While it lasted, I had finally come to the full realization that 464 Juliet was on her way home. We all burst into shouts of excitement and satisfaction.

"Maiquetia Control ... Maiquetia Control ... Learjet November 464 Juliet is entering your airspace at 3:23 ... level 11,500 ... eighty miles southwest of Aruba on the two-five-six-degree radial Aruba VOR."

I tried five or six times and got no reply.

"Never mind, Bob," Sam suggested, "try Aruba tower. We need to start our descent in five minutes or so."

"Frequency 118.0," I said to Dave, who promptly set it for me.

"Aruba tower ... Learjet November 464 Juliet."

Several moments passed. I repeated the call. Finally, the response came back.

"Go ahead, 464 Juliet ... I read you loud and clear."

It was a relief to hear the voice. No Spanish accent on the other end.

"Yes, sir, Aruba tower ... 464 Juliet. We're about sixty DME on the two-five-six-degree radial. Inbound for landing. Unable to reach Maiquetia Control. They don't answer."

"464 Juliet ... Do you have Aruba in sight?"

"464 Juliet, negative," I replied.

"Report when airport in sight."

Sam eased the power back and started our descent.

"How far, Bob?" he asked. "Do you have the island in sight?"

"According to my watch, we're about thirty miles out."

Sam, Dave, and I strained our eyes looking for Aruba. All we could see were scattered clouds: 10,000—9,000—8,000—all the way down to 3,000 feet.

"Straight ahead," I shouted, pointing. "There she is, still about eighteen miles away."

"Aruba tower … Learjet 464 Juliet."

"Aruba tower … 464 Juliet go ahead."

"Airport in sight, 464 Juliet approximately fifteen miles west south west … request landing information." "Learjet 454 Juliet … Join the localizer approach twelve DME. Out. Report when established."

"Aruba tower … 464 Juliet unable … repeat … unable. We have no navigation equipment on board."

Several seconds of silence.

"Learjet 464 Juliet … report on three-mile final for runway eleven. Wind zero nine zero at fourteen knots. Altimeter 30.01."

"464 Juliet … Roger."

"There's the runway, Sam," I pointed.

"Yes, I've got it, Bob."

Sam pulled back the power to 80 percent and started down.

"Be ready to blow the gear down," Sam ordered as he sat up and leaned forward, taking a firm grip on the yoke, and, then, "OK, Bob, run the checklist."

I quickly spat out all the items except gear and flaps.

Hydraulic pressure—OK. Emergency air—OK.

"Aruba tower … Learjet 464 Juliet … Aruba tower … go ahead, Learjet 464 Juliet."

"Yes, sir, 464 Juliet on three-mile final for runway one one."

"Learjet 464 Juliet, clear to land. Wind 080, twelve knots. Altimeter 30.10."

"Check your bug, Bob," Sam said, asking me to check the airspeed, "and make sure it's set at 125 knots. Give me approach flaps."

"OK. Flaps approach."

"Gear down."

"Come on," I coaxed, "don't fail me now, baby … Gear down and three greens."

"Watch my speed, Bob," Sam warned, "don't let me get under 135."

"150 … 145 … ," I kept calling out, "135 … 135 … 130 … Power!

Power, Sam! Power! ... 135 ... 135 ... "

"Full flaps."

"OK, flaps full."

On short final, Sam eased the power back.

"125 ... 125 ... "

Again easing the power back, Sam gently brought the yoke back. Several small chirps of the tires and we were down.

There was no time for rejoicing.

"Spoilers," Sam snapped.

"Spoilers out. Hydraulic pressure ... OK."

Sam lowered her nose down to a perfect landing.

"Learjet 464 Juliet ... next left turn ... park at fuel depot."

"Learjet 464 Juliet, Roger."

"Retract spoiler ... checklist," Sam said, as he wiped the sweat from his forehead.

After we turned off the runway, Sam hit the pressurization dump switch. Instantly, the cockpit filled with fog. Sam slammed on the brakes; he couldn't see. Within several seconds the fog began to clear. Raul was wheezing and moaning in abject terror, and I was close behind. I thought we had a fire.

"Relax, Bob," Sam said, "I had to dump the cabin pressure. You'd have blown the door off if you had tried to open it."

As we slowed down, Dave was bent over, laughing hysterically. He knew what had happened.

We taxied over to the fuel depot and shut 464 Juliet down. Dave opened the door, and as soon as I could unbend my legs I jumped out and actually kissed the ground. Sam, Dave, Raul, and I stood around hugging each other, shaking hands and grinning foolishly. We had done the impossible.

We were just beginning to calm down when two Latin looking men approached us. One was dressed in a uniform similar to that of a policeman. The other wore slacks and a white casual shirt worn loose. They took out badges.

"Where did you come from?" the first asked sternly.

"From Santa Marta, Colombia," I answered.

"You entered here illegally," he snapped. "You didn't notify Maiquetia Control or Curacao Control. They have no flight plan on you."

"Hold on," I snapped back. "I called Maiquetia Control several times, and they didn't answer. And I did call Aruba. Check with the tower. Furthermore, I did file a flight plan. And I sent a telex—two, as a matter of fact—to the Civil Aeronautics Department here in Aruba, two weeks ago, notifying them of my arrival."

"Where are your documents?" he insisted.

I opened my briefcase and handed him the flight plan, the telex from Bogotá, and a copy of the telex I had sent to Aruba, along with my ferry permit.

"Look. Everything here is legal and in order. This plane has been in Colombia for three years. I removed it for Lloyd's of London. If you have any questions about who I am, call the FAA office in Miami, Florida. They are monitoring this flight. Ask for Mr. Red Garglay. He knows all the details about this flight. In fact, if you don't mind, I need to phone right now and advise him we are here in Aruba.

I was stretching the truth a little with these two officials and talking a little bigger than I felt, but I was getting to be a connoisseur of bullshit after my long days in Colombia. I was plowing right in and putting them on the defensive. Letting them know from the moment they had sounded their battle-cry that I was sure of my ground and was not backing down.

"We'll check these out," he grunted. "In the meantime, remove all the contents of this jet. Put the stuff outside. Right here," and he then pointed to the spot he had chosen.

"Take a look inside," I protested. "It took us hours to load it! Are you serious?"

"Right now, Mr. Wood," he insisted. "Empty the plane."

"OK, you guys. Let's get to it."

The two men stood by while we sweated and tugged and strained, trying our best to remember where the pieces belonged so we didn't have to rethink the puzzle when we repacked. Finally, every part, piece, box, bag, and tool was neatly stacked in the chosen spot.

The men moved in and opened every single thing we had, including taped boxes. It was a complete shakedown. Obviously, someone had tipped them off that we were coming, and they had expected to find more interesting cargo than our rag-tag collection of parts and worn clothing.

The agent with the white shirt climbed inside 464 Juliet and eased his broad rear into the right front passenger seat, smoking his cigarette and dropping ashes on the floor. Motioning the uniformed agent to enter, the latter climbed inside and dived under the instrument panel. I had a sinking feeling of something like paranoia—a premonition that he would emerge with a fifty-gram packet of cocaine and that the clock would mysteriously be turned backward to a day over three years earlier, like a rerun of an already viewed movie.

It truly looked like another perfect set up. I watched them carefully, bracing myself for a fake surprised announcement from the uniformed man emerging from under the instrument panel saying, "Well, look what I found."

I walked over to the door and said that I would have to notify the FAA in Miami and was going to find a telephone. The FAA office would soon be closed.

"Get back over there," the white shirt ordered.

As I turned around, I could see the other agent was still under the panel. Finally, they stepped out.

"Give me all your passports and driver's licenses," he ordered.

I couldn't believe this—it was just like Colombia.

Gathering up all our papers, they walked away. I silently cursed their retreating backs. I knew we were being hustled, but I didn't know a thing about their rules. However, I was intensely relieved to find that they hadn't planted anything on the airplane—at least not yet.

Some thirty minutes later they were back, handing us our papers and informing us that we could now clear customs and immigration. Not a word of apology for the inconvenience or that a mistake had been made.

Nothing made any sense. I had no idea of what they were looking for or what they thought they would find.

We spent the next hour and a half repacking the boxes they had rummaged. Then we had to crank 464 Juliet and move her across the field to Oduber Aviation. After clearing customs and immigration, who were extremely courteous, we went straight to the telephone office, where I called my wife, Terry. She knew I was to be home that day, with 464 Juliet in tow.

She was surprised to hear my voice and elated to know that I was already in Aruba—with 464 Juliet. She had a large reception waiting for us at Air Unlimited and was anxious for us to get there. However, the fact that 464 Juliet and Bobby Wood were both out of Colombia was good enough news to erase any disappointment about canceling that day's reception.

The meal I had that night was the best I have ever tasted. I had a New York strip and a baked potato. We sat around eating and talking for over three hours. It was a night I would never forget.

Thursday, August 28, 1980

We were up early, ringing bells. We were in Oduber Aviation by eight thirty. Raul and Sam were putting our bags back inside the jet when Dave called to me.

"Bobby, we have a problem," and he indicated a spot under 464 Juliet. There was a big puddle of hydraulic fluid on the ground, beneath the clear doors. Removing the tool box, we immediately dropped the right gear door and immediately spotted the problem. An aluminum hydraulic line had a pinhole in it. Dave had removed it in a few minutes. The line was a special one made of aluminum with compound bends.

"I have an idea, Dave," I said. "Oduber Aviation is a Cessna dealer. Let's go to the parts department and see if they have an oil pressure line. This is a No. 4 line, and Cessna uses some the same size. It won't be just like this one—it'll be a steel-braided flex—but we can still connect it up and stuff the excess hose into the wheel well and then tie-wrap it."

"You ain't bad for a redneck," Dave laughed.

After an hour, 464 Juliet was airworthy again with her makeshift hose patch, a tank topped with fuel, and our flight plan filed, we then departed for Port-au-Prince, Haiti. It was 450 miles over water with only a whisky compass; we cruised along at twenty thousand feet. God blessed us again with extremely clear skies, sprinkled with only a few puffy white clouds. Juliet whispered along like a happy angel in her element.

Finally, an hour and twenty-nine minutes later, we spotted Haiti. We dodged several large build-ups and landed with no problem on runway nine.

Sam was acting more confident now. There were no problems at customs; so, we quickly fueled 464 Juliet and filed our flight plan.

"How's the weather in Miami, Sam?" I asked.

"Thirty-five hundred feet scattered, Bob. Should be real good. We have to go to thirty thousand, though."

"Why? What for?" I inquired.

"Hell, we won't make it otherwise, even stuffed with fuel. It's 750 miles! Even at thirty thousand, we'll be blowing fuel out the tailpipes. It would be no problem at forty-one thousand—we would have plenty of fuel, but, remember, we don't have oxygen."

I turned to Dave. "What about the pressurization?" I asked, "Will it work at thirty thousand feet?"

"I don't know, Bobby, we'll have to see."

One thing we knew for sure. There was no place, on the way, to stop for jet fuel; so, we'd damned well have to do our best.

As we walked outside to leave, I glanced at the sky.

"Shit, Sam, look at those clouds. There's a lot of bad stuff up there," and I pointed to the build-ups over the mountain that stretched as far as the eye could see. We examined the build-ups carefully.

"Look," I indicated a stretch to the east of the thunderheads, "I think if we get up fast enough we can pick our way through those."

We were given runway nine for our takeoff. We really didn't want it. It would put our takeoff right into the mountains, but we had no choice. It was very hot as 464 Juliet roared down the runway. We could feel that she was heavy as the runway flashed by underneath us. We had used up almost five thousand feet before I called out, "Rotate."

Juliet eased off.

"Gear up"—several seconds—"Flaps up," Sam sang out.

Climbing at maximum rate, we turned on a heading of about 040 to pick our way through the clouds. We were outbound almost seventy degrees off course. Not to mention the fact that whisky compasses are completely inaccurate when climbing or turning. We had no idea of our actual heading. As we picked our way around the buildups, I knew we should have a small island, the Ile de la Tortue, on our right when we were to reach the northwest corner of Haiti.

Sam leveled her off at thirty thousand. We were on top of most of the clouds. We had been airborne for almost twenty minutes. Knowing our fuel could become critical, all of us were looking for the north coast of Haiti, which should have been below us. The cloud cover was almost 90 percent. Landmark navigation was almost impossible. I spotted a section of the north coast and fearfully searched for Ile de la Tortue. We were over the coast now, heading out to sea. The coastline to my right was clear, no clouds. But still no Ile de la Tortue.

I checked and rechecked my chart.

"Sam, this is impossible. Ile de la Tortue is not there. It's got to be on your left."

Both of us were breaking our necks trying to peer through the broken clouds to find the islands. Several minutes passed.

"Sam," I shouted, finally, "turn left; I think I saw it."

We turned left. A minute later, there it was. "Shit, Sam, we're almost thirty miles off course. It's that damned whisky compass. All that climbing and turning through the clouds and the SOB isn't accurate."

We were flying at six-and-one-half miles a minute for almost twenty minutes, and, at that speed, it didn't take long to get off course. Once we had our heading, though, the skies opened up again.

All of us relaxed. In another twenty minutes, we spotted another air landmark: Great Inagua. Gently, Sam turned to a heading of 315 degrees after passing over the island. Dave was monitoring the pressurization; it was still fluctuating between eight thousand to fifteen thousand cabin altitude. With the Bahamas off to our right, I carefully checked our position.

The day was sunny and now the sky held only puffy white scattered clouds. Another thirty minutes passed. I was feeling strange.

"Sam, are you OK?" I asked curiously.

"Sure—why?" He turned to look at me.

"Dave, Raul—are you two OK?" I continued.

They were fine, too.

"It must be me," I said. "I'm getting dizzy. My head's not clear. I think I'm getting hypoxia."

Dave checked the cabin altitude.

"It's about fifteen thousand feet," he announced.

"Sam, are you sure you're OK?" I persisted.

Sam was perfect, he reported. I was alarmed that our pilot might soon be stricken as I was and warned him to be careful.

"Don't worry about me, Bob," he assured me, "it's the cigarettes that are bothering you. You're a smoker."

"I know, but so is Dave. Just be careful."

My dizziness came and went for the next few minutes and I just prayed it wouldn't incapacitate me for the balance of the flight back home. We were so close.

"Do you see what I see, Sam?" I was suddenly alert.

Looming ahead of us was a large front over forty thousand feet high, stretching to our right and left as far as the eye could see. We both knew there was no way around or over it.

"Sam," I said, "we just passed Georgetown to my right. Let's keep going and try to find a hole. If we can't, let's turn around and land at Georgetown."

As we came closer, the cloud looked even more solid. We would reach it in less than twenty minutes.

Miraculously, I saw a small hole off to my right. I pointed it out to Sam. It looked to be about half a mile wide and down at about twenty thousand feet.

"OK, Bob, let's try it," and Sam eased the power back to about 80 percent to start down. Juliet became a slim, swift-moving shuttle, tracing her way in a complicated pattern down through the small opening in the clouds until she was finally under the front at sixteen thousand feet.

"There's Andros, right ahead," I yelled.

"They haven't moved the old swamp an inch," Sam said, with his eyes glued to the fuel indicator, "but I'd better get this baby upstairs. She's gobbling up close to 60 percent more fuel down here," and he took her back up to thirty thousand feet.

Even Raul was now eye-ball navigating, with a "Look, there's Miami" as he tapped a finger on his window, pointing at the pollution smear that sat like a dirty thumbprint on the horizon to the northwest. Next came Bimini, like a weathered shell in the shallow blue-green waters of its reefs, with the deep blue Gulf Stream sweeping by in the deeper waters.

"Bimini," I shouted, "11:30 A.M. We're practically in our own backyard."

As we swept by Bimini, I turned to Sam, "Hey captain, we're still at thirty thousand feet—Miami Center is going to have a heart attack. I told them we were at twelve thousand. They have us on radar."

"I know, Bob, but look at the fuel," Sam said, pointing a finger at the quantity indicator. It was dangerously low by this time. Holding my breath, my eyes began scouring the Miami shoreline, less than thirty miles away, identifying familiar landmarks.

"I feel like Moses looking at the Promised Land," I remarked, feeling the microphone cutting into my hand from gripping it so tightly in anticipation of communicating with home base.

Sam eased the power back and extended the spoilers.

Everyone began yelling, as if on signal. "We've done it!"—"We're home!"—"We made it!"—"Gracias a Dios!"

I glanced at the airspeed indicator as 464 Juliet began diving steeply and at twenty-five thousand feet I called out a warning.

"Sam, slow her down. You're twenty knots over the red line."

Sam glanced down, 330 knots, and grinned, "Hell, Bob, she's just, in a big hurry to get home."

The shoreline zoomed toward us as we descended. My throat was tight and my eyes burned with tears as I stared ahead hungrily.

Freedom. Learjet 464 Juliet leveled off at twenty-five hundred feet. I lifted the microphone to my mouth, my voice shaking as I called, "Opa-Locka tower ... Learjet November 464 Juliet."

"Opa-Locka tower ... Go ahead, 464 Juliet."

"Yes, sir, 464 Juliet is at the shoreline at twenty-five hundred feet. VFR. Request nine left for landing."

"Learjet 464 Juliet ... ," there was a slight hesitation in the controller's voice, "Say again ... Did you say VFR?"

No wonder he was puzzled, Learjets are always IFR, handed on from approach.

"Sam," I laughed, "he must think we're some student pilots calling in from the beach," and to the controller, "Affirmative, VFR it is."

"Four six four Juliet, enter left downwind for landing ... nine left ... Report at the Twin Drive Inns."

"Four six four Juliet, Roger."

Everyone was crowding his head into the cockpit, drinking in familiar sights like soldiers home from the wars.

"There's ole I-95," Dave said as it shot below us in a flash.

"I can see Air Unlimited," Raul crowed in relief.

We were approaching Twin Drive Inns, and I reported to the tower again, "Opa-Locka tower ... 464 Juliet at the Twins."

"Four six four Juliet ... clear to land ... ," and we all listened reverently, as if to a benediction, " ... wind zero eight zero at six ... Altimeter 30.1."

"464 Juliet ... Roger."

"OK, Bob, gear down. Flaps approach," Sam called out, then, "Hydraulic pressure check."

Dave and I anxiously watched 464 Juliet's instrument panel.

"Everything green … hydraulic pressure OK," Dave and I chanted, almost in unison, and I added, under my breath, *Juliet, don't fail us now.*

We sat holding our breath as Sam banked her to the left and turned her obedient head toward the final for runway nine left.

I began calling out softly, "140—135—135," glancing from side to side to ward off any possible last-minute bad luck, "—130—125—120."

"Full flaps," Sam also spoke in a gentle voice, as if he could read my thoughts.

Everything was perfect; Juliet needed nothing more, she was pointed straight as an arrow at the runway. Sam eased the power back and pulled the yoke back. Ever so gently the tires chirped. There was a breathless hush as she sped down the runway and reduced speed. I was trembling as we turned right, clear of the runway, on Opa-Locka ground. Again we burst into a loud cheer, as if by common consent.

"Learjet 464 Juliet … clear off nine left … taxi to customs … 464 Juliet … taxi to customs," the radio crackled.

Mission completed: Home. We could hardly believe it. The engines shutoff and we opened the door.

My youngest son, Jeff, was running down the ramp as I stepped out. Close behind were Terry, my older son, Jay, my oldest daughter, Terri, Jim Burkett and his wife Kitty. Jeff was in tears as he hugged me, and my family swarmed over me in a tidal wave of love.

It was like moving into a peaceful dream at the end of a long nightmare. No one, including me, could grasp that we were finally home.

I had managed the impossible. And in doing so, I had distilled and confirmed a trinity of eternal truths—

Believe in God. Believe in Yourself. Make it Happen.